A Civil War spy faces death . . . a World War I veteran tries to readjust to an unchanged civilian society

the charming . . .

what a young ... ed generation" ... pop-ularity . . .

the poignant ... m-hand for a se... . . .

the turn-of-th... . . .

and the consummate product of contemporary American life—the search for a way to understand our experience . . .

These are but a few of the themes of the American short story, that uniquely American literary genre through which the American character has found full expression. Shaped by many influences—initiation rites of adolescence, participation in war, the need to escape society or find a place within it, the sudden loss of an illusion once firmly held—the American character has emerged, survived, and grown. With its intensely heightened and compact vision, the American short story has most effectively captured and conveyed the painful, poignant lessons that have shaped our character. Here, from Hemingway to Updike, Fitzgerald to O'Connor, Anderson to Wright, are nine of the best works in the genre, all reflecting the great diversity and the common ground of the American experience.

CALVIN SKAGGS is Professor of English at Drew University and Associate Producer of *The American Short Story*.

LAUREL BOOKS OF INTEREST:

AMERICAN FILM GENRES
Stuart M. Kaminsky

GREAT AMERICAN SHORT STORIES
Edited by Wallace and Mary Stegner

INNOVATIVE FICTION
Edited by Jerome Klinkowitz and John Somer

SHORT STORY MASTERPIECES
Edited by Robert Penn Warren and Albert Erskine

DELTA BOOKS OF INTEREST:

AMERICA IN THE MOVIES
Michael Wood

FICTION INTO FILM
Rachel Maddux, Stirling Silliphant
and Neil D. Isaacs

THE AMERICAN SHORT STORY

Edited by
Calvin Skaggs

A LAUREL BOOK

Published by
Dell Publishing Co., Inc.
1 Dag Hammarskjold Plaza
New York, New York 10017

Photo of Ron Weyand as Alfred Schweigen
in *The Music School* by Drew Takahasi.

Laurel ® TM 674623, Dell Publishing Co., Inc.

ISBN: 0-440-30294-3

Printed in the United States of America
First Laurel printing—May 1979

ACKNOWLEDGMENTS
"I'M A FOOL" by Sherwood Anderson: Reprinted by permission of Harold Ober Associates, Incorporated. Copyright © 1922 by Dial Publishing Company, Inc. Renewed 1949 by Eleanor Copenhaver Anderson. Script excerpt reprinted by permission of Harold Ober Associates, Incorporated.

"BERNICE BOBS HER HAIR" by F. Scott Fitzgerald: Reprinted from *Flappers and Philosophers* by permission of Charles Scribner's Sons. Copyright 1920 Curtis Publishing Co. Script reprinted by permission of Harold Ober Associates, Incorporated.

"SOLDIER'S HOME" by Ernest Hemingway: Reprinted from *In Our Time* by permission of Charles Scribner's Sons. Copyright 1925 Charles Scribner's Sons. Script reprinted by permission of Alfred Rice.

"ALMOS' A MAN" by Richard Wright: Copyright © 1960, 1941 by Richard Wright. "The Man Who Was Almost a Man" from *Eight Men* by Richard Wright, published originally by World Publishing Company, reprinted by permission of Thomas Y. Crowell Company, Inc. Script excerpt reprinted by permission of Paul R. Reynolds, Inc.

CONTENTS

FOREWORD

by Robert Geller
Executive Producer,
The American Short Story series

The short story, an indigenous American form like the movie, has been called an act of "artful audacity" because of its marvelous compression, and its ability to heighten feelings and evoke human responses. Its characters are fully drawn in relatively few pages, often resembling the uncertain but appealing nature of our own neighbors: those people we see in hurried glimpses and might someday want to know more deeply.

That compression, that appeal to the private sense in our nature, gave the short story its popularity—and the fact that Americans have always loved a good yarn. It is what compelled the varied talents of Anderson, Bierce, James, O'Connor, and Hemingway to write short stories.

But it is a craft that has suffered from growing neglect. The demise of newspaper serialization, the collapse of hundreds of literary magazines and periodicals in the last two decades, and the insatiable hunger for banal television "shows" have diminished serious motivation for newer short story writers. It has also relegated our master writers to obligatory anthologies or to rainy-day diversions for the vanishing liberal arts majors.

In part to redress that neglect, the National Endowment for the Humanities generously supported the creation of The American Short Story series. The selection by eminent scholars of nine stories and their faithful rendering into film by outstanding artists express a strong concern for reflecting the historical and cultural forces which shaped our writers over a century, and which they in turn honed into fiction through their own perceptions and passions.

INTRODUCTION

by Calvin Skaggs,
Literary Advisor,
The American Short Story series
Professor of English,
Drew University

The short story has thrived in America from the moment that we began to develop our own secular literature, free from slavish imitation of Anglo-European forms and from subordination to religious function. From Nathaniel Hawthorne and Henry James in the nineteenth century to Ernest Hemingway and William Faulkner in the twentieth, most of our greatest novelists have also written great short stories. Many other American writers, without achieving equal mastery in the longer novel, have excelled in the short story. Such writers as Edgar Allan Poe, Sherwood Anderson, and Katherine Anne Porter come immediately to mind.

Indeed, Americans are said to have invented the short story. Not that people haven't always told one another stories or that the brief tale or sketch hasn't had a long literary history. But American writers were the first to define the short story as a specific literary form, different from the novel or the long narrative poem not only in length but also in kind. American writers were the first to be conscious of working in a particular literary genre, with its own rules and values, in a way their predecessors had not been.

It was Edgar Allan Poe who, in 1842, provided the critical definitions for this new literary form. The popular sketches of Washington Irving, which added Ichabod Crane and Rip Van Winkle to the gallery of American character types, had preceded Poe's own highly polished stories. Vividly imagined personalities had also been developed in essay form, such as Benjamin Franklin's Poor Richard. But it was in reviews of the tales of his contemporary, Hawthorne, that Poe formalized the nature and the demands of the short story, thereby defining this new literary form. First, he praised the story as the prose form most suitable for the exercise of "ambitious genius" in a writer. Next, he defined its central characteristic as a singleness or unity of effect attained by subordinating all characters, incidents, and even sentences, to a single purpose. Finally, he declared the well-constructed story capable of leaving "in the mind of him who contemplates it with a kindred art, a sense of the fullest satisfaction."

For over a century after Poe's statement, this satisfaction was relished by millions of readers. The short story became a staple of the American magazine. Almost every general magazine, whether popular enough to be read by millions or restricted to a subscription list of a few hundred, included short stories in its table of contents. Only in the past twenty years or so have the more popular showcases for short stories disappeared: magazines such as *Collier's*, *Liberty*, and *The Saturday Evening Post* ceased publication.

What remains, however, are both a conception of a literary form demanding the highest craft that still attracts some of our most talented writers, and a heritage of short fiction that all Americans can view with pride. Enriching our shared knowledge of this heritage has been a primary purpose of The American Short Story series. The first task of those who shaped this series was to choose a few stories to represent the many fine ones. The stories filmed and then collected here, reflecting one hundred years of American experience, are carefully chosen samples of the diverse types our authors have published. Granted this diversity, it may be useful to discuss some of the themes that link these stories, for there are few better reflectors of the continuously evolving character-types and values that have haunted the American mind than the short story.

To understand this evolution, it seems logical to begin with the earliest story in the volume, Ambrose Bierce's "Parker Adderson, Philosopher," published in 1891. It is interesting to observe that three of the nine stories collected here present some experience of war, though they vary in directness of treatment. Bierce's story depicts a wartime event, its only characters Civil War soldiers. Ernest Hemingway's "Soldier's Home" looks back on World War I, as a returning veteran tempered by that war attempts to readjust to an unchanged civilian society. Flannery O'Connor's "The Displaced Person" refracts the experience of World War II, as a refugee from that war revivifies the characters' memories of the mass destruction and exile it caused.

At the heart of Bierce's tale is the irony concerning the difference between theory and practice or between philosophy and experience. Parker Adderson's philosophical detachment toward the idea of death crumbles once he faces it on terms other than his own. The general, who has been awed, if not frightened, by the idea of death, accepts his own dying with philosophical detachment.

Similar ironies characterize other works included here, for the short story usually has space for only a single revelation, and this revelation often surprises us in an ironic way. In Stephen Crane's "The Blue Hotel," the Swede's announcement that he will be killed at first appears absurd. That his prophecy is fulfilled is doubly ironic, for he seems determined to destroy himself if only to make real his own fears. In Sherwood Anderson's "I'm a Fool," the lie the young hero tells to attract a girl becomes the means by which he loses all hope of seeing her again.

In all these stories the central irony springs from a cluster of themes frequently developed in American short fiction: the loss of illusions as to the nature of one's own experience or identity, and the forging of a different identity from the insight gained through disillusionment. Often this process involves an adolescent whose experience provides a means of initiation into adulthood. One of the best examples of such a rite of passage occurs in F. Scott Fitzgerald's "Bernice Bobs Her Hair," but the stories by Anderson, Hemingway, and Richard Wright also deal with this situation. In each case the central initiatory process touches on different problems, ideas, and values in American cultural history.

Fitzgerald's story presents the coming of age of a young woman. Unattractive and unpopular, Bernice apprentices herself to her highly attractive and popular cousin, Marjorie. As Bernice learns to mimic, equal, and then outdistance her cousin's model, Fitzgerald outlines a conception of female identity based solely on a woman's capacity to attract the attention of men, to capture the heart of a specific man, and to make a successful match. Though Bernice's attitude toward this means of self-definition remains entirely implicit, never directly articulated by either character or narrator, she appears to reject male approval as the only means of female identification when she rejects her cousin's model at the end of the story. Once she has undergone the ritual of hair-bobbing, Bernice strikes out for new territory, a new life, as do so many young heroes and heroines in American fiction, from Huckleberry Finn to the present. What they make of their new lives we never get to see.

For the young heroes of Anderson and Hemingway, the initiatory experience has already happened, though neither has yet integrated its meaning fully into a new conception of selfhood. Torn between his mother's vision of middle-class respectability, involving a good-paying job in a store or factory, and his own desire to work outdoors in the world of stablemen and horses, Anderson's young man has chosen the latter. Once he meets a respectable young woman, however, he pretends to be what he has rejected: respectable, wealthy, and successful. Anderson's ironical treatment of his hero's emergence into adulthood leaves the young man confused if not embittered. And Anderson finds in his hero's lie a way of treating several themes prominent in American short fiction: the confusions of adult sexuality; the conflicts between the values of a mercantile and an agricultural society; and the barriers of class structure.

Hemingway also uses the initiatory experience of a single individual to reflect upon larger social issues. Returning to his small home town after World War I, Harold Krebs finds it exactly as he left it, as if the war had never happened. He, however, has changed. He has grown into an honest maturity. Facing death in battle, he functioned efficiently, without the panic of fear. Facing sexual need, he found a woman. Now, the mores of his home town require him to falsify his own experience in retrospect by pretending to a fear he never felt or a romantic heroism he never indulged in; by engaging in courtship rituals he has outgrown; and by giving allegiance to a religious dogma he no longer believes. In presenting this opposition between two value systems, Hemingway reveals the confusions felt by returning veterans after most American wars. He specifically questions the rigid moral and social codes of post-World War I America that seemed out of touch with recent human experience.

Richard Wright's hero also undergoes an initiatory experience in "Almos' a Man," one that again reflects broad social and political issues. David Glover's desire to be treated as a man is frustrated not only by his youth and poverty but also by his being black. In Wright's view it is precisely the traits we associate with manhood that black males are prevented from developing. Such achievements as economic security and the related freedom of choice and sense of self-sufficiency are also denied to David's father. David's means of escaping the situation that keeps him trapped in boyhood only tightens the trap, as he is faced with two more years of enforced servitude in payment for the accidental death of his employer's mule. Like Bernice, he lights out, to start over elsewhere, though we never see beyond his first step into adulthood.

All four of these initiation stories exemplify another important characteristic of American short fiction: its detailed observation of manners and social texture, and its careful examination of their relation to moral values. One finds such precise detailing especially noteworthy in Henry James's "The Jolly Corner" and John Updike's "The Music School." The obverse of this emphasis on social history is the careful psychological exploration dominating several of these stories.

Probably no work included here manages to intertwine these two strands more intricately than James's story. James shows that an American of middle age can also be required to redefine his self, and that the sense of selfhood in flux, uncertain and changeable, is not confined to adolescents but shared by people of all ages. Returning to New York after many years abroad, James's protagonist finds the city thoroughly altered. In many ways he is confused by the new effects of industrialism, by the "skyscrapers" and the bustling crowds. But these social changes also stimulate the discovery of unsuspected talents in himself, talents that might have flowered had he remained in America. His uncertainty concerning what he might have been is intensified by a renewed sense of his past, which he gains by nightly visits to his deserted childhood home. He develops an obsession which takes the form of a ghostly presence, a double, an alter ego he must confront in order to know himself. James's treatment of this confrontation, and the journey that leads to it, awakens us to the unknown forces at work in the human psyche. For James plunges us into the turmoil of the American self which is constantly in the process of redefinition.

James's sense of the unknown at work in human life is personal and psychological. In Crane's "The Blue Hotel" and Flannery O'Connor's "The Displaced Person," the unknown is cosmic and abstract. Crane depicts a world with a universal disregard for man, a place where human beings are blown about like the snow, where chance and accident reign, where there is no governing force at all and man is left to his own self-destructive devices. In "The Displaced Person" Flannery O'Connor creates a world dense with sociological and psychological detail. Her stories can teach as much about the class structure, the ruling beliefs, and the social gestures and habits of the modern South, as the best documented works of social history. But what O'Connor's stories present most forcefully is the irruption into this mundane world of a transcendent force so powerful, so awful, and so unknowable by limited human minds that it sometimes seems demonic—unrecognizable as the grace of an omniscient and omnipotent God.

In most of the stories in this volume, the abstract impersonal forces of history, of myth, of religion or of social convention intersect with the intricate personal details of individual lives. For the essence of the short story is detail—detail so carefully selected, artfully ordered, and evocatively expressed that a moment in a character's life can suggest the whole life, a day or a year suggest a whole segment of our national history. John Updike's "The Music School," the only contemporary story in this volume, perhaps best illustrates this important characteristic of the short story. In Alfred Schweigen's meditation on the details of his everyday life—on remembered fragments of conversation, chance meetings, newspaper reports; on the sights and sounds of his home, his daughter's music school, his host's living room—we learn much about our own moral uncertainties, our thirsts for belief, our desires for understanding and for a world-view that will allow us to make sense of our lives.

Short stories exist to be read, to be experienced; and reading a story is an act of interpretation. The contents of this volume, in addition to the nine stories themselves, represent other forms of interpretation. First, there are nine essays of literary history and criticism, one for each story. These represent a highly developed form of interpretation consisting of description, analysis, and evaluation of the individual stories, their authors, and their historical contexts. Second, there are the film scripts, or scenes from them, by which these stories were translated from one medium into another. These scripts also represent an act of interpreting the original stories. And the scripts exist to be unfolded further, for they too are words on a page meant to be transmuted into visual images by directors, actors, designers, cameramen, and other film craftspersons.

Both the writing of a script and the making of a film require several different kinds of interpretation. The first is to find a dramatic form. Stories with a straightforward narrative line like "Parker Adderson, Philosopher" and "Bernice Bobs Her Hair" contain clearly defined plots. To turn these into dramatic form requires a selectivity and a heightening of detail by the script-writer that differs from the invention required by stories containing little plot, such as Hemingway's "Soldier's Home," or those in which most of the action occurs within a character's mind, such as "The Jolly Corner" or "The Music School." Also, stories told retrospectively require a reconstruction on the part of the script-writer unnecessary when a story unfolds in consecutive linear form. This is especially true when the story is internalized by being reported in the first person, as is "I'm a Fool."

But after these interpretive acts have been performed, there remains the interpretation that is the filmmaking process itself. To suggest the nature of this process, this book contains three interviews with representative film artists involved in The American Short Story series—a writer, a director, and a writer-director. These interviews are only the tip of the iceberg, however, for the collaboration that is filmmaking requires the imaginations of several dozen artists and craftspersons, and each of these makes a contribution to the interpretive act of filming a story. The details of a location may stimulate a designer or cameraperson or director to approach a scene differently than either story or script indicates. The limitations of a budget may require a producer to restage in one spot scenes meant for three locations. In such cases the interpretive act differs merely in degree from that which the individual reader performs. For the same reader reads the same story differently at age twenty and age forty, just as the son of a Polish immigrant will react to "The Displaced Person" otherwise than the daughter of a Southern farmer.

The glory of the American short story is that it lends itself to ever-recurring acts of interpretation, for like all art it relates simultaneously to the past, present, and future. These stories exist here on the pages of this book, in the present, to be experienced. They exist as a compendium of knowledge about our collective past as a people. And they exist to be reinterpreted when we need them to understand our future.

PARKER ADDERSON, PHILOSOPHER

by Ambrose Bierce

"Prisoner, what is your name?"

"As I am to lose it at daylight to-morrow morning it is hardly worth while concealing it. Parker Adderson."

"Your rank?"

"A somewhat humble one; commissioned officers are too precious to be risked in the perilous business of a spy. I am a sergeant."

"Of what regiment?"

"You must excuse me; my answer might, for anything I know, give you an idea of whose forces are in your front. Such knowledge as that is what I came into your lines to obtain, not to impart."

"You are not without wit."

"If you have the patience to wait you will find me dull enough to-morrow."

"How do you know that you are to die to-morrow morning?"

"Among spies captured by night that is the custom. It is one of the nice observances of the profession."

The general so far laid aside the dignity appropriate to a Confederate officer of high rank and wide renown as to smile. But no one in his power and out of his favor would have drawn any happy augury from that outward and visible sign of approval. It was neither genial nor infectious; it did not communicate itself to the other persons exposed to it—the caught spy who had provoked it and the armed guard who had brought him into the tent and now stood a little apart, watching his prisoner in the yellow candle-light. It was no part of that warrior's duty to smile; he had been detailed for another purpose. The conversation was resumed; it was in character a trial for a capital offense.

"You admit, then, that you are a spy—that you came into my camp, disguised as you are in the uniform of a

Confederate soldier, to obtain information secretly regarding the numbers and disposition of my troops."

"Regarding, particularly, their numbers. Their disposition I already knew. It is morose."

The general brightened again; the guard, with a severer sense of his responsibility, accentuated the austerity of his expression and stood a trifle more erect than before. Twirling his gray slouch hat round and round upon his forefinger, the spy took a leisurely survey of his surroundings. They were simple enough. The tent was a common "wall tent," about eight feet by ten in dimensions, lighted by a single tallow candle stuck into the haft of a bayonet, which was itself stuck into a pine table at which the general sat, now busily writing and apparently forgetful of his unwilling guest. An old rag carpet covered the earthen floor; an older leather trunk, a second chair and a roll of blankets were about all else that the tent contained; in General Clavering's command Confederate simplicity and penury of "pomp and circumstance" had attained their highest development. On a large nail driven into the tent pole at the entrance was suspended a sword-belt supporting a long sabre, a pistol in its holster and, absurdly enough, a bowie-knife. Of that most unmilitary weapon it was the general's habit to explain that it was a souvenir of the peaceful days when he was a civilian.

It was a stormy night. The rain cascaded upon the canvas in torrents, with the dull, drum-like sound familiar to dwellers in tents. As the whooping blasts charged upon it the frail structure shook and swayed and strained at its confining stakes and ropes.

The general finished writing, folded the half-sheet of paper and spoke to the soldier guarding Adderson: "Here, Tassman, take that to the adjutant-general; then return."

"And the prisoner, General?" said the soldier, saluting, with an inquiring glance in the direction of that unfortunate.

"Do as I said," replied the officer, curtly.

The soldier took the note and ducked himself out of the tent. General Clavering turned his handsome face toward the Federal spy, looked him in the eyes, not unkindly, and said: "It is a bad night, my man."

"For me, yes."

"Do you guess what I have written?"

"Something worth reading, I dare say. And—perhaps it is my vanity—I venture to suppose that I am mentioned in it."

"Yes; it is a memorandum for an order to be read to the troops at *reveille* concerning your execution. Also some notes for the guidance of the provost-marshal in arranging the details of that event."

"I hope, General, the spectacle will be intelligently arranged, for I shall attend it myself."

"Have you any arrangements of your own that you wish to make? Do you wish to see a chaplain, for example?"

"I could hardly secure a longer rest for myself by depriving him of some of his."

"Good God, man! do you mean to go to your death with nothing but jokes upon your lips? Do you know that this is a serious matter?"

"How can I know that? I have never been dead in all my life. I have heard that death is a serious matter, but never from any of those who have experienced it."

The general was silent for a moment; the man interested, perhaps amused him—a type not previously encountered.

"Death," he said, "is at least a loss—a loss of such happiness as we have, and of opportunities for more."

"A loss of which we shall never be conscious can be borne with composure and therefore expected without apprehension. You must have observed, General, that of all the dead men with whom it is your soldierly pleasure to strew your path none shows signs of regret."

"If the being dead is not a regrettable condition, yet the becoming so—the act of dying—appears to be distinctly disagreeable to one who has not lost the power to feel."

"Pain is disagreeable, no doubt. I never suffer it without more or less discomfort. But he who lives longest is most exposed to it. What you call dying is simply the last pain—there is really no such thing as dying. Suppose, for illustration, that I attempt to escape. You lift the revolver that you are courteously concealing in your lap, and—"

The general blushed like a girl, then laughed softly, disclosing his brilliant teeth, made a slight inclination of his handsome head and said nothing. The spy continued: "You fire, and I have in my stomach what I did not swallow. I fall, but am not dead. After a half-hour of agony I am dead. But at any given instant of that half-hour I was either alive or dead. There is no transition period.

"When I am hanged to-morrow morning it will be quite the same; while conscious I shall be living; when dead, unconscious. Nature appears to have ordered the matter quite in my interest—the way that I should have ordered it myself. It is so simple," he added with a smile, "that it seems hardly worth while to be hanged at all."

At the finish of his remarks there was a long silence. The general sat impassive, looking into the man's face, but apparently not attentive to what had been said. It was as if his eyes had mounted guard over the prisoner while his mind concerned itself with other matters. Presently he drew a long, deep breath, shuddered, as one awakened from a dreadful dream, and exclaimed almost inaudibly: "Death is horrible!"—this man of death.

"It was horrible to our savage ancestors," said the spy, gravely, "because they had not enough intelligence to dissociate the idea of consciousness from the idea of the physical forms in which it is manifested—as an even lower order of intelligence, that of the monkey, for example, may be unable to imagine a house without inhabitants, and seeing a ruined hut fancies a suffering occupant. To us it is horrible because we have inherited the tendency to think it so, accounting for the notion by wild and fanciful theories of another world—as names of places give rise to legends explaining them and reasonless conduct to philosophies in justification. You can hang me, General, but there your power of evil ends; you cannot condemn me to heaven."

The general appeared not to have heard; the spy's talk had merely turned his thoughts into an unfamiliar channel, but there they pursued their will independently to conclusions of their own. The storm had ceased, and something of the solemn spirit of the night had imparted itself to his reflections, giving them the sombre tinge of a supernatural dread. Perhaps there was an element of prescience in it. "I should not like to die," he said—"not to-night."

He was interrupted—if, indeed, he had intended to speak further—by the entrance of an officer of his staff, Captain Hasterlick, the provost-marshal. This recalled him to himself; the absent look passed away from his face.

"Captain," he said, acknowledging the officer's salute,

"this man is a Yankee spy captured inside our lines with incriminating papers on him. He has confessed. How is the weather?"

"The storm is over, sir, and the moon shining."

"Good; take a file of men, conduct him at once to the parade ground, and shoot him."

A sharp cry broke from the spy's lips. He threw himself forward, thrust out his neck, expanded his eyes, clenched his hands.

"Good God!" he cried hoarsely, almost inarticulately; "you do not mean that! You forget—I am not to die until morning."

"I have said nothing of morning," replied the general, coldly; "that was an assumption of your own. You die now."

"But, General, I beg—I implore you to remember; I am to hang! It will take some time to erect the gallows—two hours—an hour. Spies are hanged; I have rights under military law. For Heaven's sake, General, consider how short—"

"Captain, observe my directions."

The officer drew his sword and fixing his eyes upon the prisoner pointed silently to the opening of the tent. The prisoner hesitated; the officer grasped him by the collar and pushed him gently forward. As he approached the tent pole the frantic man sprang to it and with cat-like agility seized the handle of the bowie-knife, plucked the weapon from the scabbard and thrusting the captain aside leaped upon the general with the fury of a madman, hurling him to the ground and falling headlong upon him as he lay. The table was overturned, the candle extinguished and they fought blindly in the darkness. The provost-marshal sprang to the assistance of his superior officer and was himself prostrated upon the struggling forms. Curses and inarticulate cries of rage and pain came from the welter of limbs and bodies; the tent came down upon them and beneath its hampering and enveloping folds the struggle went on. Private Tassman, returning from his errand and dimly conjecturing the stiuation, threw down his rifle and laying hold of the flouncing canvas at random vainly tried to drag it off the men under it; and the sentinel who paced up and down in front, not daring to leave his beat though the skies should fall, discharged his rifle. The report alarmed the camp;

drums beat the long roll and bugles sounded the assembly, bringing swarms of half-clad men into the moonlight, dressing as they ran, and falling into line at the sharp commands of their officers. This was well; being in line the men were under control; they stood at arms while the general's staff and the men of his escort brought order out of confusion by lifting off the fallen tent and pulling apart the breathless and bleeding actors in that strange contention.

Breathless, indeed, was one: the captain was dead; the handle of the bowie-knife, protruding from his throat, was pressed back beneath his chin until the end had caught in the angle of the jaw and the hand that delivered the blow had been unable to remove the weapon. In the dead man's hand was his sword, clenched with a grip that defied the strength of the living. Its blade was streaked with red to the hilt.

Lifted to his feet, the general sank back to the earth with a moan and fainted. Besides his bruises he had two sword-thrusts—one through the thigh, the other through the shoulder.

The spy had suffered the least damage. Apart from a broken right arm, his wounds were such only as might have been incurred in an ordinary combat with nature's weapons. But he was dazed and seemed hardly to know what had occurred. He shrank away from those attending him, cowered upon the ground and uttered unintelligible remonstrances. His face, swollen by blows and stained with gouts of blood, nevertheless showed white beneath his disheveled hair—as white as that of a corpse.

"The man is not insane," said the surgeon, preparing bandages and replying to a question; "he is suffering from fright. Who and what is he?"

Private Tassman began to explain. It was the opportunity of his life; he omitted nothing that could in any way accentuate the importance of his own relation to the night's events. When he had finished his story and was ready to begin it again nobody gave him any attention.

The general had now recovered consciousness. He raised himself upon his elbow, looked about him, and, seeing the spy crouching by a camp-fire, guarded, said simply:

"Take that man to the parade ground and shoot him."

"The general's mind wanders," said an officer standing near.

"His mind does *not* wander," the adjutant-general said. "I have a memorandum from him about this business; he had given that same order to Hasterlick"—with a motion of the hand toward the dead provost-marshal—"and, by God! it shall be executed."

Ten minutes later Sergeant Parker Adderson, of the Federal army, philosopher and wit, kneeling in the moonlight and begging incoherently for his life, was shot to death by twenty men. As the volley rang out upon the keen air of the midnight, General Clavering, lying white and still in the red glow of the camp-fire, opened his big blue eyes, looked pleasantly upon those about him and said: "How silent it all is!"

The surgeon looked at the adjutant-general, gravely and significantly. The patient's eyes slowly closed, and thus he lay for a few moments; then, his face suffused with a smile of ineffable sweetness, he said, faintly: "I suppose this must be death," and so passed away.

SCENES FROM *PARKER ADDERSON, PHILOSOPHER*,

*a film script based on the Bierce story, by Arthur Barron**

Parker Adderson, a Yankee spy, captured during the Civil War, is brought into camp, delivered into the hands of a smartly uniformed young lieutenant, and described to the commanding general of the camp. The following excerpt begins as the general and an aide approach the detention area:

9. WHEN THE GENERAL IS CLOSE . . .

LIEUTENANT. Attention!

[ADDERSON *stands at attention. He and the* GENERAL *regard each other*.]

GENERAL. Prisoner, what is your name?

ADDERSON. Parker Adderson. As I am to lose it at daylight tomorrow morning, it is hardly worth concealing.

GENERAL. Your rank?

ADDERSON. A somewhat humble one; I am a sergeant. Commissioned officers are too precious to be risked in the perilous business of a spy.

GENERAL. Of what regiment?

ADDERSON. You must excuse me; such knowledge is what I am into your lines to obtain, not impart.

GENERAL. You are not without wit.

ADDERSON. If you have the patience to wait, you will find me dull enough tomorrow.

GENERAL. [*laughs*]. I dare say I will. . . . I repeat, of what regiment?

ADDERSON. And I repeat, sir, that I cannot tell you.

GENERAL. You force me to be hard, man.

---

* After establishing a reputation as one of America's leading documentary filmmakers, Arthur Barron wrote and directed such dramatic films as *Orville and Wilbur* and *Jeremy*. He is also the director of the recent feature film, *Brothers*.

ADDERSON. Harder than the noose? With all due respect, I think not.

[*Pause. Silence. They measure each other.*]

GENERAL. [to LIEUTENANT]. I will have my supper now, I think. . . . Lieutenant, conduct this gentleman to my tent in an hour.

LIEUTENANT. Yes, sir.

[*The* GENERAL *begins to leave. Then he turns to issue a command.*]

GENERAL. And put him in leg irons!

LIEUTENANT. Yes, sir.

CUT TO

10. EXTERIOR. THE CAMP. DAY.

CU a chicken's head. It is squawking loudly. CUT TO private holding the bird in his hands. The corporal is with him and other soldiers are watching, including the drummer boy.

Private demonstrates to drummer boy how to calm chicken, then chops its head off with an axe.

CUT TO

11. INTERIOR. GENERAL'S TENT. DAY.

The cooked bird on a platter in front of the General. He dines alone, with an attendant standing by. He eats off good china, with silver.

[*The* GENERAL *bows his head.*]

GENERAL. Bless us Lord, and these gifts, which we have received this day, from thy bounty, and through our Lord, Jesus Christ, Amen.

[*The* GENERAL *begins to eat. He eats outside his tent, under a lean-to with an attendant standing by.*]

12. INTERIOR. DETENTION AREA. DAY.

Adderson steps out of doorway of detention house, hands and legs shackled. He is holding a tin mess plate filled with pork ribs, gravy and biscuits.

GUARD. Get back inside, Yankee.

ADDERSON. It's not a very pleasant place to dine.

GUARD. Can't help it. If the general came by, there'd be hell to pay!

[ADDERSON *turns inside and hobbles back to his seat. He toys with his food. Three men with shovels march past the window, followed by the* LIEUTENANT, *who enters the detention house moments later.*]

ADDERSON. Why, Lieutenant, this is a fine meal you've arranged.

LIEUTENANT. Thank you.

ADDERSON. Pork—I don't know where on earth you got it.

LIEUTENANT. It wasn't easy.

ADDERSON. Does everyone in camp eat this well?

LIEUTENANT. No, except the General.

ADDERSON. Generals and spies. . . . well, it's a fine last supper. [*Awkward look from* LIEUTENANT.] I'm sorry. . . . It appears my thoughts have a morose coloration. Have you eaten?

LIEUTENANT. Why no.

ADDERSON. Will you join me? [LIEUTENANT *holds back.*] Please, I can't eat all of this. It's very good.

LIEUTENANT. Well, all right.

[ADDERSON *motions and the* LIEUTENANT *walks over, bends and takes a rib and chews it.*]

ADDERSON. Tasty?

LIEUTENANT. Mmmmm, yes.

ADDERSON. Here, have a biscuit. [LIEUTENANT *obliges.*] Get some gravy. [LIEUTENANT *obliges.*] Sit down. [LIEUTENANT *sits.*]

13. EXTERIOR. CAMP. DAY.

General is being shaved by an attendant. No dialogue.

14. INTERIOR. DETENTION TENT. DAY.

Adderson and the Lieutenant have finished eating. They are drinking coffee. At an appropriate point in their conversation, the Lieutenant gives Adderson a cigar, lights it for him, lights his own. They smoke and talk.

LIEUTENANT. Where are you from?

ADDERSON. Boston.

LIEUTENANT. Do you have family there?

ADDERSON. Yes. The question is, does my family have me?

LIEUTENANT. I don't understand.

ADDERSON. Let us say there is some distance between us, something more than miles. Perhaps they have not been altogether pleased with the life of their wayward son.

LIEUTENANT. Yet they would be proud of you. It takes a brave man to do what you have done.

ADDERSON [*pause*]. Perhaps. In any event, I preferred spying to soldiering.

LIEUTENANT [*kindly*]. Perhaps I could write to them.

ADDERSON. You are very kind, but . . . I think not.

[*A little off from them, heard but not seen, a soldier begins to sing. The song is "Barbara Allen." He is accompanied on harmonica.*]

ADDERSON. And you? Are there loved ones waiting for you?

LIEUTENANT. Yes. Parents, brothers, and sisters . . . a large family.

ADDERSON. They must be proud of such a fine son.

LIEUTENANT. I'm new to the service, but I hope they will have cause to be proud of me.

ADDERSON. Are you afraid, Lieutenant?

LIEUTENANT. Of death?

ADDERSON. Yes. . . .

LIEUTENANT [*innocent, naive, sincere*]. No . . . of course not.

ADDERSON [*pause and then gently*]. No . . . of course not.

LIEUTENANT. And you . . . are you afraid?

ADDERSON. Of death, no. Of pain and cruelty? Why, yes. . . .

[*Pause.*]

ADDERSON. And is there someone else who waits for you back home? Someone pretty?

LIEUTENANT. Yes.

ADDERSON. Do you have a picture?

[*Involuntarily, the* LIEUTENANT'S *hand goes to his chest.*]

ADDERSON. May I see it? [*The* LIEUTENANT *hesitates.*] I would deem it a privilege, a comfort.

LIEUTENANT. Yes, of course.

ADDERSON. Thank you.

[*The* LIEUTENANT *removes a locket from the inside of his*

tunic. He opens it and shows Adderson the picture of a young, pretty, Lillian Gish–type *woman.*]

ADDERSON. She is very beautiful.

14A. MONTAGE OF CAMP LIFE WHILE SONG "BARBARA ALLEN."

MUSIC UP (the song) and LONG DISSOLVE to the soldier who is singing the ballad. He is seated with companions around a campfire. He has a high, clear, sweet voice. . . . The song ends . . . and . . .

ON AMBROSE BIERCE and "PARKER ADDERSON, PHILOSOPHER"

Alfred Kazin

Ambrose Bierce (1842–1914?) was only seventeen years old when he entered the Union Army during the Civil War. The war was the great experience of his life, and everything he was to write would be colored by this experience.

Bierce's writing is thus distinguished by a particular point of view, a slant, an angle of vision, that is somehow more original and more compelling than his narrative art itself. Unlike his contemporary, Henry James, who virtually created the modern realistic, psychological novel in America, Bierce was not a great craftsman in fiction and invented nothing that was to have a technical influence on the development of modern fiction. As will be seen, even so acute a story as "Parker Adderson, Philosopher" depends on Bierce's favorite device, a sudden reversal of character, rather than on a deeply worked out plot.

But Bierce's "point of view," his particular slant on life, was his ace in the hole. This was something new in American history and American literature. It was a form of war-hardened cynicism, as we so lightly say; it was the profoundest kind of disbelief, as we should say, a disbelief that overturned the usual balance of things as the American mind considered it. Bierce delighted in bringing into his *dénouement*, in story after story, not a *deus ex machina*, but the crunch of a devil out of the machine—a devil not so much in man as a steady accuser of man, a perpetual adversary of our poor human nature that delighted in showing up man as a hypocrite, self-deluder, sentimentalist, fool.

The secret of the world, Emerson once wrote with the typical confidence of his "spiritual" generation before the Civil War, is the tie between person and event. Character is fate, said Heraclitus. These are moral statements that suggest that the reason why human beings fail, why they fail themselves, is that they are not "good" enough. This was certainly the belief of American writers before the Civil War. Emerson, the prince of them all, thought that a man properly in touch with the gods—a man, that is, in touch with his supposedly "immortal" nature—could accomplish everything he meant to.

Bierce, like so many writers in his later generation, believed that we are ruled by circumstances. But this subservience to circumstances is not due to a lack of morality or higher purpose, as Emerson and other sages before the Civil War would have said. To Bierce the law of things (and there is an unyielding design that makes us do not what we want but what circumstances beyond our control invariably compel) is to trip man up, to show him up. The law of life is what the literary naturalists, the imitators of science in literature, liked to call determinism. We are determined by the formula inherent in things, by forces that operate on us as if we were inorganic particles—in short, by circumstances. Even when these circumstances are in ourselves, and display themselves as some corrupting, shameful, above all unexpected and contradictory weakness, this weakness is rooted in our psyches and hereditary nature, so that it works on us as if it were outside.

No one can really say why Ambrose Bierce of Ohio, who grew up on the old frontier and served in the Civil War, became a professional newspaperman mocker and iconoclast, became "Bitter Bierce," as a biographer in the twentieth century was to call him. No one can really say why Bierce made a point of parodying and inverting the status quo in his many columns, sketches, and stories for San Francisco papers, or why he made a point of scaring his Victorian audience, invariably showing human nature at its worst. He had been wounded in the head during the Civil War, and it would be tempting to say of him, as of twentieth-century war writers like Hemingway and Céline, who never recovered from the wounds they suffered in the First World War, that he was a permanent victim of war. But it might be truer to say that Bierce was somehow not altogether sorry to suffer terrible wounds in war because of the literary capital he could wrest out of his disillusionment.

The central fact about Bierce, as about Hemingway after him, is that he very early found his one distinctive note—

skepticism about the prevailing ethos of American life—that he pursued this, with unequal success, through one story after another, for the pleasure of accomplishing a particular emotional and pictorial effect.

Bierce specialized in the "piece," the column, the squib, the satire, the story that was often a very short story indeed. He was never a novelist, but rather a natural writer of newspaper articles, stories, and satire. He was a man with a specific design on the reader, as all journalists must be. This explains Bierce's startling, provocative effect on readers. It does not explain the peculiarly obsessive, almost fanatically unyielding quality of his work.

Bierce wanted to create specific effects, and he did. He wanted in some way to unsettle the reader, to transmit his own taste of bitterness. The effect of a Bierce story can be described as the surprise ending made into a moral quality, a principle of life according to Ambrose Bierce. There is invariably a sudden reversal, usually in a few lines near the end, that takes the story away from the reader, as it were, that overthrows his confidence in the nature of what he has been reading, that indeed overthrows his confidence. Bierce intends to leave the reader with a dizzying feeling that life is a trick, and that the only sure element in it is a totally mischievous, insidious kind of surprise.

But we must grant Bierce a higher degree of artistry, above all of intellectual purpose, than is suggested by the words "trick," or "surprise ending." For Bierce spoke for a whole generation of writers after the Civil War when, in his repeated use of this trick ending, he made clear his absolute belief that life itself at the end of the nineteenth century had become, for a nation of proverbial innocents and believers, a game that human beings are not allowed to win. In one important respect, however, Bierce differs from other realists of his generation who shared something of Bierce's general view of life, though in a considerably subtler form. Bierce has a kind of strictness, or monomania, about what he believes, that is unlike relatively more genial writers like Henry James and Mark Twain, for whom the contest between the individual and his fate demands the expansive working out that is a novel.

Bierce is not a great writer, for he described life as an ordeal without dealing with the individual nature of each ordeal. He does not deal with character in depth; indeed, he never explores character for its own sake. His interest is all too much in shocking the reader. By writing straight at the reader, by working on his feelings, Bierce himself becomes the trickster rather than the uncoverer of life as a trick.

But in Bierce's "Parker Adderson, Philosopher" we see brought to its highest level of ironic concentration Bierce's mischievous design, his scornful kind of narrative economy. "Parker Adderson" is one of Bierce's best stories. The trick or surprise *dénouement* at the end is original. The captured Federal spy is philosophic and even condescending to the Confederate general because he knows that spies are shot at sunrise. He goes to pieces as soon as he discovers that he is to be shot right away. Falling upon his captors, he manages to kill the general's aide and to wound mortally the general himself. The general becomes the real "philosopher" of the story, but this—surprise again!—only because of his weary, unconscious death wish.

"Parker Adderson" succeeds without question (as too many of Bierce's stories do not) because both the captured spy and the general have their characters defined with some care. And of course Bierce's most brilliant thrust is to show that while Parker Adderson is not superior to his own death, the general, brought down from his lofty detachment about other men's deaths, somehow welcomes the death that he must share with Parker Adderson himself. The point made is again the old Greek adage that "character is fate." In some way that is closer to Freud than the Greeks, the general in "Parker Adderson" has unconsciously wished for death. In this brilliant, tough little story, Bierce makes once again the point American writers in the generation that followed his were to swear by, that although life is full of accidents and reversals, nothing that happens is simply arbitrary. It is we, sooner or later, who somehow help to dislodge the rock that falls on us. There is a merciless pattern of cause and effect to human life. We are in the hands of forces beyond ourselves—though it is we, every time, who somehow (surprise!) set these forces in motion.

SUGGESTIONS FOR FURTHER READING

By Ambrose Bierce:

Collected Writings of Ambrose Bierce. New York: Citadel Press, 1960.

Fantastic Fables. New York: Dover, 1970.

In the Midst of Life and Other Stories. New York: New American Library, 1961.

About Ambrose Bierce:

Grattan, Clinton Hartley. *Bitter Bierce: A Mystery of American Letters*. New York: Cooper Square Publishers, 1966.

O'Connor, Richard. *Ambrose Bierce: A Biography*. Boston: Little, Brown & Co., 1967.

Woodruff, Stuart C. *The Short Stories of Ambrose Bierce: A Study in Polarity*. Pittsburgh: University of Pittsburgh Press, 1964.

THE BLUE HOTEL

by Stephen Crane

I

The Palace Hotel at Fort Romper was painted a light blue, a shade that is on the legs of a kind of heron, causing the bird to declare its position against any background. The Palace Hotel, then, was always screaming and howling in a way that made the dazzling winter landscape of Nebraska seem only a gray swampish hush. It stood alone on the prairie, and when the snow was falling the town two hundred yards away was not visible. But when the traveler alighted at the railway station he was obliged to pass the Palace Hotel before he could come upon the company of low clapboard houses which composed Fort Romper, and it was not to be thought that any traveler could pass the Palace Hotel without looking at it. Pat Scully, the proprietor, had proved himself a master of strategy when he chose his paints. It is true that on clear days, when the great transcontinental expresses, long lines of swaying Pullmans, swept through Fort Romper, passengers were overcome at the sight, and the cult that knows the brown-reds and the subdivisions of the dark greens of the East expressed shame, pity, horror, in a laugh. But to the citizens of this prairie town and to the people who would naturally stop there, Pat Scully had performed a feat. With this opulence and splendor, these creeds, classes, egotisms, that streamed through Romper on the rails day after day, they had no color in common.

As if the displayed delights of such a blue hotel were not sufficiently enticing, it was Scully's habit to go every morning and evening to meet the leisurely trains that stopped at Romper and work his seductions upon any man that he might see wavering, gripsack in hand.

One morning, when a snow-crusted engine dragged its long string of freight cars and its one passenger coach to the station, Scully performed the marvel of catching three men. One was a shaky and quick-eyed Swede, with a great shining cheap valise; one was a tall bronzed cowboy, who was on his way to a ranch near the Dakota line; one was a little silent man from the East, who didn't look it, and didn't announce it. Scully practically made them prisoners. He was so nimble and merry and kindly that each probably felt it would be the height of brutality to try to escape. They trudged off over the creaking board sidewalks in the wake of the eager little Irishman. He wore a heavy fur cap squeezed tightly down on his head. It caused his two red ears to stick out stiffly, as if they were made of tin.

At last, Scully, elaborately, with boisterous hospitality, conducted them through the portals of the blue hotel. The room which they entered was small. It seemed to be merely a proper temple for an enormous stove, which, in the center, was humming with godlike violence. At various points on its surface the iron had become luminous and glowed yellow from the heat. Beside the stove Scully's son Johnnie was playing High-Five with an old farmer who had whiskers both gray and sandy. They were quarreling. Frequently the old farmer turned his face toward a box of sawdust—colored brown from tobacco juice—that was behind the stove, and spat with an air of great impatience and irritation. With a loud flourish of words Scully destroyed the game of cards, and bustled his son upstairs with part of the baggage of the new guests. He himself conducted them to three basins of the coldest water in the world. The cowboy and the Easterner burnished themselves fiery red with this water, until it seemed to be some kind of metal polish. The Swede, however, merely dipped his fingers gingerly and with trepidation. It was notable that throughout this series of small ceremonies the three travelers were made to feel that Scully was very benevolent. He was conferring great favors upon them. He handed the towel from one to the other with an air of philanthropic impulse.

Afterward they went to the first room, and, sitting about the stove, listened to Scully's officious clamor at his daughters, who were preparing the midday meal. They reflected in the silence of experienced men who tread carefully amid new people. Nevertheless, the old farmer, stationary, invincible in his chair near the warmest part of the stove, turned his face from the sawdust box frequently and addressed a glowing commonplace to the strangers. Usually he was answered in short but adequate sentences by either the cowboy or the Easterner. The Swede said nothing. He seemed to be occupied in making furtive estimates of each man in the room. One might have thought that he had the sense of silly suspicion which comes to guilt. He resembled a badly frightened man.

Later, at dinner, he spoke a little, addressing his conversation entirely to Scully. He volunteered that he had come from New York, where for ten years he had worked as a tailor. These facts seemed to strike Scully as fascinating, and afterward he volunteered that he had lived at Romper for fourteen years. The Swede asked about the crops and the price of labor. He seemed barely to listen to Scully's extended replies. His eyes continued to rove from man to man.

Finally, with a laugh and a wink, he said that some of these Western communities were very dangerous; and after his statement he straightened his legs under the table, tilted his head, and laughed again, loudly. It was plain that the demonstration had no meaning to the others. They looked at him wondering and in silence.

II

As the men trooped heavily back into the front room, the two little windows presented views of a turmoiling sea of snow. The huge arms of the wind were making attempts —mighty, circular, futile—to embrace the flakes as they sped. A gatepost like a still man with a blanched face stood aghast amid this profligate fury. In a hearty voice Scully announced the presence of a blizzard. The guests of the blue hotel, lighting their pipes, assented with grunts of lazy masculine contentment. No island of the sea could be exempt in the degree of this little room with its humming stove. Johnnie, son of Scully, in a tone which defined his opinion of his ability as a card player, challenged the old farmer of both gray and sandy whiskers to a game of High-Five. The farmer agreed with a contemptuous and bitter scoff. They sat close to the stove, and squared their knees under a wide board. The cowboy and the Easterner watched the game with interest. The Swede remained near the window, aloof, but with a countenance that showed signs of an inexplicable excitement.

The play of Johnnie and the graybeard was suddenly ended by another quarrel. The old man arose while casting a look of heated scorn at his adversary. He slowly buttoned his coat, and then stalked with fabulous dignity from the room. In the discreet silence of all other men the Swede laughed. His laughter rang somehow childish. Men by this time had begun to look at him askance, as if they wished to inquire what ailed him.

A new game was formed jocosely. The cowboy volunteered to become the partner of Johnnie, and they all then turned to ask the Swede to throw in his lot with the little Easterner. He asked some questions about the game, and, learning that it wore many names, and that he had played it when it was under an alias, he accepted the invitation. He strode toward the men nervously, as if he expected to be assaulted. Finally, seated, he gazed from face to face and laughed shrilly. This laugh was so strange that the Easterner looked up quickly, the cowboy sat intent and with his mouth open, and Johnnie paused, holding the cards with still fingers.

Afterward there was a short silence. Then Johnnie said, "Well, let's get at it. Come on now!" They pulled their chairs forward until their knees were bunched under the board. They began to play, and their interest in the game caused the others to forget the manner of the Swede.

The cowboy was a board-whacker. Each time that he held superior cards he whanged them, one by one, with exceeding force, down upon the improvised table, and took the tricks with a glowing air of prowess and pride that sent thrills of indignation into the hearts of his opponents. A game with a board-whacker in it is sure to become intense. The countenances of the Easterner and the Swede were miserable whenever the cowboy thundered down his aces and kings, while Johnnie, his eyes gleaming with joy, chuckled and chuckled.

Because of the absorbing play none considered the strange ways of the Swede. They paid strict heed to the game. Finally, during a lull caused by a new deal, the Swede suddenly addressed Johnnie: "I suppose there have been a good many men killed in this room." The jaws of the others dropped and they looked at him.

"What in hell are you talking about?" said Johnnie.

The Swede laughed again his blatant laugh, full of a kind of false courage and defiance. "Oh, you know what I mean all right," he answered.

"I'm a liar if I do!" Johnnie protested. The card was halted, and the men stared at the Swede. Johnnie evidently felt that as the son of the proprietor he should make a direct inquiry. "Now, what might you be drivin' at, mister?" he asked. The Swede winked at him. It was a wink full of cunning. His fingers shook on the edge of the board. "Oh, maybe you think I have been to nowheres. Maybe you think I'm a tenderfoot?"

"I don't know nothin' about you," answered Johnnie, "and I don't give a damn where you've been. All I got to say is that I don't know what you're driving at. There hain't never been nobody killed in this room."

The cowboy, who had been steadily gazing at the Swede, then spoke: "What's wrong with you, mister?"

Apparently it seemed to the Swede that he was formidably menaced. He shivered and turned white near the corners of his mouth. He sent an appealing glance in the direction of the little Easterner. During these moments he did not forget to wear his air of advanced pot-valor. "They say they don't know what I mean," he remarked mockingly to the Easterner.

The latter answered after prolonged and cautious reflection. "I don't understand you," he said, impassively.

The Swede made a movement then which announced that he thought he had encountered treachery from the only quarter where he had expected sympathy, if not help. "Oh, I see you are all against me. I see—"

The cowboy was in a state of deep stupefaction. "Say," he cried, as he tumbled the deck violently down upon the board, "say, what are you gittin' at, hey?"

The Swede sprang up with the celerity of a man escaping from a snake on the floor. "I don't want to fight!" he shouted. "I don't want to fight!"

The cowboy stretched his long legs indolently and deliberately. His hands were in his pockets. He spat into the sawdust box. "Well, who the hell thought you did?" he inquired.

The Swede backed rapidly toward a corner of the room. His hands were out protectingly in front of his chest, but he was making an obvious struggle to control his fright. "Gentlemen," he quavered, "I suppose I am going to be killed before I can leave this house! I suppose I am going to be killed before I can leave this house!" In his eyes was the dying-swan look. Through the windows could be seen the snow turning blue in the shadow of dusk. The wind tore at the house, and some loose thing beat regularly against the clapboards like a spirit tapping.

A door opened, and Scully himself entered. He paused in surprise as he noted the tragic attitude of the Swede. Then he said, "What's the matter here?"

The Swede answered him swiftly and eagerly: "These men are going to kill me."

"Kill you!" ejaculated Scully. "Kill you! What are you talkin'?"

The Swede made the gesture of a martyr.

Scully wheeled sternly upon his son. "What is this, Johnnie?"

The lad had grown sullen. "Damned if I know," he answered. "I can't make no sense to it." He began to shuffle the cards, fluttering them together with an angry snap. "He says a good many men have been killed in this room, or something like that. And he says he's goin' to be killed here too. I don't know what ails him. He's crazy, I shouldn't wonder."

Scully then looked for explanation to the cowboy, but the cowboy simply shrugged his shoulders.

"Kill you?" said Scully again to the Swede. "Kill you? Man, you're off your nut."

"Oh, I know," burst out the Swede. "I know what will happen. Yes, I'm crazy—yes. Yes, of course, I'm crazy—yes. But I know one thing—" There was a sort of sweat of misery and terror upon his face. "I know I won't get out of here alive."

The cowboy drew a deep breath, as if his mind was passing into the last stages of dissolution. "Well, I'm dog-goned," he whispered to himself.

Scully wheeled suddenly and faced his son. "You've been troublin' this man!"

Johnnie's voice was loud with its burden of grievance. "Why, good Gawd, I ain't done nothin' to 'im."

The Swede broke in. "Gentlemen, do not disturb yourselves. I will leave this house. I will go away, because"—he accused them dramatically with his glance—"because I do not want to be killed."

Scully was furious with his son. "Will you tell me what is the matter, you young divil? What's the matter, anyhow? Speak out!"

"Blame it!" cried Johnnie in despair, "don't I tell you I don't know? He—he says we want to kill him, and that's all I know. I can't tell what ails him."

The Swede continued to repeat: "Never mind, Mr. Scully; never mind. I will leave this house. I will go away, because I do not wish to be killed. Yes, of course, I am crazy—yes. But I know one thing! I will go away. I will leave this house. Never mind, Mr. Scully; never mind. I will go away."

"You will not go 'way," said Scully. "You will not go 'way until I hear the reason of this business. If anybody has troubled you I will take care of him. This is my house. You are under my roof, and I will not allow any peaceable man to be troubled here." He cast a terrible eye upon Johnnie, the cowboy, and the Easterner.

"Never mind, Mr. Scully; never mind. I will go away. I do not wish to be killed." The Swede moved toward the door which opened upon the stairs. It was evidently his intention to go at once for his baggage.

"No, no," shouted Scully peremptorily; but the white-faced man slid by him and disappeared. "Now," said Scully severely, "what does this mane?"

Johnnie and the cowboy cried together: "Why, we didn't do nothin' to 'im!"

Scully's eyes were cold. "No," he said, "you didn't?"

Johnnie swore a deep oath. "Why, this is the wildest loon I ever see. We didn't do nothin' at all. We were jest sittin' here playin' cards, and he—"

The father suddenly spoke to the Easterner. "Mr. Blanc," he asked, "what has these boys been doin'?"

The Easterner reflected again. "I didn't see anything wrong at all," he said at last, slowly.

Scully began to howl. "But what does it mane?" He

stared ferociously at his son. "I have a mind to lather you for this, me boy."

Johnnie was frantic. "Well, what have I done?" he bawled at his father.

III

"I think you are tongue-tied," said Scully finally to his son, the cowboy, and the Easterner; and at the end of this scornful sentence he left the room.

Upstairs the Swede was swiftly fastening the straps of his great valise. Once his back happened to be half turned toward the door, and, hearing a noise there, he wheeled and sprang up, uttering a loud cry. Scully's wrinkled visage showed grimly in the light of the small lamp he carried. This yellow effulgence, streaming upward, colored only his prominent features, and left his eyes, for instance, in mysterious shadow. He resembled a murderer.

"Man! man!" he exclaimed, "have you gone daffy?"

"Oh, no! Oh, no!" rejoined the other. "There are people in this world who know pretty nearly as much as you do—understand?"

For a moment they stood gazing at each other. Upon the Swede's deathly pale cheeks were two spots brightly crimson and sharply edged, as if they had been carefully painted. Scully placed the light on the table and sat himself on the edge of the bed. He spoke ruminatively. "By cracky, I never heard of such a thing in my life. It's a complete muddle. I can't, for the soul of me, think how you ever got this idea into your head." Presently he lifted his eyes and asked: "And did you sure think they were going to kill you?"

The Swede scanned the old man, as if he wished to see into his mind. "I did," he said at last. He obviously suspected that this answer might precipitate an outbreak. As he pulled on a strap his whole arm shook, the elbow wavering like a bit of paper.

Scully banged his hand impressively on the footboard of the bed. "Why, man, we're goin' to have a line of ilictric streetcars in this town next spring."

" 'A line of electric streetcars,' " repeated the Swede, stupidly.

"And," said Scully, "there's a new railroad goin' to be built down from Broken Arm to here. Not to mintion the four churches and the smashin' big brick schoolhouse. Then there's the big factory, too. Why, in two years Romper'll be a met-tro-*pol*-is."

Having finished the preparation of his baggage, the Swede straightened himself. "Mr. Scully," he said, with sudden hardihood, "how much do I owe you?"

"You don't owe me anythin'," said the old man, angrily.

"Yes, I do," retorted the Swede. He took seventy-five cents from his pocket and tendered it to Scully; but the latter snapped his fingers in disdainful refusal. However, it happened that they both stood gazing in a strange fashion at three silver pieces on the Swede's open palm.

"I'll not take your money," said Scully at last. "Not after what's been goin' on here." Then a plan seemed to strike him. "Here," he cried, picking up his lamp and moving toward the door. "Here! Come with me a minute."

"No," said the Swede, in overwhelming alarm.

"Yes," urged the old man. "Come on! I want you to come and see a picter—just across the hall—in my room."

The Swede must have concluded that his hour was come. His jaw dropped and his teeth showed like a dead man's. He ultimately followed Scully across the corridor, but he had the step of one hung in chains.

Scully flashed the light high on the wall of his own chamber. There was revealed a ridiculous photograph of a little girl. She was leaning against a balustrade of gorgeous decoration, and the formidable bang to her hair was prominent. The figure was as graceful as an upright sled-stake, and, withal, it was of the hue of lead. "There," said Scully, tenderly, "that's the picter of my little girl that died. Her name was Carrie. She had the purtiest hair you ever saw! I was that fond of her, she—"

Turning then, he saw that the Swede was not contemplating the picture at all, but, instead, was keeping keen watch on the gloom in the rear.

"Look, man!" cried Scully, heartily. "That's the picter of my little gal that died. Her name was Carrie. And then here's the picter of my oldest boy, Michael. He's a lawyer in Lincoln, an' doin' well. I gave that boy a grand eddycation, and I'm glad for it now. He's a fine boy. Look at 'im now. Ain't he bold as blazes, him there in Lincoln, an honored an' respicted gintleman! An honored and respicted gintleman," concluded Scully with a flourish. And, so saying, he smote the Swede jovially on the back.

The Swede faintly smiled.

"Now," said the old man, "there's only one more thing." He dropped suddenly to the floor and thrust his head beneath the bed. The Swede could hear his muffled voice. "I'd keep it under me piller if it wasn't for that boy Johnnie. Then there's the old woman— Where is it now? I never put it twice in the same place. Ah, now come out with you!"

Presently he backed clumsily from under the bed, dragging with him an old coat rolled into a bundle. "I've fetched him," he muttered. Kneeling on the floor, he unrolled the coat and extracted from its heart a large yellow-brown whiskey bottle.

His first maneuver was to hold the bottle up to the light. Reassured, apparently, that nobody had been tampering with it, he thrust it with a generous movement toward the Swede.

The weak-kneed Swede was about to eagerly clutch this element of strength, but he suddenly jerked his hand away and cast a look of horror upon Scully.

"Drink," said the old man affectionately. He had risen to his feet, and now stood facing the Swede.

There was a silence. Then again Scully said: "Drink!"

The Swede laughed wildly. He grabbed the bottle, put it to his mouth; and as his lips curled absurdly around the opening and his throat worked, he kept his glance, burning with hatred, upon the old man's face.

IV

After the departure of Scully the three men, with the cardboard still upon their knees, preserved for a long time an astounded silence. Then Johnnie said: "That's the doddangedest Swede I ever see."

"He ain't no Swede," said the cowboy, scornfully.

"Well, what is he then?" cried Johnnie. "What is he then?"

"It's my opinion," replied the cowboy deliberately, "he's some kind of a Dutchman." It was a venerable custom of the country to entitle as Swedes all light-haired men who spoke with a heavy tongue. In consequence the idea of the cowboy was not without its daring. "Yes, sir," he repeated. "It's my opinion this feller is some kind of a Dutchman."

"Well, he says he's a Swede, anyhow," muttered Johnnie, sulkily. He turned to the Easterner: "What do you think, Mr. Blanc?"

"Oh, I don't know," replied the Easterner.

"Well, what do you think makes him act that way?" asked the cowboy.

"Why, he's frightened." The Easterner knocked his pipe against a rim of the stove. "He's clear frightened out of his boots."

"What at?" cried Johnnie and the cowboy together.

The Easterner reflected over his answer.

"What at?" cried the others again.

"Oh, I don't know, but it seems to me this man has been reading dime novels, and he thinks he's right out in the middle of it—the shootin' and stabbin' and all."

"But," said the cowboy, deeply scandalized, "this ain't Wyoming, ner none of them places. This is Nebrasker."

"Yes," added Johnnie, "an' why don't he wait till he gits *out West?*"

The traveled Easterner laughed. "It isn't different there even—not in these days. But he thinks he's right in the middle of hell."

Johnnie and the cowboy mused long.

"It's awful funny," remarked Johnnie at last.

"Yes," said the cowboy. "This is a queer game. I hope we don't git snowed in, because then we'd have to stand this here man bein' around with us all the time. That wouldn't be no good."

"I wish pop would throw him out," said Johnnie.

Presently they heard a loud stamping on the stairs, accompanied by ringing jokes in the voice of old Scully, and laughter, evidently from the Swede. The men around the stove stared vacantly at each other. "Gosh!" said the cowboy. The door flew open, and old Scully, flushed and anecdotal, came into the room. He was jabbering at the Swede, who followed him, laughing bravely. It was the entry of two roisterers from a banquet hall.

"Come now," said Scully sharply to the three seated men, "move up and give us a chance at the stove." The cowboy and the Easterner obediently sidled their chairs to make room for the newcomers. Johnnie, however, simply arranged himself in a more indolent attitude, and then remained motionless.

"Come! Git over, there," said Scully.

"Plenty of room on the other side of the stove," said Johnnie.

"Do you think we want to sit in the draught?" roared the father.

But the Swede here interposed with a grandeur of confidence. "No, no. Let the boy sit where he likes," he cried in a bullying voice to the father.

"All right! All right!" said Scully, deferentially. The cowboy and the Easterner exchanged glances of wonder.

The five chairs were formed in a crescent about one side of the stove. The Swede began to talk; he talked arrogantly, profanely, angrily. Johnnie, the cowboy, and the Easterner maintained a morose silence, while old Scully appeared to be receptive and eager, breaking in constantly with sympathetic ejaculations.

Finally the Swede announced that he was thirsty. He moved in his chair, and said that he would go for a drink of water.

"I'll git it for you," cried Scully at once.

"No," said the Swede, contemptuously. "I'll get it for myself." He arose and stalked with the air of an owner off into the executive parts of the hotel.

As soon as the Swede was out of hearing Scully sprang to his feet and whispered intensely to the others: "Upstairs he thought I was tryin' to poison 'im."

"Say," said Johnnie, "this makes me sick. Why don't you throw 'im out in the snow?"

"Why, he's all right now," declared Scully. "It was only that he was from the East, and he thought this was a tough place. That's all. He's all right now."

The cowboy looked with admiration upon the Easterner. "You were straight," he said. "You were on to that there Dutchman."

"Well," said Johnnie to his father, "he may be all right now, but I don't see it. Other time he was scared, but now he's too fresh."

Scully's speech was always a combination of Irish brogue and idiom, Western twang and idiom, and scraps of curiously formal diction taken from the story-books and newspapers. He now hurled a strange mass of language at the head of his son. "What do I keep? What do I keep? What do I keep?" he demanded, in a voice of thunder. He slapped his knee impressively, to indicate that he himself was going to make reply, and that all should heed. "I keep a hotel," he shouted. "A hotel, do you mind? A guest under my roof has sacred privileges. He is to be intimidated by none. Not one word shall he hear that would prijudice him in favor of goin' away. I'll not have it. There's no place in this here town where they can say they iver took in a guest of mine because he was afraid to stay here." He wheeled suddenly upon the cowboy and the Easterner. "Am I right?"

"Yes, Mr. Scully," said the cowboy, "I think you're right."

"Yes, Mr. Scully," said the Easterner, "I think you're right."

V

At six-o'clock supper, the Swede fizzed like a fire-wheel. He sometimes seemed on the point of bursting into riotous song, and in all his madness he was encouraged by old Scully. The Easterner was encased in reserve; the cowboy sat in wide-mouthed amazement, forgetting to eat, while Johnnie wrathily demolished great plates of food. The daughters of the house, when they were obliged to replenish the biscuits, approached as warily as Indians, and, having succeeded in their purpose, fled with ill-concealed trepidation. The Swede domineered the whole feast, and he gave it the appearance of a cruel bacchanal. He seemed to have grown suddenly taller; he gazed, brutally disdainful, into every face. His voice rang through the room. Once when he jabbed out harpoon-fashion with his fork to pinion a biscuit, the weapon nearly impaled the hand of the Easterner, which had been stretched quietly out for the same biscuit.

After supper, as the men filed toward the other room, the Swede smote Scully ruthlessly on the shoulder. "Well, old boy, that was a good, square meal." Johnnie looked hopefully at his father; he knew that shoulder was tender from an old fall; and, indeed, it appeared for a moment as if Scully was going to flame out over the matter, but in the end he smiled a sickly smile and remained silent. The others understood from his manner that he was admitting his responsibility for the Swede's new viewpoint.

Johnnie, however, addressed his parent in an aside. "Why don't you license somebody to kick you downstairs?" Scully scowled darkly by way of reply.

When they were gathered about the stove, the Swede insisted on another game of High-Five. Scully gently deprecated the plan at first, but the Swede turned a wolfish glare upon him. The old man subsided, and the Swede canvassed the others. In his tone there was always a great threat. The cowboy and the Easterner both remarked indifferently that they would play. Scully said that he would presently have to go to meet the 6:58 train, and so the Swede turned menacingly upon Johnnie. For a moment their glances crossed like blades, and then Johnnie smiled and said, "Yes, I'll play."

They formed a square, with the little board on their knees. The Easterner and the Swede were again partners. As the play went on, it was noticeable that the cowboy was not board-whacking as usual. Meanwhile, Scully, near the lamp, had put on his spectacles and, with an appearance curiously like an old priest, was reading a newspaper. In time he went out to meet the 6:58 train, and, despite his precautions, a gust of polar wind whirled into the room as he opened the door. Besides scattering the cards, it chilled the players to the marrow. The Swede cursed frightfully. When Scully returned, his entrance disturbed a cozy and friendly scene. The Swede again cursed. But presently they were once more intent, their heads bent forward and their hands moving swiftly. The Swede had adopted the fashion of board-whacking.

Scully took up his paper and for a long time remained immersed in matters which were extraordinarily remote from him. The lamp burned badly, and once he stopped to adjust the wick. The newspaper, as he turned from page to page, rustled with a slow and comfortable sound. Then suddenly he heard three terrible words: "You are cheatin'!"

Such scenes often prove that there can be little of dramatic import in environment. Any room can present a tragic front; any room can be comic. This little den was now hideous as a torture chamber. The new faces of the men themselves had changed it upon the instant. The Swede held a huge fist in front of Johnnie's face, while the latter looked steadily over it into the blazing orbs of his accuser. The Easterner had grown pallid; the cowboy's jaw had dropped in that expression of bovine amazement which was one of his important mannerisms. After the three words, the first sound in the room was made by Scully's paper as it floated forgotten to his feet. His spectacles had also fallen from his nose, but by a clutch he had saved them in air. His hand, grasping the spectacles, now remained poised awkwardly and near his shoulder. He stared at the card-players.

Probably the silence was while a second elapsed. Then, if the floor had been suddenly twitched out from under the men they could not have moved quicker. The five had projected themselves headlong toward a common point. It happened that Johnnie, in rising to hurl himself upon the Swede, had stumbled slightly because of his curiously instinctive care for the cards and the board. The loss of the moment allowed time for the arrival of Scully, and also allowed the cowboy time to give the Swede a great push which sent him staggering back. The men found tongue together, and hoarse shouts of rage, appeal, or fear burst from every throat. The cowboy pushed and jostled feverishly at the Swede, and the Easterner and Scully clung wildly to Johnnie; but, through the smoky air, above the swaying bodies of the peace-compellers, the eyes of the two warriors ever sought each other in glances of challenge that were at once hot and steely.

Of course the board had been overturned, and now the whole company of cards was scattered over the floor, where the boots of the men trampled the fat and painted kings and queens as they gazed with their silly eyes at the war that was waging above them.

Scully's voice was dominating the yells. "Stop now! Stop, I say! Stop, now—"

Johnnie, as he struggled to burst through the rank formed by Scully and the Easterner, was crying, "Well, he says I cheated! He says I cheated! I won't allow no man to say I cheated! If he says I cheated, he's a——!"

The cowboy was telling the Swede, "Quit, now! Quit, d'ye hear—"

The screams of the Swede never ceased: "He did cheat! I saw him! I saw him—"

As for the Easterner, he was importuning in a voice that was not heeded: "Wait a moment, can't you? Oh, wait a moment. What's the good of a fight over a game of cards? Wait a moment—"

In this tumult no complete sentences were clear. "Cheat" —"Quit"—"He says"—these fragments pierced the uproar and rang out sharply. It was remarkable that, whereas Scully undoubtedly made the most noise, he was the least heard of any of the riotous band.

Then suddenly there was a great cessation. It was as if each man had paused for breath; and although the room was still lighted with the anger of men, it could be seen that there was no danger of immediate conflict, and at once Johnnie, shouldering his way forward, almost succeeded in confronting the Swede. "What did you say I cheated for? What did you say I cheated for? I don't cheat, and I won't let no man say I do!"

The Swede said, "I saw you! I saw you!"

"Well," cried Johnnie, "I'll fight any man what says I cheat!"

"No, you won't," said the cowboy. "Not here."

"Ah, be still, can't you?" said Scully, coming between them.

The quiet was sufficient to allow the Easterner's voice to be heard. He was repeating, "Oh, wait a moment, can't you? What's the good of a fight over a game of cards? Wait a moment!"

Johnnie, his red face appearing above his father's shoulder, hailed the Swede again. "Did you say I cheated?"

The Swede showed his teeth. "Yes."

"Then," said Johnnie, "we must fight."

"Yes, fight," roared the Swede. He was like a demoniac. "Yes, fight! I'll show you what kind of a man I am! I'll show you who you want to fight! Maybe you think I can't fight! Maybe you think I can't! I'll show you, you skin, you card-sharp! Yes, you cheated! You cheated! You cheated!"

"Well, let's go at it, then, mister," said Johnnie, coolly.

The cowboy's brow was beaded with sweat from his efforts in intercepting all sorts of raids. He turned in despair to Scully. "What are you goin' to do now?"

A change had come over the Celtic visage of the old man. He now seemed all eagerness; his eyes glowed.

"We'll let them fight," he answered, stalwartly. "I can't put up with it any longer. I've stood this damned Swede till I'm sick. We'll let them fight."

VI

The men prepared to go out-of-doors. The Easterner was so nervous that he had great difficulty in getting his arms into the sleeves of his new leather coat. As the cowboy drew his fur cap down over his ears his hands trembled. In fact, Johnnie and old Scully were the only ones who displayed no agitation. These preliminaries were conducted without words.

Scully threw open the door. "Well, come on," he said. Instantly a terrific wind caused the flame of the lamp to struggle at its wick, while a puff of black smoke sprang from the chimney-top. The stove was in mid-current of the blast, and its voice swelled to equal the roar of the storm. Some of the scarred and bedabbled cards were caught up from the floor and dashed helplessly against the farther wall. The men lowered their heads and plunged into the tempest as into a sea.

No snow was falling, but great whirls and clouds of flakes, swept up from the ground by the frantic winds, were streaming southward with the speed of bullets. The covered land was blue with the sheen of an unearthly satin, and there was no other hue save where, at the low, black railway station—which seemed incredibly distant—one light gleamed like a tiny jewel. As the men floundered into a thigh-deep drift, it was known that the Swede was bawling out something. Scully went to him, put a hand on his shoulder, and projected an ear. "What's that you say?" he shouted.

"I say," bawled the Swede again, "I won't stand much show against this gang. I know you'll all pitch on me."

Scully smote him reproachfully on the arm. "Tut, man!" he yelled. The wind tore the words from Scully's lips and scattered them far alee.

"You are all a gang of—" boomed the Swede, but the storm also seized the remainder of this sentence.

Immediately turning their backs upon the wind, the men had swung around a corner to the sheltered side of the hotel. It was the function of the little house to preserve here, amid this great devastation of snow, an irregular V-shape of heavily encrusted grass, which crackled beneath the feet. One could imagine the great drifts piled against the windward side. When the party reached the comparative peace of this spot it was found that the Swede was still bellowing.

"Oh, I know what kind of a thing this is! I know you'll all pitch on me. I can't lick you all!"

Scully turned upon him panther-fashion. "You'll not have to whip all of us. You'll have to whip my son Johnnie. An' the man what troubles you durin' that time will have me to dale with."

The arrangements were swiftly made. The two men faced each other, obedient to the harsh commands of Scully, whose face, in the subtly luminous gloom, could be seen set in the austere impersonal lines that are pictured on the countenances of the Roman veterans. The Easterner's teeth were chattering, and he was hopping up and down like a mechanical toy. The cowboy stood rock-like.

The contestants had not stripped off any clothing. Each was in his ordinary attire. Their fists were up, and they eyed each other in a calm that had the elements of leonine cruelty in it.

During this pause, the Easterner's mind, like a film, took lasting impressions of three men—the iron-nerved master of the ceremony; the Swede, pale, motionless, terrible; and Johnnie, serene yet ferocious, brutish yet heroic. The entire prelude had in it a tragedy greater than the tragedy of action, and this aspect was accentuated by the long, mellow cry of the blizzard, as it sped the tumbling and wailing flakes into the black abyss of the south.

"Now!" said Scully.

The two combatants leaped forward and crashed together like bullocks. There was heard the cushioned sound of blows, and of a curse squeezing out from between the tight teeth of one.

As for the spectators, the Easterner's pent-up breath exploded from him with a pop of relief, absolute relief from the tension of the preliminaries. The cowboy bounded into the air with a yowl. Scully was immovable as from supreme amazement and fear at the fury of the fight which he himself had permitted and arranged.

For a time the encounter in the darkness was such a perplexity of flying arms that it presented no more detail than would a swiftly revolving wheel. Occasionally a face, as if illumined by a flash of light, would shine out, ghastly and marked with pink spots. A moment later, the men might have been known as shadows, if it were not for the involuntary utterance of oaths that came from them in whispers.

Suddenly a holocaust of warlike desire caught the cowboy, and he bolted forward with the speed of a broncho. "Go it, Johnnie! go it! Kill him! Kill him!"

Scully confronted him. "Kape back," he said; and by his glance the cowboy could tell that this man was Johnnie's father.

To the Easterner there was a monotony of unchangeable fighting that was an abomination. This confused mingling was eternal to his sense, which was concentrated in a longing for the end, the priceless end. Once the fighters lurched near him, and as he scrambled hastily backward he heard them breathe like men on the rack.

"Kill him, Johnnie! Kill him! Kill him! Kill him!" The cowboy's face was contorted like one of those agony masks in museums.

"Keep still," said Scully, icily.

Then there was a sudden loud grunt, incomplete, cut short, and Johnnie's body swung away from the Swede and fell with sickening heaviness to the grass. The cowboy was barely in time to prevent the mad Swede from flinging himself upon his prone adversary. "No, you don't," said the cowboy, interposing an arm. "Wait a second."

Scully was at his son's side. "Johnnie! Johnnie, me boy!" His voice had a quality of melancholy tenderness. "Johnnie! Can you go on with it?" He looked anxiously down into the bloody, pulpy face of his son.

There was a moment of silence, and then Johnnie answered in his ordinary voice, "Yes, I—it—yes."

Assisted by his father he struggled to his feet. "Wait a bit now till you git your wind," said the old man.

A few paces away the cowboy was lecturing the Swede. "No, you don't! Wait a second!"

The Easterner was plucking at Scully's sleeve. "Oh, this is enough," he pleaded. "This is enough! Let it go as it stands. This is enough!"

"Bill," said Scully, "git out of the road." The cowboy stepped aside. "Now." The combatants were actuated by a new caution as they advanced toward collision. They glared at each other, and then the Swede aimed a lightning blow that carried with it his entire weight. Johnnie was evidently half stupid from weakness, but he miraculously dodged, and his fist sent the overbalanced Swede sprawling.

The cowboy, Scully, and the Easterner burst into a cheer that was like a chorus of triumphant soldiery, but before its conclusion the Swede had scuffled agilely to his feet and come in berserk abandon at his foe. There was another perplexity of flying arms, and Johnnie's body again swung away and fell, even as a bundle might fall from a roof. The Swede instantly staggered to a little wind-waved tree and leaned upon it, breathing like an engine, while his savage and flame-lit eyes roamed from face to face as the men bent over Johnnie. There was a splendor of isolation in his situation at this time which the Easterner felt once when, lifting his eyes from the man on the ground, he beheld that mysterious and lonely figure, waiting.

"Are you any good yet, Johnnie?" asked Scully in a broken voice.

The son gasped and opened his eyes languidly. After a moment he answered, "No—I ain't—any good—any—more." Then, from shame and bodily ill, he began to weep, the tears furrowing down through the bloodstains on his face. "He was too—too—too heavy for me."

Scully straightened and addressed the waiting figure. "Stranger," he said, evenly, "it's all up with our side." Then his voice changed into that vibrant huskiness which is commonly the tone of the most simple and deadly announcements. "Johnnie is whipped."

Without replying, the victor moved off on the route to the front door of the hotel.

The cowboy was formulating new and unspellable blasphemies. The Easterner was startled to find that they were out in a wind that seemed to come direct from the shadowed arctic floes. He heard again the wail of the snow as it was flung to its grave in the south. He knew now that all this time the cold had been sinking into him deeper and deeper, and he wondered that he had not perished. He felt indifferent to the condition of the vanquished man.

"Johnnie, can you walk?" asked Scully.

"Did I hurt—hurt him any?" asked the son.

"Can you walk, boy? Can you walk?"

Johnnie's voice was suddenly strong. There was a robust

impatience in it. "I asked you whether I hurt him any!"

"Yes, yes, Johnnie," answered the cowboy, consolingly; "he's hurt a good deal."

They raised him from the ground, and as soon as he was on his feet he went tottering off, rebuffing all attempts at assistance. When the party rounded the corner they were fairly blinded by the pelting of the snow. It burned their faces like fire. The cowboy carried Johnnie through the drift to the door. As they entered, some cards again rose from the floor and beat against the wall.

The Easterner rushed to the stove. He was so profoundly chilled that he almost dared to embrace the glowing iron. The Swede was not in the room, Johnnie sank into a chair and, folding his arms on his knees, buried his face in them. Scully, warming one foot and then the other at a rim of the stove, muttered to himself with Celtic mournfulness. The cowboy had removed his fur cap, and with a dazed and rueful air he was running one hand through his tousled locks. From overhead they could hear the creaking of boards, as the Swede tramped here and there in his room.

The sad quiet was broken by the sudden flinging open of a door that led toward the kitchen. It was instantly followed by an inrush of women. They precipitated themselves upon Johnnie amid a chorus of lamentation. Before they carried their prey off to the kitchen, there to be bathed and harangued with that mixture of sympathy and abuse which is a feat of their sex, the mother straightened herself and fixed old Scully with an eye of stern reproach. "Shame be upon you, Patrick Scully!" she cried. "Your own son, too. Shame be upon you!"

"There, now! Be quiet, now!" said the old man, weakly.

"Shame be upon you, Patrick Scully!" The girls, rallying to this slogan, sniffed disdainfully in the direction of those trembling accomplices, the cowboy and the Easterner. Presently they bore Johnnie away, and left the three men to dismal reflection.

VII

"I'd like to fight this here Dutchman myself," said the cowboy, breaking a long silence.

Scully wagged his head sadly. "No, that wouldn't do. It wouldn't be right. It wouldn't be right."

"Well, why wouldn't it?" argued the cowboy. "I don't see no harm in it."

"No," answered Scully, with mournful heroism. "It wouldn't be right. It was Johnnie's fight, and now we mustn't whip the man just because he whipped Johnnie."

"Yes, that's true enough," said the cowboy; "but—he better not get fresh with me, because I couldn't stand no more of it."

"You'll not say a word to him," commanded Scully, and even then they heard the tread of the Swede on the stairs. His entrance was made theatric. He swept the door back with a bang and swaggered to the middle of the room. No one looked at him. "Well," he cried, insolently, at Scully, "I s'pose you'll tell me now how much I owe you?"

The old man remained stolid. "You don't owe me nothin'."

"Huh!" said the Swede, "huh! Don't owe 'im nothin'."

The cowboy addressed the Swede. "Stranger, I don't see how you come to be so gay around here."

Old Scully was instantly alert. "Stop!" he shouted, holding his hand forth, fingers upward. "Bill, you shut up!"

The cowboy spat carelessly into the sawdust box. "I didn't say a word, did I?" he asked.

"Mr. Scully," called the Swede, "how much do I owe you?" It was seen that he was attired for departure, and that he had his valise in his hand.

"You don't owe me nothin'," repeated Scully in his same imperturbable way.

"Huh!" said the Swede. "I guess you're right. I guess if it was any way at all, you'd owe me somethin'. That's what I guess." He turned to the cowboy. " 'Kill him! Kill him! Kill him!' " he mimicked, and then guffawed victoriously. " 'Kill him!' " He was convulsed with ironical humor.

But he might have been jeering the dead. The three men were immovable and silent, staring with glassy eyes at the stove.

The Swede opened the door and passed into the storm, giving one derisive glance backward at the still group.

As soon as the door was closed, Scully and the cowboy leaped to their feet and began to curse. They trampled to and fro, waving their arms and smashing into the air with their fists. "Oh, but that was a hard minute!" wailed Scully. "That was a hard minute! Him there leerin' and scoffin'!

One bang at his nose was worth forty dollars to me that minute! How did you stand it, Bill?"

"How did I stand it?" cried the cowboy in a quivering voice. "How did I stand it? Oh!"

The old man burst into sudden brogue. "I'd loike to take that Swade," he wailed, "and hould 'im down on a shtone flure and bate 'im to a jelly wid a shtick!"

The cowboy groaned in sympathy. "I'd like to git him by the neck and ha-ammer him"—he brought his hand down on a chair with a noise like a pistol-shot—"hammer that there Dutchman until he couldn't tell himself from a dead coyote!"

"I'd bate 'im until he—"

"I'd show *him* some things—"

And then together they raised a yearning, fanatic cry—"Oh-o-oh! if we only could—"

"Yes!"

"Yes!"

"And then I'd—"

"O-o-oh!"

VIII

The Swede, tightly gripping his valise, tacked across the face of the storm as if he carried sails. He was following a line of little naked, gasping trees which, he knew, must mark the way of the road. His face, fresh from the pounding of Johnnie's fists, felt more pleasure than pain in the wind and the driving snow. A number of square shapes loomed upon him finally, and he knew them as the houses of the main body of the town. He found a street and made travel along it, leaning heavily upon the wind whenever, at a corner, a terrific blast caught him.

He might have been in a deserted village. We picture the world as thick with conquering and elate humanity, but here, with the bugles of the tempest pealing, it was hard to imagine a peopled earth. One viewed the existence of man then as a marvel, and conceded a glamor of wonder to these lice which were caused to cling to a whirling, fire-smitten, ice-locked, disease-stricken, space-lost bulb. The conceit of man was explained by this storm to be the very engine of life. One was a coxcomb not to die in it. However, the Swede found a saloon.

In front of it an indomitable red light was burning, and

the snowflakes were made blood-color as they flew through the circumscribed territory of the lamp's shining. The Swede pushed open the door of the saloon and entered. A sanded expanse was before him, and at the end of it four men sat about a table drinking. Down one side of the room extended a radiant bar, and its guardian was leaning upon his elbows listening to the talk of the men at the table. The Swede dropped his valise upon the floor and, smiling fraternally upon the barkeeper, said, "Gimme some whiskey, will you?" The man placed a bottle, a whiskey glass, and a glass of ice-thick water upon the bar. The Swede poured himself an abnormal portion of whiskey and drank it in three gulps. "Pretty bad night," remarked the bartender, indifferently. He was making the pretension of blindness which is usually a distinction of his class; but it could have been seen that he was furtively studying the half-erased bloodstains on the face of the Swede. "Bad night," he said again.

"Oh, it's good enough for me," replied the Swede, hardily, as he poured himself some more whiskey. The barkeeper took his coin and maneuvered it through its reception by the highly nickeled cash-machine. A bell rang; a card labeled "20 cts." had appeared.

"No," continued the Swede, "this isn't too bad weather. It's good enough for me."

"So?" murmured the barkeeper, languidly.

The copious drams made the Swede's eyes swim, and he breathed a trifle heavier. "Yes, I like this weather. I like it. It suits me." It was apparently his design to impart a deep significance to these words.

"So?" murmured the bartender again. He turned to gaze dreamily at the scroll-like birds and bird-like scrolls which had been drawn with soap upon the mirrors in back of the bar.

"Well, I guess I'll take another drink," said the Swede, presently. "Have something?"

"No, thanks; I'm not drinkin'," answered the bartender. Afterward he asked, "How did you hurt your face?"

The Swede immediately began to boast loudly. "Why, in a fight. I thumped the soul out of a man down here at Scully's hotel."

The interest of the four men at the table was at last aroused.

"Who was it?" said one.

"Johnnie Scully," blustered the Swede. "Son of the man what runs it. He will be pretty near dead for some weeks, I can tell you. I made a nice thing of him, I did. He couldn't get up. They carried him in the house. Have a drink?"

Instantly the men in some subtle way encased themselves in reserve. "No, thanks," said one. The group was of curious formation. Two were prominent local businessmen; one was the district attorney; and one was a professional gambler of the kind known as "square." But a scrutiny of the group would not have enabled an observer to pick the gambler from the men of more reputable pursuits. He was, in fact, a man so delicate in manner, when among people of fair class, and so judicious in his choice of victims, that in the strictly masculine part of the town's life he had come to be explicitly trusted and admired. People called him a thoroughbred. The fear and contempt with which his craft was regarded were undoubtedly the reason why his quiet dignity shone conspicuous above the quiet dignity of men who might be merely hatters, billiard-markers, or grocery clerks. Beyond an occasional unwary traveler who came by rail, this gambler was supposed to prey solely upon reckless and senile farmers, who, when flush with good crops, drove into town in all the pride and confidence of an absolutely invulnerable stupidity. Hearing at times in circuitous fashion of the despoilment of such a farmer, the important men of Romper invariably laughed in contempt of the victim, and if they thought of the wolf at all, it was with a kind of pride at the knowledge that he would never dare think of attacking their wisdom and courage. Besides, it was popular that this gambler had a real wife and two real children in a neat cottage in a suburb, where he led an exemplary home life; and when any one even suggested a discrepancy in his character, the crowd immediately vociferated descriptions of this virtuous family circle. Then men who led exemplary home lives, and men who did not lead exemplary home lives, all subsided in a bunch, remarking that there was nothing more to be said.

However, when a restriction was placed upon him—as, for instance, when a strong clique of members of the new Pollywog Club refused to permit him, even as a spectator, to appear in the rooms of the organization—the candor and gentleness with which he accepted the judgment disarmed many of his foes and made his friends more desperately partisan. He invariably distinguished between himself and a respectable Romper man so quickly and frankly that his manner actually appeared to be a continual broadcast compliment.

And one must not forget to declare the fundamental fact of his entire position in Romper. It is irrefutable that in all affairs outside his business, in all matters that occur eternally and commonly between man and man, this thieving card-player was so generous, so just, so moral, that, in a contest, he could have put to flight the consciences of nine tenths of the citizens of Romper.

And so it happened that he was seated in this saloon with the two prominent local merchants and the district attorney.

The Swede continued to drink raw whiskey, meanwhile babbling at the barkeeper and trying to induce him to indulge in potations. "Come on. Have a drink. Come on. What—no? Well, have a little one, then. By gawd, I've whipped a man tonight, and I want to celebrate. I whipped him good, too. Gentlemen," the Swede cried to the men at the table, "have a drink?"

"Ssh!" said the barkeeper.

The group at the table, although furtively attentive, had been pretending to be deep in talk, but now a man lifted his eyes toward the Swede and said, shortly, "Thanks. We don't want any more."

At this reply the Swede ruffled out his chest like a rooster. "Well," he exploded, "it seems I can't get anybody to drink with me in this town. Seems so, don't it? Well!"

"Ssh!" said the barkeeper.

"Say," snarled the Swede, "don't you try to shut me up. I won't have it. I'm a gentleman, and I want people to drink with me. And I want 'em to drink with me now. *Now*—do you understand?" He rapped the bar with his knuckles.

Years of experience had calloused the bartender. He merely grew sulky. "I hear you," he answered.

"Well," cried the Swede, "listen hard then. See those men over there? Well, they're going to drink with me, and don't you forget it. Now you watch."

"Hi!" yelled the barkeeper, "this won't do!"

"Why won't it?" demanded the Swede. He stalked over

to the table, and by chance laid his hand upon the shoulder of the gambler. "How about this?" he asked wrathfully. "I asked you to drink with me."

The gambler simply twisted his head and spoke over his shoulder. "My friend, I don't know you."

"Oh, hell!" answered the Swede, "come and have a drink."

"Now, my boy," advised the gambler, kindly, "take your hand off my shoulder and go 'way and mind your own business." He was a little, slim man, and it seemed strange to hear him use this tone of heroic patronage to the burly Swede. The other men at the table said nothing.

"What! You won't drink with me, you little dude? I'll make you, then! I'll make you!" The Swede had grasped the gambler frenziedly at the throat, and was dragging him from his chair. The other men sprang up. The barkeeper dashed around the corner of his bar. There was a great tumult, and then was seen a long blade in the hand of the gambler. It shot forward, and a human body, this citadel of virtue, wisdom, power, was pierced as easily as if it had been a melon. The Swede fell with a cry of supreme astonishment.

The prominent merchants and the district attorney must have at once tumbled out of the place backward. The bartender found himself hanging limply to the arm of a chair and gazing into the eyes of a murderer.

"Henry," said the latter, as he wiped his knife on one of the towels that hung beneath the bar rail, "you tell 'em where to find me. I'll be home, waiting for 'em." Then he vanished. A moment afterward the barkeeper was in the street dinning through the storm for help and, moreover, companionship.

The corpse of the Swede, alone in the saloon, had its eyes fixed upon a dreadful legend that dwelt atop of the cash-machine: "This registers the amount of your purchase."

IX

Months later, the cowboy was frying pork over the stove of a little ranch near the Dakota line, when there was a quick thud of hoofs outside, and presently the Easterner entered with the letters and the papers.

"Well," said the Easterner at once, "the chap that killed the Swede has got three years. Wasn't much, was it?"

"He has? Three years?" The cowboy poised his pan of pork, while he ruminated upon the news. "Three years. That ain't much."

"No. It was a light sentence," replied the Easterner as he unbuckled his spurs. "Seems there was a good deal of sympathy for him in Romper."

"If the bartender had been any good," observed the cowboy, thoughtfully, "he would have gone in and cracked that there Dutchman on the head with a bottle in the beginnin' of it and stopped all this here murderin'."

"Yes, a thousand things might have happened," said the Easterner, tartly.

The cowboy returned his pan of pork to the fire, but his philosophy continued. "It's funny, ain't it? If he hadn't said Johnnie was cheatin' he'd be alive this minute. He was an awful fool. Game played for fun, too. Not for money. I believe he was crazy."

"I feel sorry for that gambler," said the Easterner.

"Oh, so do I," said the cowboy. "He don't deserve none of it for killin' who he did."

"The Swede might not have been killed if everything had been square."

"Might not have been killed?" exclaimed the cowboy. "Everythin' square? Why, when he said that Johnnie was cheatin' and acted like such a jackass? And then in the saloon he fairly walked up to git hurt?" With these arguments the cowboy browbeat the Easterner and reduced him to rage.

"You're a fool!" cried the Easterner, viciously. "You're a bigger jackass than the Swede by a million majority. Now let me tell you one thing. Let me tell you something. Listen! Johnnie *was* cheating!"

" 'Johnnie,' " said the cowboy, blankly. There was a minute of silence, and then he said, robustly, "Why, no. The game was only for fun."

"Fun or not," said the Easterner, "Johnnie was cheating. I saw him. I know it. I saw him. And I refused to stand up and be a man. I let the Swede fight it out alone. And you—you were simply puffing around the place and wanting to fight. And then old Scully himself! We are all in it!

This poor gambler isn't even a noun. He is kind of an adverb. Every sin is the result of a collaboration. We, five of us, have collaborated in the murder of this Swede. Usually there are from a dozen to forty women really involved in every murder, but in this case it seems to be only five men—you, I, Johnnie, old Scully; and that fool of an unfortunate gambler came merely as a culmination, the apex of a human movement, and gets all the punishment."

The cowboy, injured and rebellious, cried out blindly into this fog of mysterious theory: "Well, I didn't do anythin', did I?"

SCENE FROM *THE BLUE HOTEL,*

*a film script based on the Crane story, by Harry Mark Petrakis**

A wild-eyed Swede arrives at a Nebraska hotel, along with other guests, and expresses what seems an irrational fear of being murdered. Scully, the proprietor, persuades him to remain. After drinking too much, the Swede provokes a card game and accuses Johnnie, the proprietor's son, of cheating. In the ritualized fight in the snow which follows, Johnnie is soundly beaten by the Swede. As the men return to the lobby, the climactic scene begins.

INTERIOR. LOBBY.

[*As the men enter the lobby,* SCULLY *and the* COWBOY *still dragging* JOHNNIE *between them,* SCULLY *motions toward the door leading to the other part of the house. They carry him through the door while the* EASTERNER *walks toward the fire glowing in the stove, removing his coat. From the other room can be heard the shrill, concerned voices of* SCULLY'S *daughters.*]

SCULLY [*shouting*]. He's all right! Just beaten up a little. You wash him and get him to bed!

GIRL'S VOICE [*off-camera*]. Shame on you, Pa! Letting this happen to Johnnie!

[*The second girl's voice joins the tirade against* SCULLY. *In a moment* SCULLY *and the* COWBOY *emerge from the door,* SCULLY *moving angrily toward the stove, muttering to himself with Celtic mournfulness. The* COWBOY *removes his hat and jacket and ruefully runs his fingers*

---

* Harry Mark Petrakis has published many volumes of fiction, including *Pericles on 31st Street, A Dream of Kings,* and *The Waves of Night.* He has adapted several of his novels and stories for television and film presentation.

through his hair. Overhead they can hear the groaning of the boards as the Swede tramps back and forth in his room.]

[SCULLY *shakes his fist at the ceiling.*]

SCULLY [*wailing*]. I'd like to take that Swede and hold him down on the floor and beat 'im to jelly!

COWBOY. I'd like to git him by the neck and ham-mer that damned Dutchman until you couldn't tell him from a dead coyote!

SCULLY. That's what he needs! A beating!

COWBOY. By God, I think I'll ham-mer him when he comes down.

[*The* EASTERNER *has been listening to them and now he speaks quietly, for the first time since they reentered the hotel.*]

EASTERNER. No, that wouldn't do. It wouldn't be right, you know.

[SCULLY *and the* COWBOY *stare at him.*]

COWBOY. Why in hell wouldn't it be right?

[SCULLY *shakes his head in a sudden, mournful revelation.*]

SCULLY. He's right, Bill. It wouldn't be right or fair. It was Johnnie's fight and we mustn't whip the man because he whipped Johnnie.

COWBOY. That may be true but he better not get cheeky with me!

SCULLY [*sternly*]. You'll not say a word to him, nor lay a hand on him. Whatever he done to Johnnie, he is a guest in this hotel, a guest under my roof.

[*Their discussion is interrupted by the heavy tread of the* SWEDE *descending the stairs. He is attired for departure, his valise in his hand. A certain swagger in his walk suggests he might have revisited the bottle of Bombay gin under* SCULLY'S *bed.*]

SWEDE [*loudly*]. I'm getting out of here now, going to check into a real hotel up the street. How much do I owe you?

SCULLY [*somberly*]. You don't owe me nothing.

SWEDE [*mockingly*]. Huh! Huh! You don't owe me nothing!

COWBOY [*making a mighty effort to control his temper*]. Stranger, I don't see how come you're so damn cheeky. . . .

SCULLY. Bill, you shut up!

[*The* COWBOY *spits into the sawdust box in disgust and turns away.*]

SWEDE [*harshly*]. Scully, I asked how much I owe you?

SCULLY. I told you you you don't owe me nothing.

SWEDE [*chortling*]. Huh! I guess you're right. I guess you owe me something for teaching your boy a lesson he won't forget. That's what I guess. [*Turning toward the* COWBOY *he begins to mimic his voice.*] Kill him! Kill him! Kill him! Kill him! [*He is convulsed with derisive delight.*]

[*As the* SWEDE, *still laughing loudly, moves toward the door, it bursts open and a small, slender figure of a man in a coat with a fine fur collar enters the lobby. A gust of wind sweeps in around his legs, scattering the cards that litter the table, flickering the flame of the lamps. The man turns, pushing with all his strength to close the door against the wind. With a grunt the* SWEDE *reaches out his hand and arm and slams the door closed. The stranger nods to him in thanks and turns back to the lobby. He draws the fur cap off his head. He is a pale-faced, slender man with a certain grave dignity in his bearing.*]

STRANGER. Good evening, gentlemen. They told me at the stable I might get a room here. [*Motions toward the stove.*] That looks inviting. A bad night out there.

SCULLY. Warm yourself, stranger. We'll be glad to put you up when you're ready to sleep.

SWEDE [*delighted at another witness to his triumph*]. This isn't bad weather! It's good weather for me!

[*The* STRANGER *looks calmly at the* SWEDE *and doesn't answer. He removes his greatcoat, shaking off the snowflakes on the iron planking of the floor around the stove. He is neatly and precisely attired in the frock-coat and vest of the professional gambler.*]

SWEDE [*heartily*]. Yes, I like this weather. I like it fine! [*Winks at the stranger.*] Want to know why it's been great weather for me?

[*The* STRANGER *stands warming the back of his legs at the stove, looking at the* SWEDE, *not saying a word.*]

SWEDE. I had a fight here earlier tonight. I beat the living soul out of a man right here.

[SCULLY *mutters under his breath and the* COWBOY *shakes his head. The* EASTERNER *stares from one to the other, then looks back at the* SWEDE.]

SWEDE. Johnnie Scully! Son of this man here. [*Motions to* SCULLY.] He will be near dead for some weeks, I can tell you. I made a mess of him. They had to carry him into the house. [*Finishes with a boastful and raucous laugh.*]

[*The* COWBOY *lets out a low groan and* SCULLY *rubs his cheek in a mighty effort to rein in his temper.*]

[*Through the* SWEDE'S *boasting the* STRANGER *has been watching him silently. Now he deliberately turns his back on the* SWEDE, *extending his manicured and delicate hands toward the stove.*]

SWEDE [*offended*]. Mister, I told you what I done to a man here tonight and it ain't polite to turn your back on a man who's talking to you. Hear?

SCULLY. You were just leaving. Why don't you keep going and let us alone? You done enough trouble here tonight.

COWBOY. By God, if he don't leave . . .

[*The* SWEDE *casts a look of contempt at* SCULLY *and the* COWBOY *and marches defiantly toward the* STRANGER *at the stove. He places his big hand on the slender, frock-coated shoulder of the* STRANGER.]

SWEDE. I told you it ain't polite to turn your back on a man who is talking to you. . . .

STRANGER [*quietly*]. Now, my friend, take your hand off my shoulder.

SWEDE [*shouting*]. Turn around and look at me when I'm talking to . . .

[*He clutches the* STRANGER'S *shoulder harder and begins to jerk him around.* SCULLY *and the* COWBOY *move rapidly toward them, but not quickly enough. The* STRANGER *completes turning around under his own power, moving with a sudden, catlike swiftness. For an instant the lamplight glistens on the long, slim blade of a knife that has sprung into his hand. He faces the* SWEDE, *who looms over him, and thrusts the knife upward, piercing the* SWEDE'S *chest over his heart as easily as if he were slicing into a melon. A shattered shock sweeps the* SWEDE'S *face; he opens his mouth to utter a shriek; a short, shrill whistle of breath is all that emerges. He plunges forward taking the table adjoining the stove down with him, landing with a thunderous thump, sprawled on the floor at the* STRANGER'S *feet.*]

[*For a stunned, disbelieving moment the men in the room stand transfixed. The* EASTERNER *covers his eyes with his hands.* SCULLY *tries to speak and mumbles only a few unintelligible words. The* COWBOY *walks slowly to the stove and stands staring down at the body.*]

STRANGER [*quietly*]. If there is a sheriff or marshall in this town, you can call him. I'll be waiting for him right here. You are all witnesses that this man was abusing me. . . .

[*He turns back to the stove and calmly resumes warming his hands. Camera pans the faces of each of the men in the room and then settles on the dead face of the* SWEDE.]

INTERVIEW WITH JAN KADAR*

INT: The first question I have for you concerns the aspects of the Crane story that attracted you. What about this story made you want to film it?

KADAR: Though I was not familiar with Crane before, "The Blue Hotel" is such an eminently American story with such a contemporary idea. The political content of the story is not only universal but timeless. It spoke to me very closely, and probably my position is a very personal one. As I told you once before, I felt so close to the character of the Swede because the problem of being put in an alien environment and the desire to cooperate—how difficult it is! Today people are being transported from one place to another and looking for survival and some form of identity. So the story became very contemporary. That was really what attracted me very, very strongly. And I read a lot of literary essays about Crane.

INT: Analysis of Crane?

KADAR: Yes. This literary analysis of Crane's work helped me understand an important point about his writing: the strong irony with which he deals with the myths and legends of the West, with the same illusions the Swede believes in.

INT: Had you grown up in Europe with any myths about the American West?

KADAR: Yes. Certainly yes. There was a myth of the

---

* Director of *The Blue Hotel*, Jan Kadar is the eminent Czechoslovakian-American filmmaker known in this country for such highly-acclaimed works as *The Shop on Main Street*, *Adrift*, *Angel Levine*, and *Lies My Father Told Me*. He is currently Director in Residence, American Film Institute—West, Los Angeles. This interview with Mr. Kadar was conducted by Calvin Skaggs on April 18, 1977.

West. First of all, did you ever hear of a German writer called Karl May?

INT: No, I don't think so.

KADAR: He was a German writer who never left Germany. Yet he wrote all these stories about the West, about the Indians. It was a long series, tremendously popular.

INT: And you read that as a child?

KADAR: Each child knew these books. There are movies of the series in Germany. And there were the books of James Fenimore Cooper. Everybody was attracted to the mythical adventures and legends about the West.

INT: This reminds me of that Jean Renoir film, *Le Crime de Monsieur Lange*, about a Frenchman who doesn't know a thing about the West from personal experience but creates a character called Arizona Jim for a newspaper, and the film starts with him posing for pictures in cowboy costume.

KADAR: Yes, the myth of the West is very lively in Europe everywhere. But interestingly enough, very few people know Crane. They know Mark Twain and Jack London. But they don't know Crane.

INT: Were any of your earlier films dramatizations of novels or stories?

KADAR: Oh yes. One which I did in '63 was a dramatization of a book called *Engelchen*. *Engelchen* is the German nickname for "little angel." Then I did *Adrift*, which was an adaptation of a book. *The Shop on Main Street* was based on a short story.

INT: Oh, you'd done a short story?

KADAR: Yes. But it's different though. When I make an adaptation for a feature film, I usually take the basic idea and work very freely with the material. But the purpose of *The Blue Hotel* was different. I had to be as faithful as possible to the original Crane, on one hand, and, on the other, I realized that the film adaptation should not be simply an illustration of Crane's text. I had to keep the basic philosophy of the story, but, because we were working in a short form, the dramaturgy was different from that of a feature. So *The Blue Hotel* for me was really a new challenge because I had never done a short dramatic form on film before.

INT: Can you describe the differences in how you construct a feature out of a story and a short film out of a story?

KADAR: The basic dramaturgy is different. You cannot work on the same scale in a short form as in a feature. There are differences not only in length but in the exposition of the characters, the economy and rhythm of the dialogue, and the structure of each individual scene. The best short stories often revolve around one basic incident leading to a surprise twist at the end. The short dramatic film is a unique discipline with its own specific aesthetics. Even the staging requires a special kind of choreography.

INT: You use the word *choreography*. Many people are simply amazed at how beautifully you choreograph the card game in *The Blue Hotel*.

KADAR: The drama was contained in the two card games. The beauty of Crane's story was in the mood he created with his literary images, in the description of the characters, the whole feeling of the place. In these respects, a film can hardly compete with a great work of literature. But a film requires drama; and drama is confrontation expressed in action and dialogue. In our case, the dramatic confrontations were best expressed through the card games, each one different, leading to the surprise ending. The Swede is killed, and we learn that Johnnie was cheating. The card game told the story, so it was a great challenge for me. Working out a scene with a group of people sitting around a table is sometimes more difficult than staging a great panoramic scene.

INT: And to keep it so alive! It doesn't seem static at all.

KADAR: That was the danger. In the script there were two short paragraphs describing the game. Can you imagine that there are 56-60 cuts for only about fifteen lines in the script?

INT: Yes, I can. That's what makes the scene so lively. Let's talk about the characters in the film for a bit. To the other characters the Swede's fear of being killed here in this town is just absurd. They think he's crazy. Yet he dies exactly as he fears.

KADAR: I think this story has a certain existentialist quality, which was not articulated in Crane's time, of course. Because this Swede is aiming at his own destruction. And there's a certain element of fate which affects the lives of everybody involved. What motivates the Swede is the difficulty of coping with an alien culture. Also interesting is the sense of silent conspiracy in the story.

INT: Why do you use that phrase?

KADAR: Silent conspiracy describes the phenomenon of watching consciously the destruction of a person and not doing anything. All of the characters are guilty of this, perhaps without knowing it. In my opinion, the one who is the most guilty is the Easterner, the nice guy, the intelligent guy who understands but doesn't say anything; he sees how the tragedy is building up, but he won't stop it. All participate in a kind of silent conspiracy, letting this Swede run to his own destruction. Even though I grew up in a completely different society, the attitude of people toward condemned people was the same.

INT: You're talking of not taking any kind of responsibility.

KADAR: Taking the most convenient, least painful way. In our country there was an expression for this: "It's not our man." He doesn't belong to us, he's from the outside. We can be polite to him; we can play the game with him, but he can never be part of us.

INT: And we don't have to worry about him.

KADAR: We don't have to worry about him. But the way Crane describes the whole situation is really brilliant. Crane has the Swede behave in such an obtrusive way that even the reader would like to send him to hell.

INT: He involves the reader in the destructive process too.

KADAR: Exactly.

INT: Why do you think Scully takes the Swede upstairs? He doesn't do so simply to keep him in the hotel and get his money.

KADAR: Not at all. Scully takes him up and offers him a drink not to get him drunk but to initiate him into this environment, and to help him overcome his paranoic fear.

INT: Yes, that's a good way of putting it.

KADAR: Because he sees that this man feels uneasy here. He doesn't want anyone to feel uncomfortable in his hotel. He's a good host, and he's proud of it. Scully means well, but it is the Swede who misjudges the situation.

INT: Why did you decide to change the ending, so that the Swede is killed in the hotel? He never goes to the saloon as he does in the story.

KADAR: There were many whys. One was economic, of course. But a more important reason has to do with unity of time and place. From a practical point of view, you cannot achieve so efficiently on film what Crane does in the story. In literature you can describe in one paragraph who these new people are in the saloon and whom the Swede is provoking.

INT: But in film you can't bring in new exposition at the last moment.

KADAR: That's one of the reasons. But the main purpose of placing the climax of the drama in the hotel, rather than in the saloon, was to let all of the characters witness the destruction of the Swede, since all of them are responsible for destroying him. Seeing his death is, dramatically and emotionally, more powerful than just hearing about it.

INT: Yes, that's clear, though I hadn't thought of it in that way before.

KADAR: Also, keeping the last scene in the hotel emphasizes the quality of fate and destiny, of inevitability. If the Swede had left one minute earlier, nothing would have happened to him. The stranger in our film, like the gambler in the saloon in Crane's story, is merely a dramatic device designed to serve destiny. Neither has any depth of character. As such, it makes no difference whether the stranger comes to the hotel to kill the Swede, or whether the Swede goes to the saloon to get killed.

INT: You use the word *inevitable* about the death of the Swede, and we both used the word *fate*. Yet one of the things about Crane's sense of the universe that we all live in is that it's such a chaotic place. It's a place where chance and accident rule things. There seems to be a contradiction in that. On the one hand, the universe is not set up for man; it's a place where accident rules and man is no more important than a tree or a cloud in Crane's view. On the other hand, he shows that there's almost no room for accident at all, because that Swede's death is fated from the moment we get involved in that story. Did you feel a sense of contradiction in this or not?

KADAR: It is an interesting question, but I don't feel it's a contradiction. I think that our life is full of a series of contradictions. It makes a certain logic, finally.

INT: The logic of contradiction. The logic of chance. Yes, I see what you mean. When you look at the finished film, what are you most delighted with? What gives you the greatest pleasure? You said to me earlier that one of the things that is missing is the great sense of the sweep of the snow and the wind, which your budgetary limitations kept you from capturing.

KADAR: A real blizzard would have added to the mood of the picture. No director is ever quite satisfied with the physical limitations of his production. But, to be honest, I don't think the result would have been much different. The most important thing is the drama. I like this film very much, mainly for its austerity. There is nothing superfluous in it. There is not one extra cut. The camera is always tuned to the physical attention of the audience, in the right place at the right moment. You know I did fifteen features before I did this film, but this is my first short film made on a very modest scale, which I didn't mind at all. It is told with the same economy as is the short story itself. Crane's writing is condensed and pure. I tried to achieve the same qualities and remain faithful to the story.

INT: You are talking about an economy of means.

KADAR: Economy in the way it is told.

INT: Yes. I think you've been very successful in this respect—and in the film as a whole. Thank you for sharing some of your thoughts about it.

ON STEPHEN CRANE and "THE BLUE HOTEL"

Alfred Kazin

Stephen Crane was born in Newark, New Jersey, on November 1, 1871; he died in Germany on June 5, 1900, after having vainly sought in the Black Forest some respite from lung disease. Not yet twenty-nine when he died, he was the most original, most ruthless, and perhaps the wittiest novelist of his talented generation. (Crane, Theodore Dreiser, and Frank Norris were born within a few months of each other.)

In Crane's short, tense life, he managed many different things extremely well. Of course he did not manage himself as well as he should, but Crane did not believe in managing anything. The important thing about him is that he wrote several masterpieces that will be read as long as American writing is read: *The Red Badge of Courage*, "The Open Boat," "The Blue Hotel," "Wounds in the Rain." Crane somehow brought to focus in his person, as well as in his work, the searing skepticism of a generation that was too young for the Civil War but just old enough to sense from it America's now unparalleled power in human affairs. If "God is dead," as we've heard often in recent years, he first died around the 1890s and nowhere in America with such finality as in the prose and poetry of Stephen Crane. Crane's particular theme was that the world at large is a senselessly violent cosmic process unrelated to the longings, ideas, and beliefs of the human beings who (only in their own eyes) are its favorite victims.

Crane was an original. He is one of those rare writers, like Ernest Hemingway in our century, who established a wholly new way of looking at life, of seeing. The fact that Crane was often smart-alecky, "fresh," cocky, very young indeed, should not blind anyone to the fact that he was much more mature than Hemingway, that he was indeed the most influential American spokesman for a stoicism that had to be learned by many "fine consciences" as the nineteenth century expired to the Wagnerian music of blood lust, imperialism and war.

Although Crane often seems a "fancy" writer, his style is never an end in itself—as it never is for important writers. No matter how disconcerting and even disturbing it may be to encounter Crane's very deliberate and highly colored style for the first time (we read in *The Red Badge of Courage* that "The red sun was pasted in the sky like a fierce wafer."), the point of his unforgettably active sentences is that they work as gashes on our consciousness. His intention is to work on our conventional feelings in the most provocative way. His sensibility is aggressive, stoic, humorous: How much can human beings take? He was an experimenter by profession. But he is not frivolous. He sees the world, the life process that so deceptively makes our consciousness the center of all things, in just one way and not another.

The power of literature seems to lie in the writer's ability to concentrate, to condense, to reduce, to hammer into shape certain intractable images. Whatever else writing is, it is not eclectic, diffusable, sentimentally hospitable to everybody's impression of life. Crane was a man whose head was turned in one direction and was never able or willing to look in another. He was a minister's son, so we are likely to smile over his determined denial of God and of any purpose to our existence. In the era of sensational journalism, he was a reporter fascinated by the derelicts on the Bowery, by prostitutes he quixotically defended against corrupt New York cops. He was a war correspondent, headed for Cuba at a time when that island was trying to throw off the yoke of Spain. He was forced to abandon ship, and he almost died trying to get to land with some others in an open boat. He fell in love with a remarkable "madame" in Jacksonville, Florida, who loved Crane back, joined him as a war correspondent during the Greek-Turkish war, and devoted herself to him during his short and hurried lifetime.

Yet none of these experiences, much as they explain Crane's ideas and prejudices, help to explain the tension of genius. Crane burned into his readers' minds the conviction that life is simply a state of war. Though very dramatic, the war is meaningless except in what it shows us of what human beings are like under pressure. Crane is always matter-of-fact about everything—there are too many extremes for us to think that life is anything but war. Unlike Hemingway, who was a frighteningly vulnerable man under his super-manly pose, and so sought "grace under pressure" as his main wish from life and from writing, Crane was not personal about war. He did not seek personal gratification from war. War is life and life is war. The situation in which we "modern" people find ourselves is invariably a mass scene, a collective circus. Therefore the determining factor is the invisible and indecipherable makeup of the individual that either saves or destroys him within the life situation: the pressure of others.

"Art is a child of pain," Crane said in one of his offhand, shorthand comments on the business of writing. He did not say it was *his* pain. The pain lies in the irrevocable fact. The pain also has to do with the fact that a character can deal with the pressure, an artist can describe the situation, only on the shortest possible leash, or on the slant. The idea of a "slant" was very important to Crane. Things are slanted. We see things on a slant. There is only a very narrow, and even crooked, field in which to operate. The central factor in any situation is the irreducible, intractable character of the individual, who is an accident in nature. But this accidency is everything when the individual is lined up against other characters. People are single lines of force traveling in a predetermined direction. There is nothing to be done except to show one line of human force acting on another. So in a totally disbelieving age, art is possible. Because there is nothing more to life than appears on the surface.

Once we understand how fierce Crane is about accepting what we are, where we are, about telling the truth from the inescapable slant of what we are forced to accept, we can see why "The Blue Hotel" begins and consists in a set of extreme, improbable circumstances. Into a "blue" hotel in a remote Nebraska town during a violent snowstorm wanders "a shaky and quick-eyed Swede with a great shining cheap valise." The enthusiastically enterprising owner of the hotel, Scully, has also collared a cowboy on his way to a ranch near the Dakota line and "a little silent man from the East, who didn't look it, and didn't announce it." Scully's excitable son Johnnie is also in the plot.

What happens is that everyone in the hotel is somehow pushed to the wall, rendered half-crazy, by the "crazy" Swede, who announces from the beginning that he expects to be killed before he leaves the house. One man can terrorize a group; one man alone can disturb the daily run of things. The totally unexpected character of the Swede lies in the fact that he constantly amazes. And amazement is a form of humor. It is characteristic of Crane's art, which is never emotionally on one level, that disconcerting as the Swede's storm-warnings of his approaching demise are to us—to everyone in the hotel—the Swede's immediate effect is funny, hysteria-making, for he cannot be understood, believed, or absorbed into the normal run of things.

What is equally funny in the story is Scully's amazement that such forebodings should be heard in his town. Scully is the caricature of normal business dealing with . . . Hitler. His efforts to calm the Swede down by liquoring him up turn the Swede into a quarrelsome buffoon who calls Johnnie a cheat at cards (which he is) and then knocks him out during their battle outside during a howling storm. The clumsiness of the men fighting in the snow, against the snow, is as funny as all the attempts of the others to take the Swede down, to placate and normalize him, to absorb him into the banal life of the boarding house.

The Swede will not be normalized. He sees his future death and he will not be released from his strange intuition. He makes it happen. One of Crane's favorite words, used here with significant effect, is "demonstration." The point is made at the end: every sin is a collaboration. Whether he set it up or not by his fear, the Swede was done in by the group as a whole.

But demonstration means not only the exposure of a secret pattern, but the process or logic of life itself. As the Swede, glowing with the pride of having thrashed Johnnie, takes himself off in the snow to the saloon where he will meet his death from a quiet gambler who does not like to be molested by strangers, we see that the crazy startling humor of the savage *dénouement* makes the unexpected a factor to the end. In other words, not the "moral" of the story but the weirdness of the situation is what remains with us. For what is a "blue" hotel in a snowstorm but a bad dream about ourselves? What is this exposed, lonely, shrieking Nebraska landscape but another ominous image in the bad hours of the night? What is the Swede, at once villain and victim, but the ominous fortune-teller in all of us predicting what we alone will bring to pass?

So the zany is a bridge to the horrible, and the horror remains a threat hanging over us. This is a great story, for we can recognize ourselves in it without knowing why. Crane made a world, a funny crazy American world, out of our most anxious inner consciousness.

SUGGESTIONS FOR FURTHER READING

By Stephen Crane:

Complete Novels, ed. Thomas A. Gullason. Garden City, N.Y.: Doubleday, 1967.

Complete Short Stories and Sketches, ed. Thomas A. Gullason. Garden City, N.Y.: Doubleday, 1963.

The Portable Stephen Crane, ed. Joseph Katz. New York: Viking Press, 1969.

Stephen Crane: Letters, ed. R. W. Stallman and Lillian Gilkes. New York: N.Y.U. Press, 1960.

About Stephen Crane:

Bergon, Frank. *Stephen Crane's Artistry*. New York: Columbia University Press, 1975.

Berryman, John. *Stephen Crane*. New York: Sloane, 1950.

Cady, Edwin Harrison. *Stephen Crane*. New York: Twayne Publishers, 1962.

Stallman, Robert Wooster. *Stephen Crane: A Biography*. New York: G. Braziller, 1968.

THE JOLLY CORNER

by Henry James

I

"Every one asks me what I 'think' of everything," said Spencer Brydon; "and I make answer as I can—begging or dodging the question, putting them off with any nonsense. It wouldn't matter to any of them really," he went on, "for, even were it possible to meet in that stand-and-deliver way so silly a demand on so big a subject, my 'thoughts' would still be almost altogether about something that concerns only myself." He was talking to Miss Staverton, with whom for a couple of months now he had availed himself of every possible occasion to talk; this disposition and this resource, this comfort and support, as the situation in fact presented itself, having promptly enough taken the first place in the considerable array of rather unattenuated surprises attending his so strangely belated return to America. Everything was somehow a surprise; and that might be natural when one had so long and so consistently neglected everything, taken pains to give surprises so much margin for play. He had given them more than thirty years—thirty-three, to be exact; and they now seemed to him to have organised their performance quite on the scale of that licence. He had been twenty-three on leaving New York—he was fifty-six to-day: unless indeed he were to reckon as he had sometimes, since his repatriation, found himself feeling; in which case he would have lived longer than is often allotted to man. It would have taken a century, he repeatedly said to himself, and said also to Alice Staverton, it would have taken a longer absence and a more averted mind than those even of which he had been guilty, to pile up the differences, the newnesses, the queernesses, above all the bignesses, for the better or the worse, that at present assaulted his vision wherever he looked.

The great fact all the while however had been the incalculability; since he *had* supposed himself, from decade to decade, to be allowing, and in the most liberal and intelligent manner, for brilliancy of change. He actually saw that he had allowed for nothing; he missed what he would have been sure of finding, he found what he would never have imagined. Proportions and values were upside-down; the ugly things he had expected, the ugly things of his far-away youth, when he had too promptly waked up to a sense of the ugly—these uncanny phenomena placed him rather, as it happened, under the charm; whereas the "swagger" things, the modern, the monstrous, the famous things, those he had more particularly, like thousands of ingenuous enquirers every year, come over to see, were exactly his sources of dismay. They were as so many set traps for displeasure, above all for reaction, of which his restless tread was constantly pressing the spring. It was interesting, doubtless, the whole show, but it would have been too disconcerting hadn't a certain finer truth saved the situation. He had distinctly not, in this steadier light, come over *all* for the monstrosities; he had come, not only in the last analysis but quite on the face of the act, under an impulse with which they had nothing to do. He had come—putting the thing pompously—to look at his "property," which he had thus for a third of a century not been within four thousand miles of; or, expressing it less sordidly, he had yielded to the humour of seeing again his house on the jolly corner, as he usually, and quite fondly, described it—the one in which he had first seen the light, in which various members of his family had lived and had died, in which the holidays of his overschooled boyhood had been passed and the few social flowers of his chilled adolescence gathered, and which, alienated then for so long a period, had, through the successive deaths of his two brothers and the termination of old arrangements, come wholly into his hands. He was the owner of another, not quite so "good"—the jolly corner having been, from far back, superlatively extended and consecrated; and the value of the pair represented his main capital, with an income consisting, in these later years, of their respective rents which (thanks precisely to their original excellent type) had never been depressingly low. He could live in "Europe," as he had been in the habit of living, on the product of these flourishing New York leases, and all the better since, that of the second structure, the mere number in its long row, having within a twelvemonth fallen in, renovation at a high advance had proved beautifully possible.

These were items of property indeed, but he had found himself since his arrival distinguishing more than ever between them. The house within the street, two bristling blocks westward, was already in course of reconstruction as a tall mass of flats; he had acceded, some time before, to overtures for this conversion—in which, now that it was going forward, it had been not the least of his astonishments to find himself able, on the spot, and though without a previous ounce of such experience, to participate with a certain intelligence, almost with a certain authority. He had lived his life with his back so turned to such concerns and his face addressed to those of so different an order that he scarce knew what to make of this lively stir, in a compartment of his mind never yet penetrated, of a capacity for business and a sense for construction. These virtues, so common all round him now, had been dormant in his own organism—where it might be said of them perhaps that they had slept the sleep of the just. At present, in the splendid autumn weather—the autumn at least was a pure boon in the terrible place—he loafed about his "work" undeterred, secretly agitated; not in the least "minding" that the whole proposition, as they said, was vulgar and sordid, and ready to climb ladders, to walk the plank, to handle materials and look wise about them, to ask questions, in fine, and challenge explanations and really "go into" figures.

It amused, it verily quite charmed him; and, by the same stroke, it amused, and even more, Alice Staverton, though perhaps charming her perceptibly less. She wasn't however going to be better-off for it, as *he* was—and so astonishingly much: nothing was now likely, he knew, ever to make her better-off than she found herself, in the afternoon of life, as the delicately frugal possessor and tenant of the small house in Irving Place to which she had subtly managed to cling through her almost unbroken New York career. If he knew the way to it now better than to any other address among the dreadful multiplied numberings which seemed to him to reduce the whole place to some vast ledger-page, overgrown, fantastic, of ruled and criss-crossed lines and figures—if he had formed, for his consolation, that habit, it was really not a little because of the charm of his having encountered and recognised, in the vast wilderness of the wholesale, breaking through the mere gross generalisation of wealth and force and success, a small still scene where items and shades, all delicate things, kept the sharpness of the notes of a high voice perfectly trained, and where economy hung about like the scent of a garden. His old friend lived with one maid and herself dusted her relics and trimmed her lamps and polished her silver; she stood off, in the awful modern crush, when she could, but she sallied forth and did battle when the challenge was really to "spirit," the spirit she after all confessed to, proudly and a little shyly, as to that of the better time, that of *their* common, their quite far-away and antediluvian social period and order. She made use of the street-cars when need be, the terrible things that people scrambled for as the panic-stricken at sea scramble for the boats; she affronted, inscrutably, under stress, all the public concussions and ordeals; and yet, with that slim mystifying grace of her appearance, which defied you to say if she were a fair young woman who looked older through trouble, or a fine smooth older one who looked young through successful indifference; with her precious reference, above all, to memories and histories into which he could enter, she was as exquisite for him as some pale pressed flower (a rarity to begin with), and, failing other sweetnesses, she was a sufficient reward of his effort. They had communities of knowledge, "their" knowledge (this discriminating possessive was always on her lips) of presences of the other age, presences all overlaid, in his case, by the experience of a man and the freedom of a wanderer, overlaid by pleasure, by infidelity, by passages of life that were strange and dim to her, just by "Europe" in short, but still unobscured, still exposed and cherished, under that pious visitation of the spirit from which she had never been diverted.

She had come with him one day to see how his "apartment-house" was rising; he had helped her over gaps and explained to her plans, and while they were there had happened to have, before her, a brief but lively discussion with the man in charge, the representative of the building-firm that had undertaken his work. He had found himself quite "standing-up" to this personage over a failure on the latter's part to observe some detail of one of their noted conditions, and had so lucidly argued his case that, besides ever so prettily flushing, at the time, for sympathy in his triumph, she had afterwards said to him (though to a slightly greater effect of irony) that he had clearly for too many years neglected a real gift. If he had but stayed at home he would have anticipated the inventor of the sky-scraper. If he had but stayed at home he would have discovered his genius in time really to start some new variety of awful architectural hare and run it till it burrowed in a goldmine. He was to remember these words, while the weeks elapsed, for the small silver ring they had sounded over the queerest and deepest of his own lately most disguised and most muffled vibrations.

It had begun to be present to him after the first fortnight, it had broken out with the oddest abruptness, this particular wanton wonderment: it met him there—and this was the image under which he himself judged the matter, or at least, not a little, thrilled and flushed with it—very much as he might have been met by some strange figure, some unexpected occupant, at a turn of one of the dim passages of an empty house. The quaint analogy quite hauntingly remained with him, when he didn't indeed rather improve it by a still intenser form: that of his opening a door behind which he would have made sure of finding nothing, a door into a room shuttered and void, and yet so coming, with a great suppressed start, on some quite erect confronting presence, something planted in the middle of the place and facing him through the dusk. After that visit to the house in construction he walked with his companion to see the other and always so much the better one, which in the eastward direction formed one of the corners, the "jolly" one precisely, of the street now so generally dishonoured and disfigured in its westward reaches, and of the comparatively conservative Avenue. The Avenue still had pretensions, as Miss Staverton said, to decency; the old people had mostly gone, the old names were unknown, and here and there an old association seemed to stray, all vaguely, like some very aged person, out too late, whom you might meet and feel the impulse to watch or follow, in kindness, for safe restoration to shelter.

They went in together, our friends; he admitted himself

with his key, as he kept no one there, he explained, preferring, for his reasons, to leave the place empty, under a simple arrangement with a good woman living in the neighbourhood and who came for a daily hour to open windows and dust and sweep. Spencer Brydon had his reasons and was growingly aware of them; they seemed to him better each time he was there, though he didn't name them all to his companion, any more than he told her as yet how often, how quite absurdly often, he himself came. He only let her see for the present, while they walked through the great blank rooms, that absolute vacancy reigned and that, from top to bottom, there was nothing but Mrs Muldoon's broomstick, in a corner, to tempt the burglar. Mrs Muldoon was then on the premises, and she loquaciously attended the visitors, preceding them from room to room and pushing back shutters and throwing up sashes—all to show them, as she remarked, how little there was to see. There was little indeed to see in the great gaunt shell where the main dispositions and the general apportionment of space, the style of an age of ampler allowances, had nevertheless for its master their honest pleading message, affecting him as some good old servant's, some lifelong retainer's appeal for a character, or even for a retiring-pension; yet it was also a remark of Mrs Muldoon's that, glad as she was to oblige him by her noonday round, there was a request she greatly hoped he would never make of her. If he should wish her for any reason to come in after dark she would just tell him, if he "plased," that he must ask it of somebody else.

The fact that there was nothing to see didn't militate for the worthy woman against what one *might* see, and she put it frankly to Miss Staverton that no lady could be expected to like, could she? "craping up to thim top storeys in the ayvil hours." The gas and the electric light were off the house, and she fairly evoked a gruesome vision of her march through the great grey rooms—so many of them as there were too!—with her glimmering taper. Miss Staverton met her honest glare with a smile and the profession that she herself certainly would recoil from such an adventure. Spencer Brydon meanwhile held his peace—for the moment; the question of the "evil" hours in his old home had already become too grave for him. He had begun some time since to "crape," and he knew just why a packet of candles addressed to that pursuit had been stowed by his own hand, three weeks before, at the back of a drawer of the fine old sideboard that occupied, as a "fixture," the deep recess in the dining-room. Just now he laughed at his companions—quickly however changing the subject; for the reason that, in the first place, his laugh struck him even at that moment as starting the odd echo, the conscious human resonance (he scarce knew how to qualify it) that sounds made while he was there alone sent back to his ear or his fancy; and that, in the second, he imagined Alice Staverton for the instant on the point of asking him, with a divination, if he ever so prowled. There were divinations he was unprepared for, and he had at all events averted enquiry by the time Mrs Muldoon had left them, passing on to other parts.

There was happily enough to say, on so consecrated a spot, that could be said freely and fairly; so that a whole train of declarations was precipitated by his friend's having herself broken out, after a yearning look round: "But I hope you don't mean they want you to pull *this* to pieces!" His answer came, promptly, with his re-awakened wrath: it was of course exactly what they wanted, and what they were "at" him for, daily, with the iteration of people who couldn't for their life understand a man's liability to decent feelings. He had found the place, just as it stood and beyond what he could express, an interest and a joy. There were values other than the beastly rent-values, and in short, in short—! But it was thus Miss Staverton took him up. "In short you're to make so good a thing of your sky-scraper that, living in luxury on *those* ill-gotten gains, you can afford for a while to be sentimental here!" Her smile had for him, with the words, the particular mild irony with which he found half her talk suffused; an irony without bitterness and that came, exactly, from her having so much imagination—not, like the cheap sarcasms with which one heard most people, about the world of "society," bid for the reputation of cleverness, from nobody's really having any. It was agreeable to him at this very moment to be sure that when he had answered, after a brief demur, "Well yes: so, precisely, you may put it!" her imagination would still do him justice. He explained that even if never a dollar were to come to him from the other house he would nevertheless cherish this one; and he dwelt, further, while they lingered and wandered, on the fact of the stupefaction he was already exciting, the positive mystification he felt himself create.

He spoke of the value of all he read into it, into the mere sight of the walls, mere shapes of the rooms, mere sound of the floors, mere feel, in his hand, of the old silver-plated knobs of the several mahogany doors, which suggested the pressure of the palms of the dead; the seventy years of the past in fine that these things represented, the annals of nearly three generations, counting his grandfather's, the one that had ended there, and the impalpable ashes of his long-extinct youth, afloat in the very air like microscopic motes. She listened to everything; she was a woman who answered intimately but who utterly didn't chatter. She scattered abroad therefore no cloud of words; she could assent, she could agree, above all she could encourage, without doing that. Only at the last she went a little further than he had done himself. "And then how do you know? you may still, after all, want to live here." It rather indeed pulled him up, for it wasn't what he had been thinking, at least in her sense of the words. "You mean I may decide to stay on for the sake of it?"

"Well, *with* such a home—!" But, quite beautifully, she had too much tact to dot so monstrous an *i*, and it was precisely an illustration of the way she didn't rattle. How could any one—of any wit—insist on any one else's "wanting" to live in New York?

"Oh," he said, "I *might* have lived here (since I had my opportunity early in life); I might have put in here all these years. Then everything would have been different enough—and, I dare say, 'funny' enough. But that's another matter. And then the beauty of it—I mean of my perversity, of my refusal to agree to a 'deal'—is just in the total absence of a reason. Don't you see that if I had a reason about the matter at all it would *have* to be the other way; and would then be inevitably a reason of dollars? There are no reasons here *but* of dollars. Let us therefore have none whatever—not the ghost of one."

They were back in the hall then for departure, but from where they stood the vista was large, through an open door, into the great square main saloon, with its almost antique felicity of brave spaces between windows. Her eyes came back from that reach and met his own a moment.

"Are you very sure the 'ghost' of one doesn't, much rather, serve—?"

He had a positive sense of turning pale. But it was as near as they were then to come. For he made answer, he believed, between a glare and a grin: "Oh ghosts—of course the place must swarm with them! I should be ashamed of it if it didn't. Poor Mrs Muldoon's right, and it's why I haven't asked her to do more than look in."

Miss Staverton's gaze again lost itself, and things she didn't utter, it was clear, came and went in her mind. She might even for the minute, off there in the fine room, have imagined some element dimly gathering. Simplified like the death-mask of a handsome face, it perhaps produced for her just then an effect akin to the stir of an expression in the "set" commemorative plaster. Yet whatever her impression may have been she produced instead a vague platitude. "Well, if it were only furnished and lived in—!"

She appeared to imply that in case of its being still furnished he might have been a little less opposed to the idea of a return. But she passed straight into the vestibule, as if to leave her words behind her, and the next moment he had opened the house-door and was standing with her on the steps. He closed the door and, while he re-pocketed his key, looking up and down, they took in the comparatively harsh actuality of the Avenue, which reminded him of the assault of the outer light of the Desert on the traveller emerging from an Egyptian tomb. But he risked before they stepped into the street his gathered answer to her speech. "For me it *is* lived in. For me it *is* furnished." At which it was easy for her to sigh "Ah yes—!" all vaguely and discreetly; since his parents and his favourite sister, to say nothing of other kin, in numbers, had run their course and met their end there. That represented, within the walls, ineffaceable life.

It was a few days after this that, during an hour passed with her again, he had expressed his impatience of the too flattering curiosity—among the people he met—about his appreciation of New York. He had arrived at none at all that was socially producible, and as for that matter of his "thinking" (thinking the better or the worse of anything there) he was wholly taken up with one subject of thought. It was mere vain egoism, and it was moreover, if she liked, a morbid obsession. He found all things come back to the question of what he personally might have been, how he might have led his life and "turned out," if he had not so, at the outset, given it up. And confessing for the first time to the intensity within him of this absurd speculation—which but proved also, no doubt, the habit of too selfishly thinking—he affirmed the impotence there of any other source of interest, any other native appeal. "What would it have made of me, what would it have made of me? I keep for ever wondering, all idiotically; as if I could possibly know! I see what it has made of dozens of others, those I meet, and it positively aches within me, to the point of exasperation, that it would have made something of me as well. Only I can't make out *what*, and the worry of it, the small rage of curiosity never to be satisfied, brings back what I remember to have felt, once or twice, after judging best, for reasons, to burn some important letter unopened. I've been sorry, I've hated it—I've never known what was in the letter. You may of course say it's a trifle—!"

"I don't say it's a trifle," Miss Staverton gravely interrupted.

She was seated by her fire, and before her, on his feet and restless, he turned to and fro between this intensity of his idea and a fitful and unseeing inspection, through his single eye-glass, of the dear little old objects on her chimney-piece. Her interruption made him for an instant look at her harder. "I shouldn't care if you did!" he laughed, however; "and it's only a figure, at any rate, for the way I now feel. *Not* to have followed my perverse young course—and almost in the teeth of my father's curse, as I may say; not to have kept it up, so, 'over there,' from that day to this, without a doubt or a pang; not, above all, to have liked it, to have loved it, so much, loved it, no doubt, with such an abysmal conceit of my own preference: some variation from *that*, I say, must have produced some different effect for my life and for my 'form.' I should have stuck here—if it had been possible; and I was too young, at twenty-three, to judge, *pour deux sous*, whether it *were* possible. If I had waited I might have seen it was, and then I might have been, by staying here, something nearer to one of these types who have been hammered so hard and made so keen by their conditions. It isn't that I admire them so much—the question of any charm in them, or of any charm, beyond that of the rank money-passion, exerted by their conditions *for* them, has nothing to do with the matter: it's only a question of what fantastic, yet perfectly possible, development of my own nature I mayn't have missed. It comes over me that I had then a strange *alter ego* deep down somewhere within me, as the full-blown flower is in the small tight bud, and that I just took the course, I just transferred him to the climate, that blighted him for once and for ever."

"And you wonder about the flower," Miss Staverton said. "So do I, if you want to know; and so I've been wondering these several weeks. I believe in the flower," she continued, "I feel it would have been quite splendid, quite huge and monstrous."

"Monstrous above all!" her visitor echoed; "and I imagine, by the same stroke, quite hideous and offensive."

"You don't believe that," she returned; "if you did you wouldn't wonder. You'd know, and that would be enough for you. What you feel—and what I feel *for* you—is that you'd have had power."

"You'd have liked me that way?" he asked.

She barely hung fire. "How should I not have liked you?"

"I see. You'd have liked me, have preferred me, a billionaire!"

"How should I not have liked you?" she simply again asked.

He stood before her still—her question kept him motionless. He took it in, so much there was of it; and indeed his not otherwise meeting it testified to that. "I know at least what I am," he simply went on; "the other side of the medal's clear enough. I've not been edifying—I believe I'm thought in a hundred quarters to have been barely decent. I've followed strange paths and worshipped strange gods; it must have come to you again and again—in fact you've admitted to me as much—that I was leading, at any time these thirty years, a selfish frivolous scandalous life. And you see what it has made of me."

She just waited, smiling at him. "You see what it has made of *me*."

"Oh you're a person whom nothing can have altered. You were born to be what you are, anywhere, anyway: you've the perfection nothing else could have blighted. And don't you see how, without my exile, I shouldn't have been waiting till now—?" But he pulled up for the strange pang.

"The great thing to see," she presently said, "seems to me to be that it has spoiled nothing. It hasn't spoiled your being here at last. It hasn't spoiled this. It hasn't spoiled your speaking—" She also however faltered.

He wondered at everything her controlled emotion might mean. "Do you believe then—too dreadfully!—that I *am* as good as I might ever have been?"

"Oh no! Far from it!" With which she got up from her chair and was nearer to him. "But I don't care," she smiled.

"You mean I'm good enough?"

She considered a little. "Will you believe it if I say so? I mean will you let that settle your question for you?" And then as if making out in his face that he drew back from this, that he had some idea which, however absurd, he couldn't yet bargain away: "Oh you don't care either—but very differently: you don't care for anything but yourself."

Spencer Brydon recognised it—it was in fact what he had absolutely professed. Yet he importantly qualified. "*He* isn't myself. He's the just so totally other person. But I do want to see him," he added. "And I can. And I shall."

Their eyes met for a minute while he guessed from something in hers that she divined his strange sense. But neither of them otherwise expressed it, and her apparent understanding, with no protesting shock, no easy derision, touched him more deeply than anything yet, constituting for his stifled perversity, on the spot, an element that was like breatheable air. What she said however was unexpected. "Well, *I've* seen him."

"You—?"

"I've seen him in a dream."

"Oh a 'dream'—!" It let him down.

"But twice over," she continued. "I saw him as I see you now."

"You've dreamed the same dream—?"

"Twice over," she repeated. "The very same."

This did somehow a little speak to him, as it also gratified him. "You dream about me at that rate?"

"Ah about *him!*" she smiled.

His eyes again sounded her. "Then you know all about him." And as she said nothing more: "What's the wretch like?"

She hesitated, and it was as if he were pressing her so hard that, resisting for reasons of her own, she had to turn away. "I'll tell you some other time!"

II

It was after this that there was most of a virtue for him, most of a cultivated charm, most of a preposterous secret thrill, in the particular form of surrender to his obsession and of address to what he more and more believed to be his privilege. It was what in these weeks he was living for—since he really felt life to begin but after Mrs Muldoon had retired from the scene and, visiting the ample house from attic to cellar, making sure he was alone, he knew himself in safe possession and, as he tacitly expressed it, let himself go. He sometimes came twice in the twenty-four hours; the moments he liked best were those of gathering dusk, of the short autumn twilight; this was the time of which, again and again, he found himself hoping most. Then he could, as seemed to him, most intimately wander and wait, linger and listen, feel his fine attention, never in his life before so fine, on the pulse of the great vague place: he preferred the lampless hour and only wished he might have prolonged each day the deep crepuscular spell. Later—rarely much before midnight, but then for a considerable vigil—he watched with his glimmering light; moving slowly, holding it high, playing it far, rejoicing above all, as much as he might, in open vistas, reaches of communication between rooms and by passages; the long straight chance or show, as he would have called it, for the revelation he pretended to invite. It was a practice he found he could perfectly "work" without exciting remark; no one was in the least the wiser for it; even Alice Staverton, who was moreover a well of discretion, didn't quite fully imagine.

He let himself in and let himself out with the assurance of calm proprietorship; and accident so far favoured him that, if a fat Avenue "officer" had happened on occasion to see him entering at eleven-thirty, he had never yet, to the best of his belief, been noticed as emerging at two. He walked there on the crisp November nights, arrived regularly at the evening's end; it was as easy to do this after dining out as to take his way to a club or to his hotel. When he left his club, if he hadn't been dining out, it was ostensibly to go to his hotel; and when he left his hotel, if he had spent a part of the evening there, it was ostensibly to go to his club. Everything was easy in fine; everything conspired and promoted: there was truly even in the strain of his experience something that glossed over, something that salved and simplified, all the rest of consciousness. He circulated, talked, renewed, loosely and pleasantly, old relations—met indeed, so far as he could, new expectations and seemed to make out on the whole that in spite of the career, of such different contacts, which he had spoken of to Miss Staverton as ministering so little, for those who might have watched it, to edification, he was positively rather liked than not. He was a dim secondary social success—and all with people who had truly not an idea of him. It was all mere surface sound, this murmur of their welcome, this popping of their corks—just as his gestures of response were the extravagant shadows, emphatic in proportion as they meant little, of some game of *ombres chinoises.* He projected himself all day, in thought, straight over the bristling line of hard unconscious heads and into the other, the real, the waiting life; the life that, as soon as he had heard behind him the click of his great house-door, began for him, on the jolly corner, as beguilingly as the slow opening bars of some rich music follows the tap of the conductor's wand.

He always caught the first effect of the steel point of his stick on the old marble of the hall pavement, large black-and-white squares that he remembered as the admiration of his childhood and that had then made in him, as he now saw, for the growth of an early conception of style. This effect was the dim reverberating tinkle as of some far-off bell hung who should say where?—in the depths of the house, of the past, of that mystical other world that might have flourished for him had he not, for weal or woe, abandoned it. On this impression he did ever the same thing; he put his stick noiselessly away in a corner—feeling the place once more in the likeness of some great glass bowl, all precious concave crystal, set delicately humming by the play of a moist finger round its edge. The concave crystal held, as it were, this mystical other world, and the indescribably fine murmur of its rim was the sigh there, the scarce audible pathetic wail to his strained ear, of all the old baffled forsworn possibilities. What he did therefore by this appeal of his hushed presence was to wake them into such measure of ghostly life as they might still enjoy. They were shy, all but unappeasably shy, but they weren't really sinister; at least they weren't as he had hitherto felt them—before they had taken the Form he so yearned to make them take, the Form he at moments saw himself in the light of fairly hunting on tiptoe, the points of his evening-shoes, from room to room and from storey to storey.

That was the essence of his vision—which was all rank folly, if one would, while he was out of the house and otherwise occupied, but which took on the last verisimilitude as soon as he was placed and posted. He knew what he meant and what he wanted; it was as clear as the figure on a cheque presented in demand for cash. His *alter ego* "walked"—that was the note of his image of him, while his image of his motive for his own odd pastime was the desire to waylay him and meet him. He roamed, slowly, warily, but all restlessly, he himself did—Mrs Muldoon had been right, absolutely, with her figure of their "craping"; and the presence he watched for would roam restlessly too. But it would be as cautious and as shifty; the conviction of its probable, in fact its already quite sensible, quite audible evasion of pursuit grew for him from night to night, laying on him finally a rigour to which nothing in his life had been comparable. It had been the theory of many superficially-judging persons, he knew, that he was wasting that life in a surrender to sensations, but he had tasted of no pleasure so fine as his actual tension, had been introduced to no sport that demanded at once the patience and the nerve of this stalking of a creature more subtle, yet at bay perhaps more formidable, than any beast of the forest. The terms, the comparisons, the very practices of the chase positively came again into play; there were even moments when passages of his occasional experience as a sportsman, stirred memories, from his younger time, of moor and mountain and desert, revived for him—and to the increase of his keenness—by the tremendous force of analogy. He found himself at moments—once he had placed his single light on some mantel-shelf or in some recess—stepping back into shelter or shade, effacing himself behind a door or in an embrasure, as he had sought of old the vantage of rock and tree; he found himself holding his breath and living in the joy of the instant, the supreme suspense created by big game alone.

He wasn't afraid (though putting himself the question as he believed gentlemen on Bengal tiger-shoots or in close quarters with the great bear of the Rockies had been known to confess to having put it); and this indeed—since here at least he might be frank!—because of the impression, so intimate and so strange, that he himself produced as yet a dread, produced certainly a strain, beyond the liveliest he was likely to feel. They fell for him into categories, they fairly became familiar, the signs, for his own perception, of the alarm his presence and his vigilance created; though leaving him always to remark, portentously, on his probably having formed a relation, his probably enjoying a consciousness, unique in the experience of man. People enough, first and last, had been in terror of apparitions, but who had ever before so turned the tables and become himself, in the apparitional world, an incalculable terror? He might have found this sublime had he quite dared to think of it; but he didn't too much insist, truly, on that side of his privilege. With habit and repetition he gained to an extraordinary degree the power to penetrate the dusk of distances and the darkness of corners, to resolve back into their innocence the treacheries of uncertain light, the evil-looking forms taken in the gloom by mere shadows, by accidents of the air, by shifting effects of perspective; putting down his dim luminary he could still wander on without it, pass into other rooms and, only knowing it was there behind him in case of need, see his way about, visually project for his purpose a comparative clearness. It made him feel, this acquired faculty, like some monstrous stealthy cat; he wondered if he would have glared at these moments with large shining yellow eyes, and what it mightn't verily be, for the poor hard-pressed *alter ego*, to be confronted with such a type.

He liked however the open shutters; he opened everywhere those Mrs Muldoon had closed, closing them as carefully afterwards, so that she shouldn't notice: he liked—oh this he did like, and above all in the upper rooms!—the sense of the hard silver of the autumn stars through the window-panes, and scarcely less the flare of the street-lamps below, the white electric lustre which it would have taken curtains to keep out. This was human actual social;

this was of the world he had lived in, and he was more at his ease certainly for the countenance, coldly general and impersonal, that all the while and in spite of his detachment it seemed to give him. He had support of course mostly in the rooms at the wide front and the prolonged side; it failed him considerably in the central shades and the parts at the back. But if he sometimes, on his rounds, was glad of his optical reach, so none the less often the rear of the house affected him as the very jungle of his prey. The place was there more subdivided; a large "extension" in particular, where small rooms for servants had been multiplied, abounded in nooks and corners, in closets and passages, in the ramifications especially of an ample back staircase over which he leaned, many a time, to look far down—not deterred from his gravity even while aware that he might, for a spectator, have figured some solemn simpleton playing at hide-and-seek. Outside in fact he might himself make that ironic *rapprochement;* but within the walls, and in spite of the clear windows, his consistency was proof against the cynical light of New York.

It had belonged to that idea of the exasperated consciousness of his victim to become a real test for him; since he had quite put it to himself from the first that, oh distinctly! he could "cultivate" his whole perception. He had felt it as above all open to cultivation—which indeed was but another name for his manner of spending his time. He was bringing it on, bringing it to perfection, by practice; in consequence of which it had grown so fine that he was now aware of impressions, attestations of his general postulate, that couldn't have broken upon him at once. This was the case more specifically with a phenomenon at last quite frequent for him in the upper rooms, the recognition—absolutely unmistakeable, and by a turn dating from a particular hour, his resumption of his campaign after a diplomatic drop, a calculated absence of three nights—of his being definitely followed, tracked at a distance carefully taken and to the express end that he should the less confidently, less arrogantly, appear to himself merely to pursue. It worried, it finally quite broke him up, for it proved, of all the conceivable impressions, the one least suited to his book. He was kept in sight while remaining himself—as regards the essence of his position—sightless, and his only recourse then was in abrupt turns, rapid recoveries of ground. He wheeled about, retracing his steps, as if he might so catch in his face at least the stirred air of some other quick revolution. It was indeed true that his fully dislocalised thought of these manœuvres recalled to him Pantaloon, at the Christmas farce, buffeted and tricked from behind by ubiquitous Harlequin; but it left intact the influence of the conditions themselves each time he was re-exposed to them, so that in fact this association, had he suffered it to become constant, would on a certain side have but ministered to his intenser gravity. He had made, as I have said, to create on the premises the baseless sense of a reprieve, his three absences; and the result of the third was to confirm the after-effect of the second.

On his return, that night—the night succeeding his last intermission—he stood in the hall and looked up the staircase with a certainty more intimate than any he had yet known. "He's *there*, at the top, and waiting—not, as in general, falling back for disappearance. He's holding his ground, and it's the first time—which is a proof, isn't it? that something has happened for him." So Brydon argued with his hand on the banister and his foot on the lowest stair; in which position he felt as never before the air chilled by his logic. He himself turned cold in it, for he seemed of a sudden to know what now was involved. "Harder pressed?—yes, he takes it in, with its thus making clear to him that I've come, as they say, 'to stay.' He finally doesn't like and can't bear it, in the sense, I mean, that his wrath, his menaced interest, now balances with his dread. I've hunted him till he has 'turned': that, up there, is what has happened—he's the fanged or the antlered animal brought at last to bay." There came to him, as I say—but determined by an influence beyond my notation!—the acuteness of this certainty; under which however the next moment he had broken into a sweat that he would as little have consented to attribute to fear as he would have dared immediately to act upon it for enterprise. It marked none the less a prodigious thrill, a thrill that represented sudden dismay, no doubt, but also represented, and with the self-same throb, the strangest, the most joyous, possibly the next minute almost the proudest, duplication of consciousness.

"He has been dodging, retreating, hiding, but now, worked up to anger, he'll fight!"—this intense impression made a single mouthful, as it were, of terror and applause. But what was wondrous was that the applause, for the felt fact, was so eager, since, if it was his other self he was running to earth, this ineffable identity was thus in the last resort not unworthy of him. It bristled there—somewhere near at hand, however unseen still—as the hunted thing, even as the trodden worm of the adage *must* at last bristle; and Brydon at this instant tasted probably of a sensation more complex than had ever before found itself consistent with sanity. It was as if it would have shamed him that a character so associated with his own should triumphantly succeed in just skulking, should to the end not risk the open; so that the drop of this danger was, on the spot, a great lift of the whole situation. Yet with another rare shift of the same subtlety he was already trying to measure by how much more he himself might now be in peril of fear; so rejoicing that he could, in another form, actively inspire that fear, and simultaneously quaking for the form in which he might passively know it.

The apprehension of knowing it must after a little have grown in him, and the strangest moment of his adventure perhaps, the most memorable or really most interesting, afterwards, of his crisis, was the lapse of certain instants of concentrated conscious *combat*, the sense of a need to hold on to something, even after the manner of a man slipping and slipping on some awful incline; the vivid impulse, above all, to move, to act, to charge, somehow and upon something—to show himself, in a word, that he wasn't afraid. The state of "holding-on" was thus the state to which he was momentarily reduced; if there had been anything, in the great vacancy, to seize, he would presently have been aware of having clutched it as he might under a shock at home have clutched the nearest chair-back. He had been surprised at any rate—of this he *was* aware—into something unprecedented since his original appropriation of the place; he had closed his eyes, held them tight, for a long minute, as with that instinct of dismay and that terror of vision. When he opened them the room. the other contiguous rooms, extraordinarily, seemed lighter—so light, almost, that at first he took the change for day. He stood firm, however that might be, just where he had paused; his resistance had helped him—it was as if there were something he had tided over. He knew after a little what this was—it had been in the imminent danger of flight. He had stiffened his will against going; without this he would have made for the stairs, and it seemed to him that, still with his eyes closed, he would have descended them, would have known how, straight and swiftly, to the bottom.

Well, as he had held out, here he was—still at the top, among the more intricate upper rooms and with the gauntlet of the others, of all the rest of the house, still to run when it should be his time to go. He would go at his time—only at his time: didn't he go every night very much at the same hour? He took out his watch—there was light for that: it was scarcely a quarter past one, and he had never withdrawn so soon. He reached his lodgings for the most part at two—with his walk of a quarter of an hour. He would wait for the last quarter—he wouldn't stir till then; and he kept his watch there with his eyes on it, reflecting while he held it that this deliberate wait, a wait with an effort, which he recognised, would serve perfectly for the attestation he desired to make. It would prove his courage—unless indeed the latter might most be proved by his budging at last from his place. What he mainly felt now was that, since he hadn't originally scuttled, he had his dignities—which had never in his life seemed so many—all to preserve and to carry aloft. This was before him in truth as a physical image, an image almost worthy of an age of greater romance. That remark indeed glimmered for him only to glow the next instant with a finer light; since what age of romance, after all, could have matched either the state of his mind or, "objectively," as they said, the wonder of his situation? The only difference would have been that, brandishing his dignities over his head as in a parchment scroll, he might then—that is in the heroic time—have proceeded downstairs with a drawn sword in his other grasp.

At present, really, the light he had set down on the mantle of the next room would have to figure his sword; which utensil, in the course of a minute, he had taken the requisite number of steps to possess himself of. The door between the rooms was open, and from the second another door opened to a third. These rooms, as he remembered, gave all three upon a common corridor as well, but there was a fourth, beyond them, without issue save through the preceding. To have moved, to have heard his step again, was appreciably a help; though even in recognising this he lingered once more a little by the chimney-piece on which his light had rested. When he next moved, just hesitating where to turn, he found himself considering a circumstance that, after his first and comparatively vague apprehension of it, produced in him the start that often attends some pang of recollection, the violent shock of having ceased happily to forget. He had come into sight of the door in which the brief chain of communication ended and which he now surveyed from the nearer threshold, the one not directly facing it. Placed at some distance to the left of this point, it would have admitted him to the last room of the four, the room without other approach or egress, had it not, to his intimate conviction, been closed *since* his former visitation, the matter probably of a quarter of an hour before. He stared with all his eyes at the wonder of the fact, arrested again where he stood and again holding his breath while he sounded its sense. Surely it had been *subsequently* closed—that is it had been on his previous passage indubitably open!

He took it full in the face that something had happened between—that he couldn't not have noticed before (by which he meant on his original tour of all the rooms that evening) that such a barrier had exceptionally presented itself. He had indeed since that moment undergone an agitation so extraordinary that it might have muddled for him any earlier view; and he tried to convince himself that he might perhaps then have gone into the room and, inadvertently, automatically, on coming out, have drawn the door after him. The difficulty was that this exactly was what he never did; it was against his whole policy, as he might have said, the essence of which was to keep vistas clear. He had them from the first, as he was well aware, quite on the brain: the strange apparition, at the far end of one of them, of his baffled "prey" (which had become by so sharp an irony so little the term now to apply!) was the form of success his imagination had most cherished, projecting into it always a refinement of beauty. He had known fifty times the start of perception that had afterwards dropped; had fifty times gasped to himself "There!" under some fond brief hallucination. The house, as the case stood, admirably lent itself; he might wonder at the taste, the native architecture of the particular time, which could rejoice so in the multiplication of doors—the opposite extreme to the modern, the actual almost complete proscription of them; but it had fairly contributed to provoke this obsession of the presence encountered telescopically, as he might say, focussed and studied in diminishing perspective and as by a rest for the elbow.

It was with these considerations that his present attention was charged—they perfectly availed to make what he saw portentous. He *couldn't*, by any lapse, have blocked that aperture; and if he hadn't, if it was unthinkable, why what else was clear but that there had been another agent? Another agent?—he had been catching, as he felt, a moment back, the very breath of him; but when had he been so close as in this simple, this logical, this completely personal act? It was so logical, that is, that one might have *taken* it for personal; yet for what did Brydon take it, he asked himself, while, softly panting, he felt his eyes almost leave their sockets. Ah this time at last they *were*, the two, the opposed projections of him, in presence; and this time, as much as one would, the question of danger loomed. With it rose, as not before, the question of courage—for what he knew the blank face of the door to say to him was "Show us how much you have!" It stared, it glared back at him with that challenge; it put to him the two alternatives: should he just push it open or not? Oh to have this consciousness was to *think*—and to think, Brydon knew, as he stood there, was, with the lapsing moments, not to have acted! Not to have acted—that was the misery and the pang—was even still not to act; was in fact *all* to feel the thing in another, in a new and terrible way. How long did he pause and how long did he debate? There was presently nothing to measure it; for his vibration had already changed—as just by the effect of its intensity. Shut up there, at bay, defiant, and with the prodigy of the thing palpably proveably *done*, thus giving notice like some stark signboard—under that accession of accent the situation itself had turned; and Brydon at last remarkably made up his mind on what it had turned to.

It had turned altogether to a different admonition; to a supreme hint, for him, of the value of Discretion! This slowly dawned, no doubt—for it could take its time; so perfectly, on his threshold, had he been stayed, so little as yet had he either advanced or retreated. It was the strangest of all things that now when, by his taking ten steps and applying his hand to a latch, or even his shoulder and his knee, if necessary, to a panel, all the hunger of his prime need might have been met, his high curiosity crowned, his unrest assuaged—it was amazing, but it was also exquisite and rare, that insistence should have, at a touch, quite dropped from him. Discretion—he jumped at that; and yet not, verily, at such a pitch, because it saved his nerves or his skin, but because, much more valuably, it saved the situation. When I say he "jumped" at it I feel the consonance of this term with the fact that—at the end indeed of I know not how long—he did move again, he crossed straight to the door. He wouldn't touch it—it seemed now that he might *if* he would: he would only just wait there a little, to show, to prove, that he wouldn't. He had thus another station, close to the thin partition by which revelation was denied him; but with his eyes bent and his hands held off in a mere intensity of stillness. He listened as if there had been something to hear, but this attitude, while it lasted, was his own communication. "If you won't then—good: I spare you and I give up. You affect me as by the appeal positively for pity: you convince me that for reasons rigid and sublime—what do I know?—we both of us should have suffered. I respect them then, and, though moved and privileged as, I believe, it has never been given to man, I retire, I renounce—never, on my honour, to try again. So rest for ever—and let *me!*"

That, for Brydon was the deep sense of this last demonstration—solemn, measured, directed, as he felt it to be. He brought it to a close, he turned away; and now verily he knew how deeply he had been stirred. He retraced his steps, taking up his candle, burnt, he observed, well-nigh to the socket, and marking again, lighten it as he would, the distinctness of his footfall; after which, in a moment, he knew himself at the other side of the house. He did here what he had not yet done at these hours—he opened half a casement, one of those in the front, and let in the air of the night; a thing he would have taken at any time previous for a sharp rupture of his spell. His spell was broken now, and it didn't matter—broken by his concession and his surrender, which made it idle henceforth that he should ever come back. The empty street—its other life so marked even by the great lamplit vacancy—was within call, within touch; he stayed there as to be in it again, high above it though he was still perched; he watched as for some comforting common fact, some vulgar human note, the passage of a scavenger or a thief, some night-bird however base. He would have blessed that sign of life; he would have welcomed positively the slow approach of his friend the policeman, whom he had hitherto only sought to avoid, and was not sure that if the patrol had come into sight he mightn't have felt the impulse to get into relation with it, to hail it, on some pretext, from his fourth floor.

The pretext that wouldn't have been too silly or too compromising, the explanation that would have saved his dignity and kept his name, in such a case, out of the papers, was not definite to him: he was so occupied with the thought of recording his Discretion—as an effect of the vow he had just uttered to his intimate adversary—that the importance of this loomed large and something had overtaken all ironically his sense of proportion. If there had been a ladder applied to the front of the house, even one of the vertiginous perpendiculars employed by painters and roofers and sometimes left standing overnight, he would have managed somehow, astride of the window-sill, to compass by outstretched leg and arm that mode of descent. If there had been some such uncanny thing as he had found in his room at hotels, a workable fire-escape in the form of notched cable or a canvas shoot, he would have availed himself of it as a proof—well, of his present delicacy. He nursed that sentiment, as the question stood, a little in vain, and even—at the end of he scarce knew, once more, how long—found it, as by the action on his mind of the failure of response of the outer world, sinking back to vague anguish. It seemed to him he had waited an age for some stir of the great grim hush; the life of the town was itself under a spell—so unnaturally, up and down the whole prospect of known and rather ugly objects, the blankness and the silence lasted. Had they ever, he asked himself, the hard-faced houses, which had begun to look livid in the dim dawn, had they ever spoken so little to any need of his spirit? Great builded voids, great crowded stillnesses put on, often, in the heart of cities, for the small hours, a sort of sinister mask, and it was of this large collective negation that Brydon presently became conscious—all the more that the break of day was, almost incredibly, now at hand, proving to him what a night he had made of it.

He looked again at his watch, saw what had become of his time-values (he had taken hours for minutes—not, as in other tense situations, minutes for hours) and the strange air of the streets was but the weak, the sullen flush of a dawn in which everything was still locked up. His choked appeal from his own open window had been the sole note of life, and he could but break off at last as for a worse despair. Yet while so deeply demoralised he was capable again of an impulse denoting—at least by his present measure—extraordinary resolution; of retracing his steps to the spot where he had turned cold with the extinction of his last pulse of doubt as to there being in the place another presence than his own. This required an effort strong enough to sicken him; but he had his reason, which overmastered for the moment everything else. There was the whole of the rest of the house to traverse, and how should he screw himself to that if the door he had seen closed were at present open? He could hold to the idea that the closing had practically been for him an act of mercy, a chance offered him to descend, depart, get off the ground and never again profane it. This conception held together, it worked; but what it meant for him depended now clearly on the amount of forbearance his recent action, or rather his recent inaction, had engendered. The image of the "presence," whatever it was, waiting there for him to go—this image had not yet been so concrete for his nerves as when he stopped short of the point at which certainty would have come to him. For, with all his resolution, or more exactly with all his dread, he did stop short—he hung back from really seeing. The risk was too great and his fear too definite: it took at this moment an awful specific form.

He knew—yes, as he had never known anything—that, *should* he see the door open, it would all too abjectly be the end of him. It would mean that the agent of his shame—for his shame was the deep abjection—was once more at large and in general possession; and what glared him thus in the face was the act that this would determine for him. It would send him straight about to the window he had left open, and by that window, be long ladder and dangling rope as absent as they would, he saw himself uncontrollably insanely fatally take his way to the street. The hideous chance of this he at least could avert; but he could only avert it by recoiling in time from assurance. He had the whole house to deal with, this fact was still there; only he now knew that uncertainty alone could start him. He stole back from where he had checked himself—merely to do so was suddenly like safety—and, making blindly for the greater staircase, left gaping rooms and sounding passages behind. Here was the top of the stairs, with a fine large dim descent and three spacious landings to mark off. His instinct was all for mildness, but his feet were harsh on the floors, and, strangely, when he had in a couple of minutes become aware of this, it counted somehow for help. He couldn't have spoken, the tone of his voice would have scared him, and the common conceit or resource of "whistling in the dark" (whether literally or figuratively) have appeared basely vulgar; yet he liked none the less to hear himself go, and when he had reached his first landing —taking it all with no rush, but quite steadily—that stage of success drew from him a gasp of relief.

The house, withal, seemed immense, the scale of space again inordinate; the open rooms, to no one of which his eyes deflected, gloomed in their shuttered state like mouths of caverns; only the high skylight that formed the crown of the deep well created for him a medium in which he could advance, but which might have been, for queerness of colour, some watery under-world. He tried to think of something noble, as that his property was really grand, a splendid possession; but this nobleness took the form too of the clear delight with which he was finally to sacrifice it. They might come in now, the builders, the destroyers—they might come as soon as they would. At the end of two flights he had dropped to another zone, and from the middle of the third, with only one more left, he recognised the influence of the lower windows, of half-drawn blinds, of the occasional gleam of street-lamps, of the glazed spaces of the vestibule. This was the bottom of the sea, which showed an illumination of its own and which he even saw paved—when at a given moment he drew up to sink a long look over the banisters—with the marble squares of his childhood. By that time indubitably he felt, as he might have said in a commoner cause, better; it had allowed him to stop and draw breath, and the ease increased with the sight of the old black-and-white slabs. But what he most felt was that now surely, with the element of impunity pulling him as by hard firm hands, the case was settled for what he might have seen above had he dared that last look. The closed door, blessedly remote now, was still closed—and he had only in short to reach that of the house.

He came down further, he crossed the passage forming the access to the last flight; and if here again he stopped an instant it was almost for the sharpness of the thrill of assured escape. It made him shut his eyes—which opened again to the straight slope of the remainder of the stairs. Here was impunity still, but impunity almost excessive; inasmuch as the side-lights and the high fan-tracery of the entrance were glimmering straight into the hall; an appearance produced, he the next instant saw, by the fact that the vestibule gaped wide, that the hinged halves of the inner door had been thrown far back. Out of that again the *question* sprang at him, making his eyes, as he felt, half-start from his head, as they had done, at the top of the house, before the sign of the other door. If he had left that one open, hadn't he left this one closed, and wasn't he now in *most* immediate presence of some inconceivable occult activity? It was as sharp, the question, as a knife in his side, but the answer hung fire still and seemed to lose itself in the vague darkness to which the thin admitted dawn, glimmering archwise over the whole outer door, made a semicircular margin, a cold silvery nimbus that seemed to play a little as he looked—to shift and expand and contract.

It was as if there had been something within it, protected by indistinctness and corresponding in extent with the opaque surface behind, the painted panels of the last barrier to his escape, of which the key was in his pocket. The indistinctness mocked him even while he stared, affected him as somehow shrouding or challenging certitude, so that after faltering an instant on his step he let himself go with the sense that here *was* at last something to meet, to touch, to take, to know—something all unnatural and dreadful, but to advance upon which was the condition for him either of liberation or of supreme defeat. The penumbra, dense and dark, was the virtual screen of a figure which stood in it as still as some image erect in a niche or as some black-vizored sentinel guarding a treasure. Brydon was to know afterwards, was to recall and make out, the particular thing he had believed during the rest of his descent. He saw, in its great grey glimmering margin, the central vagueness diminish, and he felt it to be taking the very form toward which, for so many days, the passion of his curiosity had yearned. It gloomed, it loomed, it was something, it was somebody, the prodigy of a personal presence.

Rigid and conscious, spectral yet human, a man of his own substance and stature waited there to measure himself with his power to dismay. This only could it be—this only till he recognised, with his advance, that what made the face dim was the pair of raised hands that covered it and in which, so far from being offered in defiance, it was buried as for dark deprecation. So Brydon, before him, took him in; with every fact of him now, in the higher light, hard and acute—his planted stillness, his vivid truth, his grizzled bent head and white masking hands, his queer actuality of evening-dress, of dangling double eye-glass, of gleaming silk lappet and white linen, of pearl button and gold watch-guard and polished shoe. No portrait by a great modern master could have presented him with more intensity, thrust him out of his frame with more art, as if there had been "treatment," of the consummate sort, in his every shade and salience. The revulsion, for our friend, had become, before he knew it, immense—this drop, in the act of apprehension, to the sense of his adversary's inscrutable manœuvre. That meaning at least, while he gaped, it offered him; for he could but gape at his other self in this other anguish, gape as a proof that *he*, standing there for the achieved, the enjoyed, the triumphant life, couldn't be faced in his triumph. Wasn't the proof in the splendid covering hands, strong and completely spread?—so spread and so intentional that, in spite of a special verity that surpassed every other, the fact that one of these hands had lost two fingers, which were reduced to stumps, as if accidentally shot away, the face was effectually guarded and saved.

"Saved," though, *would* it be?—Brydon breathed his wonder till the very impunity of his attitude and the very insistence of his eyes produced, as he felt, a sudden stir which showed the next instant as a deeper portent, while the head raised itself, the betrayal of a braver purpose. The hands, as he looked, began to move, to open; then, as if deciding in a flash, dropped from the face and left it uncovered and presented. Horror, with the sight, had leaped into Brydon's throat, gasping there in a sound he couldn't utter; for the bared identity was too hideous as *his*, and his glare was the passion of his protest. The face, *that* face, Spencer Brydon's?—he searched it still, but looking away from it in dismay and denial, falling straight from his height of sublimity. It was unknown, inconceivable, awful, disconnected from any possibility—! He had been "sold," he inwardly moaned, stalking such game as this: the presence before him was a presence, the horror within him a horror, but the waste of his nights had been only grotesque and the success of his adventure an irony. Such an identity fitted his at *no* point, made its alternative monstrous. A thousand times yes, as it came upon him nearer now—the face was the face of a stranger. It came upon him nearer now, quite as one of those expanding fantastic images projected by the magic lantern of childhood; for the stranger, whoever he might be, evil, odious, blatant, vulgar, had advanced as for aggression, and he knew himself give ground. Then harder pressed still, sick with the force of his shock, and falling back as under the hot breath and the roused passion of a life larger than his own, a rage of personality before which his own collapsed, he felt the whole vision turn to darkness and his very feet give way. His head went round; he was going; he had gone.

III

What had next brought him back, clearly—though after how long?—was Mrs Muldoon's voice, coming to him from quite near, from so near that he seemed presently to see her as kneeling on the ground before him while he lay looking up at her; himself not wholly on the ground, but half-raised and upheld—conscious, yes, of tenderness of support and, more particularly, of a head pillowed in extraordinary softness and faintly refreshing fragrance. He considered, he wondered, his wit but half at his service; then another face intervened, bending more directly over him, and he finally knew that Alice Staverton had made her lap an ample and perfect cushion to him, and that she had to this end seated herself on the lowest degree of the staircase, the rest of his long person remaining stretched on his old black-and-white slabs. They were cold, these marble squares of his youth; but *he* somehow was not, in this rich return of consciousness—the most wonderful hour, little by little, that he had ever known, leaving him, as it did, so gratefully, so abysmally passive, and yet as with a treasure of intelligence waiting all round him for quiet appropriation; dissolved, he might call it, in the air of the place and producing the golden glow of a late autumn afternoon. He had come back, yes—come back from further away than any man but himself had ever travelled; but it was strange how with this sense what he had come back *to* seemed really the great thing, and as if his prodigious journey had been all for the sake of it. Slowly but surely his consciousness grew, his vision of his state thus completing itself: he had been miraculously *carried* back—lifted and carefully borne as from where he had been picked up, the uttermost end of an interminable grey passage. Even with this he was suffered to rest, and what had now brought him to knowledge was the break in the long mild motion.

It had brought him to knowledge, to knowledge—yes, this was the beauty of his state; which came to resemble more and more that of a man who has gone to sleep on some news of a great inheritance, and then, after dreaming it away, after profaning it with matters strange to it, has waked up again to serenity of certitude and has only to lie and watch it grow. This was the drift of his patience—that he had only to let it shine on him. He must moreover, with intermissions, still have been lifted and borne; since why and how else should he have known himself, later on, with the afternoon glow intenser, no longer at the foot of his stairs—situated as these now seemed at that dark other end of his tunnel—but on a deep window-bench of his high saloon, over which had been spread, couch-fashion, a mantle of soft stuff lined with grey fur that was familiar to his eyes and that one of his hands kept fondly feeling as for its pledge of truth. Mrs Muldoon's face had gone, but the other, the second he had recognised, hung over him in a way that showed how he was still propped and pillowed. He took it all in, and the more he took it the more it seemed to suffice: he was as much at peace as if he had had food and drink. It was the two women who had found him, on Mrs Muldoon's having plied, at her usual hour, her latch-key—and on her having above all arrived while

Miss Staverton still lingered near the house. She had been turning away, all anxiety, from worrying the vain bell-handle—her calculation having been of the hour of the good woman's visit; but the latter, blessedly, had come up while she was still there, and they had entered together. He had then lain, beyond the vestibule, very much as he was lying now—quite, that is, as he appeared to have fallen, but all so wondrously without bruise or gash; only in a depth of stupor. What he most took in, however, at present, with the steadier clearance, was that Alice Staverton had for a long unspeakable moment not doubted he was dead.

"It must have been that I *was*." He made it out as she held him. "Yes—I can only have died. You brought me literally to life. Only," he wondered, his eyes rising to her, "only, in the name of all the benedictions, how?"

It took her but an instant to bend her face and kiss him, and something in the manner of it, and in the way her hands clasped and locked his head while he felt the cool charity and virtue of her lips, something in all this beatitude somehow answered everything. "And now I keep you," she said.

"Oh keep me, keep me!" he pleaded while her face still hung over him: in response to which it dropped again and stayed close, clingingly close. It was the seal of their situation—of which he tasted the impress for a long blissful moment in silence. But he came back. "Yet how did you know—?"

"I was uneasy. You were to have come, you remember—and you had sent no word."

"Yes, I remember—I was to have gone to you at one to-day." It caught on to their "old" life and relation—which were so near and so far. "I was still out there in my strange darkness—where was it, what was it? I must have stayed there so long." He could but wonder at the depth and the duration of his swoon.

"Since last night?" she asked with a shade of fear for her possible indiscretion.

"Since this morning—it must have been: the cold dim dawn of to-day. Where have I been," he vaguely wailed, "where have I been?" He felt her hold him close, and it was as if this helped him now to make in all security his mild moan. "What a long dark day!"

All in her tenderness she had waited a moment. "In the cold dim dawn?" she quavered.

But he had already gone on piecing together the parts of the whole prodigy. "As I didn't turn up you came straight—?"

She barely cast about. "I went first to your hotel—where they told me of your absence. You had dined out last evening and hadn't been back since. But they appeared to know you had been at your club."

"So you had the idea of *this*—?"

"Of what?" she asked in a moment.

"Well—of what has happened."

"I believed at least you'd have been here. I've known, all along," she said, "that you've been coming."

" 'Known' it—?"

"Well, I've believed it. I said nothing to you after that talk we had a month ago—but I felt sure. I knew you *would*," she declared.

"That I'd persist, you mean?"

"That you'd see him."

"Ah but I didn't!" cried Brydon with his long wail. "There's somebody—an awful beast; whom I brought, too horribly, to bay. But it's not me."

At this she bent over him again, and her eyes were in his eyes. "No—it's not you." And it was as if, while her face hovered, he might have made out in it, hadn't it been so near, some particular meaning blurred by a smile. "No, thank heaven," she repeated—"it's not you! Of course it wasn't to have been."

"Ah but it *was*," he gently insisted. And he stared before him now as he had been staring for so many weeks. "I was to have known myself."

"You couldn't!" she returned consolingly. And then reverting, and as if to account further for what she had herself done, "But it wasn't only *that*, that you hadn't been at home," she went on. "I waited till the hour at which we had found Mrs Muldoon that day of my going with you; and she arrived, as I've told you, while, failing to bring any one to the door, I lingered in my despair on the steps. After a little, if she hadn't come, by such a mercy, I should have found means to hunt her up. But it wasn't," said

Alice Staverton, as if once more with her fine intention—"it wasn't only that."

His eyes, as he lay, turned back to her. "What more then?"

She met it, the wonder she had stirred. "In the cold dim dawn, you say? Well, in the cold dim dawn of this morning I too saw you."

"Saw *me*—?"

"Saw *him*," said Alice Staverton. "It must have been at the same moment."

He lay an instant taking it in—as if he wished to be quite reasonable. "At the same moment?"

"Yes—in my dream again, the same one I've named to you. He came back to me. Then I knew it for a sign. He had come to you."

At this Brydon raised himself; he had to see her better. She helped him when she understood his movement, and he sat up, steadying himself beside her there on the window-bench and with his right hand grasping her left. "*He* didn't come to me."

"You came to yourself," she beautifully smiled.

"Ah I've come to myself now—thanks to you, dearest. But this brute, with his awful face—this brute's a black stranger. He's none of *me*, even as I *might* have been," Brydon sturdily declared.

But she kept the clearness that was like the breath of infallibility. "Isn't the whole point that you'd have been different?"

He almost scowled for it. "As different as *that*—?"

Her look again was more beautiful to him than the things of this world. "Haven't you exactly wanted to know *how* different? So this morning," she said, "you appeared to me."

"Like *him?*"

"A black stranger!"

"Then how did you know it was I?"

"Because, as I told you weeks ago, my mind, my imagination, had worked so over what you might, what you mightn't have been—to show you, you see, how I've thought of you. In the midst of that you came to me—that my wonder might be answered. So I knew," she went on; "and believed that, since the question held you too so fast, as you told me that day, you too would see for yourself.

And when this morning I again saw I knew it would be because you had—and also then, from the first moment, because you somehow wanted me. *He* seemed to tell me of that. So why," she strangely smiled, "shouldn't I like him?"

It brought Spencer Brydon to his feet. "You 'like' that horror—?"

"I *could* have liked him. And to me," she said, "he was no horror. I had accepted him."

" 'Accepted'—?" Brydon oddly sounded.

"Before, for the interest of his difference—yes. And as *I* didn't disown him, as *I* knew him—which you at last, confronted with him in his difference, so cruelly didn't, my dear—well, he must have been, you see, less dreadful to me. And it may have pleased him that I pitied him."

She was beside him on her feet, but still holding his hand—still with her arm supporting him. But though it all brought for him thus a dim light, "You 'pitied' him?" he grudgingly, resentfully asked.

"He has been unhappy, he has been ravaged," she said.

"And haven't I been unhappy? Am not I—you've only to look at me!—ravaged?"

"Ah I don't say I like him *better*," she granted after a thought. "But he's grim, he's worn—and things have happened to him. He doesn't make shift, for sight, with your charming monocle."

"No"—it struck Brydon: "I couldn't have sported mine 'downtown.' They'd have guyed me there."

"His great convex pince-nez—I saw it, I recognised the kind—is for his poor ruined sight. And his poor right hand—!"

"Ah!" Brydon winced—whether for his proved identity or for his lost fingers. Then, "He has a million a year," he lucidly added. "But he hasn't you."

"And he isn't—no, he isn't—*you!*" she murmured as he drew her to his breast.

SCENES FROM *THE JOLLY CORNER*,

*a film script based on the James story, by Arthur Barron**

After many years abroad, expatriate Spencer Brydon has returned to his native New York at the end of the nineteenth century. His nighttime visits to his now vacant family home, "the jolly corner," convince him that a ghostly presence residing there embodies the secret of what he might have been. During the weeks following his return, he resumes a relationship with Alice Staverton, a young woman with whom he shared his youth. Discovering in himself a flair for business he never realized, he becomes involved in the reconstruction of inherited property. And gradually becoming obsessed with the ghost, the double, the alter ego he senses in the jolly corner, he intensifies his pursuit of it during nightly visits. The following scenes lead up to the climactic confrontation with the ghost.

18. INTERIOR. ALICE'S DINING AND DRAWING ROOMS. DAY.

A tasteful apartment, full of art objects, bric-a-brac, antiques, paintings, etc. BRYDON sits at a table, examining objects with the eye of a connoisseur. ALICE stands nearby.

BRYDON. You are perfectly right, Alice, it has become an obsession with me. I am consumed with the mystery of what I would have been had I remained here, instead of going abroad. . . . What would it have made of me? I keep forever wondering—all idiotically—as if I could possibly know.

---

* After establishing a reputation as one of America's leading documentary filmmakers, Arthur Barron wrote and directed such dramatic films as *Orville and Wilbur* and *Jeremy*. He is also the director of the recent feature film, *Brothers*.

ALICE. And why should you care to know?

BRYDON. Ah, but I *do*, desperately, and it positively aches within me, to the point of exasperation. . . . Perhaps I should have stuck here, instead of fleeing. But at twenty-three, how was one to judge? If I had stayed, I might have become something nearer to one of those American men who have been hammered so hard and made so keen by their conditions.

ALICE. Do you admire them so?

BRYDON. No. The question of any charm in them has nothing to do with the matter; it's only a question of what fantastic, yet perfectly possible development of my own nature I might have missed. . . . It comes over me that I had then a strange alter ego within me, as the full-blown flower is in the small tight bud, and that I just transferred him to the climate that blighted him forever. [*Here he picks up an object or objects which symbolize what he is talking about.*]

ALICE. And you wonder about the flower. So do I, if you want to know; and have been these past weeks. I believe in the flower. . . . I feel it would have been quite splendid, quite huge and monstrous.

BRYDON. Monstrous above all, and, I imagine, hideous and equally offensive.

ALICE. You don't believe that. If you did you wouldn't wonder. . . . You'd know . . . and that would be enough. What you feel, and what I feel for you, is that you'd have had power.

BRYDON. You'd have liked me that way?

ALICE. How should I not have liked you?

BRYDDN. I know at least what I am. . . . This side of the medal's clear enough. Yet what I would have been . . .

[*He turns to show her a figurine, a rather voluptuous, almost erotic one, depicting a woman and an antlered stag. As he holds the piece, he notices a couple passing outside, behind her back. It is* MR. WILKES, *the contractor, cane in hand, swaggering along with a woman on his arm, a woman who evokes a strumpet quality, vulgar, and sexy.* ALICE *notices his look.*]

ALICE. What is it?

[*She whirls her head to look outside, but* WILKES *is gone.*]

DISSOLVE TO
19. EXTERIOR. YARD. DAY.

And dissolve with optical printer to . . . flashback . . . stepmotion, sepia-tinted, the quality of memory. A croquet game . . . Alice and Brydon. He twenty-two; she nineteen. They are dressed in white, she with a floppy hat, he with white, floppy hat. She is radiant, happy; he seems to be *trying* to be relaxed and happy, but has difficulty giving himself over to the pleasure, the intimacy of the game.

FREEZE FRAME.

Music under . . . And DISSOLVE TO

20. INTERIOR. BEDROOM. NIGHT.

CLOSEUP of a still, a photograph, framed and on Alice's vanity table, in her bedroom; the photo shows the croquet scene just seen. Alice is preparing for bed. She is dressed demurely, with no hint or suggestion of sensuality, covered as she is by a flannel gown. Her preparations are smoothly time-worn, habitual, almost old-maidish.

21. EXTERIOR. STREET. NIGHT.

Brydon walking along the street toward the Jolly Corner. His walking stick tapping the sidewalk.

22. INTERIOR. BEDROOM. NIGHT.

Alice walking with gas light from her vanity table to her bed.

23. INTERIOR. HOUSE. NIGHT.

Brydon enters the house, puts his walking stick in a corner. He walks to a mantel, finds a candle and match.

24. INTERIOR. BEDROOM. NIGHT.

Alice in bed. She blows the lamp out.

25. INTERIOR. HOUSE. NIGHT.

Brydon lights candle, walks with it aloft in the upper stories of the house. We hear his footsteps, and a pair of other footsteps, which are just a bit out of synch with them. He becomes aware of this sound, and stops. The other footsteps stop. He walks. The other footsteps walk. He stops again; the other footsteps stop. He stands still . . . waiting.

26. INTERIOR. BEDROOM. NIGHT.

Alice is sleeping fitfully. Her labored breathing mingles with Brydon's. She becomes more and more agitated in her sleep, as if in a nightmare.

27. INTERIOR. HOUSE. NIGHT.

Brydon moves forward again. He passes a niche in the wall, and as he moves down the corridor, someone steps out behind him, a bulky, shadowy figure. Brydon stops. One can sense the hackles rising on his neck . . . He slowly turns and peers into the darkness ahead of him . . . He is obviously frightened.

BRYDON [*hoarse whisper*] I know you are *here* [*pause . . . breathing*] . . . I have known it these many years [*fear, his voice rising*] . . . I have pursued you . . . but now I spare you and I give you up. [*In the darkness something stirs, moves toward him.*] No! I renounce—never on my honor to try again. . . . [*He walks backward, now in terror.*] So rest forever . . . and let me . . .

A door opens and slams . . . Brydon's candle is blown out . . . and . . . SHOCK CUT TO

28. INTERIOR. BEDROOM. NIGHT.

Alice comes out of her nightmare with a scream. She sits up in terror, and takes deep shuddering breaths.

29. EXTERIOR. POND. DAY.

Alice and Brydon are riding in a swan boat.

BRYDON. I have lived such a selfish frivolous life these past thirty years. You see what my wayward life has made of me.

ALICE. You see what it has made of me . . . a pale flower, was it you said? More likely a shriveled blossom, blighted on the vine.

BRYDON. Oh, you're a person whom nothing can have altered. . . . You were born to be what you are, anywhere, anyway. You're the perfection nothing could blight. And don't you see how, without my exile, I shouldn't have been waiting till now?

ALICE. The great thing to see . . . is . . . that it has spoiled nothing. It hasn't spoiled your being here at last. It hasn't spoiled this. It hasn't spoiled your speaking.

BRYDON. Do you really believe, then, that I am as good as I might ever have been?

ALICE. Oh, no. Far from it. But I don't care.

BRYDON. You mean I'm good enough?

ALICE. Will you believe it if I say so? Anyway, the other person is still you!

BRYDON. He isn't myself.

ALICE. I know. I've seen him.

BRYDON. You?

ALICE. I've seen him in a dream.

BRYDON. Oh, a dream.

ALICE. But twice over. I saw him as I see you now.

BRYDON. You've dreamed the same dream?

ALICE. Twice over. The very same.

BRYDON. You dream about me at that rate?

ALICE. Ah, about him.

BRYDON. Then you know all about him. What's the wretch like?

ALICE. How can one describe a dream?

30. EXTERIOR. PUBLIC GARDENS. DAY (LATER).

Alice and Brydon walk and talk. A montage of locations, synch, and voice-over.

The weather has turned menacing, with rumbles of an approaching electrical storm.

ALICE. What an angry sound . . .

BRYDON. Yes. I imagine it sounds like battle. I say *imagine* advisedly, of course.

ALICE. Oh?

BRYDON. I mean I have never actually heard a battle. While brother was killing brother here, I was in Europe collecting.

ALICE. How fortunate.

BRYDON [*sadly*]. Yes . . .

ALICE. Are you embarrassed by your good luck?

BRYDON [*he turns to her*]. Do you think I am a coward, Alice, as some do?

ALICE. I think you have not yet been tested. [*A loud rumble, and crack of lightning.*] Perhaps we should delay returning . . .

BRYDON. [*Firmly. As though he has made a decision.*] No . . . I've been away too long.

ALICE. Away from what?

BRYDON. From . . . [*loud crack of thunder, and since what he says is almost a whisper, it is almost drowned out*] . . . *him*!

ALICE. What?

BRYDON. Nothing . . . [*he speaks to himself*] . . . I shall see him now. I *shall*.

ON HENRY JAMES and "THE JOLLY CORNER"

Henry Nash Smith
University of California, Berkeley

Henry James, born in New York City in 1843, was educated with his elder brother William in various European schools, so that he reached maturity with a cosmopolitan outlook and a fluent command of languages, especially French. He was rendered unfit for military service in the Civil War by an injury to his back. When James found he could support himself by writing criticism and fiction for magazines, he decided to live in Europe—first in Paris, but from 1876 onward in England. He never married. The short novel *Daisy Miller* (1879) became a *cause célèbre* when he was charged with libeling the American Girl in his portrayal of the heroine. During the remainder of an immensely productive career he was never able to reach so wide an audience again, but in the eyes of discriminating readers on both sides of the Atlantic he became the supreme exponent of the novel as an art form. When the United States was slow to enter the First World War on the side of the Allies, James became a British subject. He was awarded the Order of Merit a short time before his death in 1916.

"The Jolly Corner," written in 1906, grew out of James's ten-months' visit to the United States in 1904–05. Spencer Brydon, the protagonist, resembles James in being a native New Yorker, a bachelor with a moderate income from inherited wealth who has returned to the city of his birth after many years spent in Europe. Brydon is fifty-six years old, five years younger than James himself at the time of his visit, and he lacks a vocation or profession to stand as an equivalent for the decades of hard work that had produced James's sixty volumes of impeccable prose. But the question Brydon seeks to answer—What would America have made of him?—is one with deep meaning for James.

Directed toward the outer world of social circumstances, this question provided James with his international theme, the comparison of European and American cultures that he developed in a score of stories long and short, from his first true novel, *Roderick Hudson* (1876), and his most celebrated single work, *Daisy Miller* (1879), to his last published tale, "A Round of Visits" (1910), and the novel he left unfinished at his death in 1916, *The Ivory Tower*. Directed toward the inner world of consciousness in *The Ambassadors* (1903), for example, which many critics consider James's best novel, the international theme posed the question of the relative value of a life of action, which James associated with the United States and with business, and a life of passive observation and contemplation, which he associated with Europe.

In order to represent these alternative ways of life in "The Jolly Corner," James uses the supernatural. During Spencer Brydon's long hours of restless midnight prowling through the house on lower Fifth Avenue once occupied by his family (all of whom except him are now dead), he becomes aware of an invisible presence following him about the empty rooms. The presence, however, is not a ghost in the usual sense of the spirit of a dead person, but rather the hypothetical personality that might have been Spencer Brydon's had he chosen to remain in America and go into business. Afflicted with a persistent anxiety and a fear of the unknown, Brydon nevertheless has the courage to persevere in his efforts to bring the invisible alter ego to bay, and at last manages to do so. When the phantasm actually appears to him, the confrontation is so traumatic that Brydon loses consciousness for several hours. He is revived by Alice Staverton, the woman whose love for him has endured through the decades of his absence, and as a new man he presumably begins a new life with her in the house on the Jolly Corner.

What James wishes to convey concerning the process occurring in Brydon's psyche is beyond the resources of ordinary language. The story deals with the kind of depth psychology that was just being opened up by Sigmund Freud, and, among others, by Henry James's brother William, famous in his own right as psychologist and philosopher. In *The Turn of the Screw* (1898) as well as in "The Jolly Corner," James drew upon reports of appearances of ghosts, hallucinations, instances of telepathic communication, and so on, published in the *Proceedings* of the Society for Psychical Research, of which William James was a prominent member. F. W. H. Myers, another member of the Society and a man with whom the novelist corresponded, had not only discussed the notion of "subliminal" selves, but had also introduced the term "reciprocal hallucination" to designate phenomena like the simultaneous appearances of Brydon's alter ego to him in the house on the jolly corner and to Alice Staverton in her dream.

James intends for us to understand that Spencer Brydon passes through a psychological crisis so intense it might be considered a metaphorical death and rebirth. His quest of the alter ego in the empty house demands "a rigour to which nothing in his life had been comparable." He is stalking "a creature more subtle, yet at bay perhaps more formidable, than any beast of the forest." "There were even moments," asserts the narrative voice in a surprising anticipation of Hemingway, "when passages of Brydon's occasional experiences as a sportsman, stirred memories, from his younger time, of moor and mountain and desert . . . ," moments when "he found holding his breath and living in the joy of the instant, the supreme suspense created by big game alone." Like Hemingway's protagonists, Brydon vindicates his self-respect by the discovery that "he wasn't afraid (though putting himself the question as he believed gentlemen on Bengal tiger-shoots or in close quarters with the great bear of the Rockies had been known to confess to having put it). . . ." The narrative returns repeatedly to the subject of courage. When Brydon concludes that the apparition is actually afraid of him, he enjoys "a consciousness, unique in the experience of man." There is another moment when he believes he has the phantom cornered in a room behind a closed door: "It bristles there—somewhere near at hand, however unseen still—as the hunted thing," angry (he thinks) and ready to fight. This "sensation" of Brydon, says James, was probably "more complex than had ever before found itself consistent with sanity." When he finally regains consciousness, we are assured he has made a "prodigious journey" and has "come back from further away than any man but himself had ever traveled. . . ."

These superlatives belong to a vocabulary of melodrama

such as James had seldom if ever used since his earliest apprenticeship, and they are notably vague. The combination of obscurity with almost hysterical strain in the language indicates a charge of autobiographical emotion that James has failed to deal with fully. As a consequence, although the story has made a powerful impression on many readers, it has often proved baffling for them. In a pioneering study published in 1947, F. O. Matthiessen was interested primarily in the sociological implications of the story—in James's criticism of American culture as it entered the phase of fully developed capitalist competition. According to Matthiessen, the apparition reveals to Brydon "what he might have been had he stayed at home and gone into business and become 'one of those types who have been hammered so hard and made so keen by their conditions. . . .' " The answer comes in the mutilated hand and the "evil, odious, blatant, vulgar" face of the alter ego, which reveal "his crippled spirit." While this gets at part of James's meaning, it ignores almost entirely the psychological complexity of the story.

F. W. Dupee, in a brief comment published in 1951, showed greater awareness of this complexity in declaring that Brydon, "by laying the phantom of the obscene man of business he might have become if he had passed his life in America, relieves his mind of apprehensions and frees his heart to love." Yet Dupee's reading of the story fails to explain what is meant by laying the phantom, and offers no help concerning Alice Staverton's acceptance of an alter ego that seems so repulsive to Brydon. In 1962 Dorothea Krook elaborated on Brydon's acquiring the ability to give and particularly to receive love, but still did not explain how the confrontation with the apparition has such a powerful effect on him.

Leon Edel's monumental biography of James (completed in 1972) offers the promising observation that the two identities of Spencer Brydon do not present a simple white-and-black contrast between sensitive returning exile and vulgar but fortunately nonexistent millionaire. Yet Edel makes far too sweeping an identification between Brydon and James and falls into confusion about what their conflicting natures are. His hypothesis, for example, throws no light on the strong implication in the text that Brydon's alter ego tries to lead him into suicide by impelling him to leap from a fourth-floor window. And this analysis, like earlier ones, virtually ignores the emotional relation between Brydon and Alice Staverton.

Ernest Tuveson, the most recent interpreter of "The Jolly Corner," advances the psychological investigation considerably by calling attention to the connection between Brydon's repressed personality and the remodeling of the second house he owns, on Fourteenth Street. To Tuveson, "The construction project stirs up his dormant self, as it finally receives its opportunity to manifest its real nature." The idea of Brydon's latent capacity to become a dominant figure in the construction industry implies not only an ample grasp of material realities but also a competitive power of self-assertion. Nevertheless, this still fails to do justice to all the facets of Brydon's character.

The hypothesis that Arthur Barron has built into his film version of the story, which views the buried part of Brydon's psyche as his male sexuality, carries the long-range trend of interpretation appreciably farther. The emphasis on Brydon's sexuality allows recognition of Alice Staverton's also. Her passionate love for him accounts for her being aware of the repressed alter ego before he is, and for the fact that she dreams of the phantom at the moment of Brydon's confrontation with it. Finally, Brydon's psychological crisis becomes more understandable when it is portrayed as a process in which a repressed sexual impulse is admitted to consciousness and thus reintegrated with the remainder of his psyche. In this way it ceases to be a source of anxiety and becomes instead the basis for his rebirth as a new personality.

In the end, however, it must be admitted that James has built into this story a margin of the inexplicable. Spencer Brydon's confrontation with his alter ego cannot be reduced to a simple contest of wills resulting in the defeat of the phantom. For example, the story places considerable emphasis on a moment when Brydon seems to surrender the house to his antagonist, and after overcoming the impulse to leap from the high window, he is eager only to escape from the structure. He decides that "the builders, the destroyers" who wish to tear it down and erect a more commercially profitable structure in its place "might come as soon as they would." Yet when at last the specter actually appears to Brydon, it is hiding its face in its hands as if it could not bear to look at "the achieved, the enjoyed, the triumphant life" embodied in Brydon himself.

And this is not a complete list of the undeveloped suggestions with which James has enriched the final pages of the story. Yet even if each of them could be shown to have its proper place in an analytic account of Brydon's mental processes, we should merely have made the story into a case history. "The Jolly Corner" pursues a course of psychological realism for a certain distance, but like the three great works of James's "major phase" (*The Wings of the Dove, The Ambassadors*, and *The Golden Bowl*), it belongs ultimately to a post-realistic mode of writing. That is, it looked toward the future rather than the past, a future that only a decade later would explode into technical experiments and deliberate acts of "deconstruction" in fiction, such as James Joyce's *Ulysses* (1922) and André Gide's *The Counterfeiters* (1926). James's use of parapsychology and occult phenomena is a repudiation of nineteenth-century realism rather than an effort to achieve greater precision in the realistic presentation of life. This story shows how the epoch-making psychological discoveries of Freud and his colleagues could have the paradoxical effect of causing novelists to realize how little rather than how much they and their contemporaries knew about the human mind.

SUGGESTIONS FOR FURTHER READING

By Henry James:

The American Novels and Stories of Henry James, with an Introduction by F. O. Matthiessen. New York: Alfred A. Knopf, 1951.

The Complete Tales of Henry James, ed. Leon Edel, 12 vols. Philadelphia: J. B. Lippincott Co., 1962–1965.

The Notebooks of Henry James, eds. F. O. Matthiessen and Kenneth B. Murdock. New York: Oxford University Press, 1947.

Representative Selections, ed. Lyon N. Richardson. New York: American Book Co., 1941.

About Henry James:

F. W. Dupee, *Henry James* (1951), rev. ed. New York: Dell Publishing Co., 1965.

Leon Edel, *Henry James*, 6 vols. Philadelphia: J. B. Lippincott Co., 1953–1972.

Leon Edel, ed., *Henry James: A Collection of Critical Essays* (Twentieth Century Views). Englewood Cliffs, N.J.: Prentice-Hall, Inc., 1963.

Dorothea Krook, *The Ordeal of Consciousness in Henry James* (1962). Cambridge, England: Cambridge University Press, 1967.

F. O. Matthiessen, *The James Family, Including Selections from the Writings of Henry James, Senior, William, Henry, & Alice James*. New York: Alfred A. Knopf, 1947.

Ernest Tuveson, " 'The Jolly Corner': A Fable of Redemption." *Studies in Short Fiction*, 12 (Summer 1975): 271–280.

I'M A FOOL

by Sherwood Anderson

It was a hard jolt for me, one of the most bitterest I ever had to face. And it all came about through my own foolishness, too. Even yet sometimes, when I think of it, I want to cry or swear or kick myself. Perhaps, even now, after all this time, there will be a kind of satisfaction in making myself look cheap by telling of it.

It began at three o'clock one October afternoon as I sat in the grandstand at the fall trotting and pacing meet at Sandusky, Ohio.

To tell the truth, I felt a little foolish that I should be sitting in the grandstand at all. During the summer before I had left my home town with Harry Whitehead and, with a nigger named Burt, had taken a job as swipe with one of the two horses Harry was campaigning through the fall race meets that year. Mother cried and my sister Mildred, who wanted to get a job as a school teacher in our town that fall, stormed and scolded about the house all during the week before I left. They both thought it something disgraceful that one of our family should take a place as a swipe with race horses. I've an idea Mildred thought my taking the place would stand in the way of her getting the job she'd been working so long for.

But after all I had to work, and there was no other work to be got. A big lumbering fellow of nineteen couldn't just hang around the house and I had got too big to mow people's lawns and sell newspapers. Little chaps who could get next to people's sympathies by their sizes were always getting jobs away from me. There was one fellow who kept saying to everyone who wanted a lawn mowed or a cistern cleaned, that he was saving money to work his way through college, and I used to lay awake nights thinking up ways to injure him without being found out. I kept thinking of wagons running over him and bricks falling on his head as he walked along the street. But never mind him.

I got the place with Harry and I liked Burt fine. We got along splendid together. He was a big nigger with a lazy sprawling body and soft, kind eyes, and when it came to a fight he could hit like Jack Johnson. He had Bucephalus, a big black pacing stallion that could do 2.09 or 2.10, if he had to, and I had a little gelding named Doctor Fritz that never lost a race all fall when Harry wanted him to win.

We set out from home late in July in a box car with the two horses and after that, until late November, we kept moving along to the race meets and the fairs. It was a peachy time for me, I'll say that. Sometimes now I think that boys who are raised regular in houses, and never have a fine nigger like Burt for best friend, and go to high schools and college, and never steal anything, or get drunk a little, or learn to swear from fellows who know how, or come walking up in front of a grandstand in their shirt sleeves and with dirty horsey pants on when the races are going on and the grandstand is full of people all dressed up—What's the use of talking about it? Such fellows don't know nothing at all. They've never had no opportunity.

But I did. Burt taught me how to rub down a horse and put the bandages on after a race and steam a horse out and a lot of valuable things for any man to know. He could wrap a bandage on a horse's leg so smooth that if it had been the same color you would think it was his skin, and I guess he'd have been a big driver, too, and got to the top like Murphy and Walter Cox and the others if he hadn't been black.

Gee whizz, it was fun. You got to a county seat town, maybe say on a Saturday or Sunday, and the fair began the next Tuesday and lasted until Friday afternoon. Doctor Fritz would be, say in the 2.25 trot on Tuesday afternoon and on Thursday afternoon Bucephalus would knock 'em cold in the "free-for-all" pace. It left you a lot of time to hang around and listen to horse talk, and see Burt knock some yap cold that got too gay, and you'd find out about horses and men and pick up a lot of stuff you could use all the rest of your life, if you had some sense and salted down what you heard and felt and saw.

And then at the end of the week when the race meet was over, and Harry had run home to tend up to his livery stable business, you and Burt hitched the two horses to carts and drove slow and steady across country, to the place for the next meeting, so as to not overheat the horses, etc., etc., you know.

Gee whizz, Gosh amighty, the nice hickorynut and beechnut and oaks and other kinds of trees along the roads, all brown and red, and the good smells, and Burt singing a song that was called Deep River, and the country girls at the windows of houses and everything. You can stick your colleges up your nose for all me. I guess I know where I got my education.

Why, one of those little burgs of towns you come to on the way, say now on a Saturday afternoon, and Burt says, "let's lay up here." And you did.

And you took the horses to a livery stable and fed them, and you got your good clothes out of a box and put them on.

And the town was full of farmers gaping, because they could see you were race-horse people, and the kids maybe never see a nigger before and was afraid and run away when the two of us walked down their main street.

And that was before prohibition and all that foolishness, and so you went into a saloon, the two of you, and all the yaps come and stood around, and there was always someone pretended he was horsey and knew things and spoke up and began asking questions, and all you did was to lie and lie all you could about what horses you had, and I said I owned them, and then some fellow said "will you have a drink of whisky" and Burt knocked his eye out the way he could say, offhand-like, "Oh well, all right, I'm agreeable to a little nip. I'll split a quart with you." Gee whizz.

But that isn't what I want to tell my story about. We got home late in November and I promised mother I'd quit the race horses for good. There's a lot of things you've got to promise a mother because she don't know any better.

And so, there not being any work in our town any more than when I left there to go to the races, I went off to Sandusky and got a pretty good place taking care of horses for a man who owned a teaming and delivery and storage and coal and real estate business there. It was a pretty good place with good eats, and a day off each week, and sleeping on a cot in a big barn, and mostly just shoveling in hay and oats to a lot of big good-enough skates of horses, that couldn't have trotted a race with a toad. I wasn't dissatisfied and I could send money home.

And then, as I started to tell you, the fall races come to Sandusky and I got the day off and I went. I left the job at noon and had on my good clothes and my new brown derby hat, I'd just bought the Saturday before, and a stand-up collar.

First of all I went downtown and walked about with the dudes. I've always thought to myself, "put up a good front" and so I did it. I had forty dollars in my pocket and so I went into the West House, a big hotel, and walked up to the cigar stand. "Give me three twenty-five cent cigars," I said. There was a lot of horsemen and strangers and dressed-up people from other towns standing around in the lobby and in the bar, and I mingled amongst them. In the bar there was a fellow with a cane and a Windsor tie on, that it made me sick to look at him. I like a man to be a man and dress up, but not to go put on that kind of airs. So I pushed him aside, kind of rough, and had me a drink of whisky. And then he looked at me, as though he thought maybe he'd get gay, but he changed his mind and didn't say anything. And then I had another drink of whisky, just to show him something, and went out and had a hack out to the races, all to myself, and when I got there I bought myself the best seat I could get up in the grandstand, but didn't go in for any of these boxes. That's putting on too many airs.

And so there I was, sitting up in the grandstand as gay as you please and looking down on the swipes coming out with their horses, and with their dirty horsey pants on and the horse blankets swung over their shoulders, same as I had been doing all the year before. I liked one thing about the same as the other, sitting up there and feeling grand and being down there and looking up at the yaps and feeling grander and more important, too. One thing's about as good as another, if you take it just right. I've often said that.

Well, right in front of me, in the grandstand that day, there was a fellow with a couple of girls and they was about my age. The young fellow was a nice guy all right. He was the kind maybe that goes to college and then comes to be a lawyer or maybe a newspaper editor or something like that, but he wasn't stuck on himself. There are some of that kind are all right and he was one of the ones.

He had his sister with him and another girl and the sister looked around over his shoulder, accidental at first, not intending to start anything—she wasn't that kind—and her eyes and mine happened to meet.

You know how it is. Gee, she was a peach! She had on a soft dress, kind of a blue stuff and it looked carelessly made, but was well sewed and made and everything. I knew that much. I blushed when she looked right at me and so did she. She was the nicest girl I've ever seen in my life. She wasn't stuck on herself and she could talk proper grammar without being like a school teacher or something like that. What I mean is, she was O. K. I think maybe her father was well-to-do, but not rich to make her chesty because she was his daughter, as some are. Maybe he owned a drugstore or a drygoods store in their home town, or something like that. She never told me and I never asked.

My own people are all O. K. too, when you come to that. My grandfather was Welsh and over in the old country, in Wales he was— But never mind that.

The first heat of the first race come off and the young fellow setting there with the two girls left them and went down to make a bet. I knew what he was up to, but he didn't talk big and noisy and let everyone around know he was a sport, as some do. He wasn't that kind. Well, he come back and I heard him tell the two girls what horse he'd bet on, and when the heat was trotted they all half got to their feet and acted in the excited, sweaty way people do when they've got money down on a race, and the horse they bet on is up there pretty close at the end, and they think maybe he'll come on with a rush, but he never does because he hasn't got the old juice in him, come right down to it.

And then, pretty soon, the horses came out for the 2.18 pace and there was a horse in it I knew. He was a horse Bob French had in his string but Bob didn't own him. He was a horse owned by a Mr. Mathers down at Marietta, Ohio.

This Mr. Mathers had a lot of money and owned some

coal mines or something, and he had a swell place out in the country, and he was stuck on race horses, but was a Presbyterian or something, and I think more than likely his wife was one, too, maybe a stiffer one than himself. So he never raced his horses hisself, and the story round the Ohio race tracks was that when one of his horses got ready to go to the races he turned him over to Bob French and pretended to his wife he was sold.

So Bob had the horses and he did pretty much as he pleased and you can't blame Bob, at least, I never did. Sometimes he was out to win and sometimes he wasn't. I never cared much about that when I was swiping a horse. What I did want to know was that my horse had the speed and could go out in front, if you wanted him to.

And, as I'm telling you, there was Bob in this race with one of Mr. Mathers' horses, was named "About Ben Ahem" or something like that, and was fast as a streak. He was a gelding and had a mark of 2.21, but could step in .08 or .09.

Because when Burt and I were out, as I've told you, the year before, there was a nigger, Burt knew, worked for Mr. Mathers and we went out there one day when we didn't have no race on at the Marietta Fair and our boss Harry was gone home.

And so everyone was gone to the fair but just this one nigger and he took us all through Mr. Mathers' swell house and he and Burt tapped a bottle of wine Mr. Mathers had hid in his bedroom, back in a closet, without his wife knowing, and he showed us this Ahem horse. Burt was always stuck on being a driver but didn't have much chance to get to the top, being a nigger, and he and the other nigger gulped that whole bottle of wine and Burt got a little lit up.

So the nigger let Burt take this About Ben Ahem and step him a mile in a track Mr. Mathers had all to himself, right there on the farm. And Mr. Mathers had one child, a daughter, kinda sick and not very good-looking, and she came home and we had to hustle and get About Ben Ahem stuck back in the barn.

I'm only telling you to get everything straight. At Sandusky, that afternoon I was at the fair, this young fellow with the two girls was fussed, being with the girls and losing his bet. You know how a fellow is that way. One of them was his girl and the other his sister. I had figured that out.

"Gee whizz," I says to myself, "I'm going to give him the dope."

He was mighty nice when I touched him on the shoulder. He and the girls were nice to me right from the start and clear to the end. I'm not blaming them.

And so he leaned back and I give him the dope on About Ben Ahem. "Don't bet a cent on this first heat because he'll go like an oxen hitched to a plow, but when the first heat is over go right down and lay on your pile." That's what I told him.

Well, I never saw a fellow treat anyone sweller. There was a fat man sitting beside the little girl, that had looked at me twice by this time, and I at her, and both blushing, and what did he do but have the nerve to turn and ask the fat man to get up and change places with me so I could set with his crowd.

Gee whizz, craps amighty. There I was. What a chump I was to go and get gay up there in the West House bar, and just because that dude was standing there with a cane and that kind of a necktie on, to go and get all balled up and drink that whisky, just to show off.

Of course she would know, me setting right beside her and letting her smell of my breath. I could have kicked myself right down out of that grandstand and all around that race track and made a faster record than most of the skates of horses they had there that year.

Because that girl wasn't any mutt of a girl. What wouldn't I have give right then for a stick of chewing gum to chew, or a lozenger, or some liquorice, or most anything. I was glad I had those twenty-five cent cigars in my pocket and right away I give that fellow one and lit one myself. Then that fat man got up and we changed places and there I was, plunked right down beside her.

They introduced themselves and the fellow's best girl, he had with him, was named Miss Elinor Woodbury, and her father was a manufacturer of barrels from a place called Tiffin, Ohio. And the fellow himself was named Wilbur Wessen and his sister was Miss Lucy Wessen.

I suppose it was their having such swell names got me off my trolley. A fellow, just because he has been a swipe with a race horse, and works taking care of horses for a man in the teaming, delivery, and storage business, isn't any better or worse than anyone else. I've often thought that, and said it too.

But you know how a fellow is. There's something in that kind of nice clothes, and the kind of nice eyes she had, and the way she had looked at me, awhile before, over her brother's shoulder, and me looking back at her, and both of us blushing.

I couldn't show her up for a boob, could I?

I made a fool of myself, that's what I did. I said my name was Walter Mathers from Marietta, Ohio, and then I told all three of them the smashingest lie you ever heard. What I said was that my father owned the horse About Ben Ahem and that he had let him out to this Bob French for racing purposes, because our family was proud and had never gone into racing that way, in our own name, I mean. Then I had got started and they were all leaning over and listening, and Miss Lucy Wessen's eyes were shining, and I went the whole hog.

I told about our place down at Marietta, and about the big stables and the grand brick house we had on a hill, up above the Ohio River, but I knew enough not to do it in no bragging way. What I did was to start things and then let them drag the rest out of me. I acted just as reluctant to tell as I could. Our family hasn't got any barrel factory, and, since I've known us, we've always been pretty poor, but not asking anything of anyone at that, and my grandfather, over in Wales—but never mind that.

We set there talking like we had known each other for years and years, and I went and told them that my father had been expecting maybe this Bob French wasn't on the square, and had sent me up to Sandusky on the sly to find out what I could.

And I bluffed it through I had found out all about the 2.18 pace, in which About Ben Ahem was to start.

I said he would lose the first heat by pacing like a lame cow and then he would come back and skin 'em alive after that. And to back up what I said I took thirty dollars out of my pocket and handed it to Mr. Wilbur Wessen and asked him, would he mind, after the first heat, to go down and place it on About Ben Ahem for whatever odds he could get. What I said was that I didn't want Bob French to see me and none of the swipes.

Sure enough the first heat come off and About Ben Ahem went off his stride, up the back stretch, and looked like a wooden horse or a sick one, and come in to be last. Then this Wilbur Wessen went down to the betting place under the grandstand and there I was with the two girls, and when that Miss Woodbury was looking the other way once, Lucy Wessen kinda, with her shoulder you know, kinda touched me. Not just tucking down, I don't mean. You know how a woman can do. They get close, but not getting gay either. You know what they do. Gee whizz.

And then they give me a jolt. What they had done, when I didn't know, was to get together, and they had decided Wilbur Wessen would bet fifty dollars, and the two girls had gone and put in ten dollars each, of their own money, too. I was sick then, but I was sicker later.

About the gelding, About Ben Ahem, and their winning their money, I wasn't worried a lot about that. It come out O. K. Ahem stepped the next three heats like a bushel of spoiled eggs going to market before they could be found out, and Wilbur Wessen had got nine to two for the money. There was something else eating at me.

Because Wilbur come back, after he had bet the money, and after that he spent most of his time talking to that Miss Woodbury, and Lucy Wessen and I was left alone together like on a desert island. Gee, if I'd only been on the square or if there had been any way of getting myself on the square. There ain't any Walter Mathers, like I said to her and them, and there hasn't ever been one, but if there was, I bet I'd go to Marietta, Ohio, and shoot him tomorrow.

There I was, big boob that I am. Pretty soon the race was over, and Wilbur had gone down and collected our money, and we had a hack downtown, and he stood us a swell supper at the West House, and a bottle of champagne beside.

And I was with that girl and she wasn't saying much, and I wasn't saying much either. One thing I know. She wasn't stuck on me because of the lie about my father being rich and all that. There's a way you know. . . . Craps amighty. There's a kind of girl, you see just once in your life, and if you don't get busy and make hay, then you're gone for good and all, and might as well go jump off a bridge. They give you a look from inside of them somewhere, and it ain't no vamping, and what it means is—you want that girl to be your wife, and you want nice things around her like flowers and swell clothes, and you want her to have the kids you're going to have, and you want good music played and no ragtime. Gee whizz.

There's a place over near Sandusky, across a kind of bay, and it's called Cedar Point. And after we had supper we went over to it in a launch, all by ourselves. Wilbur and Miss Lucy and that Miss Woodbury had to catch a ten o'clock train back to Tiffin, Ohio, because, when you're out with girls like that you can't get careless and miss any trains and stay out all night, like you can with some kinds of Janes.

And Wilbur blowed himself to the launch and it cost him fifteen cold plunks, but I wouldn't never have knew if I hadn't listened. He wasn't no tin horn kind of a sport.

Over at the Cedar Point place, we didn't stay around where there was a gang of common kind of cattle at all.

There was big dance halls and dining places for yaps, and there was a beach you could walk along and get where it was dark, and we went there.

She didn't talk hardly at all and neither did I, and I was thinking how glad I was my mother was all right, and always made us kids learn to eat with a fork at table, and not swill soup, and not be noisy and rough like a gang you see around a race track that way.

Then Wilbur and his girl went away up the beach and Lucy and I sat down in a dark place, where there was some roots of old trees, the water had washed up, and after that the time, till we had to go back in the launch and they had to catch their trains, wasn't nothing at all. It went like winking your eye.

Here's how it was. The place we were setting in was dark, like I said, and there was the roots from that old stump sticking up like arms, and there was a watery smell, and the night was like—as if you could put your hand out and feel it—so warm and soft and dark and sweet like an orange.

I most cried and I most swore and I most jumped up and danced, I was so mad and happy and sad.

When Wilbur come back from being alone with his girl, and she saw him coming, Lucy she says, "we got to go to the train now," and she was most crying too, but she never knew nothing I knew, and she couldn't be so all busted up. And then, before Wilbur and Miss Woodbury got up to where we was, she put her face up and kissed me quick and put her head up against me and she was all quivering and—Gee whizz.

Sometimes I hope I have cancer and die. I guess you know what I mean. We went in the launch across the bay to the train like that, and it was dark, too. She whispered and said it was like she and I could get out of the boat and walk on the water, and it sounded foolish, but I knew what she meant.

And then quick we were right at the depot, and there was a big gang of yaps, the kind that goes to the fairs, and crowded and milling around like cattle, and how could I tell her? "It won't be long because you'll write and I'll write to you." That's all she said.

I got a chance like a hay barn afire. A swell chance I got.

And maybe she would write me, down at Marietta that way, and the letter would come back, and stamped on the front of it by the U.S.A. "there ain't any such guy," or something like that, whatever they stamp on a letter that way.

And me trying to pass myself off for a bigbug and a swell—to her, as decent a little body as God ever made. Craps amighty—a swell chance I got!

And then the train come in, and she got on it, and Wilbur Wessen he come and shook hands with me, and that Miss Woodbury was nice too and bowed to me, and I at her, and the train went and I busted out and cried like a kid.

Gee, I could have run after that train and made Dan Patch look like a freight train after a wreck but, socks amighty, what was the use? Did you ever see such a fool?

I'll bet you what—if I had an arm broke right now or a train had run over my foot—I wouldn't go to no doctor at all. I'd go set down and let her hurt and hurt—that's what I'd do.

I'll bet you what—if I hadn't a drunk that booze I'd a never been such a boob as to go tell such a lie—that couldn't never be made straight to a lady like her.

I wish I had that fellow right here that had on a Windsor tie and carried a cane. I'd smash him for fair. Gosh darn his eyes. He's a big fool—that's what he is.

And if I'm not another you just go find me one and I'll quit working and be a bum and give him my job. I don't care nothing for working, and earning money, and saving it for no such boob as myself.

SCENE FROM *I'M A FOOL,*

a film script based on the Anderson story,
*by Ron Cowen**

In his late teens at the beginning of this century, Andy has spent the summer wandering through Ohio in the company of Burt, a fellow racetrack swipe older than he. Together they drive a horse or two from track to track, caring for them en route. As the summer ends, they stop to visit George, a friend of Burt's and a stablehand on the estate of a wealthy man, Mr. Walter Mathers. There Andy drinks a bit and reveals his desire for a woman, and Burt wears himself out racing Big Ben, Mr. Mather's prize horse, on the sly. A day or two later Andy decides to view a race from the grandstand. Already feeling rather insecure in his fine clothes, he becomes more so when taunted by a dude in a bar. As a result, he drinks a couple of neat whiskies and buys some fine cigars just before the following scene begins.

EXTERIOR. RACETRACK. GRANDSTAND. DAY.

Andy weaves past small crowd.

CUT TO

Andy making way across an aisle of grandstand.

ANDY. 'Scuse me . . . beg pardon.
He sits down and wipes sweat from his forehead. Beginning to feel effects of liquor. Squints into sun.

CUT TO

EXTERIOR. RACETRACK.

---

* Ron Cowen's first dramatic success was *Summertree,* produced at Lincoln Center in New York City. He has written extensively for the stage and for television.

Andy sees George leading Big Ben. He rubs his eyes and squints again. Looks in pocket for a candy and pops it in his mouth. Eyes people sitting on either side of him, older and well dressed. Straightens his tie.

In boxes, just four or five rows below, Andy sees Wilbur Wesson, Lucy Wesson and Elinor Woodbury take their seats. They are his age. Attractive and well dressed.

Lucy turns to adjust her hat and her eyes meet Andy's. They stare at each other. Then look away. Embarrassed.

The sound of gunshot.

EXTERIOR. RACETRACK. DAY.

An empty stretch of track. The sound of horses thundering off in distance growing louder. Finally we see a horse race across the screen, momentarily filling blank stretch of track. Then they're gone again and the track is empty.

CUT TO

Andy POV—sees Wilbur and Elinor shake heads in disappointment. Lucy slowly tears losing tickets into small pieces.

Andy gets up and excuses himself. POV of spectators who are perturbed.

Andy finds a seat just behind Wesson. Leans forward and taps Wilbur on the shoulder.

ANDY. 'Scuse me. Hope I'm not bein' too forward. I couldn't help noticin' your bad luck. I've had it on several occasions at the races myself. If you're thinkin' about placin' another bet, you might take a look at a horse comin' up named Big Ben. Right below.

WILBUR [*big smile*]. Why, thanks. Big Ben. My, he is a handsome horse. Isn't he, Lucy?

[*They are looking at the warmups.*]

LUCY [*demurely*]. He certainly is.

WILBUR. Have you bet on him before?

ANDY. Wouldn't be fair if I said right now. But I can tell

you he's got a time of 2:18 and he'll come in well under that.

WILBUR. You sure?

ANDY. I'm positive. But don't bet a cent on this first heat 'cause he'll run it like . . . like a mule in a snowstorm. After that, he'll skin 'em alive.

WILBUR. Why thank you . . . Mr. . . . Mr.?

ANDY. Don't mention it. [*Hesitates and doesn't identify himself.*]

WILBUR [*offering his hand*]. My name's Wilbur Wesson and this is my sister Lucy Wesson and my fiancée, Miss Elinor Woodbury.

[ANDY *shakes* WILBUR'S *hand and tips his hat to both ladies.* ANDY'S *expression glazes over as his eyes and* LUCY'S *meet.*]

ANDY. How do you do. I'm—uh . . , Mr. Walter Mathers Jr. of Marietta, Ohio . . . Our family has this place nearby, a grand old brick house up on a hill, and big stables . . . [*His hesitancy gives way to bravado.*]

ELINOR. What brings you up to Sandusky, Mr. Mathers?

ANDY. What brings me? Well . . . you see, my father owns that horse, Big Ben . . . which he lets out to a Mr. Bob French for racing purposes. You see, being Presbyterian, our family's never gone into racing that way. In our own name, I mean. . . .

[*He smiles at* LUCY. *She smiles back.*]

Well, my father thinks this Bob French may not be on the square, so he's sent me up here to Sandusky on the sly . . .

ELINOR. You mean you're a spy? How exciting! Isn't that exciting, Lucy?

[LUCY *smiles at* ANDY. ANDY *smiles back.*]

ANDY. Wilbur, can I offer you a cigar?

[*He reaches in his pocket and pulls out two cigars.*]

WILBUR. Thank you, Walter. Don't mind if I do.

[ANDY *lights the two cigars.*]

ANDY. And, Wilbur, I was wonderin' if you wouldn't mind placin' this for me on Big Ben for the second heat. Might not look right for me to . . . ownin' him and all.

[*He takes three ten-dollar bills from his pocket and hands them one by one to* WILBUR.]

. . . for whatever odds you can get.

[WILBUR *starts to leave.*]

LUCY. Wait, Wilbur! After what Mr. Mathers has told us, Elinor and I would be missing a golden opportunity if we didn't each put in something.

ELINOR. That's right, Wilbur. We all want to be millionaires.

LUCY. Is ten dollars enough?

CUT TO Andy's face. His large smile vanishes.

CUT TO

EXTERIOR. RACETRACK. THE FIELD. DAY.

A pack of horses crosses the finish line. The sequence is repeated two more times, possibly from different points of view.

CUT TO

Andy's sigh of relief and hysterics and hugging. Wilbur and Elinor Hug. Andy and Lucy want to hug. He pulls back slightly.

CUT TO

EXTERIOR. DUSK.

Montage of four young people walking slowly along bankside of lake. In the distance, soft colored lights are strung out at the fair across the lake. They are supposed to be choosing a picnic spot but are more engrossed in enjoying one another's company during the leisurely stroll, as we hear Andy in voice over:

ANDY. So Big Ben came through and all, then what am I gettin' so worked up for, right? Well, I'll tell you. Miss Lucy wasn't stuck on me 'count of the lie about my father being rich. She really liked me! Now that's the kind of girl you see just once in your life, and if you don't make hay, then she's gone and you may as well jump off a bridge. They give you a look from inside them somewhere, and it ain't no vampin'. What it means is . . . you want that girl to be your wife and you want nice things around her and you want her to have your kids and you want good music played and no ragtime!

ON SHERWOOD ANDERSON and "I'M A FOOL"

Jordon Pecile
Fairfield University, Connecticut

The myth about Sherwood Anderson (1876–1941)—that in the middle of a successful advertising career he repudiated the money-making ethics and the regimentation of business in order to realize himself as a writer—has become part of our literary tradition, an ironic reversal of the Horatio Alger myth.

The crisis which gave rise to this myth occurred in 1912, when Anderson was thirty-six and living with his wife and three children in Elyria, Ohio. By that time he had been in advertising some twelve years, working his way up from copy and sales to become president of his own firm. The Anderson Manufacturing Company mixed paints and roofing compounds and sold them by direct mail advertising. But money and management problems were harassing the Roof-Fix Man, as Anderson called himself in his ads; he had been using cheap ingredients in order to increase profits, and business was falling off. He was also having marital difficulties. Some of these troubles he escaped at night, when he retreated to a desk in his attic to write. Long hours of compulsive, almost automatic writing on four radical novels about business began to affect his health, as the financial burdens of his manufacturing company were depressing his spirits. The crisis came one autumn morning before Thanksgiving.

He was in his office that morning "buying and selling as usual," dictating letters, when suddenly he had a moment of terrible clarity, an epiphanal moment when the fraudulent quality of his life was revealed to him and he realized that he was being dishonest with words and dishonest with himself. He wanted to uproot himself, to walk out the door and out of that baleful phase of his life. Thinking of his feet, he turned to his secretary and said, "I have been wad-ing in a long river, and my feet are wet." Then he walked, trancelike, away from his desk and out of town.

The words are recorded in one of the three moody autobiographies in which he labored to create the image of himself as an upwardly mobile businessman who pursued, for half his life, the American dream of making money, only to find that in the cutthroat competition he was losing his compassion for his fellow men.

Actually, the choice Anderson made to chuck his business and try to make it as a writer was heroic in his time, the time of the Tin Lizzie. In the first decades of this century the country was changing rapidly from an agrarian to an industrial economy with its new methods of mass production, its efficient assembly lines, its standardization of parts and of lives. In this change, and in the greedy pursuit of money that paralleled it, Anderson foresaw the consequent impoverishment of the spirit and estrangement of the individual. From his own experiences as a dedicated go-getter, he concluded that as the nation became mechanized men would become less gentle because they would not have their hands in the soil, their roots in the earth. In the stories he came to write, he lamented this waning of the pastoral life, and he warned against the shrinking significance of the human being in the expansion of industrial, urban society.

But the sad truth behind the Anderson myth is that, four days after his flight from Elyria, he turned up, dazed and incoherent, in a Cleveland hospital. The doctor's diagnosis was nervous exhaustion and temporary amnesia.

After his recovery, Anderson returned to his business only to close it, and in 1913 he separated from his wife and joined his older brother Karl, an illustrator working in Chicago. Through Karl he came to know the avant-garde painters and writers of the bohemian South Side and was exposed to the vitality and the liberating influences of what has become known as the Chicago Renaissance, the literary flowering of the Midwest. In lofts and studios in the Jackson Park area, he discussed the new theories of Freud and the new prose of Gertrude Stein; he read *Spoon River Anthology* and Theodore Dreiser's novels: "The books jolted me. 'Look homeward, angel,' they shouted at me. They did, I felt, turn me away from books, from other writers, to the life about me, as I had myself seen and felt it."

In that brief decade when he wrote his best stories, he did look homeward. In his attic room in a boarding house near Michigan Boulevard, he returned in his imagination to his unhappy childhood, to the years he spent growing up in Clyde, Ohio, and to the memories of his dour, self-sacrificing mother and of that smiling failure, his father. Though he always chastised himself for it, he never really got over his feelings of shame because his mother had to take in washing and because other louts ridiculed the clownish antics and drunken vagaries of his cornet-playing father. In a fresh and beautiful story of those days called "The Sad Horn Blowers," he wrote, "Young boys growing up and merging into manhood do not fancy fathers being too boyish."

Young boys growing up and merging into manhood is the central concern of the stories for which Anderson is celebrated today. It's the linking theme of his classic cycle of related stories about Winesburg, Ohio, and it's the subject of the three famous monologues which recapture his summers at the race tracks: "I Want to Know Why," "The Man Who Became a Woman," and "I'm a Fool."

In these oral narratives, the race-track setting and the sounds and earthy smells of the stables, the closeness of horses and men, represent the easy, intimate and idyllic relationship which Anderson was convinced existed between human beings and the natural world before the onslaught of the machine. Like the raft and the river in *Huckleberry Finn*, the stables and the race track are places of contentment and escape, Edenic oases for the Adamic adolescent. Horses in this context embody the noble fulfillment of purposeful nature; they are dependable and honest and fine, whereas adults are ambiguous, devious and phony. Each of these three monologues is a tale of resistance to the loss of boyhood innocence and of reluctant initiation into the complexities of manhood, especially the shadowy complexities of adult sexuality.

The emotional tone of these tales, on which so much of their lasting appeal is based, mixes boyish bewilderment, frustration, and vulnerability. The boy-man in each suffers from feelings of inferiority (social and sexual), and he speaks from the depths of his being, confessing his burden of guilt and confusion "in order to get everything straight," to come to terms with it and to subdue it forever. His pitiful search for the meaning of the experience, for understanding, is his reason for telling the story, for taking us into his confidence.

Though the main incident in "I'm a Fool"—what happened to a youth who made himself out to be richer than he was and got away with it, to his own chagrin—has occurred some time before the telling of the tale, the big lumbering fellow who confesses it still doesn't understand why it happened. He blames his foolishness on the dude in the Windsor tie and on being slightly drunk, not on the unresolved conflict of values which is tearing him up inside, the conflict between life in the stables and life in the grandstand. As a swipe at heart, he is in mild revolt against the false airs of the dude, and against the false respectability of his middle-class mother and his schoolteacher sister—respectability imposed by a binding morality and a restrictive society where money and position are at stake: "I've an idea Mildred thought my taking the place [as swipe at the tracks] would stand in the way of her getting the job she'd been working so long for," he admits. Yet even he capitulates to the social importance of appearances when he meets the girl in the soft blue dress that "looked carelessly made but was well-sewed and made and everything." And when he has to, he too can put up a good front; it's easy to deceive, when one is at the mercy of economic and social forces beyond his control. It is only after, on the beach, against the background of a clump of roots "sticking up like arms," that he realizes that his denial of his origins, of who he is, will hold him back from the fulfillment of the tenderness, the love he feels. But he never understands why.

The main challenges in dramatizing "I'm a Fool" are to convert the oral monologue into a dialogue and a series of incremental dramatic scenes, and to rearrange time in an orderly manner. The unskilled speaker in the story, unable to control his responses, rambles and runs on, in and out of time, telling about events which took place in the past, and events which took place on the day of the races (which was some time ago, before Prohibition), and telling about now, his compulsive desire to make himself look cheap. That the story should adapt to a dramatic form as faithfully as it does is further evidence of Anderson's painstaking, original craftsmanship, and of his finesse in making colloquial conversation—essentially an ancient way of story telling—serve the needs of modern fiction and drama. In Anderson's dramatic monologue, the artless rambling of the boy-man not only continuously reveals his character in ways he doesn't even suspect, but it artfully pushes the action forward all the time.

"I'm a Fool" was sold to the little literary magazine *Dial* for less than a hundred dollars because Anderson couldn't peddle it successfully to the mass market, where editors found it unfinished, vague, groping. But so was life, Anderson argued, and he continued to write stories that an admiring Virginia Woolf was later to call "shell-less"—stories that exposed the vulnerable areas, the secrets, of thwarted lives, and that illuminated the obscure realm of personal relationships.

By the example of the crisis in his own life, Sherwood Anderson is said to have liberated man from timetable servitude to business; by the example of his art, he is said to have liberated the short story from its previous dependence on slick plots and trick endings. Generations of writers have and will follow his example in both areas. Almost all good modern fiction writers, including Hemingway and Faulkner whom he so generously helped get started, are beholden to him. For though Sherwood Anderson was a provincial in his choice of subject matter, in his concentration on the limited lives of limited human beings, he was a pioneer in his narrative techniques.

Study people, don't try to think out plots, was his advice to a young writer; "it seems to me that the stories and the drama of the stories should come out of the real lives of people." It's easy now to understand why.

SUGGESTIONS FOR FURTHER READING

By Sherwood Anderson:

The Portable Sherwood Anderson, ed. Horace Gregory. New York: Viking Press, 1949.

Sherwood Anderson: Short Stories, ed. Maxwell Geismar. New York: Hill and Wang, 1962.

Winesburg, Ohio, ed. Malcolm Cowley. New York: Viking Press, 1960.

About Sherwood Anderson:

Anderson, David D. *Sherwood Anderson*. New York: Holt, Rinehart and Winston, 1967.

Burbank, Rex. *Sherwood Anderson*. New York: Twayne Publishers, 1964.

Howe, Irving. *Sherwood Anderson*. New York: William Sloane, 1951; Stanford University Press, 1966.

Rideout, Walter B., ed. *Sherwood Anderson, A Collection of Critical Essays*. Englewood Cliffs, New Jersey: Prentice-Hall, 1974.

Weber, Brom. *Sherwood Anderson*. Minneapolis: University of Minnesota Press, 1964.

White, Ray Lewis, ed. *The Achievement of Sherwood Anderson: Essays in Criticism*. Chapel Hill: University of North Carolina Press, 1966.

BERNICE BOBS HER HAIR

by F. Scott Fitzgerald

After dark on Saturday night one could stand on the first tee of the golf-course and see the country-club windows as a yellow expanse over a very black and wavy ocean. The waves of this ocean, so to speak, were the heads of many curious caddies, a few of the more ingenious chauffeurs, the golf professional's deaf sister—and there were usually several stray, diffident waves who might have rolled inside had they so desired. This was the gallery.

The balcony was inside. It consisted of the circle of wicker chairs that lined the wall of the combination club-room and ballroom. At these Saturday-night dances it was largely feminine; a great babel of middle-aged ladies with sharp eyes and icy hearts behind lorgnettes and large bosoms. The main function of the balcony was critical. It occasionally showed grudging admiration, but never approval, for it is well known among ladies over thirty-five that when the younger set dance in the summer-time it is with the very worst intentions in the world, and if they are not bombarded with stony eyes stray couples will dance weird barbaric interludes in the corners, and the more popular, more dangerous, girls will sometimes be kissed in the parked limousines of unsuspecting dowagers.

But, after all, this critical circle is not close enough to the stage to see the actors' faces and catch the subtler byplay. It can only frown and lean, ask questions and make satisfactory deductions from its set of postulates, such as the one which states that every young man with a large income leads the life of a hunted partridge. It never really appreciates the drama of the shifting, semicruel world of adolescence. No; boxes, orchestra-circle, principals, and chorus are represented by the medley of faces and voices that sway to the plaintive African rhythm of Dyer's dance orchestra.

From sixteen-year-old Otis Ormonde, who has two more years at Hill School, to G. Reece Stoddard, over whose bureau at home hangs a Harvard law diploma; from little Madeleine Hogue, whose hair still feels strange and uncomfortable on top of her head, to Bessie MacRae, who has been the life of the party a little too long—more than ten years—the medley is not only the centre of the stage but contains the only people capable of getting an unobstructed view of it.

With a flourish and a bang the music stops. The couples exchange artificial, effortless smiles, facetiously repeat "*la*-de-*da*-*da* dum-*dum*," and then the clatter of young feminine voices soars over the burst of clapping.

A few disappointed stags caught in midfloor as they had been about to cut in subsided listlessly back to the walls, because this was not like the riotous Christmas dances—these summer hops were considered just pleasantly warm and exciting, where even the younger marrieds rose and performed ancient waltzes and terrifying fox trots to the tolerant amusement of their younger brothers and sisters.

Warren McIntyre, who casually attended Yale, being one of the unfortunate stags, felt in his dinner-coat pocket for a cigarette and strolled out onto the wide, semidark veranda, where couples were scattered at tables, filling the lantern-hung night with vague words and hazy laughter. He nodded here and there at the less absorbed and as he passed each couple some half-forgotten fragment of a story played in his mind, for it was not a large city and every one was Who's Who to every one else's past. There, for example, were Jim Strain and Ethel Demorest, who had been privately engaged for three years. Every one knew that as soon as Jim managed to hold a job for more than two months she would marry him. Yet how bored they both looked, and how wearily Ethel regarded Jim sometimes, as if she wondered why she had trained the vines of her affection on such a wind-shaken poplar.

Warren was nineteen and rather pitying with those of his friends who hadn't gone East to college. But, like most boys, he bragged tremendously about the girls of his city when he was away from it. There was Genevieve Ormonde, who regularly made the rounds of dances, house-parties, and football games at Princeton, Yale, Williams, and Cornell; there was black-eyed Roberta Dillon, who was quite as famous to her own generation as Hiram Johnson or Ty Cobb; and, of course, there was Marjorie Harvey, who besides having a fairylike face and a dazzling, bewildering tongue was already justly celebrated for having turned five cart-wheels in succession during the past pump-and-slipper dance at New Haven.

Warren, who had grown up across the street from Marjorie, had long been "crazy about her." Sometimes she seemed to reciprocate his feeling with a faint gratitude, but she had tried him by her infallible test and informed him gravely that she did not love him. Her test was that when she was away from him she forgot him and had affairs with other boys. Warren found this discouraging, especially as Marjorie had been making little trips all summer, and for the first two or three days after each arrival home he saw great heaps of mail on the Harveys' hall table addressed to her in various masculine handwritings. To make matters worse, all during the month of August she had been visited by her cousin Bernice from Eau Claire, and it seemed impossible to see her alone. It was always necessary to hunt round and find some one to take care of Bernice. As August waned this was becoming more and more difficult.

Much as Warren worshipped Marjorie, he had to admit that Cousin Bernice was sorta dopeless. She was pretty, with dark hair and high color, but she was no fun on a party. Every Saturday night he danced a long arduous duty dance with her to please Marjorie, but he had never been anything but bored in her company.

"Warren"—a soft voice at his elbow broke in upon his thoughts, and he turned to see Marjorie, flushed and radiant as usual. She laid a hand on his shoulder and a glow settled almost imperceptibly over him.

"Warren," she whispered, "do something for me—dance with Bernice. She's been stuck with little Otis Ormonde for almost an hour."

Warren's glow faded.

"Why—sure," he answered half-heartedly.

"You don't mind, do you? I'll see that you don't get stuck."

" 'Sall right."

Marjorie smiled—that smile that was thanks enough.

"You're an angel, and I'm obliged loads."

With a sigh the angel glanced round the veranda, but Bernice and Otis were not in sight. He wandered back inside, and there in front of the women's dressing-room he found Otis in the centre of a group of young men who were convulsed with laughter. Otis was brandishing a piece of timber he had picked up, and discoursing volubly.

"She's gone in to fix her hair," he announced wildly. "I'm waiting to dance another hour with her."

Their laughter was renewed.

"Why don't some of you cut in?" cried Otis resentfully. "She likes more variety."

"Why, Otis," suggested a friend, "you've just barely got used to her."

"Why the two-by-four, Otis?" inquired Warren, smiling.

"The two-by-four? Oh, this? This is a club. When she comes out I'll hit her on the head and knock her in again."

Warren collapsed on a settee and howled with glee.

"Never mind, Otis," he articulated finally. "I'm relieving you this time."

Otis simulated a sudden fainting attack and handed the stick to Warren.

"If you need it, old man," he said hoarsely.

No matter how beautiful or brilliant a girl may be, the reputation of not being frequently cut in on makes her position at a dance unfortunate. Perhaps boys prefer her company to that of the butterflies with whom they dance a dozen times an evening, but youth in this jazz-nourished generation is temperamentally restless, and the idea of fox-trotting more than one full fox trot with the same girl is distasteful, not to say odious. When it comes to several dances and the intermissions between she can be quite sure that a young man, once relieved, will never tread on her wayward toes again.

Warren danced the next full dance with Bernice, and finally, thankful for the intermission, he led her to a table on the veranda. There was a moment's silence while she did unimpressive things with her fan.

"It's hotter here than in Eau Claire," she said.

Warren stifled a sigh and nodded. It might be for all he knew or cared. He wondered idly whether she was a poor conversationalist because she got no attention or got no attention because she was a poor conversationalist.

"You going to be here much longer?" he asked, and then

turned rather red. She might suspect his reasons for asking.

"Another week," she answered, and stared at him as if to lunge at his next remark when it left his lips.

Warren fidgeted. Then with a sudden charitable impulse he decided to try part of his line on her. He turned and looked at her eyes.

"You've got an awfully kissable mouth," he began quietly.

This was a remark that he sometimes made to girls at college proms when they were talking in just such half dark as this. Bernice distinctly jumped. She turned an ungraceful red and became clumsy with her fan. No one had ever made such a remark to her before.

"Fresh!"—the word had slipped out before she realized it, and she bit her lip. Too late she decided to be amused, and offered him a flustered smile.

Warren was annoyed. Though not accustomed to have that remark taken seriously, still it usually provoked a laugh or a paragraph of sentimental banter. And he hated to be called fresh, except in a joking way. His charitable impulse died and he switched the topic.

"Jim Strain and Ethel Demorest sitting out as usual," he commented.

This was more in Bernice's line, but a faint regret mingled with her relief as the subject changed. Men did not talk to her about kissable mouths, but she knew that they talked in some such way to other girls.

"Oh, yes," she said, and laughed. "I hear they've been mooning round for years without a red penny. Isn't it silly?"

Warren's disgust increased. Jim Strain was a close friend of his brother's, and anyway he considered it bad form to sneer at people for not having money. But Bernice had had no intention of sneering. She was merely nervous.

II

When Marjorie and Bernice reached home at half after midnight they said good night at the top of the stairs. Though cousins, they were not intimates. As a matter of fact Marjorie had no female intimates—she considered girls stupid. Bernice on the contrary all through this parent-arranged visit had rather longed to exchange those confidences flavored with giggles and tears that she considered an indispensable factor in all feminine intercourse. But in this respect she found Marjorie rather cold; felt somehow the same difficulty in talking to her that she had in talking to men. Marjorie never giggled, was never frightened, seldom embarrassed, and in fact had very few of the qualities which Bernice considered appropriately and blessedly feminine.

As Bernice busied herself with tooth-brush and paste this night she wondered for the hundredth time why she never had any attention when she was away from home. That her family were the wealthiest in Eau Claire; that her mother entertained tremendously, gave little dinners for her daughter before all dances and bought her a car of her own to drive round in, never occurred to her as factors in her home-town social success. Like most girls she had been brought up on the warm milk prepared by Annie Fellows Johnston and on novels in which the female was beloved because of certain mysterious womanly qualities, always mentioned but never displayed.

Bernice felt a vague pain that she was not at present engaged in being popular. She did not know that had it not been for Marjorie's campaigning she would have danced the entire evening with one man; but she knew that even in Eau Claire other girls with less position and less pulchritude were given a much bigger rush. She attributed this to something subtly unscrupulous in those girls. It had never worried her, and if it had her mother would have assured her that the other girls cheapened themselves and that men really respected girls like Bernice.

She turned out the light in her bathroom, and on an impulse decided to go in and chat for a moment with her aunt Josephine, whose light was still on. Her soft slippers bore her noiselessly down the carpeted hall, but hearing voices inside she stopped near the partly opened door. Then she caught her own name, and without any definite intention of eavesdropping lingered—and the thread of the conversation going on inside pierced her consciousness sharply as if it had been drawn through with a needle.

"She's absolutely hopeless!" It was Marjorie's voice. "Oh, I know what you're going to say! So many people have told you how pretty and sweet she is, and how she can cook! What of it? She has a bum time. Men don't like her."

"What's a little cheap popularity?"

Mrs. Harvey sounded annoyed.

"It's everything when you're eighteen," said Marjorie emphatically. "I've done my best. I've been polite and I've made men dance with her, but they just won't stand being bored. When I think of that gorgeous coloring wasted on such a ninny, and think what Martha Carey could do with it—oh!"

"There's no courtesy these days."

Mrs. Harvey's voice implied that modern situations were too much for her. When she was a girl all young ladies who belonged to nice families had glorious times.

"Well," said Marjorie, "no girl can permanently bolster up a lame-duck visitor, because these days it's every girl for herself. I've even tried to drop her hints about clothes and things, and she's been furious—given me the funniest looks. She's sensitve enough to know she's not getting away with much, but I'll bet she consoles herself by thinking that she's very virtuous and that I'm too gay and fickle and will come to a bad end. All unpopular girls think that way. Sour grapes! Sarah Hopkins refers to Genevieve and Roberta and me as gardenia girls! I'll bet she'd give ten years of her life and her European education to be a gardenia girl and have three or four men in love with her and be cut in on every few feet at dances."

"It seems to me," interrupted Mrs. Harvey rather wearily, "that you ought to be able to do something for Bernice. I know she's not very vivacious."

Marjorie groaned.

"Vivacious! Good grief! I've never heard her say anything to a boy except that it's hot or the floor's crowded or that she's going to school in New York next year. Sometimes she asks them what kind of car they have and tells them the kind she has. Thrilling!"

There was a short silence, and then Mrs. Harvey took up her refrain:

"All I know is that other girls not half so sweet and attractive get partners. Martha Carey, for instance, is stout and loud, and her mother is distinctly common. Roberta Dillon is so thin this year that she looks as though Arizona were the place for her. She's dancing herself to death."

"But, mother," objected Marjorie impatiently, "Martha is cheerful and awfully witty and an awfully slick girl, and

Roberta's a marvellous dancer. She's been popular for ages!"

Mrs. Harvey yawned.

"I think it's that crazy Indian blood in Bernice," continued Marjorie. "Maybe she's a reversion to type. Indian women all just sat round and never said anything."

"Go to bed, you silly child," laughed Mrs. Harvey. "I wouldn't have told you that if I'd thought you were going to remember it. And I think most of your ideas are perfectly idiotic," she finished sleepily.

There was another silence, while Marjorie considered whether or not convincing her mother was worth the trouble. People over forty can seldom be permanently convinced of anything. At eighteen our convictions are ills from which we look; at forty-five they are caves in which we hide.

Having decided this, Marjorie said good night. When she came out into the hall it was quite empty.

III

While Marjorie was breakfasting late next day Bernice came into the room with a rather formal good morning, sat down opposite, stared intently over and slightly moistened her lips.

"What's on your mind?" inquired Marjorie, rather puzzled.

Bernice paused before she threw her hand-grenade.

"I heard what you said about me to your mother last night."

Marjorie was startled, but she showed only a faintly heightened color and her voice was quite even when she spoke.

"Where were you?"

"In the hall. I didn't mean to listen—at first."

After an involuntary look of contempt Marjorie dropped her eyes and became very interested in balancing a stray cornflake on her finger.

"I guess I'd better go back to Eau Claire—if I'm such a nuisance." Bernice's lower lip was trembling violently and she continued on a wavering note: "I've tried to be nice, and—and I've been first neglected and then insulted. No one ever visited me and got such treatment."

Marjorie was silent.

"But I'm in the way, I see. I'm a drag on you. Your friends don't like me." She paused, and then remembered another one of her grievances. "Of course I was furious last week when you tried to hint to me that that dress was unbecoming. Don't you think I know how to dress myself?"

"No," murmured Marjorie less than half-aloud.

"What?"

"I didn't hint anything," said Marjorie succinctly. "I said, as I remember, that it was better to wear a becoming dress three times straight than to alternate it with two frights."

"Do you think that was a very nice thing to say?"

"I wasn't trying to be nice." Then after a pause: "When do you want to go?"

Bernice drew in her breath sharply.

"Oh!" It was a little half-cry.

Marjorie looked up in surprise.

"Didn't you say you were going?"

"Yes, but——"

"Oh, you were only bluffing!"

They stared at each other across the breakfast-table for a moment. Misty waves were passing before Bernice's eyes, while Marjorie's face wore that rather hard expression that she used when slightly intoxicated undergraduates were making love to her.

"So you were bluffing," she repeated as if it were what she might have expected.

Bernice admitted it by bursting into tears. Marjorie's eyes showed boredom.

"You're my cousin," sobbed Bernice. "I'm v-v-visiting you. I was to stay a month, and if I go home my mother will know and she'll wah-wonder——"

Marjorie waited until the shower of broken words collapsed into little sniffles.

"I'll give you my month's allowance," she said coldly, "and you can spend this last week anywhere you want. There's a very nice hotel——"

Bernice's sobs rose to a flute note, and rising of a sudden she fled from the room.

An hour later, while Marjorie was in the library absorbed in composing one of those non-committal, marvellously elusive letters that only a young girl can write,

Bernice reappeared, very red-eyed and consciously calm. She cast no glance at Marjorie but took a book at random from the shelf and sat down as if to read. Marjorie seemed absorbed in her letter and continued writing. When the clock showed noon Bernice closed her book with a snap.

"I suppose I'd better get my railroad ticket."

This was not the beginning of the speech she had rehearsed upstairs, but as Marjorie was not getting her cues —wasn't urging her to be reasonable; it's all a mistake—it was the best opening she could muster.

"Just wait till I finish this letter," said Marjorie without looking round. "I want to get it off in the next mail."

After another minute, during which her pen scratched busily, she turned round and relaxed with an air of "at your service." Again Bernice had to speak.

"Do you want me to go home?"

"Well," said Marjorie, considering, "I suppose if you're not having a good time you'd better go. No use being miserable."

"Don't you think common kindness——"

"Oh, please don't quote 'Little Women'!" cried Marjorie impatiently. "That's out of style."

"You think so?"

"Heavens, yes! What modern girl could live like those inane females?"

"They were the models for our mothers."

Marjorie laughed.

"Yes, they were—not! Besides, our mothers were all very well in their way, but they know very little about their daughters' problems."

Bernice drew herself up.

"Please don't talk about my mother."

Marjorie laughed.

"I don't think I mentioned her."

Bernice felt that she was being led away from her subject.

"Do you think you've treated me very well?"

"I've done my best. You're rather hard material to work with."

The lids of Bernice's eyes reddened.

"I think you're hard and selfish, and you haven't a feminine quality in you."

"Oh, my Lord!" cried Marjorie in desperation. "You little nut! Girls like you are responsible for all the tiresome colorless marriages; all those ghastly inefficiencies that pass as feminine qualities. What a blow it must be when a man with imagination marries the beautiful bundle of clothes that he's been building ideals round, and finds that she's just a weak, whining, cowardly mass of affectations!"

Bernice's mouth had slipped half open.

"The womanly woman!" continued Marjorie. "Her whole early life is occupied in whining criticisms of girls like me who really do have a good time."

Bernice's jaw descended farther as Marjorie's voice rose.

"There's some excuse for an ugly girl whining. If I'd been irretrievably ugly I'd never have forgiven my parents for bringing me into the world. But you're starting life without any handicap—" Marjorie's little fist clinched. "If you expect me to weep with you you'll be disappointed. Go or stay, just as you like." And picking up her letters she left the room.

Bernice claimed a headache and failed to appear at luncheon. They had a matinée date for the afternoon, but the headache persisting, Marjorie made explanations to a not very downcast boy. But when she returned late in the afternoon she found Bernice with a strangely set face waiting for her in her bedroom.

"I've decided," began Bernice without preliminaries, "that maybe you're right about things—possibly not. But if you'll tell me why your friends aren't—aren't interested in me I'll see if I can do what you want me to."

Marjorie was at the mirror shaking down her hair.

"Do you mean it?"

"Yes."

"Without reservations? Will you do exactly what I say?"

"Well, I——"

"Well nothing! Will you do exactly as I say?"

"If they're sensible things."

"They're not! You're no case for sensible things."

"Are you going to make—to recommend—"

"Yes, everything. If I tell you to take boxing lessons you'll have to do it. Write home and tell your mother you're going to stay another two weeks."

"If you'll tell me——"

"All right—I'll just give you a few examples now. First, you have no ease of manner. Why? Because you're never sure about your personal appearance. When a girl feels that she's perfectly groomed and dressed she can forget that part of her. That's charm. The more parts of yourself you can afford to forget the more charm you have."

"Don't I look all right?"

"No; for instance, you never take care of your eyebrows. They're black and lustrous, but by leaving them straggly they're a blemish. They'd be beautiful if you'd take care of them in one-tenth the time you take doing nothing. You're going to brush them so that they'll grow straight."

Bernice raised the brows in question.

"Do you mean to say that men notice eyebrows?"

"Yes—subconsciously. And when you go home you ought to have your teeth straightened a little. It's almost imperceptible, still——"

"But I thought," interrupted Bernice in bewilderment, "that you despised little dainty feminine things like that."

"I hate dainty minds," answered Marjorie. "But a girl has to be dainty in person. If she looks like a million dollars she can talk about Russia, ping-pong, or the League of Nations and get away with it."

"What else?"

"Oh, I'm just beginning! There's your dancing."

"Don't I dance all right?"

"No, you don't—you lean on a man; yes, you do—ever so slightly. I noticed it when we were dancing together yesterday. And you dance standing up straight instead of bending over a little. Probably some old lady on the side-line once told you that you looked so dignified that way. But except with a very small girl it's much harder on the man, and he's the one that counts."

"Go on." Bernice's brain was reeling.

"Well, you've got to learn to be nice to men who are sad birds. You look as if you'd been insulted whenever you're thrown with any except the most popular boys. Why, Bernice, I'm cut in on every few feet—and who does most of it? Why, those very sad birds. No girl can afford to neglect them. They're the big part of any crowd. Young boys too shy to talk are the very best conversational practice. Clumsy boys are the best dancing practice. If you can follow them and yet look graceful you can follow a baby tank across a barb-wire sky-scraper."

Bernice sighed profoundly, but Marjorie was not through.

"If you go to a dance and really amuse, say, three sad birds that dance with you; if you talk so well to them that they forget they're stuck with you, you've done something. They'll come back next time, and gradually so many sad birds will dance with you that the attractive boys will see there's no danger of being stuck—then they'll dance with you."

"Yes," agreed Bernice faintly. "I think I begin to see."

"And finally," concluded Marjorie, "poise and charm will just come. You'll wake up some morning knowing you've attained it, and men will know it too."

Bernice rose.

"It's been awfully kind of you—but nobody's ever talked to me like this before, and I feel sort of startled."

Marjorie made no answer but gazed pensively at her own image in the mirror.

"You're a peach to help me," continued Bernice.

Still Marjorie did not answer, and Bernice thought she had seemed too grateful.

"I know you don't like sentiment," she said timidly.

Marjorie turned to her quickly.

"Oh, I wasn't thinking about that. I was considering whether we hadn't better bob your hair."

Bernice collapsed backward upon the bed.

IV

On the following Wednesday evening there was a dinner-dance at the country club. When the guests strolled in Bernice found her place-card with a slight feeling of irritation. Though at her right sat G. Reece Stoddard, a most desirable and distinguished young bachelor, the all-important left held only Charley Paulson. Charley lacked height, beauty, and social shrewdness, and in her new enlightenment Bernice decided that his only qualification to be her partner was that he had never been stuck with her. But this feeling of irritation left with the last of the soup-plates, and Marjorie's specific instruction came to her. Swallowing her pride she turned to Charley Paulson and plunged.

"Do you think I ought to bob my hair, Mr. Charley Paulson?"

Charley looked up in surprise.

"Why?"

"Because I'm considering it. It's such a sure and easy way of attracting attention."

Charley smiled pleasantly. He could not know this had been rehearsed. He replied that he didn't know much about bobbed hair. But Bernice was there to tell him.

"I want to be a society vampire, you see," she announced coolly, and went on to inform him that bobbed hair was the necessary prelude. She added that she wanted to ask his advice, because she had heard he was so critical about girls.

Charley, who knew as much about the psychology of women as he did of the mental states of Buddhist contemplatives, felt vaguely flattered.

"So I've decided," she continued, her voice rising slightly, "that early next week I'm going down to the Sevier Hotel barber-shop, sit in the first chair, and get my hair bobbed." She faltered, noticing that the people near her had paused in their conversation and were listening; but after a confused second Marjorie's coaching told, and she finished her paragraph to the vicinity at large. "Of course I'm charging admission, but if you'll all come down and encourage me I'll issue passes for the inside seats."

There was a ripple of appreciative laughter, and under cover of it G. Reece Stoddard leaned over quickly and said close to her ear: "I'll take a box right now."

She met his eyes and smiled as if he had said something surpassingly brilliant.

"Do you believe in bobbed hair?" asked G. Reece in the same undertone.

"I think it's unmoral," affirmed Bernice gravely. "But, of course, you've either got to amuse people or feed 'em or shock 'em." Marjorie had culled this from Oscar Wilde. It was greeted with a ripple of laughter from the men and a series of quick, intent looks from the girls. And then as though she had said nothing of wit or moment Bernice turned again to Charley and spoke confidentially in his ear.

"I want to ask you your opinion of several people. I imagine you're a wonderful judge of character."

Charley thrilled faintly—paid her a subtle compliment by overturning her water.

Two hours later, while Warren McIntyre was standing passively in the stag line abstractedly watching the dancers and wondering whither and with whom Marjorie had disappeared, an unrelated perception began to creep slowly upon him—a perception that Bernice, cousin to Marjorie, had been cut in on several times in the past five minutes. He closed his eyes, opened them and looked again. Several minutes back she had been dancing with a visiting boy, a matter easily accounted for; a visiting boy would know no better. But now she was dancing with some one else, and there was Charley Paulson headed for her with enthusiastic determination in his eye. Funny—Charley seldom danced with more than three girls an evening.

Warren was distinctly surprised when—the exchange having been effected—the man relieved proved to be none other than G. Reece Stoddard himself. And G. Reece seemed not at all jubilant at being relieved. Next time Bernice danced near, Warren regarded her intently. Yes, she was pretty, distinctly pretty; and to-night her face seemed really vivacious. She had that look that no woman, however histrionically proficient, can successfully counterfeit—she looked as if she were having a good time. He liked the way she had her hair arranged, wondered if it was brilliantine that made it glisten so. And that dress was becoming—a dark red that set off her shadowy eyes and high coloring. He remembered that he had thought her pretty when she first came to town, before he had realized that she was dull. Too bad she was dull—dull girls unbearable—certainly pretty though.

His thoughts zigzagged back to Marjorie. This disappearance would be like other disappearances. When she reappeared he would demand where she had been—would be told emphatically that it was none of his business. What a pity she was so sure of him! She basked in the knowledge that no other girl in town interested him; she defied him to fall in love with Genevieve or Roberta.

Warren sighed. The way to Marjorie's affections was a labyrinth indeed. He looked up. Bernice was again dancing with the visiting boy. Half unconsciously he took a step out from the stag line in her direction, and hesitated. Then he said to himself that it was charity. He walked toward her—collided suddenly with G. Reece Stoddard.

"Pardon me," said Warren.

But G. Reece had not stopped to apologize. He had again cut in on Bernice.

That night at one o'clock Marjorie, with one hand on the electric-light switch in the hall, turned to take a last look at Bernice's sparkling eyes.

"So it worked?"

"Oh, Marjorie, yes!" cried Bernice.

"I saw you were having a gay time."

"I did! The only trouble was that about midnight I ran short of talk. I had to repeat myself—with different men of course. I hope they won't compare notes."

"Men don't," said Marjorie, yawning, "and it wouldn't matter if they did—they'd think you were even trickier."

She snapped out the light, and as they started up the stairs Bernice grasped the banister thankfully. For the first time in her life she had been danced tired.

"You see," said Marjorie at the top of the stairs, "one man sees another man cut in and he thinks there must be something there. Well, we'll fix up some new stuff tomorrow. Good night."

"Good night."

As Bernice took down her hair she passed the evening before her in review. She had followed instructions exactly. Even when Charley Paulson cut in for the eighth time she had simulated delight and had apparently been both interested and flattered. She had not talked about the weather or Eau Claire or automobiles or her school, but had confined her conversation to me, you, and us.

But a few minutes before she fell asleep a rebellious thought was churning drowsily in her brain—after all, it was she who had done it. Marjorie, to be sure, had given her her conversation, but then Marjorie got much of her conversation out of things she read. Bernice had bought the red dress, though she had never valued it highly before Marjorie dug it out of her trunk—and her own voice had said the words, her own lips had smiled, her own feet had danced. Marjorie nice girl—vain, though—nice evening—

nice boys—like Warren—Warren—Warren—what's-his-name—Warren——

She fell asleep.

V

To Bernice the next week was a revelation. With the feeling that people really enjoyed looking at her and listening to her came the foundation of self-confidence. Of course there were numerous mistakes at first. She did not know, for instance, that Draycott Deyo was studying for the ministry; she was unaware that he had cut in on her because he thought she was a quiet, reserved girl. Had she known these things she would not have treated him to the line which began "Hello, Shell Shock!" and continued with the bathtub story—"It takes a frightful lot of energy to fix my hair in the summer—there's so much of it—so I always fix it first and powder my face and put on my hat; then I get into the bathtub, and dress afterward. Don't you think that's the best plan?"

Though Draycott Deyo was in the throes of difficulties concerning baptism by immersion and might possibly have seen a connection, it must be admitted that he did not. He considered feminine bathing an immoral subject, and gave her some of his ideas on the depravity of modern society.

But to offset that unfortunate occurrence Bernice had several signal successes to her credit. Little Otis Ormonde pleaded off from a trip East and elected instead to follow her with a puppylike devotion, to the amusement of his crowd and to the irritation of G. Reece Stoddard, several of whose afternoon calls Otis completely ruined by the disgusting tenderness of the glances he bent on Bernice. He even told her the story of the two-by-four and the dressing-room to show her how frightfully mistaken he and every one else had been in their first judgment of her. Bernice laughed off that incident with a slight sinking sensation.

Of all Bernice's conversation perhaps the best known and most universally approved was the line about the bobbing of her hair.

"Oh, Bernice, when you goin' to get the hair bobbed?"

"Day after to-morrow maybe," she would reply, laughing. "Will you come and see me? Because I'm counting on you, you know."

"Will we? You know! But you better hurry up."

Bernice, whose tonsorial intentions were strictly dishonorable, would laugh again.

"Pretty soon now. You'd be surprised."

But perhaps the most significant symbol of her success was the gray car of the hypercritical Warren McIntyre, parked daily in front of the Harvey house. At first the parlor-maid was distinctly startled when he asked for Bernice instead of Marjorie; after a week of it she told the cook that Miss Bernice had gotta holda Miss Marjorie's best fella.

And Miss Bernice had. Perhaps it began with Warren's desire to rouse jealousy in Marjorie; perhaps it was the familiar though unrecognized strain of Marjorie in Bernice's conversation; perhaps it was both of these and something of sincere attraction besides. But somehow the collective mind of the younger set knew within a week that Marjorie's most reliable beau had made an amazing face-about and was giving an indisputable rush to Marjorie's guest. The question of the moment was how Marjorie would take it. Warren called Bernice on the 'phone twice a day, sent her notes, and they were frequently seen together in his roadster, obviously engrossed in one of those tense, significant conversations as to whether or not he was sincere.

Marjorie on being twitted only laughed. She said she was mighty glad that Warren had at last found some one who appreciated him. So the younger set laughed, too, and guessed that Marjorie didn't care and let it go at that.

One afternoon when there were only three days left of her visit Bernice was waiting in the hall for Warren, with whom she was going to a bridge party. She was in rather a blissful mood, and when Marjorie—also bound for the party—appeared beside her and began casually to adjust her hat in the mirror, Bernice was utterly unprepared for anything in the nature of a clash. Marjorie did her work very coldly and succinctly in three sentences.

"You may as well get Warren out of your head," she said coldly.

"What?" Bernice was utterly astounded.

"You may as well stop making a fool of yourself over

Warren McIntyre. He doesn't care a snap of his fingers about you."

For a tense moment they regarded each other—Marjorie scornful, aloof; Bernice astounded, half-angry, half-afraid. Then two cars drove up in front of the house and there was a riotous honking. Both of them gasped faintly, turned, and side by side hurried out.

All through the bridge party Bernice strove in vain to master a rising uneasiness. She had offended Marjorie, the sphinx of sphinxes. With the most wholesome and innocent intentions in the world she had stolen Marjorie's property. She felt suddenly and horribly guilty. After the bridge game, when they sat in an informal circle and the conversation became general, the storm gradually broke. Little Otis Ormonde inadvertently precipitated it.

"When you going back to kindergarten, Otis?" some one had asked.

"Me? Day Bernice gets her hair bobbed."

"Then your education's over," said Marjorie quickly. "That's only a bluff of hers. I should think you'd have realized."

"That a fact?" demanded Otis, giving Bernice a reproachful glance.

Bernice's ears burned as she tried to think up an effectual comeback. In the face of this direct attack her imagination was paralyzed.

"There's a lot of bluffs in the world," continued Marjorie quite pleasantly. "I should think you'd be young enough to know that, Otis."

"Well," said Otis, "maybe so. But gee! With a line like Bernice's——"

"Really?" yawned Marjorie. "What's her latest bon mot?"

No one seemed to know. In fact, Bernice, having trifled with her muse's beau, had said nothing memorable of late.

"Was that really all a line?" asked Roberta curiously.

Bernice hesitated. She felt that wit in some form was demanded of her, but under her cousin's suddenly frigid eyes she was completely incapacitated.

"I don't know," she stalled.

"Splush!" said Marjorie. "Admit it!"

Bernice saw that Warren's eyes had left a ukulele he had been tinkering with and were fixed on her questioningly.

"Oh, I don't know!" she repeated steadily. Her cheeks were glowing.

"Splush!" remarked Marjorie again.

"Come through, Bernice," urged Otis. "Tell her where to get off."

Bernice looked round again—she seemed unable to get away from Warren's eyes.

"I like bobbed hair," she said hurriedly, as if he had asked her a question, "and I intend to bob mine."

"When?" demanded Marjorie.

"Any time."

"No time like the present," suggested Roberta.

Otis jumped to his feet.

"Good stuff!" he cried. "We'll have a summer bobbing party. Sevier Hotel barber-shop, I think you said."

In an instant all were on their feet. Bernice's heart throbbed violently.

"What?" she gasped.

Out of the group came Marjorie's voice, very clear and contemptuous.

"Don't worry—she'll back out!"

"Come on, Bernice!" cried Otis, starting toward the door.

Four eyes—Warren's and Marjorie's—stared at her, challenged her, defied her. For another second she wavered wildly.

"All right," she said swiftly, "I don't care if I do."

An eternity of minutes later, riding down-town through the late afternoon beside Warren, the others following in Roberta's car close behind, Bernice had all the sensations of Marie Antoinette bound for the guillotine in a tumbrel. Vaguely she wondered why she did not cry out that it was all a mistake. It was all she could do to keep from clutching her hair with both hands to protect it from the suddenly hostile world. Yet she did neither. Even the thought of her mother was no deterrent now. This was the test supreme of her sportsmanship; her right to walk unchallenged in the starry heaven of popular girls.

Warren was moodily silent, and when they came to the hotel he drew up at the curb and nodded to Bernice to precede him out. Roberta's car emptied a laughing crowd into the shop, which presented two bold plate-glass windows to the street.

Bernice stood on the curb and looked at the sign, Sevier Barber-Shop. It was a guillotine indeed, and the hangman was the first barber, who, attired in a white coat and smoking a cigarette, leaned nonchalantly against the first chair. He must have heard of her; he must have been waiting all week, smoking eternal cigarettes beside that portentous, too-often-mentioned first chair. Would they blindfold her? No, but they would tie a white cloth around her neck lest any of her blood—nonsense—hair—should get on her clothes.

"All right, Bernice," said Warren quickly.

With her chin in the air she crossed the sidewalk, pushed open the swinging screen-door, and giving not a glance to the uproarious, riotous row that occupied the waiting bench, went up to the first barber.

"I want you to bob my hair."

The first barber's mouth slid somewhat open. His cigarette dropped to the floor.

"Huh?"

"My hair—bob it!"

Refusing further preliminaries, Bernice took her seat on high. A man in the chair next to her turned on his side and gave her a glance, half lather, half amazement. One barber started and spoiled little Willy Schuneman's monthly haircut. Mr. O'Reilly in the last chair grunted and swore musically in ancient Gaelic as a razor bit into his cheek. Two bootblacks became wide-eyed and rushed for her feet. No, Bernice didn't care for a shine.

Outside a passer-by stopped and stared; a couple joined him; half a dozen small boys' noses sprang into life, flattened against the glass; and snatches of conversation borne on the summer breeze drifted in through the screen-door.

"Lookada long hair on a kid!"

"Where'd yuh get 'at stuff? 'At's a bearded lady he just finished shavin'."

But Bernice saw nothing, heard nothing. Her only living sense told her that this man in the white coat had removed one tortoise-shell comb and then another; that his fingers were fumbling clumsily with unfamiliar hairpins; that this hair, this wonderful hair of hers, was going—she would never again feel its long voluptuous pull as it hung in a dark-brown glory down her back. For a second she was near breaking down, and then the picture before her swam mechanically into her vision—Marjorie's mouth curling in a faint ironic smile as if to say:

"Give up and get down! You tried to buck me and I called your bluff. You see you haven't got a prayer."

And some last energy rose up in Bernice, for she clinched her hands under the white cloth, and there was a curious narrowing of her eyes that Marjorie remarked on to some one long afterward.

Twenty minutes later the barber swung her round to face the mirror, and she flinched at the full extent of the damage that had been wrought. Her hair was not curly, and now it lay in lank lifeless blocks on both sides of her suddenly pale face. It was ugly as sin—she had known it would be ugly as sin. Her face's chief charm had been a Madonna-like simplicity. Now that was gone and she was —well, frightfully mediocre—not stagy; only ridiculous, like a Greenwich Villager who had left her spectacles at home.

As she climbed down from the chair she tried to smile—failed miserably. She saw two of the girls exchange glances; noticed Marjorie's mouth curved in attenuated mockery —and that Warren's eyes were suddenly very cold.

"You see"—her words fell into an awkward pause—"I've done it."

"Yes, you've—done it," admitted Warren.

"Do you like it?"

There was a half-hearted "Sure" from two or three voices, another awkward pause, and then Marjorie turned swiftly and with serpent-like intensity to Warren.

"Would you mind running me down to the cleaners?" she asked. "I've simply got to get a dress there before supper. Roberta's driving right home and she can take the others."

Warren stared abstractedly at some infinite speck out the window. Then for an instant his eyes rested coldly on Bernice before they turned to Marjorie.

"Be glad to," he said slowly.

VI

Bernice did not fully realize the outrageous trap that had been set for her until she met her aunt's amazed glance just before dinner.

"Why, Bernice!"

"I've bobbed it, Aunt Josephine."

"Why, child!"

"Do you like it?"

"Why, Ber-nice!"

"I suppose I've shocked you."

"No, but what'll Mrs. Deyo think to-morrow night? Bernice, you should have waited until after the Deyos' dance—you should have waited if you wanted to do that."

"It was sudden, Aunt Josephine. Anyway, why does it matter to Mrs. Deyo particularly?"

"Why, child," cried Mrs. Harvey, "in her paper on 'The Foibles of the Younger Generation' that she read at the last meeting of the Thursday Club she devoted fifteen minutes to bobbed hair. It's her pet abomination. And the dance is for you and Marjorie!"

"I'm sorry."

"Oh, Bernice, what'll your mother say? She'll think I let you do it."

"I'm sorry."

Dinner was an agony. She had made a hasty attempt with a curling-iron, and burned her finger and much hair. She could see that her aunt was both worried and grieved, and her uncle kept saying, "Well, I'll be darned!" over and over in a hurt and faintly hostile tone. And Marjorie sat very quietly, intrenched behind a faint smile, a faintly mocking smile.

Somehow she got through the evening. Three boys called; Marjorie disappeared with one of them, and Bernice made a listless unsuccessful attempt to entertain the two others—sighed thankfully as she climbed the stairs to her room at half past ten. What a day!

When she had undressed for the night the door opened and Marjorie came in.

"Bernice," she said, "I'm awfully sorry about the Deyo dance. I'll give you my word of honor I'd forgotten all about it."

" 'Sall right," said Bernice shortly. Standing before the mirror she passed her comb slowly through her short hair.

"I'll take you down-town to-morrow," continued Marjorie, "and the hairdresser'll fix it so you'll look slick. I didn't imagine you'd go through with it. I'm really mighty sorry."

"Oh, 'sall right!"

"Still it's your last night, so I suppose it won't matter much."

Then Bernice winced as Marjorie tossed her own hair over her shoulders and began to twist it slowly into two long blond braids until in her cream-colored negligee she looked like a delicate painting of some Saxon princess. Fascinated, Bernice watched the braids grow. Heavy and luxurious they were, moving under the supple fingers like restive snakes—and to Bernice remained this relic and the curling-iron and a to-morrow full of eyes. She could see G. Reece Stoddard, who liked her, assuming his Harvard manner and telling his dinner partner that Bernice shouldn't have been allowed to go to the movies so much; she could see Draycott Deyo exchanging glances with his mother and then being conscientiously charitable to her. But then perhaps by to-morrow Mrs. Deyo would have heard the news; would send round an icy little note requesting that she fail to appear—and behind her back they would all laugh and know that Marjorie had made a fool of her; that her chance at beauty had been sacrificed to the jealous whim of a selfish girl. She sat down suddenly before the mirror, biting the inside of her cheek.

"I like it," she said with an effort. "I think it'll be becoming."

Marjorie smiled.

"It looks all right. For heaven's sake, don't let it worry you!"

"I won't."

"Good night, Bernice."

But as the door closed something snapped within Bernice. She sprang dynamically to her feet, clinching her hands, then swiftly and noiselessly crossed over to her bed and from underneath it dragged out her suitcase. Into it she tossed toilet articles and a change of clothing. Then she turned to her trunk and quickly dumped in two drawerfuls of lingerie and summer dresses. She moved quietly, but with deadly efficiency, and in three-quarters of an hour her trunk was locked and strapped and she was fully dressed in a becoming new travelling suit that Marjorie had helped her pick out.

Sitting down at her desk she wrote a short note to Mrs. Harvey, in which she briefly outlined her reasons for going. She sealed it, addressed it, and laid it on her pillow. She glanced at her watch. The train left at one, and she knew that if she walked down to the Marborough Hotel two blocks away she could easily get a taxicab.

Suddenly she drew in her breath sharply and an expression flashed into her eyes that a practiced character reader might have connected vaguely with the set look she had worn in the barber's chair—somehow a development of it. It was quite a new look for Bernice—and it carried consequences.

She went stealthily to the bureau, picked up an article that lay there, and turning out all the lights stood quietly until her eyes became accustomed to the darkness. Softly she pushed open the door to Marjorie's room. She heard the quiet, even breathing of an untroubled conscience asleep.

She was by the bedside now, very deliberate and calm. She acted swiftly. Bending over she found one of the braids of Marjorie's hair, followed it up with her hand to the point nearest the head, and then holding it a little slack so that the sleeper would feel no pull, she reached down with the shears and severed it. With the pigtail in her hand she held her breath. Marjorie had muttered something in her sleep. Bernice deftly amputated the other braid, paused for an instant, and then flitted swiftly and silently back to her own room.

Down-stairs she opened the big front door, closed it carefully behind her, and feeling oddly happy and exuberant stepped off the porch into the moonlight, swinging her heavy grip like a shopping-bag. After a minute's brisk walk she discovered that her left hand still held the two blond braids. She laughed unexpectedly—had to shut her mouth hard to keep from emitting an absolute peal. She was passing Warren's house now, and on the impulse she set down her baggage, and swinging the braids like pieces of rope flung them at the wooden porch, where they landed with a slight thud. She laughed again, no longer restraining herself.

"Huh!" she giggled wildly. "Scalp the selfish thing!"

Then picking up her suitcase she set off at a half-run down the moonlit street.

F. SCOTT FITZGERALD'S
BERNICE BOBS HER HAIR

*Screenplay by Joan Micklin Silver**

A midwestern town of medium size in the late summer of 1919.

1. INT. COUNTRY CLUB. WOMEN'S DRESSING ROOM. SATURDAY NIGHT.

The room is empty. Faint band music can be heard . . . a Saturday night country club combo. As the door opens, and Marjorie Harvey and Roberta Dillon enter, the music blares briefly, becoming faint again as they close the door after them.

Marjorie is eighteen, dark-haired and pretty. Roberta is seventeen, small and thin with a delicate lisp. Like all the women in the script, they wear their long, thick hair piled on top of their heads in an arrangement of tendrils and curls. Numerous tortoise shell combs support these hair-dos.

If Marjorie and Roberta are not yet flappers, it is only because full-scale flapperdom hasn't reached their particular corner of the Midwest.

Still, they are close to it, impudent, good-looking, self-assured, not at all giggly, girlish or demure.

A long horizontal mirror against one wall; beneath it a long table on which women have left their purses. Marjorie finds hers, opens it and carefully removes her handerchief. We move in for an ECU as she opens the handkerchief. In it is

---

* Joan Micklin Silver's first feature film was the highly successful *Hester Street*, which she wrote and directed after learning her craft as writer-director of a number of short films. Most recently she has directed the contemporary comedy *Between the Lines*.

. . . a red jelly bean. She offers it to Roberta, who takes it eagerly.

ROBERTA. Marjorie, you saved my life.

[*The two girls sit at the mirror.* ROBERTA *licks the jelly bean, then uses it as a lipstick. It leaves a faint red stain on her lips.* MARJORIE *has a fresh gardenia; idly she positions it here and there on her dress, in her hair, all the while staring intently at herself in the mirror.*]

ROBERTA. Who gave you that gardenia?
MARJORIE. Warren.
ROBERTA. Warren McIntyre? I thought he'd get over you when he went away to Yale.
MARJORIE. No. All that happened was I got over him.
ROBERTA. I know about three girls in the East that are wild about him.
MARJORIE [*profoundly, as she gazes at herself in the mirror*]. Roberta, when you've grown up across the street from someone, he loses his mystery.
[*A brief flurry as the door opens and several young women enter . . . among them* GENEVIEVE ORMONDE, *eighteen, and along with* MARJORIE *and* ROBERTA *one of the popular set.* GENEVIEVE *hurries over to her friends.*]
GENEVIEVE [*sotto voce*]. Honestly, Marjorie, my brother has been stuck with your cousin Bernice for an hour.
MARJORIE [*sighs*]. All right.
[*She drops the gardenia in the wastebasket, rises.*]
GENEVIEVE. Roberta, is that your jelly bean?
MARJORIE. It's mine but you can borrow it.
[MARJORIE *starts toward dressing room door;* GENEVIEVE *sits down, starts to apply jelly bean.*]

2. INT. COUNTRY CLUB. OUTSIDE DRESSING ROOM. NIGHT.

Several young men are milling around waiting for their girls. Little Otis Ormonde, a small sixteen-year-old with an unchanged voice, moves through this bunch with Marjorie's cousin Bernice, who is almost eighteen. Though Bernice is pretty, in an old-fashioned lace-valentine sort of way, she is a bit of a deadhead, a little boring . . . "Dopeless," the boys call her.

When she and Otis are close to the dressing room door . . .

BERNICE. Excuse me, Otis.
OTIS. Certainly, Bernice.
BERNICE. I won't be but a few minutes.
OTIS. That's all right. Take your time, Bernice.
[*He watches as she enters the dressing room. As soon as the door closes behind her . . .*]
OTIS. Why don't some of you cut in? She likes more variety.
CHARLEY PAULSON. Why, Otis, you've just barely got used to her.
[*Everyone laughs but* OTIS.]
OTIS. Ha-ha.

3. INT. DRESSING ROOM.

[*As* BERNICE *moves to find a place at the mirror, she passes* MARJORIE, *who is on her way out.*]

BERNICE. Oh, Marjorie . . .
MARJORIE. 'Lo, Bernice.
[*And* MARJORIE *is out the door.*]

4. INT. AREA OUTSIDE DRESSING ROOM.

[*As* MARJORIE *comes out.*]

OTIS. *Marjorie . . .*
MARJORIE. I know, Otis, I know. I'm going to take care of it right now.
[*Her glance falls on* CHARLEY PAULSON.]
CHARLEY. Not me, Marjorie.
[MARJORIE *looks at* CARPENTER THOMPSON, *who is standing next to* CHARLEY.]
CARPENTER. Sorry, Marjorie, I'm waiting for Sara Hughes.
[MARJORIE *moves off.* CHARLEY *and* CARPENTER *exchange a look of relief.*]

5. INT. DRESSING ROOM.

Bernice sits down between Roberta and Genevieve, searches in her purse for her handkerchief. She blots her face and neck carefully.

Women and girls move back and forth through the scene, a chattering background.

BERNICE [*although no one asked*]. It's so much warmer here than in Eau Claire. In Eau Claire we have a breeze even in the hottest part of the summer.

ROBERTA. I'll bet you do. Coming, Genevieve?

[*The two girls rise and move off.* BERNICE *continues to search out any tell-tale signs of perspiration on her face, neck, even the insides of her arms which she pats delicately with the lace handkerchief. She repairs her hair though it's not much out of place.*]

6. EXT. VERANDA OF COUNTRY CLUB. NIGHT.

Marjorie, still looking for someone to dance with Bernice, walks out on the veranda. It is semidark with Japanese lanterns, couples scattered at tables. We hear vague snatches of conversation, lazy laughter.

Marjorie sees Warren McIntyre, nineteen, tall, blond and conventionally handsome, a walking Arrow shirt ad. Warren is casually at Yale, but now home for the summer vacation and bewildered that his old flame Marjorie is no longer interested. Like a puppy dog, Warren keeps wagging his tail, sure that Marjorie will have a change of heart. In fact, the more faithful and devoted he is, the less he interests the capricious Marjorie. But Warren is slow to catch on to such matters.

He is opening his cigarette case, taking out a cigarette, as Marjorie approaches.

MARJORIE. Warren?

[*His face lights up. He can't help it, so "crazy" is he about* MARJORIE.]

WARREN. Marjorie, I was looking for yøu.

MARJORIE [*intimately*]. Were you?

[*She puts her hand on his arm.*]

MARJORIE. Warren, do something for me, will you?

WARREN. Sure.

MARJORIE. Dance with Bernice. [*His face falls.*] She's been stuck with little Otis Ormonde for almost an hour. Please?

[WARREN'S *face expresses his acquiescence . . . though it's a half-hearted one.*]

MARJORIE. You don't mind, do you Warren? I'll see to it that you don't get stuck.

WARREN. 'S all right.

MARJORIE. You're an angel! She's in the dressing room.

[MARJORIE *smiles, gives his arm a little squeeze.*]

7. INT. AREA OUTSIDE DRESSING ROOM.

We are moving with Warren toward the small group surrounding Otis, who is now brandishing a two-by-four.

CARPENTER. Patience, Otis.

CHARLEY. That's right, Otis, as soon as she fixes her hair you'll get your chance.

WARREN. What chance? What's that for?

OTIS. This? It's a club. When Bernice comes out, I'll hit her on the head and knock her in again.

[*A roar of laughter, which increases as* OTIS *demonstrates.* WARREN *also finds it very funny.*]

WARREN. Good news, Otis, I'm your relief hitter.

[OTIS, *simulating a fainting attack, falls onto the wicker settee.*]

OTIS. I'll never forget this, old man, never [*handing* WARREN *the two-by-four*]. In case you need it.

[*And* OTIS *scuttles off as fast as he can, the others laughing as they watch him go.*]

[*The music starts up again and we hear it clearly.* CHARLEY *and the others head in its direction.*]

CHARLEY [*over his shoulder, to* WARREN]. Have fun, chum . . . p.

[WARREN *waits on the settee, his feet tapping in time to the music. At last* BERNICE *comes out . . . and looks unsure when she doesn't see* OTIS.]

WARREN [*stands*]. Bernice?

BERNICE. Oh . . . is Otis . . . I mean I'm looking for Otis.

WARREN. I told him this is my dance.

[BERNICE *is flustered. She likes the handsome* WARREN.]

BERNICE. Oh. It's just that it's so hot in there. The floor's crowded.

[*Not at all what she meant to say.*]

WARREN. Let's sit out on the veranda. Might be a breeze.

BERNICE. I don't think so. In Eau Claire we have a breeze even in the hottest summer.
WARREN. Well, if you don't want to dance, and you don't want to sit out, have you got a better idea?
BERNICE. No, I didn't mean that. I meant . . . well, let's try the veranda.
WARREN. We can always change our minds.
BERNICE. That's right, we can, can't we?
[*As she precedes* WARREN *to the veranda, he raises his brows. Conversation with* BERNICE *isn't exactly easy.*]

8. EXT. VERANDA. NIGHT.

Bernice and Warren are seated at one of the tables. Silence as she does unimpressive things with her fan.

Band music in the background.

BERNICE. It's the humidity.
WARREN [*who has been looking around for* MARJORIE]. Hunh?
BERNICE. As compared to Eau Claire.
WARREN. Oh yes, as compared to Eau Claire.
BERNICE. The temperature could be the same but you don't feel it as much.
WARREN. Unh-hunh . . .
[*From the other room we hear voices,* "La-*de*-da-*dah*, *dum-dum" which signal the end of a dance. Several couples drift out on the veranda;* WARREN *spots* MARJORIE. *She is having an animated conversation with the tall attractive* G. REECE STODDARD. G. REECE *has finished Harvard Law School but his diploma is still hanging above his dresser. Not yet ready to take on the larger world, where he would no doubt be regarded as an insignificant fledgling, he amuses himself with the younger set, who accord him appropriate admiration.*]
BERNICE. When do you go back to New Haven? Warren?
WARREN. Hmm? Oh. Mid-September. A few more weeks.
BERNICE. Do you like Yale?
WARREN. It has its points.
[*The music starts again. Annoyed at* MARJORIE *and vaguely sorry for* BERNICE, WARREN *decides to turn his full attention on* BERNICE.]

WARREN. [*quietly*]. Bernice, you've got an awfully kissable mouth.

BERNICE [*jumps*]. Fresh!

[*A pained expression crosses* WARREN'S *face. He likes to banter and joke around with girls. And girls usually like to banter and joke around with him.* BERNICE *may be* MARJORIE'S *cousin, but she certainly is dopeless, all right.*]

9. UPSTAIRS BATHROOM, HARVEY HOUSE. NIGHT.

Bernice is in her bathrobe. She turns off the water in the sink, dries her hands, hangs the towel neatly on the rack. She turns off the light, exits the bathroom.

10. UPSTAIRS HALL, HARVEY HOUSE. NIGHT.

The Harvey house is a large turn-of-the-century structure with various wings and ample halls. Bernice pads along noiselessly; she is heading toward her bedroom. She starts to call good-night, but she hears voices . . . those of Marjorie and Mrs. Harvey . . . and she can't resist moving closer to listen.

MARJORIE'S VOICE. She's ruining my summer.

MRS. HARVEY'S VOICE. Marjorie, she's your first cousin and I wish you wouldn't talk like that.

11. INT. MARJORIE'S ROOM.

Marjorie is seated at her dressing table. Around its mirror are snapshots, postcards, invitations. Marjorie is brushing out her long dark hair.

Mrs. Harvey is seated nearby on a comfortable chair with a footstool. She is a mild woman of forty or so with a vague, slightly distracted air. Their dialogue overlaps, the energy coming from Marjorie, her mother's remarks like a soft background drone.

MARJORIE. No one *ever* cuts in on her. I have to go out and *lasso* men to get them to dance with her.

MRS. HARVEY. Why, Mrs. Ormonde was saying just yesterday . . .

MARJORIE. Yes, don't tell me, all your friends think she's "so sweet" and "so pretty." What difference does *that* make? Men don't like her.

[INTERCUT *with* BERNICE *listening at the door.*]

MRS. HARVEY. Come here, dear, I'll do that for you [*meaning brush the back of her hair*].

[MARJORIE *moves to sit on the footstool near her mother, gives her the brush.* MRS. HARVEY *sets to work; when she finishes,* MARJORIE *begins plaiting her hair into two heavy braids for the night. Dialogue continuous from above.*]

MRS. HARVEY. I know Bernice isn't very vivacious.

MARJORIE. Vivacious! Good grief! I've never heard her say anything to a boy except it's hot or the floor's crowded or that she's going away to school next year. Sometimes she asks them what kind of car they have and tells them what kind she has. Thrilling!

12. INT. UPSTAIRS HALL.

Bernice has finally heard enough. She moves down the hall to her room, closes the door quietly after her.

13. INT. BERNICE'S ROOM.

Bernice is sitting on her bed, braiding her hair for the night. She doesn't cry.

14. EXT. ELM STREET. DAY.

Big trees, big houses, a serene street of the upper middle class.

Warren McIntyre exits his house and walks across to the Harvey house. He rings the bell.

Annie, the Harvey's housemaid, comes to the door.

ANNIE. I'm sorry, Mr. Warren, Miss Marjorie isn't up yet.

[*A twinge of disappointment crosses* WARREN'S *handsome tanned face.*]

WARREN. Thanks, Annie. [*He turns away, then back again.*] You wouldn't happen to know if she's free this afternoon.

ANNIE. No, I believe she's going to a matinee this afternoon. Is there a message?
WARREN. No . . . never mind, thanks.

15. INT. HARVEY HOUSE. FRONT HALL. DAY.

We stay with Annie as she moves to the dining room.

16. INT. DINING ROOM. DAY.

Marjorie is seated alone at the large table. She is pouring milk on her corn flakes.

ANNIE. I told him you wasn't up yet.
MARJORIE. Aren't there any berries?
[ANNIE *moves to the sideboard, brings a bowl of blueberries.* MARJORIE *drops a large spoonful onto her corn flakes.* ANNIE *is about to return the bowl to the sideboard, but at just this moment,* BERNICE *enters. She has had a bad night and it shows.*
BERNICE [*her tone is formal*]. Good morning.
MARJORIE. Morning.
BERNICE. I don't care for breakfast this morning, Annie.
ANNIE [*surprised*]. No?
BERNICE. No, thank you.
[*She glances at* ANNIE, *who takes the hint and exits to kitchen.* BERNICE *wets her lips, stares intently at* MARJORIE, *who is eating her corn flakes.*]
BERNICE. I heard what you said about me to your mother last night.
MARJORIE [*startled, but replies evenly*]. Where were you?
BERNICE. In the hall. I didn't mean to listen . . . at first.
[MARJORIE *continues to eat.*]
BERNICE [*her voice quavering*]. I guess I better go home. I'm a drag on you. Your friends don't like me.
[BERNICE *expects sympathy, of course, but she's come to the wrong place for it.*]
MARJORIE [*thoughtfully*]. Well . . . if you aren't having a good time, I suppose you better go. No use being miserable.
[BERNICE *bursts into tears, rapidly exits the dining room.* ANNIE *enters from the kitchen.*]
ANNIE [*who has to know everything*]. Is something wrong with Miss Bernice?

MARJORIE [*calmly*]. Probably. I'll have some more berries.

17. INT. HARVEY SITTING ROOM. DAY. A LITTLE LATER.

Marjorie is at the desk writing a letter. Bernice enters, red-eyed, but with a studied calmness. Marjorie continues to write. Bernice takes a book down from the shelf, sits down and pretends to read it. Finally . . .

BERNICE. Do you think you've treated me very well?
MARJORIE [*still preoccupied with her letter*]. I've done my best; you're rather hard material to work with. [*Suddenly looks up at Bernice.*] There's some excuses for an ugly girl whining. But you're starting life without any handicap. Don't expect me to weep for you.
BERNICE. I should think common kindness . . .
MARJORIE. Oh please don't quote *Little Women.* What modern girl could live like those ninnies?
BERNICE. They were models for our mothers.
MARJORIE. Our *mothers!* Our mothers were all very well in their day, but they know next to nothing when it comes to their daughters.
BERNICE [*stiffening*]. Please don't talk about my mother.
[MARJORIE *bursts out laughing, which only feeds* BERNICE'S *growing anger.*]
BERNICE [*it finally spills out*]. I think you're hard and selfish and you haven't a feminine quality in you.
MARJORIE. Oh, my Lord. You know, Bernice, girls our age divide into two groups. The ones like me that have a good time and the ones like you that sit around and criticize us for it. Go or stay just as you like.
[*And* MARJORIE *exits. We stay on* BERNICE.]

18. INT. MARJORIE'S BEDROOM. DAY.

Marjorie is before her mirror pinning on a hat. Her mother enters.

MRS. HARVEY. Marjorie dear, Bernice must not be feeling well. At least I assume so . . . all she said is for you to go along to the matinee without her.
MARJORIE. I think it's that crazy Indian blood in Bernice.

Maybe she's a reversion to type. Indian women all just sat around and never said anything.

MRS. HARVEY. Marjorie! I wouldn't have told you that if I thought you were going to remember it.

19. INT. STAIRCASE.

Marjorie, who enjoys nothing more than an audience, has one as she walks down the stairs . . . Carpenter Thompson and G. Reece Stoddard, who are waiting for her in the front hall.

MARJORIE. Who let these two parlor snakes in my house? [*They grin*]. My cousin can't go. She's sick or something.

REECE [*politely*]. Sorry to hear that.

CARPENTER. Gee whiz, that's uh . . . too bad.

[*By now* MARJORIE *is at the bottom of the stairs. She whispers intimately to the young men . . .*

MARJORIE. Hurry up, she might recover.

[*And they laugh as they exit the house.*]

20. EXT. HARVEY HOUSE. DAY.

The three of them move to Reece's car, get in. They are full of high spirits, happy. They put Marjorie into the car, close the doors.

21. INT. BERNICE'S ROOM. DAY.

She looks down at the trio from her window.

From her POV, we see Carpenter, then Reece, jump over the car door without opening it, landing one on either side of Marjorie.

Nothing will do but for Marjorie to try it. The boys demur, she insists, standing up on the car seat, until Carpenter gets out, Marjorie following.

Carpenter closes the car door. Marjorie now gets in by jumping over it. She pats her hair delicately. Before Carpenter can follow suit, Reece pulls the car out. Carpenter must now enter in a flying leap, landing half on Marjorie, who yelps.

Bernice watches the car until it is out of view, then with a sigh she pulls the curtain closed, as if to shut out the pain of the outside world.

Bernice sits down at her desk. We hear the front door chimes. Bernice takes stationery and pen and begins a letter. She gets as far as the date, "August 20, 1919" and "Dear Mother," when there is a knock on her door.

MRS. HARVEY'S VOICE. Bernice?
BERNICE. Come in.
[MRS. HARVEY *enters.*]
MRS. HARVEY. Are you feeling better, dear?
BERNICE. I'm all right, Aunt Josephine.
MRS. HARVEY. Will you come down? Young Draycott Deyo is here.

DISSOLVE TO

22. INT. SITTING ROOM. DAY.

Draycott Deyo and Bernice are seated on the sofa, a chaste space between them. Draycott, a pale young man with eyeglasses and a stiff, pedantic manner, looks straight ahead.

BERNICE. How are your studies coming along, Draycott?
DRAYCOTT. Very well, thank you.
BERNICE. You're going to be a doctor?
DRAYCOTT. A minister.
BERNICE. Oh.
[*Some awkward silence.*]
BERNICE. You weren't at the dance last night, were you?
DRAYCOTT. At the country club? No. I understand it was even noisier than usual.
BERNICE. The floor was crowded.
DRAYCOTT. A noisy, crowded dance floor is my pet abomination. In my opinion, some of our generation will end up dancing themselves to death.
BERNICE. Oh, no.
DRAYCOTT. Oh, yes. Present company excepted, of course. No one could ever accuse you of such a thing.
[DRAYCOTT *means it as a compliment, of course, but it makes* BERNICE *feel worse than ever.*]

DRAYCOTT. Next thing you know, one of them will bob her hair.
BERNICE. Oh, I don't think things will go that far, do you?
DRAYCOTT [*ominously*]. One thing has a way of leading to another.

23. INT. MARJORIE'S BEDROOM. SOMETIME LATER THAT AFTERNOON.

Bernice is sitting in the armchair. Her face is strangely set. Marjorie enters . . . she is just home from the matinee.

MARJORIE. Well . . . come right in.
[MARJORIE *sits down at her dressing table, removes her hat.*]
BERNICE. [*with no other preliminaries*]. I've decided that maybe you're right about things . . . possibly.
[MARJORIE *continues repairing her hairdo.*]
BERNICE. If you'll tell me why your friends don't like me, what I do wrong . . . I'll see what I can do.
[MARJORIE *turns and looks at* BERNICE *with a hard-eyed stare.*]
MARJORIE. Do you mean it?
BERNICE. Yes.
MARJORIE. Without reservations? Will you do exactly as I say?
BERNICE. If they're sensible things.
MARJORIE. You're no case for sensible things. Yes or no?
BERNICE. Are you going to make . . . to recommend . . .
MARJORIE. Everything. If I tell you to take boxing lessons you'll have to do it. Well? [BERNICE nods.] Write home and tell your mother you're going to stay for another two weeks. [BERNICE *stands.*] Where are you going?
BERNICE. To write my mother.
MARJORIE. Sit down. You can do that later. I have so much work to do on you, I can't lose a minute. The first thing is your personal appearance.
BERNICE. Don't I look all right?
MARJORIE. No [*counting on her fingers*]. You're also a bad conversationalist and you lean on men when you dance. Your personality is boring. You haven't the vaguest idea of how to make a man fall in love with you. Are you willing to admit all that?

BERNICE. Maybe.
MARJORIE. No maybes.
BERNICE. All right, but how are you going to fix all that in two weeks?
MARJORIE. If you'll pay attention, I can fix it in two days.
[BERNICE *is bewildered, surprised, and yes, hopeful.*]

[MARJORIE *has moved toward* BERNICE *and now scrutinizes her carefully. Embarrassed,* BERNICE *grins.*]
MARJORIE. When you go home, you ought to have your teeth straightened. Meanwhile, smile with your mouth closed.
[*Again* BERNICE *grins loonily.* MARJORIE *glares. Quickly* BERNICE *closes her lips over her imperfect teeth.*]
MARJORIE. Just think about Mona Lisa.
BERNICE. Is that why Mona Lisa . . . you mean her teeth were crooked?
MARJORIE. Of course.
BERNICE. How do you know things like that?
MARJORIE. Oh . . . you just learn them along the way.

24. INT. HARVEY DINING ROOM. EVENING.

Mrs. Harvey, Marjorie and Bernice at table. Annie is passing dessert.

MRS. HARVEY. Marjorie, did you hear that Draycott Deyo was over this afternoon? You were at the matinee.
MARJORIE. Luckily.
MRS. HARVEY. I think young Draycott has a case on Bernice.
MARJORIE. Let's not talk about it at table.
[BERNICE *and* ANNIE *smile.* MARJORIE *frowns at* BERNICE, *who quickly closes her lips à la Mona Lisa.*]
MRS. HARVEY [*mildly*]. Now, Marjorie . . .
MARJORIE. Mother, I've asked Bernice to stay an extra week.
MRS. HARVEY [*surprised, as is* ANNIE]. Why, how nice!
BERNICE. If my mother says it's all right.
MRS. HARVEY. I'm sure she will. That's just fine, Bernice.
MARJORIE. Mother, can we be excused?
MRS. HARVEY. Why, I don't think Bernice . . .
MARJORIE. Yes, she is, aren't you?

[BERNICE *puts down her fork.*]

BERNICE. Yes, thank you, Aunt Josephine.

[*The two girls rise and start to exit.*]

MARJORIE. If any men call or come by tonight, tell them I'm busy.

MRS. HARVEY. Why, Marjorie . . .

MARJORIE. Bernice and I want to have a quiet evening.

MRS. HARVEY. That's a good idea, dear. You could both use a good rest.

[*The girls exit.*]

MRS. HARVEY [*pleased*]. You see, Annie, I knew the girls would get to like each other in time.

ANNIE. Awful sudden, isn't it?

MRS. HARVEY. That's the way youngsters are.

ANNIE. Yes ma'am.

25. INT. HARVEY STAIRCASE. EVENING.

As the two girls ascend, Marjorie stares at Bernice.

MARJORIE. Your eyebrows are all straggly. You're going to brush them every night.

BERNICE. Do men really notice eyebrows?

MARJORIE. Yes . . . subconsciously.

26. INT. BERNICE'S ROOM. NIGHT.

Marjorie is examining the contents of Bernice's steamer trunk. Most of the clothes displease her and she tosses them aside.

MARJORIE. You see, Bernice, if a girl looks like a million dollars, she can talk about Russia, Ping Pong or the League of Nations and get away with it [*examining a dress*]. Ugh. [*She tosses it out.*]

[MARJORIE *comes upon the dress* BERNICE *wore to the country club dance the previous night.*]

MARJORIE. Don't ever put this on again as long as you live.

BERNICE. But my mother . . .

MARJORIE. Bernice, let's get something straight. Your mother's advice was just fine from one to fourteen. You are going to be eighteen on your next birthday.

[BERNICE *takes the offending dress from* MARJORIE *and throws it upon the pile.*]

27. INT. MARJORIE'S ROOM. NIGHT.

Bernice is seated at Marjorie's dressing table. Marjorie offers her a jar of cream.

MARJORIE. Now, I want you to use this cream every night.
BERNICE. On my face?
MARJORIE. Your face, your hands, your elbows and your knees.
BERNICE. Who will ever see my knees?
MARJORIE. Lots of people if you work it right.
[MARJORIE *is standing behind* BERNICE. *She looks at herself in the mirror.*]
BERNICE. Marjorie? Is it true you turned three cartwheels at the Pump-and-Slipper dance?
MARJORIE. Five.
[BERNICE *is awed.*]
MARJORIE. That's old hat. We'll think up something better for you.
[MARJORIE *continues to gaze at herself pensively in the mirror.*]
MARJORIE. I know. We could bob your hair.
[BERNICE *looks shocked.* MARJORIE *glances at her, then back at herself.*]
MARJORIE. All right, it was just a thought. Tell you what . . . it'll make a terrific line!

28. INT. SITTING ROOM. DAY.

Marjorie and Bernice are dancing to gramophone music. Marjorie is leading.

MARJORIE. Don't lean.
BERNICE. I'm not.
MARJORIE. Yes, you are.
[BERNICE *straightens with an unnatural erectness.*]
MARJORIE. Bend in a little.
[*Finally* MARJORIE *seems satisfied. As they continue to dance . . .*]
MARJORIE. Why aren't you saying anything?
BERNICE. Well, you aren't either.

MARJORIE. I'm the man. The girl *always* has to make the conversation.

[*After a few beats of silence*:]

BERNICE. It's hard to think of something.

MARJORIE. Bernice, when you're with a man, there are only three topics of conversation: you, me and us.

BERNICE. All right. [*After more silence.*] Maybe it would be better if I knew who you were.

MARJORIE. Just pick someone then.

BERNICE. You pick.

MARJORIE. Anybody. Warren McIntyre.

[BERNICE *is tongue-tied as she is with the real* WARREN.]

MARJORIE. Go on.

BERNICE. Are you . . . going back to college soon?

MARJORIE. Oh, thrilling.

[*Disgusted,* MARJORIE *moves to the phonograph, lifts the needle from the record.*]

BERNICE [*bewildered*]. You said you, me, and us.

MARJORIE. But what can he say except yes, I am, or no, I'm not, and who cares anyway?

29. EXT. PORCH. DAY.

The girls are now rocking back and forth on the porch glider.

MARJORIE. If you must mention college, do it like this. You be Warren. [BERNICE *nods.*] Is it true what I hear about Yale men, Warren McIntyre? [*Nudges* BERNICE.]

BERNICE. What did you hear?

MARJORIE [*with great charm*]. That they're fickler than other men. He'd probably say, who told you, and I'd say, never mind, I just hope it's true, because I think fickle men are more interesting, more of a challenge.

[BERNICE *drinks this in as though it is the revealed word.*]

MARJORIE. That's sure fire, actually. I use it all the time.

BERNICE [*with a studied casualness*]. What would you say if he said something like, you've got an awfully kissable mouth.

MARJORIE [*again, intensely charming and flirtatious*]. What's your criterion for a kissable mouth? One that looks like it's been kissed a lot or one you'd like to kiss?

[BERNICE *is shocked but ashamed to let* MARJORIE *know it.*

She pretends to be busy with a strand of wayward hair. Suddenly . . .]

BERNICE. Marjorie, have you ever . . .

MARJORIE. Lots of times.

[BERNICE *thinks this over.*]

BERNICE. But if you're a nice girl from a good family . . .

MARJORIE. . . . you like to have as much fun as anybody else.

BERNICE. Did you ever kiss Warren?

MARJORIE [*a bored tone*]. Oh Warren . . . I have an infallible test and he flunked it. I think if you really love someone, you love them even when they aren't around. When Warren went away to school, I fell in love with four men before he got home for Christmas.

[BERNICE *listens closely.*]

MARJORIE. I'm afraid he'll never get over me, though. Poor thing.

30. INT. HARVEY DINING ROOM. EARLY EVENING.

The dining room is decorated for a party. Bernice, in one of Marjorie's dresses, looking very pretty, enters the room. Marjorie, not yet dressed, is worrying over the place cards. She changes some, puts them back where they were, etc. The table is set for eight.

BERNICE. Who did you put me by?

[*She finds her card, checks those on either side of it.*]

BERNICE [*pleased*]. G. Reece Stoddard. [*Not so pleased.*] Charley Paulson!

MARJORIE. Sad birds like Charley are a big part of any crowd and you can't afford to neglect them. If you can get three sad birds to dance with you and they keep coming back, the attractive men will see there's no danger of being stuck and they'll dance with you.

BERNICE. I never thought of that.

[MARJORIE *continues to fuss around the table.*]

BERNICE [*nervously*]. You better get dressed. It's almost time.

MARJORIE. I think I'll put Roberta on the other side of Charley Paulson. It will be good practice for you. If you can get a man to pay attention to you when Roberta

Dillon is on his other side, you'll know you have what it takes.

[*The door chimes.*]

BERNICE. Marjorie!

MARJORIE. Good. Now I can go get dressed.

[BERNICE *now realizes that* MARJORIE *set it up this way. She is paralyzed.* MARJORIE *exits through kitchen to take back stairs.* BERNICE *is almost hiding in the dining room.*]

[*Again the door chimes. Finally she moves to the front door.*]

31. INT. DOWNSTAIRS HALL. EVENING.

At the door are Roberta, Genevieve, Charley and Carpenter. And Warren and G. Reece are walking up the steps. Bernice opens the door for them. She may be dressed more prettily, but she is shy as ever.

Ad lib greetings.

REECE. 'Lo, Bernice.

WARREN. Where's Marjorie?

BERNICE. She'll be right down.

[*The six young people stand in the hall, yammering away. The conversation* (to be worked out on the set) *concerns one Babs Finley and whether she was fired from Miss Walker's for cheating on her exams, sneaking out after hours, or flunking hygiene. An impassioned discussion, which* BERNICE, *standing to one side, is totally out of. She is smiling the old dumb smile.*]

ANGLE AT TOP OF STAIRS. MARJORIE *is leaning over banister. She is finishing her hairdo while observing that* BERNICE *is out of it, both geographically and conversationally.* MARJORIE *is annoyed.*]

MARJORIE *starts down the stairs. She looks gay and lovely. She is greeted by all and she quickly is surrounded.*]

MARJORIE. If you want to know about Babs Finley, you should ask Teddy Roberson.

[*Ad lib* . . . "Ted! She wouldn't go out with him after that time at Princeton!" "That's what you think." Etc., etc.]

MARJORIE. Bernice, could I see you for just a minute?

32. INT. KITCHEN. EVENING.

The cook is busy taking something out of the oven and Annie is arranging a tray. They listen while Marjorie chews Bernice out.

MARJORIE. You aren't even trying!
[BERNICE *is embarrassed and unhappy.*]
MARJORIE. If you've just been wasting my time . . . I'll never forgive you!
[BERNICE *says nothing; she glances miserably at* COOK *and* ANNIE.]
MARJORIE. You might as well go home!
BERNICE. No!
[MARJORIE *looks at* BERNICE *sternly.* BERNICE *is almost flinching.*]
ANNIE. Everything's ready, Miss Marjorie.
[MARJORIE *whips out of the kitchen,* BERNICE *slinks after her.*]

33. INT. DINING ROOM. EVENING.

The table is arranged as follows: Marjorie and Bernice are on either end; Reece and Charley on either side of Bernice; Warren and Carpenter on either side of Marjorie; Genevieve and Roberta in the middle on either side.

General conversation over the soup course . . . a jellied madrilène . . . concerns Roger Partington. Will he get tapped for Skull and Bones? After all, his brother made it. "You're a cinch for it, Warren." "I don't know about that." . . . etc.

Marjorie glares across the table at Bernice. Bernice takes a deep breath, turns to Charley.

BERNICE. Mr. Charley Paulson, do you think I ought to bob my hair? [CHARLEY *looks at her blankly.*] My hair. Do you think I ought to bob it?
CHARLEY. Why?
BERNICE. I want to be a society vampire. And I don't see how I can unless I bob my hair, do you?

[CHARLEY *is looking at her with more interest.* BERNICE *lowers her voice intimately.*]

BERNICE. I decided to ask your advice because I heard you were so critical of girls.

[CHARLEY *is now definitely hooked. He can't wait for* BERNICE *to tell him more.*]

MARJORIE. What are you all talking about down there?

[*Everyone is looking at* BERNICE *now. She falters but quickly gets going again.*]

BERNICE [*pertly*]. I was telling Charley that first thing next week I'm going to go down to the Sevier Hotel barbershop, sit in the first chair, and get my hair bobbed.

[*During* BERNICE'S *last speech we will make a* QUICK CUT *to* MARJORIE, *who is mouthing the words along with* BERNICE. *After all,* MARJORIE *not only made it up but coached* BERNICE *in the proper inflections.*]

BERNICE [*glancing around at everyone*]. Of course, I'm charging admission, but if you'll all come down and encourage me, I'll issue passes for the inside seats.

[*Appreciative laughter from all.*]

REECE [*in an undertone*]. I'll take one front and center right now.

[BERNICE *turns and smiles her Mona Lisa smile at* REECE *as though he has said something surpassingly brilliant.*]

CARPENTER. I thought bobbed hair was just for movie vamps. Would you really do it, Bernice?

BERNICE. I know it's unmoral. But my philosophy is that you have to amuse people, feed 'em or shock 'em.

[*General laughter from the boys.* ROBERTA *and* GENEVIEVE *give* BERNICE *quick and intent looks.*]

BERNICE [*in a confidential tone to* CHARLEY]. Charley, I've been wanting to ask your opinion of several people. I hear you're a wonderful judge of character.

[CHARLEY *is faintly thrilled, and he shows it by overturning his water glass.*]

34. INT. SITTING ROOM. NIGHT.

The gramophone is on, the rug rolled up, and they are dancing.

On Bernice, who is dancing with Charley.

CHARLEY. What did you mean before when you said I'm critical of girls?

BERNICE. That's what I heard, I heard it practically the minute I got to town.
CHARLEY. Who'd you hear it from?
BERNICE. Several people.
CHARLEY. Who?
BERNICE. Guess.
CHARLEY. Male or female?
[*Before she can answer,* CARPENTER *cuts in.*]
CHARLEY. Aw, wait a minute.
CARPENTER. Nuts to you.
[*He sweeps* BERNICE *around.*]
CARPENTER. Are you really going to bob your hair?
BERNICE. First thing next week. Can you come?
CARPENTER. I wouldn't miss it.
BERNICE. Carpenter, I heard something about the men who go to the U. of Minnesota and I want to know if it's true. Will you be honest with me?
CARPENTER. Sure.
[*Realizing they are dancing close to* ROBERTA *and* REECE STODDARD, BERNICE *raises her voice a little.*]
BERNICE. Just promise me you won't tell Mr. G. Reece Stoddard.
REECE. Tell me what?
BERNICE. Oh-oh.
[CARPENTER *dances her off,* REECE *looking after her with interest.*]
CARPENTER. He can't hear. Go ahead.
[BERNICE *starts to talk, then stops.*]
BERNICE. I'm afraid you'll get mad at me.
CARPENTER. No I won't, tell me.
[BERNICE *looks around, then whispers something in his ear.*]
CARPENTER [*intrigued*]. Who told you that?
BERNICE. Never mind. I hope it's true because fickle men are the only kind that interest me. They're more of a challenge.
[*On* WARREN, *who is following* MARJORIE *around.* MARJORIE *stops by the gramophone, examines some records.*]
WARREN. But you were the one who said you wanted to drive out to the lake.
MARJORIE. I did?
WARREN. Weeks ago.
MARJORIE. Oh, Warren, quit being such a pest.
[*Although* WARREN'S *handsome face is impassive, he has*

suddenly had enough of MARJORIE. *He turns, looks at the dance floor.*]

[*From* WARREN'S *point of view:* CHARLEY PAULSON *is cutting back in on* BERNICE. *Just as he does so the music ends.*]

CHARLEY. Hurry up, Marjorie.

MARJORIE. I'm trying to find something good.

[REECE, *still with* ROBERTA, *excuses himself, sidles over to* WARREN.]

REECE. Cut in on me and Roberta, will you?

WARREN. Sure. Why?

REECE. I want to dance with Bernice. [REECE *goes back to* ROBERTA.]

[WARREN *is perplexed.* BERNICE? *The music starts, a slower piece than the last one.*]

[REECE *and* ROBERTA, BERNICE *and* CHARLEY. CARPENTER *hangs against the wall watching his chance to cut in on* BERNICE *again.* MARJORIE *and* GENEVIEVE *are examining* GENEVIEVE'S *sash, which seems to have come loose.*]

MARJORIE. Do you want to sew it or pin it?

GENEVIEVE. Pin it, if it won't show.

MARJORIE. Come on upstairs.

[*The two girls exit.*]

[WARREN *moves toward* REECE *and* ROBERTA. . . . REECE *looks at him expectantly. But* WARREN *moves past them and cuts in on* BERNICE *instead. They dance for a few beats.*]

BERNICE. How do you think I'll look with my hair bobbed?

WARREN. You weren't serious, were you?

BERNICE. Of course! Did you think it was just a line? [WARREN *shrugs.*] The one in this room with a line is Mr. Warren McIntyre.

WARREN. Why do you say that?

BERNICE. "You know, Bernice, you've got an awfully kissable mouth." [WARREN *grins.*] I meant to ask you, what's your criterion for a kissable mouth . . . one that looks like it's been kissed a lot or one you'd like to kiss?

WARREN. Why . . . one I'd like to kiss.

BERNICE. I see. Thank you, Warren, that's very handy information. [*Both laugh.*]

35. INT. HARVEY STAIRCASE. NIGHT.

The party is over, Bernice is still sparkling as she walks upstairs with Marjorie.

MARJORIE. So it worked?
BERNICE. Oh, Marjorie, yes!
MARJORIE. I could tell you were having a good time.
BERNICE. The only trouble was I ran short about midnight. I had to repeat myself with different men. I hope they don't compare notes.
MARJORIE [*yawning*]. Men don't. And it wouldn't matter if they did. They'd think you were even trickier. I'll fix you up some new stuff tomorrow.
[BERNICE *feels slightly rebellious.*]
BERNICE. Maybe *I* could. I mean I thought up some myself, right on the spur of the moment.
MARJORIE [*not too interested*]. Good-night.
[*She goes into her own room, leaving* BERNICE *somewhat annoyed.*]

36. EXT. HARVEY HOUSE. DAY.

Otis, in his tennis clothes, runs up the steps to the Harvey house. He rings the bell; Annie answers.

ANNIE. Miss Marjorie's gone downtown with her mother.
OTIS. That's funny. Charley Paulson's sister said he was over here.
ANNIE. He is.
OTIS. What's he doing here if Marjorie's downtown?
[ANNIE *holds door open.* OTIS *looks perplexed. He enters.*]

37. INT. SITTING ROOM. DAY.

Charley and Bernice. Bernice is wearing one of Marjorie's dresses; she looks very young and very pretty. Charley is obviously enjoying himself, as he tells her an old school story. Bernice laughs as though it is the most hilarious story she's ever heard. Otis enters and with no preliminaries . . .

OTIS. Hey, Paulson, what about our game? 'Lo, Bernice.
BERNICE. Hello, Otis.

[CHARLEY *looks nonplussed.*]

CHARLEY. I forgot all about it.

OTIS. 'S all right. If you hurry we can still play a set or two.

CHARLEY. I'll take a rain check, Otis, sorry.

OTIS. Whaddya' mean?

CHARLEY. I mean I'm busy right now.

OTIS. Doing what?

CHARLEY [*pointedly*]. I'll see you later, Otis.

38. EXT. HARVEY PORCH. DAY.

Otis doesn't understand but he exits. As he comes out front door, Carpenter Thompson is coming in.

OTIS. Marjorie's downtown.

CARPENTER. Where's Bernice?

OTIS. Bernice?

[CARPENTER *passes him and heads into the house.* OTIS *is talking to himself. He mouths the word* "BERNICE?" *He turns and re-enters the house.*]

FLIP FRAME

39. INT. HARVEY SITTING ROOM. EVENING.

A bridge party. Bernice, Marjorie, G. Reece, and Charley.

CHARLEY. Four clubs.

BERNICE. Four hearts.

MARJORIE. Pass.

CHARLEY. Pass.

[*As* REECE *lays out the dummy's hand . . .*]

REECE. Say, Bernice, when are you going to bob your hair?

BERNICE. Day after tomorrow, maybe. You're coming, aren't you? I'm counting on you. Your lead, Marjorie. [*As they play.*] I have such a frightful lot of hair, and it takes so much energy to fix it, do you know what I've taken to doing? First I fix my hair, then I put on my hat, then I get into the bathtub and then I get dressed.

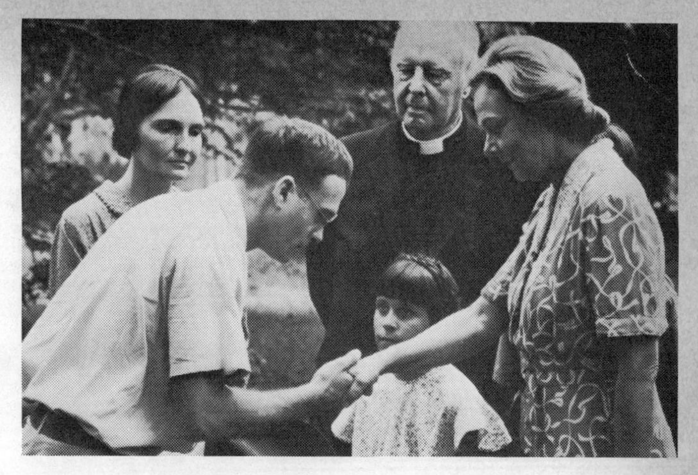

The arrival of *The Displaced Person*. L–R: Carolyn Bloodworth (Mrs. Guizac), Noam Yerushalmi (Mr. Guizac), John Houseman (Father Flynn), Dina Herrington (Sledgewig Guizac), and Irene Worth (Mrs. McIntyre). (PHOTO BY ARTHUR SIRDOFSKY)

The Shortley family, from *The Displaced Person*. Standing, L–R: Deborah Lee Jones (Sarah Mae) and Vicki Tooke (Annie Maude); seated, L–R: Lane Smith (Mr. Shortley) and Shirley Stoler (Mrs. Shortley). (PHOTO BY BARBARA MCKENZIE)

Filming front porch scene in *The Displaced Person*. Clockwise, from upper left: Tom Kane (Second Assistant Director), Terry Donnelly (Assistant Director), Glenn Jordan (Director), George Mooradian (Production Assistant), Todd Crandall (Assistant Cameraman), Joe Rivers (Gaffer), Ken Van Sickle (Director of Photography), John Houseman (Father Flynn), and Irene Worth (Mrs. McIntyre). (PHOTO BY ARTHUR SIRDOFSKY)

Scene from *Bernice Bobs Her Hair*. Shelley Duvall (Bernice) and Dennis Christopher (Charley Paulson). (PHOTO BY PAUL CRUZ)

No spades, Charley?

CHARLEY [*mesmerized*]. Huh? Oh. Sorry.

BERNICE [*continuing to play*]. Don't you think that's a good plan? My bathtub plan?

REECE [*grinning*]. First rate.

[BERNICE *smiles her Mona Lisa smile, then glances at* MARJORIE, *who nods approvingly.*]

FLIP FRAME

40. INT. MARJORIE'S ROOM. NIGHT.

The two girls are brushing and braiding their hair for the night. They sit on Marjorie's bed.

MARJORIE. You've got the smile down pat, but you've got to perfect a pathetic look, too.

BERNICE. Why?

MARJORIE. You need it sometimes in certain situations.

BERNICE [*puzzled*]. With men?

MARJORIE. Of course with men. Next year when you go East to school, you'll run into Babs Finley.

BERNICE. The one who got fired from Miss Walker's?

MARJORIE. Oh, she's been fired from three schools that I know of and maybe more. Anyway, she's probably got the greatest pathetic look of any girl in our generation.

BERNICE [*awestruck*]. How do you do it?

MARJORIE. Open your eyes wide. That's it. Now droop your mouth a little. Now . . . [MARJORIE *tips her head slightly and* BERNICE *copies her*] . . . look right in the man's eyes and say, "I hardly have any beaux at all."

BERNICE. I hardly have any beaux at all.

MARJORIE. Not bad.

BERNICE. But I thought the idea was to seem popular.

MARJORIE. It only works if you're popular. An unpopular girl couldn't use it at all. If she said, "I don't have any beaux," what could a man say? But if a popular girl says it . . . see?

BERNICE [*nods*]. Do you think I'll ever know all these things like you do?

MARJORIE. I don't know. You got a late start.

BERNICE [*that rebellious feeling again*]. I think I'm

doing all right. How did you like my bathtub line?

MARJORIE. Snazzy.

BERNICE [*feeling better*]. You can use it if you want to.

MARJORIE. Bernice, I don't have to use other people's lines.

[BERNICE *feels the implicit put-down, of course; she frowns just a little.*]

41. EXT. HARVEY PORCH. DAY.

Draycott Deyo and Bernice. Across the way, Warren is polishing his car. Bernice swings slowly back and forth on the porch glider, her eye on Warren while she listens to Draycott.

BERNICE [*stifling a yawn*]. How are your studies coming, Draycott?

DRAYCOTT. I'm working on a difficult matter. Baptism by immersion. It's a controversial area in the church, you know.

BERNICE. Baptism?

DRAYCOTT. Immersion.

BERNICE [*dreamily*]. Draycott, you know what I do sometimes? I fix my hair, put on my hat, immerse myself in the bathtub and then I get dressed.

[DRAYCOTT *is shocked . . . and faintly thrilled.*]

DRAYCOTT [*clears his throat*]. Bernice?

[*At just this minute,* BERNICE *catches* WARREN'S *eye. He waves; she waves back.*]

BERNICE. Yes, Draycott?

FLIP FRAME

42. EXT. FRONT DOOR OF HARVEY HOUSE. DAY.

Annie and Warren

ANNIE [*startled*]. Miss Bernice?

[*Before* WARREN *can reply,* BERNICE *comes out.*]

BERNICE. Hello, Shell Shock.

WARREN. Ready?

BERNICE. Annie, would you tell Aunt Josephine I'm going for a ride?

[BERNICE *and* WARREN *run down the steps toward his car, which is parked in front.*]

43. INT. KITCHEN. DAY.

Cook is icing a cake or something similar. Annie, eager to tell her news, pushes open the swinging door.

ANNIE. Looks like Miss Bernice has got ahold of Miss Marjorie's best fella!

[*Before* ANNIE *can continue, we hear* MRS. HARVEY'S *voice:*]

MRS. HARVEY [O.S.] Annie?

[ANNIE *is disappointed . . . but she looks at* COOK *as though to say, be right back.*]

44. INT. HALL. DAY.

Annie comes into the front hall. Mrs. Harvey is leaning over the banister.

MRS. HARVEY. Who was at the door?

ANNIE. Mr. Warren. He and Miss Bernice went for a ride.

MRS. HARVEY. Warren McIntyre?

45. INT. MARJORIE'S ROOM. DAY.

Marjorie in her chemise and a skirt which is being fitted. On the floor sits the dressmaker, pins in her mouth. Mrs. Harvey enters.

MARJORIE. Who was it?

MRS. HARVEY. Warren.

MARJORIE. Well, I can't see him now.

MRS. HARVEY. It seems he came for Bernice. Did you know he telephoned her twice yesterday?

MARJORIE. I'm glad he's finally found someone who appreciates him.

MRS. HARVEY. As long as you don't mind . . .

MARJORIE. Mind! If she gets him off my neck, I'll give her my next month's allowance. [*Now about her skirt.*] This still isn't right.

MRS. HARVEY. I agree. It's too short.

MARJORIE. No, it's too long. [*To the long-suffering dressmaker.*] Take it up another quarter of an inch.

46. EXT. LAKE. DAY.

A picnic by the lake. Bernice, Marjorie, Roberta, Genevieve, Warren, Reece, Otis, Charley, Carpenter. The group has come in two cars, Warren's and Roberta's. The cars can be seen parked to one side.

The young people have fanned out and are engaged in various pursuits. Some are down by the dock, some are tossing a football, Otis sits in a tree strumming on his ukulele, and so on.

Warren and Bernice are rowing on the lake and engaged in a tensely significant conversation about you, me and us. Bernice is trailing her fingers in the water and using her newly mastered pathetic look.

BERNICE. You're just saying that, Warren. How do I know you're sincere?

CUT TO

[MARJORIE *and* ROBERTA *at the dock. They are watching* BERNICE *and* WARREN *in the distance.*]
MARJORIE. I could get him back like that [*she snaps her fingers*].
ROBERTA. Could you?
[ROBERTA *doesn't sound so sure.* MARJORIE'S *eyes narrow.*]

CUT TO

[*A croquet game is under way. Four or five players, including* BERNICE, MARJORIE *and* WARREN. BERNICE *swings, walks to where her ball has landed. As she reaches it . . .*]
BERNICE. Oh!
[*Another ball has hit her ball. She turns, sees* MARJORIE *advancing, a determined look in her eye. As she nears* BERNICE, *in a low but firm voice . . .*]
MARJORIE. You may as well get Warren out of your head.
BERNICE [*astounded*]. What!
[MARJORIE *puts her foot on her own ball (which touches* BERNICE'S *ball) and gives it a sharp hit.* BERNICE'S *ball*

goes rolling off. As MARJORIE *does this, she says . . .*]

MARJORIE. Stop making a fool of yourself. Warren McIntyre doesn't care a [*hits the ball*] *fig* for you.

[BERNICE *looks after her ball, then back to* MARJORIE.]

BERNICE. You act like I stole your private property.

[MARJORIE *gives her own ball a sharp thwack. It goes sailing off toward the next wicket.*]

MARJORIE [*succinctly*]. I'm not interested in discussing it, now or later.

[*And* MARJORIE *moves on, leaving* BERNICE *unnerved.*]

CUT TO

[OTIS *sitting on a blanket, tinkering with his uke.*]

OTIS [*sings*]. My dog has fleas Right on his knees Each time I find one
I give it a squeeze.

[*We* WIDEN OUT *during* OTIS'S *"song" to show all the nice young people sprawled about, finishing their picnic lunch. General groans . . . "Cork it,* OTIS," *etc.*]

REECE. When you going back to kindergarten, Otis?

OTIS. Me? The day Bernice gets her hair bobbed.

MARJORIE. Then your education's over.

OTIS. Huh?

MARJORIE. That's only a bluff, I thought you realized.

[BERNICE *sniffs danger, but she isn't adroit enough to do anything about it.*]

ROBERTA. You mean that was just a line?

[*All eyes are on* BERNICE.]

BERNICE [*an embarrassed grin*]. I don't know.

MARJORIE. Splush! Admit it.

[BERNICE *glances around. Everyone is looking at her curiously, especially* WARREN.]

MARJORIE. Splush!

OTIS. Tell her where to get off, Bernice.

[*Again* BERNICE *looks around. Again she sees* WARREN'S *quizzical look.*]

BERNICE. I like bobbed hair and I intend to bob mine.

MARJORIE. When?

BERNICE. Any time.

ROBERTA. No time like the present.

CHARLEY [*jumps up*]. Good stuff! We'll have a summer

bobbing party. Sevier Barber Shop, isn't that what you said, Bernice?
[*Everyone is on his feet, ready to leave, except* BERNICE.]
MARJORIE. Don't worry, she'll back out!
[*Again everyone is looking at* BERNICE.]
OTIS. Come on, Bernice.
BERNICE [*with a sudden swiftness*]. All right. I don't care if I do.
[*And she leads the way to the cars.*]

47. EXT. STREET. DAY.

A two-car caravan heads downtown to the barber shop. In the lead, Warren is driving Bernice, Marjorie and Charley The rest are crammed into Roberta's car.

Warren is moodily silent. Bernice, seated next to him, is having the sensations of Marie Antoinette bound for the guillotine in a tumbrel. In the back seat, Charley and Marjorie are singing.

Involuntarily, Bernice's hands reach up toward her hair. She puts them back on her lap, grips them tightly together. She glances at Warren, but all she sees is his impassive profile.

48. INT. BARBER SHOP. DAY.

All nine of them crowd in. It's a three-chair barber shop. Two chairs are occupied; in the third, the barber sits reading the newspaper. A cigarette hangs from his mouth.

Bernice approaches him. He looks up.
BERNICE. I want you to bob my hair.
[*Puzzled, the* BARBER *stands up. She climbs up into the chair.*]
BARBER. Miss?
BERNICE. My hair. Bob it!
[*The* BARBER *looks worriedly at the other barbers.*]
BERNICE [*reaches for the shears hanging by the mirror; she hands it to him*]. You know how, don't you?
BARBER. Men's hair, yes; but I haven't ever . . .
BERNICE. Good heavens! Just do it.
[*The circle of her companions spreads around to get a good view. The second and third barbers and their clients are*

equally intrigued. Out of habit, the BARBER *shakes out a white cloth and proceeds to tie it around her neck.*]

OTIS. That's so you won't get blood on your clothes, Bernice!

[*The crowd laughs.* BERNICE *assumes her Mona Lisa smile. Clumsily, the* BARBER *removes the hair pins and tortoise-shell combs one at a time. Little by little, her golden brown hair spreads around her shoulders and down her back. Her face has a Madonna-like simplicity, framed as it is by the thick long hair.* BERNICE *looks at herself in the mirror. For a second she wavers. But her glance wanders to* MARJORIE, *gazing into the mirror at her.* MARJORIE'S *lips curl in a faintly ironic smile . . .*]

MARJORIE. You can still back down.

[BERNICE'S *expression hardens.*]

BERNICE. Why should I? [*Looks at the* BARBER.] What are you waiting for?

BARBER. I want to make sure all the pins was out. I don't want to break my shears.

[BERNICE *reaches out from under the white cloth and runs her fingers through her hair, a sensuous pleasure which in a very short time will no longer be available to her. She catches* WARREN'S *expression in the mirror, and that of the other boys, almost hypnotized at the wondrous mass of hair.*]

BERNICE. You got them all.

[*The* BARBER *takes a handful of hair and chops it off. He drops it on the ground where it lies in a pitiful clump.*]

[*From now on we will be looking not at* BERNICE, *but at the reactions of the young people and the others in the barbershop, cutting quickly from one to another. One of the customers motions* CHARLEY *aside so he can get a better view. The sound of the shears punctuates everything.*]

[*The faces of the onlookers might best be described as expressionless. They are at the scene of the accident, in the first row at the theater, nonparticipants who won't be denied their viewing. None takes his eyes from the barber chair.*]

BARBER. Well, Miss, I think that's it.

[*He spins the chair around so that* BERNICE *(and we) can finally see the damage. Her hair hangs in lifeless hanks.*

It no longer seems to go with her face. BERNICE *stares at herself. It hardly looks like the same face. The* BARBER *unties the cloth and* BERNICE *gets down from the chair. She is trying to smile confidently, but she fails miserably.* GENEVIEVE *and* ROBERTA *exchange a glance.* BERNICE *sees it, of course.*]

BERNICE. Well, . . . I did it.

[*She looks around at everyone.*]

BERNICE. Do you like it?

[*A few half-hearted "Sures" and "Yesses."*]

[*The* BARBER *is already sweeping up the hair on the floor.* BERNICE *sees this, too.*]

[MARJORIE *turns to* WARREN.]

MARJORIE. Would you mind running me down to the cleaners? I've simply got to get a dress there before supper. Roberta is driving right home and she can take the others.

[WARREN *seems distracted.*]

WARREN [*slowly*]. What? Oh, sure, be glad to.

49. INT. HARVEY DINING ROOM. EVENING.

Bernice, Marjorie and Mrs. Harvey. They eat in silence; the sounds of silverware and china are all we hear. Annie passes the vegetables from one to the next. Finally . . .

MRS. HARVEY. Oh, Bernice, what will your parents say? They'll think I let you do it.

BERNICE. I'm sorry, Aunt Josephine.

[MARJORIE *continues to eat in stolid silence.*]

50. INT. BERNICE'S BEDROOM. NIGHT.

Bernice is in her nightgown. Standing before her mirror, she passes a comb through her short hair. A knock on the door and Marjorie enters. She wears a negligée and her hair is down and has been carefully brushed.

MARJORIE. Bernice? I'm awfully sorry.

BERNICE. It's all right.

[*As* MARJORIE *talks, she braids her long dark hair for the night.* BERNICE *is fascinated as she watches the heavy luxurious braids forming.*]

MARJORIE. Maybe we can wet it or something so it won't stick out like that.

BERNICE. It's all right. [*She watches the braids grow.*]

MARJORIE. I didn't think you'd really go through with it.

BERNICE. Doesn't matter.

MARJORIE. You'll get used to it, maybe.

BERNICE [*oddly confident*]. I'm used to it now. I like it.

MARJORIE [*smiles.*] For heaven's sake, don't let it worry you.

BERNICE. I won't.

MARJORIE. Life's too short.

BERNICE. Yes.

MARJORIE. Good night, Bernice.

BERNICE. Good night, Marjorie.

[MARJORIE *exits,* BERNICE *looks at herself again in the mirror. Suddenly she takes a suitcase from the closet, opens it, begins tossing things into it. She pulls a drawer from the dresser, dumps it upside down into the suitcase.*]

CUT TO

[BERNICE *licks an envelope, puts it on her pillow. It reads "Aunt Josephine." She is now dressed in a traveling suit.* BERNICE *opens the bureau drawer, takes out something that we don't see. Now she turns out the light and slips stealthily from her room.*]

51. INT. UPSTAIRS HALL. NIGHT.

Bernice tiptoes through the hall which is dark except for one night light. She reaches Marjorie's door, opens it quietly. The night light gives off just enough light so that we can see Marjorie, sound asleep in her bed. Bernice goes in.

52. INT. MARJORIE'S ROOM. NIGHT.

Now we see what Bernice has in her hand as she moves close to Marjorie's bed . . . a pair of scissors. Bending over the bed, she holds up one braid, snips it off. Next the second braid is deftly amputated.

53. EXT. HARVEY HOUSE. STREET. NIGHT.

Bernice, braids in one hand, suitcase in the other, slips out. She goes down the stairs, along the walk, until she reaches the sidewalk.

Her POV, Warren's house in the dim street light.

ON Bernice again. She is grinning. We stay with her as she crosses the street. Winding the braids up as if they were pieces of rope, she slings them onto Warren's porch. They fall with a slight thud.

Bernice laughs unexpectedly . . . as she sets off at a half-run down the moonlit street. In the distance, the lights of the city, the sound of a train whistle. Bernice hurries toward it.

INTERVIEW WITH JOAN MICKLIN SILVER

INT: Why do you think so many films have been made of works by F. Scott Fitzgerald? What's so appealing—the dialogue, the characters, the situations, the mythical quality in Fitzgerald?

SILVER: As a filmmaker I would never have been drawn to trying most of the things of Fitzgerald that have been filmed. What's beautiful about *The Great Gatsby* is the way he wrote it.

INT: The style.

SILVER: Yes. But I'd rather not try to put something like that on film. One reason I really enjoyed this project is that "Bernice Bobs Her Hair" is a minor story written when Fitzgerald was very young, written for a popular magazine. It is a charming story, with a nice narrative line, and I didn't have to have that sort of reverential attitude one ends up having toward a master work. I wanted to capture certain Fitzgeraldian themes and characters, but "Bernice" is a kind of charming trifle and I never had the feeling I might be doing something damaging or unfaithful to Fitzgerald.

INT: What else attracted you to it?

SILVER: Well, it gave me the opportunity to make a stylish little comedy.

INT: Had you done a comedy before?

SILVER: No. I would consider *Hester Street* a comedy in the sense of the classic definitions of tragedy and comedy, but it's very different. In "Bernice" there's such a tremendous amount of humor and good will toward the

---

Joan Micklin Silver's first feature film was the highly successful *Hester Street*, which she wrote and directed after learning her craft as writer-director of a number of short films. Most recently she has directed the contemporary comedy, *Between the Lines*. This interview was conducted by Calvin Skaggs on April 19, 1977.

characters, and it's fun to work on something like that, something that has such a light, effervescent quality. It's hard to achieve on film, but that sort of effervescence was something I was trying to achieve, both in the summer-like quality of the way it looked and the way it felt and in the performances.

INT: What else appealed to you?

SILVER: Thematically, I'm obviously interested in the stories of women, in what they have done to themselves in the name of popularity.

INT: Could you talk about that a bit?

SILVER: Well, right up to the present time women have always been coached by their mothers and their aunts and their cousins and grannies, first how to attract and then how to capture the hearts of the males all about them. And if one were to add up all the energy that has been devoted to that particular endeavor, it probably would be enough to rebuild New York City. I grew up in the late '40s, early '50s, and certainly that sort of thing, silly as it seems from our vantage point now, was very much in vogue. There were all sorts of girls' magazines which coached you in how to behave on dates; talk about him, ask him questions, laugh at his jokes—that kind of stuff. As light and humorous as "Bernice" is, it shows how many women have that freight to unload. Also, I was very much taken by the character of Marjorie. She is obviously able and aggressive and assertive, but one knows she will end up doing nothing but throwing all this energy into things that will not be satisfactory to her in the end. One of the saddest parts about Fitzgerald's women is that they feel their highest moment comes when they are nineteen or twenty.

INT: As they're achieving the capture.

SILVER: Yes. It seemed to me, though, that those themes were there and would be apparent to a viewer without leaning on them. My own preference in style is understatement.

INT: Oh, they're clear, I think. One thing that's really interesting is that the year "Bernice" was published was the year that the Amendment allowing women to vote was signed by Congress. Yet I don't think Fitzgerald had any evaluative sense of the theme. The theme is there; he created it; but I don't think he took a value stance toward it.

SILVER: I don't either. It was the given. That is the way it was when I was young too. There was a certain schizophrenia about it, but it was the given: if you wanted to go to high-school proms, if you wanted to be popular, there was a certain way in which you had to behave. You either mastered that style, or you stayed home. I guess I was one of those schizophrenic teenagers that wanted to go to the prom but always had some part of me saying, "Pretty silly stuff!"

INT: What were the challenges you remember most in adapting the story into a script—as a writer, I mean, before the film was produced?

SILVER: Because I was also going to direct it and was aware of the budgetary limitations of the project, I was constantly thinking in terms of how to create a certain effect without the number of extras it would take, for instance, to reproduce the opening at the country-club dance. The story opens with a delightful description of the matrons up on the balcony peering over and commenting on the younger folks dancing below, and it seemed apparent that we did not have the budget to really stage that. So I decided we could perhaps get the same effect by going into all the corners showing what was going on—in the ladies' dressing room, on the porch, in the hallway outside of the dressing room, and so on—giving a sense of a great dance going on without having to hire a band and the many, many extra players necessary to stage such a dance.

INT: Did you do any research for the script? What sort of reading did you do?

SILVER: Far beyond what was necessary; it was my pleasure; I just enjoyed doing the research. I read the two Fitzgerald biographies and many of his letters and got one of the scene ideas from a letter to his younger sister, in which he discusses the pathetic look. There was some pictorial material to go through in the book that had just come out about the Fitzgeralds. And, of course, I reread *Zelda* and *Save Me the Waltz*—things I didn't have to do at all, except for the fun of it.

INT: Had you as a student read Fitzgerald?

SILVER: Oh, definitely. As a matter of fact, I had once taken this story to an educational film company, for which I wrote and directed the first films I made, to see if they would be willing to make it as a short film. But I got turned down. So it was for me a very happy coincidence that a story in which I had always been interested was a story that Learning in Focus wanted to do.

INT: Would you compare the difference between dramatizing a short story into a feature, as in *Hester Street*, and into a short film, as in *Bernice Bobs Her Hair*. What is the difference in the way you work, both as writer and as director?

SILVER: Well, *Hester Street* was based on a novella, a very long story, and had much more incident and much more material. It was not really a short story. So there was that difference to begin with. But with all the projects that I have worked on so far—*Hester Street* and *Bernice* and *Between the Lines*—the materials seemed infinitely capable of expansion. I could have gone on and written many more scenes, I know. But, you know, we used to joke around on the set about writing a sequel called "Marjorie Goes to Eau Claire." I would have felt quite up to it, but I would have needed lots more happening. Other themes.

INT: One thing people often remark about *Bernice*, is the degree to which all the minor characters have a kind of individuality. How did you manage this?

SILVER: I would give a lot of credit to casting. We were very lucky with the cast. We were especially lucky because they became very close; they fell into those peer relationships that the story deals with; they liked each other on and off set. As a matter of fact, they hung around on the set even when they were not shooting, and they were just tremendously involved. They liked the material, and they got a kick out of it.

INT: How did you encourage their involvement?

SILVER: The whole responsibility of a director, I guess, is to create a feeling on the set and during rehearsals that makes the actors feel very comfortable and very alive, makes them feel that they may indeed fall backwards because you will catch them. That is to say, they can try things. One of the nice moments in the film is one between Roberta and Charley Paulson when he asks her to put on another record so he can have a dance with Bernice. While we were waiting for another set-up, they came to me and told me what they had developed, and I made some suggestions. And suddenly we had a wonderful little moment. I think that happened because the actors felt they were part of it. Some directors work differently. They don't want that sort of thing from the actor. They want to stay with what they have sketched out in their minds or stay with the script, but I always prefer to work that way.

INT: By encouraging improvisation, you mean.

SILVER: Yes. Another example of what a lovely moment can happen is the car scene between Bernice and Warren. Early on it was quite clear to me that Shelley (Duvall) and Bud (Cort) played very well together and that we would be missing a wonderful opportunity not to have them do an extended scene together. So you and I went to my room at the Ramada Inn, with our tape-recorder, and had Bud and Shelley do several improvisations, out of which we plucked a really nice scene. I love the scene. Part of working this way is having actors who are comfortable doing this, and many good actors are not.

INT: They want to stick to the script.

SILVER: Definitely. In fact, they're thrown if you ask them to make the slightest changes.

INT: Do you use improvisation in other ways? Can it help keep the actors' energy up or the characters fresh and vital?

SILVER: Well, one thing I would always do on this film—and I don't quite know what made me do it—was that just before an actor was to shoot a scene I would begin to talk to him as though he were his character. That is to say, I would be addressing Bud as Warren, and I would ask him questions that had really nothing to do with the script. I might say, "Warren, you never mentioned your mother. How is she?" And he would begin to think as Warren about how his mother was. So that by the time they came to doing the scene, they felt very much in their characters already. By the time things have been rehearsed and blocked and the lighting changed and so on, any actor may be tired or he may not be as fresh with the material as he may have been when he was first looking at it, so this is a way to continue to reinvigorate the actor.

INT: How do you control the improvisation? What sets its boundaries?

SILVER: Actors can be the most inventive, the most creative, can do the most imaginative things, and I think I love the art of acting as much as I love anything in the world. But actors are not screenwriters. They really must have a clearly written character at the beginning. Of course, the director has the usual problem of how to combine different acting styles to make it all one seamless thing. That is a constant.

INT: It's part of the job.

SILVER: Exactly. I've always said that directing in the end is a matter of making choices. And one has to find a way to let an actor know that this thing he thought of is a good idea. And this one isn't. Yet, in fact, it's only my judgment. Someone's judgment has to prevail, and it's the director's.

INT: Let's talk about the structure of both the story and the film. What has always interested me is that it really has two kinds of dramatic movement, in the same direction. One is the training of Bernice, after you get the character convinced that she has to be trained; another is the triumph of Bernice. And what I think the film does beautifully is to develop both of those just to the right degree. Was keeping both interesting a challenge? Did one tend to become more important than the other?

SILVER: Fitzgerald gives very good hints in the story about ways to avoid such a problem. That is, all the while Marjorie is training Bernice, she is managing to let Bernice know that she (Marjorie) does not need that sort of assistance. This gives the audience a little extra motivation to want to see Bernice triumph.

INT: What was the most difficult sequence in the film?

SILVER: Well, the barber shop was difficult because we had a lot to shoot and only one day to shoot it in. Another hard scene to shoot, certainly, was the scene in which Marjorie teaches Bernice to dance, because of the problems of talking while they dance. And we didn't play music because I wanted to be able to cut. So they were dancing to a sort of rhythm in their own minds and had to sustain a certain beat so that, in fact, I could cut from one thing to another.

INT: Was the dance scene between Bernice and the various boys just as difficult?

SILVER: Yes, indeed it was, because there were more things going on. But we were often so lucky. Recently I was thinking about how budgetary limitations can be an advantage, in a way. A very good dancer and choreographer named Gilda Mullette came to my house to teach me how to do the One-Step, the dance used in the film. Naturally I thought how much fun it would've been to take her with us. She would have drilled the actors, and they would have done that One-Step quite well. But by the time it was sifted through me and I taught them what I remembered Gilda had taught me, somehow the dance seemed a little funnier and a little less professional and less perfect and I think in the long run, more appropriate.

INT: Much more natural.

SILVER: Yes.

INT: More like different kids learning the same dance in different ways rather than all being choreographed.

SILVER: Yes.

INT: Let's talk a bit about the ending, the cutting of Marjorie's hair. It always surprises audiences, but they don't feel it's a trick.

SILVER: By that time you really want Bernice to have her small triumph. We always talked about what happened at the barber shop as being a sort of joke that goes too far. Marjorie actually does go up to Bernice and say she doesn't have to go through with it. But by that time Bernice feels she does have to go through with it, and I think you sort of want her to. One doesn't quite know how Bernice feels. She seems very distraught at the barber shop. But we are not quite sure. We know she is upset, but she is not devastated obviously. There is something a little bit mysterious about it. She says it's all right; I like it now; it doesn't matter. That sort of thing, which seemed to be a better way to lead into what happens.

INT: How do you keep that ending from seeming vindictive?

SILVER: It depends upon how you feel about human emotion. To me those are human things. If you decide to get back at someone who has made you feel unhappy and ridiculous, that's human. And I don't see any reason why people should only be portrayed in their glory. They also have all sorts of other sides to them. I personally enjoy characters like that. That's my own taste in material.

INT: People sometimes want to talk about what happens to Bernice after the film. There's a sense that she is free. That she came into the story the least free person, while the other characters know what they are doing, where they are going, what they want. Yet when the film ends you feel that it is she who is freed by the whole experience and that it has been tremendously to her benefit.

SILVER: Bernice is very pleased because she attempted to learn how to do something, and she learned how to do it. So she feels a little sense of confidence. But there is also obviously a side of her that sees where all this leads.

INT: When you look at the film now, what pleases you most?

SILVER: I'm very proud of the cast. I like the look and the feel of the film. It is quite appropriate to the material.

INT: You had done period films before.

SILVER: Yes. I like doing period films, and I feel comfortable doing them.

INT: Had you ever shot a film before totally on location?

SILVER: No, and I never have since, and I loved it. Having all of us there together in Savannah, I think, gave the film a tremendous feeling of camaraderie, as evidenced by the fact that the cast and crew went out dancing nightly. I went back to my room to brood. I guess that is a directorial fault; I don't know. It must be my nature. Anyway, I love to do films with a strong sense of milieu, films that evoke a place and time, whether today or sometime in the past. One thing I liked about *Bernice* and *Hester Street* and *Between the Lines* is that in different ways each of them had a very specific world in which the action was taking place. I like to create that sense of a world. I think *Bernice* does that, and that's one of the things that pleases me most.

ON F. SCOTT FITZGERALD and "BERNICE BOBS HER HAIR"

Matthew J. Bruccoli
Jeffries Professor of English
University of South Carolina

Francis Scott Key Fitzgerald (1896–1940) is one of the most compelling figures in American literature, and his reputation has taken dramatic turns. During his writing years—1920–1940—he was widely regarded as a promising novelist who squandered his talent in popular short stories and alcoholic dissipation. His masterpiece, *The Great Gatsby* (1925), had a disappointing reception; and his most ambitious novel, *Tender Is the Night* (1934), was a comparative failure. After the mental breakdown of his wife, Zelda, and his own "crack-up" in the 'thirties, Fitzgerald went to Hollywood as a screen writer. Following his death in 1940 he seemed forgotten. But in the 'fifties a remarkable revival began that eventually raised Fitzgerald to a position among the greatest American writers—where he belongs.

Fitzgerald and his work are identified with the nineteen twenties—which he named "The Jazz Age." It was a decade of reaction against the betrayed idealism of the First World War, of seemingly unlimited American prosperity, of striking social change, of "wonderful nonsense"—and a decade of brilliant achievement in American literature. It is instructive to consider the roster of American novelists whose work flourished in the 'twenties: Ernest Hemingway, William Faulkner, John Dos Passos, Sinclair Lewis, Ring Lardner, Thomas Wolfe—these are only the dominant names among the group.

More than any other American writer Fitzgerald personified the paradoxes of the 'twenties: He was both a celebrated participant in the festivities and a serious literary craftsman. Although he is identified with the expatriate movement because of his extended residence in France, he was not in fact involved in it as a writer. Fitzgerald was never an experimental artist, and he did not publish in the little magazines of Paris. His techniques were traditional, and he wrote for a large readership. In fact, the strongest influences on Fitzgerald's style were the English poets—especially Keats.

The chief qualities of Fitzgerald's work are his natural yet richly evocative style, his sharp observation of contemporary manners, his "heightened sensitivity to the promises of life," and—surprisingly—his capacity for moral judgment. Fitzgerald sat in judgment while chronicling the "greatest, gaudiest spree in history." To read his stories as expressing an uncritical worship of wealth, as is sometimes done, is to misread them. Although he wrote almost exclusively about middle- and upper-class people, he was a severe critic of them—showing how their lives failed to live up to their advantages. He undoubtedly admired the grace and charm of the very rich at their best, but there was a Puritan streak in Fitzgerald that made him sensitive to their lapses from sound conduct and failures of responsibility. In his best work he was one of the most American of American writers—keenly aware of America's history and deeply committed to American ideals and aspirations. However, most good fiction succeeds in terms of character—not ideas—and Fitzgerald added a roster of enduring characters to our literature. He also gave permanence to a whole generation of young people like those in "Bernice Bobs Her Hair."

In the fall of 1919 while awaiting publication of his first novel, *This Side of Paradise*, Fitzgerald wrote a long story he called "Barbara Bobs Her Hair." After this story was declined by several magazines, he shortened it, injected "a snappy climax," and retitled it. "Bernice Bobs Her Hair" was one of six Fitzgerald stories bought by *The Saturday Evening Post* in 1920, appearing in the issue of May 1, 1920.

Fitzgerald admittedly wrote his short stories for money, but they were not just hack-work. They were written for a highly competitive magazine market, and he took great pains with them. Moreover, the stories draw on much the same material as the novels. One of the qualities of Fitzgerald's early fiction is that it takes the concerns of youth with utter seriousness. He did not patronize his young people, for he understood that their games were played in deadly earnest. The result is that while Booth Tarkington's Penrod now seems merely cute, Bernice and her companions are still believable.

One of the reasons why Fitzgerald has been called "The Laureate of the Jazz Age" is because of his achievement as a social historian. Acutely sensitive to the moods and values of his time, he was a master of selective detail. "Bernice Bobs Her Hair" tells us as much about manners and morals, class and caste, in the Midwest after the First World War as a shelf of sociology texts. It was a time when a young woman's chief ambition was to marry well, when her popularity seemed the promise of a prosperous marriage. The popular girls in Fitzgerald's stories understand that they are arranging for the rest of their lives, and they can be quite practical about love and courtship. It was also a time of what now seems like colossal innocence. The young men regarded success in college as preparation for success in life—and they defined success largely in terms of money. Today's readers will find no evidence that Fitzgerald's young people were concerned about "relevant" problems.

The source for "Bernice Bobs Her Hair" can be seen in the detailed instructions for achieving popularity that Fitzgerald—then a Princeton undergraduate—wrote for his younger sister Annabel around 1917:

"You are as you know, not a good conversationalist and you might very naturally ask 'What do boys like to talk about?' Boys like to talk about themselves—much more than girls. Here are some leading questions for a girl to use. . . . (a) You dance so much better than you did last year. (b) How about giving me that sporty necktie when you're thru with it? (c) You've got the longest eyelashes! (This will embarrass him, but he likes it.) (d) I hear you've got a 'line'! (e) Well who's your latest crush? *Avoid* (a) When do you go back to school? (b) How long have you been home? (c) It's warm or the orchestra's good or the floor's good. . . ."

The story-line of "Bernice Bobs Her Hair" combines two familiar plot ideas: the master excelled by the pupil, and the trickster tricked. Marjorie, who prides herself on being hard (she thinks of it as being realistic), trains a prodigy who learns the lessons of popularity too well. Not only does Bernice rival Marjorie at her own game, but she ultimately proves to be as hard as her teacher. When Marjorie attempts to humiliate Bernice, in order to rid herself of the threat to her social domination that Bernice has become, Bernice is capable of striking back. Perhaps Marjorie never fully realized what she was up against, for at the end of the story Fitzgerald ironically suggests that Bernice has reverted to what Marjorie has jokingly called her "crazy Indian blood." The last words Bernice speaks after shearing Marjorie's braids are: "Scalp the selfish thing!"

"Bernice Bobs Her Hair" is not one of Fitzgerald's greatest stories, although it is one of his most popular. It was written as an entertainment. But even in an obviously commercial form, Fitzgerald's work passes the tests of his best fiction: the characters are convincing; the social details are right; there is a current of ideas; and the prose is wonderfully readable.

SUGGESTIONS FOR FURTHER READING

By F. Scott Fitzgerald:

This Side of Paradise. New York: Scribners, 1920.

Flappers and Philosophers. New York: Scribners, 1920.

The Beautiful and Damned. New York: Scribners, 1922.

Tales of the Jazz Age. New York: Scribners, 1922.

The Great Gatsby. New York: Scribners, 1925.

All the Sad Young Men. New York: Scribners, 1926.

Tender Is the Night. New York: Scribners, 1934.

Taps at Reveille. New York: Scribners, 1935.

The Last Tycoon. New York: Scribners, 1941.

About F. Scott Fitzgerald:

Andrew Turnbull, *Scott Fitzgerald*. New York: Scribners, 1962.

The Letters of F. Scott Fitzgerald, ed. Andrew Turnbull. New York: Scribners, 1963.

Scottie Fitzgerald Smith, Matthew J. Bruccoli & Joan P. Kerr, *The Romantic Egoists: A Pictorial Autobiography of F. Scott and Zelda Fitzgerald*. New York: Scribners, 1974.

SOLDIER'S HOME

by Ernest Hemingway

Krebs went to the war from a Methodist college in Kansas. There is a picture which shows him among his fraternity brothers, all of them wearing exactly the same height and style collar. He enlisted in the Marines in 1917 and did not return to the United States until the second division returned from the Rhine in the summer of 1919.

There is a picture which shows him on the Rhine with two German girls and another corporal. Krebs and the corporal look too big for their uniforms. The German girls are not beautiful. The Rhine does not show in the picture.

By the time Krebs returned to his home town in Oklahoma the greeting of heroes was over. He came back much too late. The men from the town who had been drafted had all been welcomed elaborately on their return. There had been a great deal of hysteria. Now the reaction had set in. People seemed to think it was rather ridiculous for Krebs to be getting back so late, years after the war was over.

At first Krebs, who had been at Belleau Wood, Soissons, the Champagne, St. Mihiel and in the Argonne did not want to talk about the war at all. Later he felt the need to talk but no one wanted to hear about it. His town had heard too many atrocity stories to be thrilled by actualities. Krebs found that to be listened to at all he had to lie, and after he had done this twice he, too, had a reaction against the war and against talking about it. A distaste for everything that had happened to him in the war set in because of the lies he had told. All of the times that had been able to make him feel cool and clear inside himself when he thought of them; the times so long back when he had done the one thing, the only thing for a man to do, easily and naturally, when he might have done something else, now lost their cool, valuable quality and then were lost themselves.

His lies were quite unimportant lies and consisted in

attributing to himself things other men had seen, done or heard of, and stating as facts certain apocryphal incidents familiar to all soldiers. Even his lies were not sensational at the pool room. His acquaintances, who had heard detailed accounts of German women found chained to machine guns in the Argonne forest and who could not comprehend, or were barred by their patriotism from interest in, any German machine gunners who were not chained, were not thrilled by his stories.

Krebs acquired the nausea in regard to experience that is the result of untruth or exaggeration, and when he occasionally met another man who had really been a soldier and they talked a few minutes in the dressing room at a dance he fell into the easy pose of the old soldier among other soldiers: that he had been badly, sickeningly frightened all the time. In this way he lost everything.

During this time, it was late summer, he was sleeping late in bed, getting up to walk down town to the library to get a book, eating lunch at home, reading on the front porch until he became bored and then walking down through the town to spend the hottest hours of the day in the cool dark of the pool room. He loved to play pool.

In the evening he practised on his clarinet, strolled down town, read and went to bed. He was still a hero to his two young sisters. His mother would have given him breakfast in bed if he had wanted it. She often came in when he was in bed and asked him to tell her about the war, but her attention always wandered. His father was non-committal.

Before Krebs went away to the war he had never been allowed to drive the family motor car. His father was in the real estate business and always wanted the car to be at his command when he required it to take clients out into the country to show them a piece of farm property. The car always stood outside the First National Bank building where his father had an office on the second floor. Now, after the war, it was still the same car.

Nothing was changed in the town except that the young girls had grown up. But they lived in such a complicated world of already defined alliances and shifting feuds that Krebs did not feel the energy or the courage to break into it. He liked to look at them, though. There were so many good-looking young girls. Most of them had their hair cut short. When he went away only little girls wore their hair like that or girls that were fast. They all wore sweaters and shirt waists with round Dutch collars. It was a pattern. He liked to look at them from the front porch as they walked on the other side of the street. He liked to watch them walking under the shade of the trees. He liked the round Dutch collars above their sweaters. He liked their silk stockings and flat shoes. He liked their bobbed hair and the way they walked.

When he was in town their appeal to him was not very strong. He did not like them when he saw them in the Greek's ice cream parlor. He did not want them themselves really. They were too complicated. There was something else. Vaguely he wanted a girl but he did not want to have to work to get her. He would have liked to have a girl but he did not want to have to spend a long time getting her. He did not want to get into the intrigue and the politics. He did not want to have to do any courting. He did not want to tell any more lies. It wasn't worth it.

He did not want any consequences. He did not want any consequences ever again. He wanted to live along without consequences. Besides he did not really need a girl. The army had taught him that. It was all right to pose as though you had to have a girl. Nearly everybody did that. But it wasn't true. You did not need a girl. That was the funny thing. First a fellow boasted how girls mean nothing to him, that he never thought of them, that they could not touch him. Then a fellow boasted that he could not get along without girls, that he had to have them all the time, that he could not go to sleep without them.

That was all a lie. It was all a lie both ways. You did not need a girl unless you thought about them. He learned that in the army. Then sooner or later you always got one. When you were really ripe for a girl you always got one. You did not have to think about it. Sooner or later it would come. He had learned that in the army.

Now he would have liked a girl if she had come to him and not wanted to talk. But here at home it was all too complicated. He knew he could never get through it all again. It was not worth the trouble. That was the thing about French girls and German girls. There was not all this talking. You couldn't talk much and you did not need to talk. It was simple and you were friends. He thought about France and then he began to think about Germany. On the whole he had liked Germany better. He did not want to leave Germany. He did not want to come home. Still, he had come home. He sat on the front porch.

He liked the girls that were walking along the other side of the street. He liked the look of them much better than the French girls or the German girls. But the world they were in was not the world he was in. He would like to have one of them. But it was not worth it. They were such a nice pattern. He liked the pattern. It was exciting. But he would not go through all the talking. He did not want one badly enough. He liked to look at them all, though. It was not worth it. Not now when things were getting good again.

He sat there on the porch reading a book on the war. It was a history and he was reading about all the engagements he had been in. It was the most interesting reading he had ever done. He wished there were more maps. He looked forward with a good feeling to reading all the really good histories when they would come out with good detail maps. Now he was really learning about the war. He had been a good soldier. That made a difference.

One morning after he had been home about a month his mother came into his bedroom and sat on the bed. She smoothed her apron.

"I had a talk with your father last night, Harold," she said, "and he is willing for you to take the car out in the evenings."

"Yeah?" said Krebs, who was not fully awake. "Take the car out? Yeah?"

"Yes. Your father has felt for some time that you should be able to take the car out in the evenings whenever you wished but we only talked it over last night."

"I'll bet you made him," Krebs said.

"No. It was your father's suggestion that we talk the matter over."

"Yeah. I'll bet you made him," Krebs sat up in bed.

"Will you come down to breakfast, Harold?" his mother said.

"As soon as I get my clothes on," Krebs said.

His mother went out of the room and he could hear her frying something downstairs while he washed, shaved and dressed to go down into the dining-room for breakfast. While he was eating breakfast his sister brought in the mail.

"Well, Hare," she said. "You old sleepy-head. What do you ever get up for?"

Krebs looked at her. He liked her. She was his best sister.

"Have you got the paper?" he asked.

She handed him *The Kansas City Star* and he shucked off its brown wrapper and opened it to the sporting page. He folded *The Star* open and propped it against the water pitcher with his cereal dish to steady it, so he could read while he ate.

"Harold," his mother stood in the kitchen doorway, "Harold, please don't muss up the paper. Your father can't read his *Star* if it's been mussed."

"I won't muss it," Krebs said.

His sister sat down at the table and watched him while he read.

"We're playing indoor over at school this afternoon," she said. "I'm going to pitch."

"Good," said Krebs. "How's the old wing?"

"I can pitch better than lots of the boys. I tell them all you taught me. The other girls aren't much good."

"Yeah?" said Krebs.

"I tell them all you're my beau. Aren't you my beau, Hare?"

"You bet."

"Couldn't your brother really be your beau just because he's your brother?"

"I don't know."

"Sure you know. Couldn't you be my beau, Hare, if I was old enough and if you wanted to?"

"Sure. You're my girl now."

"Am I really your girl?"

"Sure."

"Do you love me?"

"Uh, huh."

"Will you love me always?"

"Sure."

"Will you come over and watch me play indoor?"

"Maybe."

"Aw, Hare, you don't love me. If you loved me, you'd want to come over and watch me play indoor."

Kreb's mother came into the dining-room from the

kitchen. She carried a plate with two fried eggs and some crisp bacon on it and a plate of buckwheat cakes.

"You run along, Helen," she said. "I want to talk to Harold."

She put the eggs and bacon down in front of him and brought in a jug of maple syrup for the buckwheat cakes. Then she sat down across the table from Krebs.

"I wish you'd put down the paper a minute, Harold," she said.

Krebs took down the paper and folded it.

"Have you decided what you are going to do yet, Harold?" his mother said, taking off her glasses.

"No," said Krebs.

"Don't you think it's about time?" His mother did not say this in a mean way. She seemed worried.

"I hadn't thought about it," Krebs said.

"God has some work for every one to do," his mother said. "There can be no idle hands in His Kingdom."

"I'm not in His Kingdom," Krebs said.

"We are all of us in His Kingdom."

Krebs felt embarrassed and resentful as always.

"I've worried about you so much, Harold," his mother went on. "I know the temptations you must have been exposed to. I know how weak men are. I know what your own dear grandfather, my own father, told us about the Civil War and I have prayed for you. I pray for you all day long, Harold."

Krebs looked at the bacon fat hardening on his plate.

"Your father is worried, too," his mother went on. "He thinks you have lost your ambition, that you haven't got a definite aim in life. Charley Simmons, who is just your age, has a good job and is going to be married. The boys are all settling down; they're all determined to get somewhere; you can see that boys like Charley Simmons are on their way to being really a credit to the community."

Krebs said nothing.

"Don't look that way, Harold," his mother said. "You know we love you and I want to tell you for your own good how matters stand. Your father does not want to hamper your freedom. He thinks you should be allowed to drive the car. If you want to take some of the nice girls out riding with you, we are only too pleased. We want you to enjoy yourself. But you are going to have to settle down to work, Harold. Your father doesn't care what you start in at. All work is honorable as he says. But you've got to make a start at something. He asked me to speak to you this morning and then you can stop in and see him at his office."

"Is that all?" Krebs said.

"Yes. Don't you love your mother, dear boy?"

"No," Krebs said.

His mother looked at him across the table. Her eyes were shiny. She started crying.

"I don't love anybody," Krebs said.

It wasn't any good. He couldn't tell her, he couldn't make her see it. It was sillly to have said it. He had only hurt her. He went over and took hold of her arm. She was crying with her head in her hands.

"I didn't mean it," he said. "I was just angry at something. I didn't mean I didn't love you."

His mother went on crying. Krebs put his arm on her shoulder.

"Can't you believe me, mother?"

His mother shook her head.

"Please, please, mother. Please believe me."

"All right," his mother said chokily. She looked up at him. "I believe you, Harold."

Krebs kissed her hair. She put her face up to him.

"I'm your mother," she said. "I held you next to my heart when you were a tiny baby."

Krebs felt sick and vaguely nauseated.

"I know, Mummy," he said. "I'll try and be a good boy for you."

"Would you kneel and pray with me, Harold?" his mother asked.

They knelt down beside the dining-room table and Krebs's mother prayed.

"Now, you pray, Harold," she said.

"I can't," Krebs said.

"Try, Harold."

"I can't."

"Do you want me to pray for you?"

"Yes."

So his mother prayed for him and then they stood up and Krebs kissed his mother and went out of the house. He had tried so to keep his life from being complicated. Still, none of it had touched him. He had felt sorry for his mother and she had made him lie. He would go to Kansas City and get a job and she would feel all right about it. There would be one more scene maybe before he got away. He would not go down to his father's office. He would miss that one. He wanted his life to go smoothly. It had just gotten going that way. Well, that was all over now, anyway. He would go over to the schoolyard and watch Helen play indoor baseball.

ERNEST HEMINGWAY'S *SOLDIER'S HOME*

*Screenplay by Robert Geller**

1. PROLOGUE. IN SEPIA.

Eight or ten young men are being huddled together for a fraternity picture. All dressed in high white collars. Most wear silver-rimmed glasses. Austere building in background. No laughter or chatter.

NARRATOR [*off camera*]. Krebs went to the war from a Methodist college in Kansas. There is a picture which shows him among his fraternity brothers. . . .

Photographer motions them to close ranks, and sheep-like they shuffle closer. One young man, Harold Krebs, stands slightly to the side and moves just a fraction after the command "hold it."

NARRATOR [*off camera*]. He enlisted in the Army in 1917. . . .

CUT TO

Photographer and "explosion" of his camera gun.

CUT TO

2. Stock footage of WWI, expository in nature, and of returning veterans. Not meant to editorialize about the war.

NARRATOR [*off camera*]. . . . and did not return to the United States until the second division returned from the Rhine in 1919.

---

* Robert Geller is the Executive Producer of The American Short Story series. In addition to other film scripts, he has written many articles on film, television, and other media.

3. EXTERIOR. DUSK.

Empty train depot in rural town. Krebs with duffle bag. Platform is deserted, with the exception of the station master and one passenger, neither of whom pays Krebs any attention.

Krebs crosses tracks deftly. Stops at depot to catch breath. Tattered signs flap in wind: "Buy U.S. Bonds," etc. At the front end of the platform a banner with "WELCOME HOME YANKS" droops limply from a worn cornice.

NARRATOR [*off camera*]. By the time Krebs returned to his home town the greeting of heroes was over. He came back much too late.

4. INTERIOR. NIGHT.

Dissolve to dining room of Krebs house. Dinner is over. Harold is still in uniform. Mr. and Mrs. Krebs and Marge hunt for words. There is no real jubilation or ease. Harold is lighting up. Faces of family watch.

MR. KREBS. Son . . . You smoke lots in battle? You seem to do it . . . naturally.

HAROLD. Not really . . . I just picked it up.

MARGE [*enthusiastic*]. Did you actually smoke, in the war, Hare? Didn't they see you lighting up? The Germans?

HAROLD. Uh . . . uh. We smoked mostly when we were bored.

MRS. KREBS. Bored! Little chance you had to be bored . . .

HAROLD. We were. I was. A lot of the time.

[*Silence. Ticking of clock. It is after 11:00 p.m.*]

MRS. KREBS. Harold, you must be tired . . . All that traveling. And we've asked so many questions.

HAROLD. I'm fine.

MR. KREBS. Well . . . it's gettin' late. I gotta go out in the county tomorrow. We'll get to talk . . . about what you wanna be doin'. Plenty of time.

HAROLD. Yes . . . I'll need a week or so . . .

MRS. KREBS. Of course. Let's just be thankful that you're home safe. Let us be thankful to our Dear Lord [*her eyes are raised*] that you're back home. Oh, Harold, we did pray for you. And each Sunday Reverend Nelson . . .

MR. KREBS [*interrupts with a yawn*]. Folks . . . I'm goin' up. Welcome home, Harold.

[*Mr. Krebs extends his hand.*]

HAROLD. Night, Dad . . . It was a fine dinner . . . Guess I'll go on up, too. [*He starts to follow* MR. KREBS *out.*]

5. INTERIOR. HALLWAY AT FOOT OF STAIRS.

MRS. KREBS [*to Harold at the foot of the stairs*]. Son . . . Marjorie and I could fix up a special breakfast. Serve it to you in bed. Remember when you had those awful winter coughs and . . .

HAROLD. Not tomorrow, Mom . . . I'll want to get up early, and . . .

MRS. KREBS. Hare?

HAROLD. Mom?

MRS. KREBS [*moves to hug him*]. Sleep well.

HAROLD [*stiffens, hugs her back*]. I will . . . thanks . . . for everything.

CUT TO

6. INTERIOR. NIGHT. HAROLD'S ROOM. DIMLY LIT. FLOWERED WALLPAPER.

Pan to boyhood mementos, which are sparse save for some scouting medals and a trophy for track & field. Harold unpacks. Looks at photo of college fraternity at Methodist school. Considers replacing it with picture of himself and another soldier with two coarse, older German women. The military uniforms are too large.

Krebs moves around his smallish room. Picks up the trophy and buffs it. Takes out a clarinet from a book shelf and slowly assembles it. Tinkers tentatively with some scales. Begins to undress and neatly pile clothes on chair near his bed. Cranks up his phonograph. It still works. He smiles. Climbs into bed with a record playing.

Krebs lights cigarette and leans on elbow, staring out at the quiet, empty streets.

MR. KREBS [*off camera*] [*knocking at Harold's door*]. Harold. Could you turn it down? It's late, and I need to be fresh and ginger tomorrow.

7. The following shots take place in one day, during which we get the feelings and rhythms of Harold being home contrasted against the rhythms of the town.

EXTERIOR. POV KREBS HOUSE. DAY. HAROLD'S WINDOW.

We see the shade, which is pulled half down with the tassle hanging. We hear the sound of footsteps on the porch and the rattling of bottles as the milkman puts the milk on the porch and takes the old bottles.

CUT TO

INTERIOR. HAROLD'S BEDROOM. DAY.

Close-up of Harold's face. He's lying awake in bed listening to the sounds of the milkman. He's been up for a while.

CUT TO

INTERIOR/EXTERIOR. HAROLD'S WINDOW. DAY.

Harold moves into frame, raises the shade, then looks down, out the window. Then Harold's face, CU. Then the sound of a factory whistle in the distance.

EXTERIOR. KREBS HOUSE. DAY.

Harold's POV. Looking down at the milkman walking away from the house carrying empty bottles away in a rack.

EXTERIOR. KREBS PORCH AND HOUSE. DAY.

Harold has a cup of coffee. He's wearing his army overcoat to protect him against the morning cold. Sits on the edge of the step and leans back against the pillar. Lights up a cigarette. The early morning sun comes through the trees.

Then the procession of men going to work begins. Through the bushes and through the empty spaces between the trees, Harold sees the working-class men of the town on their way to the factory. The procession begins with only a few, but builds in tempo as it gets closer to the hour to be in the factory. Then a few stragglers, and then it is quiet again.

Some of the images we see are two men walking carrying lunch pails. A third man behind them runs to catch up with them, and they then walk on together. Some of the figures are partially masked—seen through the screen of bushes—so we PAN with them, seeing their lunch pails swinging and their footsteps on the pavement.

A car goes by carrying some workmen. The sounds of other cars are heard going to work and their image/presence is suggested in the movement of Harold's eyes as they go by up the street. As the procession ends, in the distance the sound of the factory whistle, which heralds the start of the day's work.

The newspaper boy throws the newspaper up the walk, and Harold picks it up.

INTERIOR. HAROLD'S BEDROOM. DAY. POVs.

A series of images of Harold follow that suggest his day, to be punctuated with some activities that take place around him, such as:

A. Marge leaves for school, maybe picked up by another girl.
B. Mr. Krebs's car leaves the house. (Perhaps this could occur earlier.)
C. Two church ladies come and pick up Mrs. Krebs. We hear their voices and see them walk away from the house.

INTERIOR. HAROLD'S ROOM. DAY.

Harold reads the sports page of the newspaper, smokes, rests, and plays his clarinet.

When Harold plays his clarinet, he plays some scales to reacquaint himself with the instrument. His playing at first is very tentative—he is feeling for the instrument and for his own voice, his own theme or melody. We would use his music as a means of expressing Harold's mood. The music creates a space for him separate from the world around him.

EXTERIOR. KREBS HOUSE. DAY.

As the day grows late, the activities are reversed. The factory whistle blows late in the day, and then we see the tracking feet again, now worn, tired, the men slump-shouldered, trailing off to their homes.

8. EXTERIOR. BRIGHT MORNING.

Harold walking to town. Is stopped by a prim old man.

MAN. Mornin', young Krebs. Welcome home. How long you back now?
HAROLD. It's two weeks, today.
MAN. Your folks said you had some very difficult times over there?
HAROLD. No . . . not that bad.
MAN. Anyhow, you must be glad to be home . . . Are you planning to go back to school?
HAROLD. No.
MAN. You going to be selling farm land with Dad? At the bank? It's a blessing when a man and his son can . . .
HAROLD [*edging away*]. 'Scuse me.
[HAROLD *walks on down street.*]
MAN. Well, I'll be! You'd think he'd killed the Kaiser. Even as a young boy . . .
[*They exit; their voices trail.*]

9. EXTERIOR. DAY.

Harold walks on to town. Nods back to few passersby who seem to remember him. Harold notices the young girls in town. He sees one through shop windows. He notices their pretty faces and the patterns that they make.

NARRATOR [*off camera*]. Nothing was changed in the town except that the young girls had grown up. There were so many good-looking young girls.

10. EXTERIOR. DAY.

Harold stops in front of bank where Mr. Krebs works as land agent.

NARRATOR [*off camera*]. Before Krebs went away to the war he had never been allowed to drive the family motor car. The car always stood outside the First National Bank building where his father had an office. Now, after the war, it was still the same car.

Harold crosses the street, walks past the car to the window of his father's office. He looks in.

REVERSE ANGLE of Mr. Krebs amiably chatting with young customers Harold's age. Offers cigar. Laughter and clapping of each other's shoulders. Harold stares for several seconds and then turns away, crossing the street quickly.

11. INTERIOR. DAY.

Signs indicate library room of YMCA. Harold is checking out books. Young male librarian, glasses, devoutly scrubbed, early 30s, is at check-out desk.

LIBRARIAN. Krebs. Are you Harold Krebs?

HAROLD [*startled*]. Yes. That's me!

LIBRARIAN. Don't you remember me? I'm Mr. Phillips. I was your youth group advisor in the lower grades.

HAROLD. Sorry. I was involved with these books.

LIBRARIAN. Are you an avid reader? Have you tried the new Booth Tarkington? I try to encourage good reading. [*The* LIBRARIAN *begins to notice the books* KREBS *has checked out.*]
My heavens. They're all books about the war. I should think that . . .

HAROLD. It helps to make sense out of things that happened. The maps and . . .

LIBRARIAN. But weren't you at Argonne? My Lord, the reports we received . . .

HAROLD [*eager to go*]. Thanks . . . I'd like them for two weeks, or longer. All right?

LIBRARIAN [*stiffly*]. Two weeks. That's all that's allowed. (*Pause.*) Krebs . . .

HAROLD [*begins to leave*]. Sir?

LIBRARIAN. Krebs . . . you might want to check the social calendar on the way out of the building. We hold socials and dances so that you young vets can catch up with community activities. This Saturday . . .

HAROLD [*looks uninterested*]. Thanks . . . I'll look. [HAROLD *exits.*]

CUT TO

12. INTERIOR. LATE AFTERNOON. SITTING ROOM.

Harold is absorbed in reading a book on the war. There is a map that he studies, trying to figure out the course of battle. Harold's mother comes in.

MRS. KREBS. I had a talk with your father last night, Harold, and he's willing for you to take the car out in the evenings.

HAROLD. Yeah? [*Still absorbed in his reading.*] Take the car out? Yeah?

MRS. KREBS. Yes. Your father has felt for some time you should be able to take the car out in the evenings whenever you wished but we only talked it over last night.

HAROLD. I'll bet you made him.

MRS. KREBS. No. It was your father's suggestion that we talk it over.

HAROLD. Yeah. I'll bet you made him.

MRS. KREBS. Harold . . . we'll be having dinner a little early this evening.

HAROLD. All right . . . Think I'll walk a little.

MRS. KREBS. Don't be late. I've cooked your favorite roast.

HAROLD [*mumbles*]. All right. [*Looks back as he leaves.*]

13. EXTERIOR. DAY.

Harold enters pool hall. [Close crop and only exterior of door is needed.]

CUT TO

14. INTERIOR. POOL HALL. COOL AND SHADED.

Proprietor is ex-pug. He and Harold shadow-box and exchange jabs. They say little. But Harold is at ease here as he picks up cue and chalks.

Harold looks relaxed and concentrates on each shot. Two younger boys admire his ease and relaxed style as he puts away each ball. He smokes casually.

FIRST BOY. Hey, Harold . . . betcha didn't get no time for pool in France . . . eh . . . didja?

[HAROLD *smiles benignly throughout their banter.*]

HAROLD. Nope, not much time for pool.

SECOND BOY. Hey . . . is it true you got home last 'cause they needed the best soldiers around to keep the Krauts in line?

[HAROLD *nods yes.* HAROLD *continues to pick off shots. Lets the ash on his cigarette grow precariously long. The younger boys edge closer, begging confidences. Smoke stings his eyes.*]

YOUNGER BOY. Hey, Harold . . . swear to the truth . . . Did you really kill Germans . . . right face to face . . . honest to God? With bayonets?

HAROLD [*nods*]. That's what we went there for. Not to see the Eiffel Tower.

[*They are silent, not wanting to break his concentration.*]

PROPRIETOR [*off camera*]. Gotta close up, Harold. Run 'em out—one, two, three—the way you always used ta . . .

NARRATOR [*off camera*]. At first Krebs did not want to talk about the war at all. Later he felt the need to talk but no one wanted to hear about it. Krebs found that to be listened to at all he had to lie, and after he had done this twice he, too, had a reaction against the war and against talking about it.

[HAROLD *sizes up the last shot. The proprietor and the younger boys huddle close behind.* HAROLD'S *eyes open wide and . . . Cut to cue ball as it explodes into last remaining ball and pushes it deftly into far pockets. Ex-pug and young boys nod in admiration.*

15. EXTERIOR. LATE AFTERNOON.

Krebs walks tall and the younger boys follow as worshippers. All, as silhouettes, pass the same crisp, white houses. They pass war monument. Their questions are heard as echoes. No other sounds but their voices.

FIRST BOY. Harold, is it true that they chained Kraut women to their machine guns for GIs to . . . you know . . . to . . .

SECOND BOY. Hey, Harold, did you bring any of them pictures back . . . you know . . . the French ones . . .

FIRST BOY. Harold, are the German women all that great? Denny's brother said all they want to do is make love to Americans . . . Don't matter where they do it, or the time of day . . .

SECOND BOY. Hey, Harold, can you come to the dance at the Y Friday? Cripes . . . everybody wants to talk to you, and the girls in town are waiting for you to give them a tumble. Might even be some hard liquor if you're in the mood . . .

[*All through these questions, there are no other sounds or street noises. It is meant to be a parade, a parodied ceremony for* HAROLD KREB'S *return. Shot almost as a dreamlike ceremony. The boys double-time like GIs to keep in step with their hero.*]

16. Same as preceding shot, but nearer to Krebs house. Harold begins to run. CU as he feels the joy of movement. Knows he's late for dinner, too.

Harold collides abruptly with young man. They both struggle for balance. The man is Charlie Simmons, tall and bulky, dressed in prosperous attire of an older businessman.

CHARLIE SIMMONS. Ouch . . . Hey, what's goin on . . .

HAROLD. Sorry . . . I wasn't looking.

CHARLIE [*recovering*]. Krebs! . . . Harold Krebs. When did you get back?

HAROLD. It's just two weeks now.

CHARLIE. You look fine, just fine.

HAROLD. Thanks.

CHARLIE. You workin' for your dad at the bank?

HAROLD [*hedging*]. Not yet.

CHARLIE. You lookin' for a permanent line of work?

HAROLD. Might be . . .

CHARLIE [*blocking* HAROLD'S *path with his bulk*]. I'm doing real well. Selling insurance. All the vets are interested and need the security. They know the future . . .

HAROLD. Makes sense.

CHARLIE. Think you'd be interested?

HAROLD. Buying some?

CHARLIE. Well . . . actually that, and maybe working with me on the selling part.

HAROLD. I'll think about it. I'm late for dinner. [*He begins to trot away.*]

CHARLIE. Hey . . . did you know I'm married now? Remember Edith Hanes? She was our class secretary and the prettiest gal in this whole town [*fishing for a compliment*].

HAROLD [*over his shoulder*]. Good luck, Charlie.

17. EXTERIOR. NIGHT OR VERY LATE AFTERNOON. KREBS PORCH.

Harold looks in window at his family at supper. All heads are bowed in grace. (The MOS of grace exaggerates the piety.) They finally finished the prayer. Mrs. Krebs nervously eyes the clock. Harold, resigned, walks in.

18. EXTERIOR. GREEK'S SODA SHOP. DAY.

Car pulls up in front of soda shop with Krebs driving. Harold gets out of car and looks in window. Sees the interior, decorated with decor of period. Marge and friends are having ice-cream sodas. They are exuberant as they "recreate" some incident from school [*in pantomime*].

Harold looks in, raps on window, and beckons Marge to come outside. She signals to Harold that she'll be out in one minute.

BILL KENNER [*off camera*]. Hey, Krebs . . . Harold Krebs . . .

[BILL KENNER: *early 20s. Dressed flamboyantly with bohemian dash. Sports cane with golden handle. He limps perceptibly into frame.*]

Remember me? William Kenner. Your fellow sufferer in geometry and Latin. C'mere, my lovelies.

[KENNER *waves to two teenagers, who obediently follow.*]

HAROLD. Sure . . . Bill Kenner. I remember you. You all right?

BILL KENNER [*with bravura*]. Sure . . . if losing a chunk of your knee on a mine is all right, then I'm just fine.

HAROLD [*embarrassed for the girls*]. That's . . . that's too bad. You seem to be doin' well though.

KENNER. Well . . . with lovelies like these, *pourquoi s'en faire?* . . . Am I right?

HAROLD [*edgy*]. I guess.

KENNER. You guess. Aren't we lucky to be alive? You know this little town had three killed? Lots of injured, too. In our graduating class alone . . .

HAROLD [*spots* MARGE]. Here . . . Right here, Marge.

KENNER. Is that lovely mademoiselle a Krebs?
[*bows*].
May I introduce myself?

MARGE. Let's go, Hare . . .

HAROLD. Well . . . goodbye, Bill.

KENNER [*not dissuaded*]. That your car?

HAROLD. My dad's.

KENNER. Splen-did work of art.

HAROLD. Thanks.

KENNER. Can you get it nights?

MARGE [*impatient*]. Har-old!

HAROLD. I guess so. Why.

KENNER. You busy this Friday?

HAROLD. Well . . . I'm not sure. Let me think about it. . . .

KENNER. Think about it! About what? Let's you and I live it up, my friend. [*Girls giggle.*] There's a dance at the Y. I might even have some gen-u-ine cognac. Come by at 8:00.

HAROLD. All right . . . I'll try.

KENNER. I'll *expect* you. [*Winks.*] Bye now.
[*To* MARGE]: Bye, lovely. See you on the Champs Elysées.
[*Tips his hat and limps away dramatically.* HAROLD *and* MARGE *drive away.*]

19. INTERIOR. NIGHT. LARGE ROOM OF YMCA.

Small crowd of fifteen to twenty is dwarfed by the place. Clusters of girls, some overly dressed and coiffed. Mr. Phillips, the librarian, and Mr. and Mrs. Charlie Simmons and chaperones are standing at punch bowl. Boys, some teenagers, busily sharing their own secrets and howling at their own jokes. Few couples are dancing.

Harold stands apart, remote from the activities, watching.

NARRATOR [*off camera*]. Vaguely he wanted a girl, but he did not want to have to work to get her. He did not want to get into the intrigue and politics . . .

[*We see the usual behavior of a dance. Boys egg on one of their fellows to ask a girl to dance. A girl moves away from a boy as he approaches to ask her for a dance—as if she is too busy. Another boy approaches a girl and then veers to another girl—the first thinking he was going to ask her. All of the little intrigues of the dance.*]

NARRATOR [*off camera*]. Besides, he did not really need a girl.

[KENNER *in dramatic cape and Tyrolian hat is "performing" for* ROSELLE SIMMONS, *who is flushed and heavily rouged.*]

NARRATOR [*off camera*]. You did not need a girl unless you thought about them.

[*She looks toward* HAROLD, *who is obviously bored. He walks toward the door and into hallway.* ROSELLE *follows.* HAROLD *lights a cigarette.*]

NARRATOR [*off camera*]. When you were really ripe for a girl you always got one. He had learned that in the army.

20. INTERIOR. HALLWAY.

Cases filled with trophies. Pictures of austere town philanthropist.

ROSELLE. Harold? Harold Krebs. [*For her, all conversation is a flirtation.*]

HAROLD. It's me.

ROSELLE. I'm Roselle, Roselle Simmons.

HAROLD. Charlie's sister . . . right?

ROSELLE. Why . . . heavens . . . have I changed all that much in two years?

HAROLD. Three years . . . actually.

ROSELLE. You don't seem to be having much fun at all.

. . . You haven't danced once. I've been spying on you.

HAROLD. Well, I'm not up to the steps . . . or all the chatter . . .

ROSELLE. You need to be taught. . . . Didn't your little sister Marge ever try? There are lots of new steps . . . I could teach you . . . It's my war effort . . . Trade for a smoke?

HAROLD [*doesn't offer her a cigarette*]. It's a waste of time. I never could get my feet straight . . .

ROSELLE. Silly . . . the feet are the easy part . . . it's the rest of your body . . . the way you lead . . . the way you hold your partner . . . I'll bet you like to command a girl . . .

HAROLD [*surprised*]. Command a girl . . . Why?

ROSELLE [*she leads to music*]. Command me, Mr. Harold Krebs . . .

HAROLD [*he responds slowly*]. Like this?

[*These scenes should be played slowly—moving from awkwardness to* HAROLD'S *own arousal and assertion.*]

ROSELLE [*Gently circling his arms around her. Emphasize physical aspects of their dancing*]. Just move one, two, three, four . . . get closer . . . Did you ever dance like this, with those foreign women?

[*Cuts to* HAROLD *dancing closer. Stroking her as he would the women he has known in Europe. The music stops, and* HAROLD *continues to caress her with sureness.*]

ROSELLE [*scared now*]. Don't . . . I've got to freshen up . . . I won't be long . . . All right? Wait out here . . . Don't!

HAROLD [*confused*]. Hey . . . Where're you going? C'mon back here, Roselle.

ROSELLE [*vampishly over her shoulder*]. Silly . . .

[ROSELLE *leaves.* HAROLD *continues to wait. The music begins. He is filled with a crushing sadness, a new confusion, a feeling of betrayal.*]

21. EXTERIOR. EVENING.

Krebs and Kenner are in the Krebs car parked out front of Kenner house.

Krebs and Kenner are getting drunk. They try to whisper, but talk loudly. Kenner is much louder in his speech and more slurred. The only real sign of drunkenness for Harold is that he's talking louder than usual and trying to tell the truth to Kenner.

KENNER. We shouldn't have left. It would've gotten better.
HAROLD. You should have stayed.
KENNER. That tart Roselle is really somethin'. Know what we'd do to girls like her in France? [*Long pause as* HAROLD *says nothing.*] Christ. What do you want to do? Just mope around forever? I can't figure you. Whenever I want to forget things, I just drink. Drink and find a woman.
HAROLD. I want to *remember*—the *good* things.
KENNER. Like being over there. Scared to death. Watching guys screamin' and bleeding to death.
HAROLD. I wasn't scared . . . not like you tell it.
KENNER. Damn . . . everybody was. Didn't you ever wake up in sweats and shivers? I used to put my blanket in my mouth and . . .
HAROLD [*shakes his head, no*].
KENNER. Well . . . I was scared. Everybody was.
HAROLD [*softly*]. That's a lie.
KENNER [*pretends not to hear*]. Everybody was. Only one thing is worth remembering over there.
HAROLD. Mmm . . .
KENNER. The damned women . . . No names or faces. Those white bodies, smelling like . . . like sweet apricots in those warm hotel rooms.
HAROLD. That isn't worth remembering.
KENNER. All right . . . all right. What is worth remembering?
HAROLD. Being a good soldier. Doing what you had to . . .
KENNER. Being a good soldier? You're crazy. You really are, Krebs.
HAROLD [*softly*]. And you lie, Kenner, about everything.
KENNER. Don't call me a liar.
HAROLD. It's not worth it.
KENNER. Shut up.
[*Kenner pulls the bottle from Harold, and almost falls out car door.*]
HAROLD. Hey . . . You all right?
KENNER [*getting out of car*]. Bastard . . . Crazy bastard. Stay away from me. I don't need a friend like you, Krebs. You spoil things.

[HAROLD *starts to follow Kenner.*]

HAROLD. Hey . . . wait! No! Go on. Go on, Kenner.

[KENNER *stumbles up front steps of his home.*]

22. INTERIOR. MORNING. HAROLD'S BEDROOM.

A knock on Harold's door. Harold wakes up. He feels miserable. His mother pokes her head in the door.

MRS. KREBS [*off camera*]. Will you come down to breakfast, Harold?

HAROLD. As soon as I get my clothes on.

23. INTERIOR. DINING ROOM. MORNING.

MARGE [*bringing in folded-up newspaper*]. Well, Hare, you old sleepy-head. What do you ever get up for?

[HAROLD *removes brown wrapper of newspaper and opens it to the sporting page. He folds* The Star *open and props it against the water pitcher with his cereal dish to steady it, so he can read while he eats.*]

MRS. KREBS [*standing in the kitchen doorway*]. Harold, please don't muss up the paper. Your father can't read his *Star* if it's been mussed.

HAROLD. I won't muss it.

MARGE [*sitting down*]. We're playing indoor over at school this afternoon. I'm going to pitch.

HAROLD. Good. How's the old wing?

MARGE. I can pitch better than lots of the boys. I tell them all you taught me. I tell them all you're my beau. Aren't you my beau, Hare?

HAROLD. You bet.

MARGE. Could your brother really be your beau if he's your brother?

HAROLD. I don't know.

MARGE. Sure you know. Couldn't you be my beau, Hare, if I was old enough and if you wanted to?

HAROLD. Sure.

MARGE. Am I really your girl?

HAROLD. Sure.

MARGE. Do you love me?

HAROLD. Uh, huh.

MARGE. Will you love me always?

HAROLD [*by now becoming impatient with* MARGE]. Sure.

MARGE. Will you come over and watch me play indoor?

HAROLD. Maybe.

MARGE. Aw, Hare, you don't love me. If you loved me, you'd definitely come over and watch me play indoor.

MRS. KREBS [*entering dining room*]. You run along. I want to talk to Harold. Harold . . . I wish you'd put down the paper a minute, Harold.

HAROLD [*glances at her, hard*]. Mmm . . .

MRS. KREBS. You acted shamefully last night. . . . The whole neighborhood could hear you, stumbling around out there.

HAROLD [*searches for the words*]. Sorry . . .

MRS. KREBS. Why? You have so much . . . our love . . . You have a fine mind and a strong body . . . Have you decided what you're going to do yet, Harold?

HAROLD. No.

MRS. KREBS. Don't you think it's about time?

HAROLD. I hadn't decided yet . . .

MRS. KREBS [*stands*]. God has some work for everyone to do. . . . There can be no idle hands in His Kingdom. . . .

HAROLD [*without malice*]. I'm not in His Kingdom. . . .

MRS. KREBS. We are all of us in His Kingdom. . . . Harold, please . . . I've worried about you so much . . . I know the temptations you must have suffered . . . I know how weak men are . . . I have prayed for you . . . I pray for you all day long, Harold . . .

[HAROLD *stares straight ahead at his food.*]

MRS. KREBS. Harold . . . your father is worried, too . . . He thinks you've lost your ambition, that you have no definite aim in life. The Simmons boy is just your age, and he's doing so well . . . The boys are all settling down . . . They're all determined to get somewhere. Boys like Charlie Simmons are on the way to being a credit to the community . . . all of them . . . You, too, Harold . . .

[MRS. KREBS *starts to get up. Shaken, she sits back down.*]

MRS. KREBS. Don't look that way, Harold . . . You know we love you, and I want to tell you, for your own good, how matters stand . . . Your father doesn't want to hamper your freedom . . . He thinks you should be allowed to drive the car . . . We want you to enjoy yourself . . . but you are going to have to settle down to work, Harold. . . . Your father doesn't care what you start in at . . .

All work is honorable as he says . . . but you've got to make a start at something . . . He didn't like . . . what you did last night . . . He asked me to speak to you this morning, and then you can stop in and see him at his office in the bank.

HAROLD [*gets up*]. Is that all, Mother? . . .

MRS. KREBS. Yes, don't you love your mother, dear?

HAROLD [*waits, not wanting to lie, just this once*]. No.

MRS. KREBS [*Her eyes grow shiny. She begins to cry*]. Oh . . . Harold . . .

HAROLD. I don't love anybody . . .

[MRS. KREBS *sits down.*]

HAROLD. I didn't mean it . . . I was just angry at something . . . I didn't mean I didn't love you . . . Can't you believe me? Please, Mother . . . Please believe me.

MRS. KREBS [*shakes her head, chokily*]. All right . . . I believe you, Harold. I'm your mother . . . I held you next to my heart when you were a tiny baby . . .

[*She presses his hand against her bosom.*]

HAROLD [*sick and vaguely nauseated*]. I know, Mom . . . I know . . . I'll try and be a good boy for you.

MRS. KREBS [*more controlled*]. Would you kneel and pray with me, Harold?

[HAROLD *and* MRS. KREBS *kneel beside the table.*]

MRS. KREBS. Now, you pray, Harold . . .

HAROLD. I can't . . .

MRS. KREBS. Try, Harold . . .

HAROLD. I can't . . .

MRS. KREBS. Do you want me to pray for you? . . .

HAROLD. Yes . . .

MRS. KREBS. Our dear heavenly Father . . .

CUT TO [over continuing prayers]

[HAROLD *stares straight ahead. Dissolves of* HAROLD *packing his battered trunk. Waiting at deserted bus or train depot and riding with face against window. Looking at flat, open lands. Dusk. Tracking shots.*]

[*Clarinet music grows louder. Up with parodied version of "When Johnny Comes Marching Home Again."*]

[*Cut to reverse angle of* MRS. KREBS *monotonously droning her prayer and* HAROLD *continuing to stare into space.*

Music fades. Freeze on HAROLD, *impassive.*]

NARRATOR [*off camera*]. He had tried to keep his life from being complicated. He had felt sorry for his mother and she had made him lie. He would go to Kansas City and get a job and she would feel all right about it. There would be one more scene maybe before he got away. He would not go down to his father's office. He would miss that one. He wanted his life to go smoothly. Well, that was all over now, anyway.

ON ERNEST HEMINGWAY and "SOLDIER'S HOME"

Earl Rovit
The City College of New York

Those few readers who leafed through Robert McAlmon's *Contact Collection of Contemporary Writers* in 1925 must have been bewildered by Ernest Hemingway's contribution, "Soldier's Home." The title would have brought to their minds a familiar enough American landmark: a large rambling building with broad splintering verandas, on the outskirts of town, surrounded by patches of ragged grass and sparsely occupied by Spanish-American War veterans, a few retired Western cavalrymen, and perhaps one or two ancient, deeply cherished ex-Civil War drummer boys. The Soldiers' Home was a peculiarly sentimental institution—like the pyramids of rusty cannonballs and the weathered memorial obelisk on the village green in the middle of town. In a nation that had never seriously felt the consequences of a foreign war, and one that possessed a very small Regular Army, the retired or invalided soldier was a highly marginal figure—almost a community mascot—to be hauled out for mock-martial display on patriotic occasions but otherwise ignored. From a practical viewpoint the ex-soldier was old or useless, and there was no place for him in the energetic America which was athletically dedicated to developing its industry and expanding its agriculture and commerce. At best, the Old Soldier was a convenient emblem for mawkish nostalgia and a stimulus for self-congratulation.

America's entry into the First World War and the massive wrench of disillusionment which followed it were to change our national attitudes not only to warfare and old soldiers, but also to the self-righteous Victorian mores of the American small town. Such shifts in deeply entrenched attitudes of this sort, however, are slow and grudging; and the attacks which threaten our deepest prejudices are likely to be met with hostility, ridicule, and honest confusion. In the decade that followed the war, those of our writers who were later to be admired as cultural ambassadors worthy of international renown had first to struggle against precisely this kind of resistance. Published just six years after the Armistice, Hemingway's "Soldier's Home" is a part of that barrage of stories, novels, plays, poems, and essays which dramatically challenged the value-system of a society that had been overly comfortable and pompously complacent in its manners and morals. Along with Hemingway's *In Our Time* (1925) and *The Sun Also Rises* (1926), we should also note, among others, Anderson's *Winesburg, Ohio* (1919), Dos Passos' *Three Soldiers* (1921), Cummings' *The Enormous Room* (1922), Eliot's *The Waste Land* (1922), Lewis' *Babbitt* (1922), Anderson and Stallings' *What Price Glory?* (1924), O'Neill's *Desire Under the Elms* (1924), Dreiser's *An American Tragedy* (1925), Fitzgerald's *The Great Gatsby* (1925), and Faulkner's *Soldier's Pay* (1926). Individually different, these works unite in mounting a firm adversary position against what they perceive to be the provincial shallowness, excessive materialism, repressiveness, and moral hypocrisy of conventional American life.

Like Harold Krebs in "Soldier's Home," Ernest Hemingway had returned to Oak Park, Illinois, in January, 1919, not yet twenty years old and still so disabled by the effects of a 420-calibre Austrian shell that he limped despite the aid of a cane. Undoubtedly drawing on his own experience in telling Krebs's story, Hemingway succeeded in moving the Old Soldiers' Home into the very center of the American community, as he confronted his readers directly with the problem of a youthful generation whose experience on the frontiers of violence had made unacceptable to them the easy pieties of YMCA sociality, the real-estate business, and the Sunday prayer meeting. The sardonic irony implicit in his title—the inherent opposition between a bucolic institution which is supported only by sentimental rhetoric and the emergence of a war-tempered generation which insisted that lies were too costly a price to pay for the boredom of stability—frames Hemingway's story and imparts a cutting edge to the inconclusive embarrassments of Krebs's homecoming.

It is a curious fact that although American literature presents many brilliant accounts of its young men going off to seek their fortunes, it has seldom chronicled the return of these heroes into the everyday rhythms and routines of social and domestic life. We are not permitted, after all, to find out what happens to Melville's Ishmael or Twain's Huck Finn or Crane's Henry Fleming after their exciting ordeals have come to an end. As a people we have been eager to insist on the primary significance of experience as a shaper of personality and a touchstone of value, but have judged such experience to be exclusively private in nature and strangely irrelevant or hostile to social norms. It is partly to this obsessive split between the social and the private that Hemingway's generation addressed themselves, and "Soldier's Home" is one of a handful of American stories (like Hawthorne's *The Scarlet Letter* and James's "The Jolly Corner") which returns the adventurer to his domestic hearth and delineates the desperate incompatibility between the now-changed hero and the old familiar environment which no longer quite fits him.

And it is appropriate that it should be Hemingway who presents this stark stalemate between a midwestern small town and its native war veteran. One of that extraordinarily talented group of American writers who came to maturity in the First World War—and, unlike Krebs, a highly acclaimed hero of that war—Hemingway was to become within a year or two after the publication of "Soldier's Home" the leading spokesman for The Lost Generation and the most influential figure among those who were demanding a new honesty and directness in life and art. Convinced that personal and public morality depended on an absolute integrity in the use of language, Hemingway had apprenticed himself to Ezra Pound and Gertrude Stein in Paris in the early 'twenties. His aspiration was to develop a prose style and a narrative technique which would hew closely to the truth of experience and, consequently, capture permanently the elusive reality of authentic emotional response. Instead of telling his reader how to feel, Hemingway aimed at so arranging the elements of the story that the reader would have no choice but to supply his own appropriate response.

To accomplish these ends Hemingway submitted his craft to a discipline of ruthless selectivity, discarding as unnecessary a good deal of what had been traditionally considered essential for plot and characterization. Further, he dispensed with editorializing and the kind of description which writers relied on to guide their readers' reactions. Employing short unadorned declarative sentences, a vocabulary purged of literary rhetoric, and exchanges of dialogue artfully flattened in tone, Hemingway tried to create objective dramatic images which would be indelible and evocative through their very power of understatement.

And temperamentally attracted to people who were, like himself, devoted to sports, Hemingway preferred subjects in which the physical skill and risk factors were of prime importance; thus he wrote of boxing, bullfighting, hunting, fishing, and—most especially—of war. Physical violence is almost always involved, or implied, in Hemingway's fiction, but rarely does the violence exist for the sake of sensational effects. Since he believed that the true measure of a man's worth lies in his capacity to face up to violence and cope with the wreckage left in its aftermath, Hemingway's treatment of violence is typically moral in its context. In his short stories and in novels like *A Farewell to Arms* (1929), *For Whom the Bell Tolls* (1940), and *The Old Man and the Sea* (1952), Hemingway projected a romantic image of heroic adventure which is almost unique in serious twentieth-century literature. The Nobel Prize Committee—awarding him the Literature Prize in 1954—called special attention to his "style-making mastery of the art of modern narration," justly reflecting the incalculable influence which his experimentation in technique has wielded throughout the world of letters. But equally important has been the life-style which his prose style was designed to express. The stoic restraint of his sentence rhythms, the tight-lipped determination of his characters to exhibit "grace under pressure," and the tempered faith that a kind of heroic individuality is possible in the technological and bureaucratic regimentation of modern life, have offered an exciting and plausible code of behavior to thousands of readers, directly challenging them to be honest, uncomplaining, and brave.

Although "Soldier's Home" dramatizes the irreconcilable ironies of Krebs's homecoming with telling effectiveness, readers have often been troubled by the ambiguities inherent in Hemingway's portrayal of his hero. So much is understated or left out in what the reader is allowed to see of Krebs that it is possible to infer radically different significances in his behavior. Some view his passivity as apathy or cowardice. Profoundly moved by his war experience, Krebs lacks the desire or the verve of spirit either to revolt effectively against, or to conform to, the rigid patterns of his home-town life. Others fail to see such a level of sensitive response in Krebs's behavior. They emphasize instead the genuine satisfaction which he took in performing his duties as an efficient fighting machine, and they interpret his inability to accommodate his military skills to a peaceful routine as a logical result of his training. If it is impossible to determine completely whether Krebs is a killer or a coward, too stubborn or not stubborn enough in maintaining his sense of self, the fault probably lies in Hemingway's over-reticence in his depiction of his character.

Certainly the story allows Krebs few options. If he remains at home, his necessary compromises with the demands of family and community life will force him to tell lies—"quite unimportant lies," in fact. These, in turn, will make him lose "the cool valuable quality" of his remembered experience; and if he can't trust in the truth of these experiences, he will then have lost everything. He can go to Kansas City for a job, but lacking a trade or professional ambitions, it is not clear how a new life and new job will safeguard the integrity of his sense of self. In Hemingway's world, only the professional has a chance to build a wall of rules and rituals around himself to ward off the venial mediocrity of the everyday world. The athlete, soldier, doctor, gambler, artist—these are some of the pursuits which Hemingway saw as potential refuges for the individual intent on retaining an autonomy and authority of spirit in modern society. Ultimately, however, Hemingway's concern in "Soldier's Home" is not so much with Krebs's character as it is with the poignant incompatibility between the ex-Marine who must live a lie if he wants to stay at home and the small town which cannot afford to have its conventional truths questioned. Oblique in its presentation, narrated in a deceptively dispassionate tone, the story makes a compelling statement about the problems that divide generations and people of different experience at an historical moment of massive and incomprehensible change.

SUGGESTIONS FOR FURTHER READING

By Ernest Hemingway:

In Our Time. New York: Scribners, 1925.

The Sun Also Rises. New York: Scribners, 1926.

A Farewell to Arms. New York: Scribners, 1929.

The First Forty-Nine Stories. New York: Scribners, 1938.

For Whom the Bell Tolls. New York: Scribners, 1940.

The Old Man and the Sea. New York: Scribners, 1952.

About Ernest Hemingway:

Baker, Carlos. *Hemingway: The Writer as Artist*. Princeton, N.J.: Princeton University Press, 1952.

Baker, Carlos. *Ernest Hemingway: A Life Story*. New York: Scribners, 1969.

Benson, Jackson J. *The Short Stories of Ernest Hemingway*. Durham, N.C.: Duke University Press, 1975.

ALMOS' A MAN

by Richard Wright

Dave struck out across the fields, looking homeward through paling light. Whut's the usa talkin wid em niggers in the field? Anyhow, his mother was putting supper on the table. Them niggers can't understan nothing. One of these days he was going to get a gun and practice shooting, then they couldn't talk to him as though he were a little boy. He slowed, looking at the ground. Shucks, Ah ain scareda them even ef they are biggern me! Aw, Ah know whut Ahma do. Ahm going by ol Joe's sto n git that Sears Roebuck catlog n look at them guns. Mebbe Ma will lemme buy one when she gits mah pay from ol man Hawkins. Ahma beg her t gimme some money. Ahm ol ernough to hava gun. Ahm seventeen. Almos a man. He strode, feeling his long loose-jointed limbs. Shucks, a man oughta hava little gun aftah he done worked hard all day.

He came in sight of Joe's store. A yellow lantern glowed on the front porch. He mounted steps and went through the screen door, hearing it bang behind him. There was a strong smell of coal oil and mackerel fish. He felt very confident until he saw fat Joe walk in through the rear door, then his courage began to ooze.

"Howdy, Dave! Whutcha want?"

"How yuh, Mistah Joe? Aw, Ah don wanna buy nothing. Ah jus wanted t see ef yuhd lemme look at tha catlog erwhile."

"Sure! You wanna see it here?"

"Nawsuh. Ah wans t take it home wid me. Ah'll bring it back termorrow when Ah come in from the fiels."

"You plannin on buying something?"

"Yessuh."

"Your ma lettin you have your own money now?"

"Shucks. Mistah Joe, Ahm gittin t be a man like anybody else!"

Joe laughed and wiped his greasy white face with a red bandanna.

"Whut you plannin on buyin?"

Dave looked at the floor, scratched his head, scratched his thigh, and smiled. Then he looked up shyly.

"Ah'll tell yuh, Mistah Joe, ef yuh promise yuh won't tell."

"I promise."

"Waal, Ahma buy a gun."

"A gun? Whut you want with a gun?"

"Ah wanna keep it."

"You ain't nothing but a boy. You don't need a gun."

"Aw, lemme have the catlog, Mistah Joe. Ah'll bring it back."

Joe walked through the rear door. Dave was elated. He looked around at barrels of sugar and flour. He heard Joe coming back. He craned his neck to see if he was bringing the book. Yeah, he's got it. Gawddog, he's got it!

"Here, but be sure you bring it back. It's the only one I got."

"Sho, Mistah Joe."

"Say, if you wanna buy a gun, why don't you buy one from me? I gotta gun to sell."

"Will it shoot?"

"Sure it'll shoot."

"Whut kind is it?"

"Oh, it's kinda old . . . a left-hand Wheeler. A pistol. A big one."

"Is it got bullets in it?"

"It's loaded."

"Kin Ah see it?"

"Where's your money?"

"Whut yuh wan fer it?"

"I'll let you have it for two dollars."

"Just two dollahs? Shucks, Ah could buy tha when Ah git mah pay."

"I'll have it here when you want it."

"Awright, suh. Ah be in fer it."

He went through the door, hearing it slam again behind him. Ahma git some money from Ma n buy me a gun! Only two dollahs! He tucked the thick catalogue under his arm and hurried.

"Where yuh been, boy?" His mother held a steaming dish of black-eyed peas.

"Aw, Ma, Ah jus stopped down the road t talk wid the boys."

"Yuh know bettah than t keep suppah waitin."

He sat down, resting the catalogue on the edge of the table.

"Yuh git up from there and git to the well n wash yosef! Ah ain feedin no hogs in mah house!"

She grabbed his shoulder and pushed him. He stumbled out of the room, then came back to get the catalogue.

"Whut this?"

"Aw, Ma, it's jusa catlog."

"Who yuh git it from?"

"From Joe, down at the sto."

"Waal, thas good. We kin use it in the outhouse."

"Naw, Ma." He grabbed for it. "Gimme ma catlog, Ma."

She held onto it and glared at him.

"Quit hollerin at me! Whut's wrong wid yuh? Yuh crazy?"

"But Ma, please. It ain mine! It's Joe's! He tol me t bring it back t im termorrow."

She gave up the book. He stumbled down the back steps, hugging the thick book under his arm. When he had splashed water on his face and hands, he groped back to the kitchen and fumbled in a corner for the towel. He bumped into a chair; it clattered to the floor. The catalogue sprawled at his feet. When he had dried his eyes he snatched up the book and held it again under his arm. His mother stood watching him.

"Now, ef yuh gonna act a fool over that ol book, Ah'll take it n burn it up."

"Naw, Ma, please."

"Waal, set down n be still!"

He sat down and drew the oil lamp close. He thumbed page after page, unaware of the food his mother set on the table. His father came in. Then his small brother.

"Whutcha got there, Dave?" his father asked.

"Jusa catlog," he answered, not looking up.

"Yeah, here they is!" His eyes glowed at blue-and-black revolvers. He glanced up, feeling sudden guilt. His father was watching him. He eased the book under the table and rested it on his knees. After the blessing was asked, he ate. He scooped up peas and swallowed fat meat without chewing. Buttermilk helped to wash it down. He did not want to mention money before his father. He would do much better by cornering his mother when she was alone. He looked at his father uneasily out of the edge of his eye.

"Boy, how come yuh don quit foolin wid tha book n eat yo suppah?"

"Yessuh."

"How you n old man Hawkins gitten erlong?"

"Suh?"

"Can't yuh hear? Why don yuh lissen? Ah ast yuh how wuz yuh n ol man Hawkins gittin erlong?"

"Oh, swell, Pa. Ah plows mo lan than anybody over there."

"Waal, yuh oughta keep yo mind on whut yuh doin."

"Yessuh."

He poured his plate full of molasses and sopped it up slowly with a chunk of cornbread. When his father and brother had left the kitchen, he still sat and looked again at the guns in the catalogue, longing to muster courage enough to present his case to his mother. Lawd, ef Ah only had tha pretty one! He could almost feel the slickness of the weapon with his fingers. If he had a gun like that he would polish it and keep it shining so it would never rust. N Ah'd keep it loaded, by Gawd!

"Ma?" His voice was hesitant.

"Hunh?"

"Ol man Hawkins give yuh mah money yit?"

"Yeah, but ain no usa yuh thinking bout throwin nona it erway. Ahm keepin tha money sos yuh kin have cloes t go to school this winter."

He rose and went to her side with the open catalogue in his palms. She was washing dishes, her head bent low over a pan. Shyly he raised the book. When he spoke, his voice was husky, faint.

"Ma, Gawd knows Ah wans one of these."

"One of whut?" she asked, not raising her eyes.

"One of these," he said again, not daring even to point. She glanced up at the page, then at him with wide eyes.

"Nigger, is yuh gone plumb crazy?"

"Aw, Ma—"

"Git outta here! Don yuh talk t me bout no gun! Yuh a fool!"

"Ma, Ah kin buy one fer two dollahs."

"Not ef Ah knows it, yuh ain!"

"But yuh promised me one—"

"Ah don care whut Ah promised! Yuh ain nothing but a boy yit!"

"Ma, ef yuh lemme buy one Ah'll *never* ast yuh fer nothing no mo."

"Ah to yuh t git outta here! Yuh ain gonna toucha penny of tha money fer no gun! Thas how come Ah has Mistah Hawkins t pay yo wages t me, cause Ah knows yuh ain got no sense."

"But, Ma, we needa gun. Pa ain got no gun. We needa gun in the house. Yuh kin never tell whut might happen."

"Now don yuh try to maka fool outta me, boy! Ef we did hava gun, yuh wouldn't have it!"

He laid the catalogue down and slipped his arm around her waist.

"Aw, Ma, Ah done worked hard alla summer n ain ast yuh fer nothin, is Ah, now?"

"Thas whut yuh spose t do!"

"But Ma, Ah wans a gun. Yuh kin lemme have two dollahs outta mah money. Please, Ma. I kin give it to Pa... Please, Ma! Ah loves yuh, Ma."

When she spoke her voice came soft and low.

"Whut yuh wan wida gun, Dave? Yuh don need no gun. Yuh'll git in trouble. N ef yo pa jus thought Ah let yuh have money t buy a gun he'd hava fit."

"Ah'll hide it, Ma. It ain but two dollahs."

"Lawd, chil, whut's wrong wid yuh?"

"Ain nothin wrong, Ma. Ahm almos a man now. Ah wans a gun."

"Who gonna sell yuh a gun?"

"Ol Joe at the sto."

"N it don cos but two dollahs?"

"Thas all, Ma. Jus two dollahs. Please, Ma."

She was stacking the plates away; her hands moved slowly, reflectively. Dave kept an anxious silence. Finally, she turned to him.

"Ah'll let yuh git tha gun ef yuh promise me one thing."

"Whut's tha, Ma?"

"Yuh bring it straight back t me, yuh hear? It be fer Pa."

"Yessum! Lemme go now, Ma."

She stooped, turned slightly to one side, raised the hem of her dress, rolled down the top of her stocking, and came up with a slender wad of bills.

"Here," she said. "Lawd knows yuh don need no gun. But yer pa does. Yuh bring it right back t me, yuh hear? Ahma put it up. Now ef yuh don, Ahma have yuh pa lick yuh so hard yuh won fergit it."

"Yessum."

He took the money, ran down the steps, and across the yard.

"Dave! Yuuuuh Daaaaave!"

He heard, but he was not going to stop now. "Naw, Lawd!"

The first movement he made the following morning was to reach under his pillow for the gun. In the gray light of dawn he held it loosely, feeling a sense of power. Could kill a man with a gun like this. Kill anybody, black or white. And if he were holding his gun in his hand, nobody could run over him; they would have to respect him. It was a big gun, with a long barrel and a heavy handle. He raised and lowered it in his hand, marveling at its weight.

He had not come straight home with it as his mother had asked; instead he had stayed out in the fields, holding the weapon in his hand, aiming it now and then at some imaginary foe. But he had not fired it; he had been afraid that his father might hear. Also he was not sure he knew how to fire it.

To avoid surrendering the pistol he had not come into the house until he knew that they were all asleep. When his mother had tiptoed to his bedside late that night and demanded the gun, he had first played possum; then he had told her that the gun was hidden outdoors, that he would bring it to her in the morning. Now he lay turning it slowly in his hands. He broke it, took out the cartridges, felt them, and then put them back.

He slid out of bed, got a long strip of old flannel from a trunk, wrapped the gun in it, and tied it to his naked thigh while it was still loaded. He did not go in to breakfast. Even though it was not yet daylight, he started for Jim

Hawkins' plantation. Just as the sun was rising he reached the barns where the mules and plows were kept.

"Hey! That you, Dave?"

He turned. Jim Hawkins stood eying him suspiciously.

"What're yuh doing here so early?"

"Ah didn't know Ah wuz gittin up so early, Mistah Hawkins. Ah wuz fixin t hitch up ol Jenny n take her t the fiels."

"Good. Since you're so early, how about plowing that stretch down by the woods?"

"Suits me, Mistah Hawkins."

"O.K. Go to it!"

He hitched Jenny to a plow and started across the fields. Hot dog! This was just what he wanted. If he could get down by the woods, he could shoot his gun and nobody would hear. He walked behind the plow, hearing the traces creaking, feeling the gun tied tight to his thigh.

When he reached the woods, he plowed two whole rows before he decided to take out the gun. Finally, he stopped, looked in all directions, then untied the gun and held it in his hand. He turned to the mule and smiled.

"Know whut this is, Jenny? Naw, yuh wouldn know! Yuhs jusa ol mule! Anyhow, this is a gun, n it kin shoot, by Gawd!"

He held the gun at arm's length. Whut t hell, Ahma shoot this thing! He looked at Jenny again.

"Lissen here, Jenny! When Ah pull this ol trigger, Ah don wan yuh t run n acka fool now!"

Jenny stood with head down, her short ears pricked straight. Dave walked off about twenty feet, held the gun far out from him at arm's length, and turned his head. Hell, he told himself, Ah ain afraid. The gun felt loose in his fingers; he waved it wildly for a moment. Then he shut his eyes and tightened his forefinger. Bloom! The report half deafened him and he thought his right hand was torn from his arm. He heard Jenny whinnying and galloping over the field, and he found himself on his knees, squeezing his fingers hard between his legs. His hand was numb; he jammed it into his mouth, trying to warm it, trying to stop the pain. The gun lay at his feet. He did not quite know what had happened. He stood up and stared at the gun as though it were a living thing. He gritted his teeth and kicked the gun. Yuh almos broke mah arm! He turned to look for Jenny; she was far over the fields, tossing her head and kicking wildly.

"Hol on there, ol mule!"

When he caught up with her she stood trembling, walling her big white eyes at him. The plow was far away; the traces had broken. Then Dave stopped short, looking, not believing. Jenny was bleeding. Her left side was red and wet with blood. He went closer. Lawd, have mercy! Wondah did Ah shoot this mule? He grabbed for Jenny's mane. She flinched, snorted, whirled, tossing her head.

"Hol on now! Hol on."

Then he saw the hole in Jenny's side, right between the ribs. It was round, wet, red. A crimson stream streaked down the front leg, flowing fast. Good Gawd! Ah wuzn't shootin at tha mule. He felt panic. He knew he had to stop that blood, or Jenny would bleed to death. He had never seen so much blood in all his life. He chased the mule for half a mile, trying to catch her. Finally she stopped, breathing hard, stumpy tail half arched. He caught her mane and led her back to where the plow and gun lay. Then he stooped and grabbed handfuls of damp black earth and tried to plug the bullet hole. Jenny shuddered, whinnied, and broke from him.

"Hol on! Hol on now!"

He tried to plug it again, but blood came anyhow. His fingers were hot and sticky. He rubbed dirt into his palms, trying to dry them. Then again he attempted to plug the bullet hole, but Jenny shied away, kicking her heels high. He stood helpless. He had to do something. He ran at Jenny; she dodged him. He watched a red stream of blood flow down Jenny's leg and form a bright pool at her feet.

"Jenny . . . Jenny," he called weakly.

His lips trembled. She's bleeding t death! He looked in the direction of home, wanting to go back, wanting to get help. But he saw the pistol lying in the damp black clay. He had a queer feeling that if he only did something, this would not be; Jenny would not be there bleeding to death.

When he went to her this time, she did not move. She stood with sleepy, dreamy eyes; and when he touched her she gave a low-pitched whinny and knelt to the ground, her front knees slopping in blood.

"Jenny . . . Jenny . . ." he whispered.

For a long time she held her neck erect; then her head

sank, slowly. Her ribs swelled with a mighty heave and she went over.

Dave's stomach felt empty, very empty. He picked up the gun and held it gingerly between his thumb and forefinger. He buried it at the foot of a tree. He took a stick and tried to cover the pool of blood with dirt—but what was the use? There was Jenny lying with her mouth open and her eyes walled and glassy. He could not tell Jim Hawkins he had shot his mule. But he had to tell him something. Yeah, Ah'll tell em Jenny started gittin wil n fell on the joint of the plow. . . . But that would hardly happen to a mule. He walked across the field slowly, head down.

It was sunset. Two of Jim Hawkins' men were over near the edge of the woods digging a hole in which to bury Jenny. Dave was surrounded by a knot of people, all of whom were looking down at the dead mule.

"I don't see how in the world it happened," said Jim Hawkins for the tenth time.

The crowd parted and Dave's mother, father, and small brother pushed into the center.

"Where Dave?" his mother called.

"There he is," said Jim Hawkins.

His mother grabbed him.

"Whut happened, Dave? Whut yuh done?"

"Nothin."

"C mon, boy, talk," his father said.

Dave took a deep breath and told the story he knew nobody believed.

"Waal," he drawled. "Ah brung ol Jenny down here sos Ah could do mah plowin. Ah plowed bout two rows, just like yuh see." He stopped and pointed at the long rows of upturned earth. "Then somethin musta been wrong wid ol Jenny. She wouldn ack right a-tall. She started snortin n kickin her heels. Ah tried t hol her, but she pulled erway, rearin n goin on. Then when the point of the plow was stickin up in the air, she swung erroun n twisted herself back on it . . . She stuck herself n started t bleed. N fo Ah could do anything, she wuz dead."

"Did you ever hear of anything like that in all your life?" asked Jim Hawkins.

There were white and black standing in the crowd. They

murmured. Dave's mother came close to him and looked hard into his face. "Tell the truth, Dave," she said.

"Looks like a bullet hole to me," said one man.

"Dave, whut yuh do wid the gun?" his mother asked.

The crowd surged in, looking at him. He jammed his hands into his pockets, shook his head slowly from left to right, and backed away. His eyes were wide and painful.

"Did he hava gun?" asked Jim Hawkins.

"By Gawd, Ah tol yuh that wuz a gun wound," said a man, slapping his thigh.

His father caught his shoulders and shook him till his teeth rattled.

"Tell whut happened, yuh rascal! Tell whut . . ."

Dave looked at Jenny's stiff legs and began to cry.

"Whut yuh do wid tha gun?" his mother asked.

"Whut wuz he doin wida gun?" his father asked.

"Come on and tell the truth," said Hawkins. "Ain't nobody going to hurt you . . ."

His mother crowded close to him.

"Did yuh shoot tha mule, Dave?"

Dave cried, seeing blurred white and black faces.

"Ahh ddinn gggo tt sshooot hher . . . Ah ssswear ffo Gawd Ahh ddin. . . . Ah wuz a-tryin t sssee ef the old gggun would sshoot—"

"Where yuh git the gun from?" his father asked.

"Ah got it from Joe, at the sto."

"Where yuh git the money?"

"Ma give it t me."

"He kept worryin me, Bob. Ah had t. Ah tol im t bring the gun right back t me . . . It was fer yuh, the gun."

"But how yuh happen to shoot that mule?" asked Jim Hawkins.

"Ah wuzn shootin at the mule, Mistah Hawkins. The gun jumped when Ah pulled the trigger . . . N fo Ah knowed anythin Jenny was there a-bleedin."

Somebody in the crowd laughed. Jim Hawkins walked close to Dave and looked into his face.

"Well, looks like you have bought you a mule, Dave."

"Ah swear fo Gawd, Ah didn go t kill the mule, Mistah Hawkins!"

"But you killed her!"

All the crowd was laughing now. They stood on tiptoe and poked heads over one another's shoulders.

"Well, boy, looks like yuh done bought a dead mule! Hahaha!"

"Ain tha ershame."

"Hohohohoho."

Dave stood, head down, twisting his feet in the dirt.

"Well, you needn't worry about it, Bob," said Jim Hawkins to Dave's father. "Just let the boy keep on working and pay me two dollars a month."

"Whut yuh wan fer yo mule, Mistah Hawkins?"

Jim Hawkins screwed up his eyes.

"Fifty dollars."

"Whut yuh do wid tha gun?" Dave's father demanded.

Dave said nothing.

"Yuh wan me t take a tree lim n beat yuh till yuh talk!"

"Nawsuh!"

"Whut yuh do wid it?"

"Ah throwed it erway."

"Where?"

"Ah . . . Ah throwed it in the creek."

"Waal, c mon home. N firs thing in the mawnin git to tha creek n fin tha gun."

"Yessuh."

"What yuh pay fer it?"

"Two dollahs."

"Take tha gun n git yo money back n carry it t Mistah Hawkins, yuh hear? N don fergit Ahma lam you black bottom good fer this! Now march yoself on home, suh!"

Dave turned and walked slowly. He heard people laughing. Dave glared, his eyes welling with tears. Hot anger bubbled in him. Then he swallowed and stumbled on.

That night Dave did not sleep. He was glad that he had gotten out of killing the mule so easily, but he was hurt. Something hot seemed to turn over inside him each time he remembered how they had laughed. He tossed on his bed, feeling his hard pillow. N Pa says he's gonna beat me . . . He remembered other beatings, and his back quivered. Naw, naw, Ah sho don wan im t beat me tha way no mo. Dam em all! Nobody ever gave him anything. All he did was work. They treat me like a mule, n then they beat me. He gritted his teeth. N Ma had t tell on me.

Well, if he had to, he would take old man Hawkins that two dollars. But that meant selling the gun. And he wanted to keep that gun. Fifty dollars for a dead mule.

He turned over, thinking how he had fired the gun. He had an itch to fire it again. Ef other men kin shoota gun, by Gawd, Ah kin! He was still, listening. Mebbe they all sleepin now. The house was still. He heard the soft breathing of his brother. Yes, now! He would go down and get that gun and see if he could fire it! He eased out of bed and slipped into overalls.

The moon was bright. He ran almost all the way to the edge of the woods. He stumbled over the ground, looking for the spot where he had buried the gun. Yeah, here it is. Like a hungry dog scratching for a bone, he pawed it up. He puffed his black cheeks and blew dirt from the trigger and barrel. He broke it and found four cartridges unshot. He looked around; the fields were filled with silence and moonlight. He clutched the gun stiff and hard in his fingers. But, as soon as he wanted to pull the trigger, he shut his eyes and turned his head. Naw, Ah can't shoot wid mah eyes closed n mah head turned. With effort he held his eyes open; then he squeezed. *Blooooom!* He was stiff, not breathing. The gun was still in his hands. Dammit, he'd done it. He fired again. *Blooooom!* He smiled. *Blooooom! Blooooom! Click, click.* There! It was empty. If anybody could shoot a gun, he could. He put the gun into his hip pocket and started across the fields.

When he reached the top of a ridge he stood straight and proud in the moonlight, looking at Jim Hawkins' big white house, feeling the gun sagging in his pocket. Lawd, ef Ah had just one mo bullet Ah'd taka shot at tha house. Ah'd like t scare ol man Hawkins jusa little . . . Jusa enough t let im know Dave Glover is a man.

To his left the road curved, running to the tracks of the Illinois Central. He jerked his head, listening. From far off came a faint *hoooof-hoooof; hoooof-hoooof; hoooof-hoooof. . . .* That's number eight. He took a swift look at Jim Hawkins' house, he thought of Pa, of Ma, of his little brother, and the boys. He thought of the dead mule and heard hoooof-hoooof; hoooof-hoooof; hoooof-hoooof. . . . He stood rigid. Two dollahs a mont. Les see now . . . Tha means it'll take bout two years. Shucks! Ah'll be dam!

He started down the road, toward the tracks. Yeah, here she comes! He stood beside the track and held himself stiffly. Here she comes, erroun the ben . . . C mon, yuh slow poke! C mon! He had his hand on his gun; something quivered in his stomach. Then the train thundered past, the gray and brown box cars rumbling and clinking. He gripped the gun tightly; then he jerked his hand out of his pocket. Ah betcha Bill wouldn't do it! Ah betcha . . . The cars slid past, steel grinding upon steel. Ahm ridin yuh ternight, so hep me Gawd! He was hot all over. He hesitated just a moment; then he grabbed, pulled atop of a car, and lay flat. He felt his pocket; the gun was still there. Ahead the long rails were glinting in the moonlight, stretching away, away to somewhere, somewhere where he could be a man . . .

SCENE FROM *ALMOS' A MAN*,

*A film script based on the Wright story, by Leslie Lee**

Pushing a plow behind a mule, fifteen-year-old David Glover hears gunshots, as his white employer, Mr. Hawkins, goes hunting. When David daydreams about owning a gun of his own, his fellow fieldhands ridicule him. But the daydreams lead him to a general store where Mr. Joe, the owner, loans him a mail-order catalogue containing pictures of guns and offers to sell him a used handgun for two dollars. David returns home to eat supper with his mother Essie, his father Bob, and his younger brother. After supper, the following scene begins.

INTERIOR. KITCHEN. A LITTLE LATER THAT EVENING.

Close shot of Essie's hands as they lather the soap on Dave's head.

CUT TO

Medium shot of the kitchen. Essie is washing Dave's hair. The kitchen is empty with the exception of the two of them. Dave kneels over a large tub filled with water, as Essie hovers above him, kneading his hair. The whistle of a train can be heard in the distance. The scene conveys a quiet intimacy. Essie's scolding ways are but her means of loving Dave.

DAVE. Momma, did—did Mr. Hawkins give you my pay yet?

* Leslie Lee is the author of the award-winning drama, *The First Breeze of Summer*, as well as of several other works for the stage and, more recently, for the screen.

ESSIE. Hold still, will you. He give it to me. Why you asking?

DAVE. Nothing . . . I was just asking, that's all. [*Pause.*] Momma, can I show you something a minute?

ESSIE. I ain't through yet, David. Now you hold still.

DAVE. Momma, just look at something a minute, will you? Just a minute—all right?

ESSIE. David—all right. Wipe the soap from your face so's you don't burn your eyes. What is it I'm supposed to be looking at?

DAVE [*wiping soap away with a towel and hurrying to the table, where the catalogue sits. He returns to her*]. You see that one, Momma? That's the one—That's what I want to have. I really . . .

ESSIE. Boy, has you lost your mind?

DAVE. Two dollars, Momma, that's what I can get it for—

ESSIE. Over my dead body you will.

DAVE. Momma, you backing down on me now. You promised me I could have one some day.

ESSIE. I know what I told you, and the one thing you ain't is a man yet, so . . .

DAVE. I'm almos'! I sure wish everybody stop saying that! It's all right when I do something wrong. You and Poppa —"Young man this, and young man that." How come I'm a man then and not now—

ESSIE. You're not too big for me to spank now, David.

DAVE [*taking a precautionary step backward*]. Momma, I mean it. If you let me, I promise I won't never ask you for nothing else . . .

ESSIE. Not one bit—you understand me? Why you think I told Mr. Hawkins to give me your pay, huh? 'Cause I know your foolishness, that's why. The money he give me is for your clothes for the winter, and ain't none of it's going for no nonsense, as hard as it is to make ends meet around here. Two dollars is a whole lot of money. [*He starts to protest.*] I don't want to hear another word, else I'm going to get your father to tan your hide. Now you get on back to the tub and let me finish what I was doing. Come on now!

CUT TO

[*Close shot of* DAVE'S *face, the disappointment, the frustration.*]

CUT TO

[*Medium shot of the kitchen.* DAVE *hesitates and then goes to the tub, kneeling.* ESSIE *resumes washing, rubbing his head tenderly, starting to speak but stopping.*]

DAVE. Momma, I—I ain't asked you for nothing all summer, has I? I done my work good . . .

ESSIE. That's what you're supposed to do, ain't it?

DAVE. Yeah, Momma . . . Momma, I just want two dollars. I'll make it up real easy. All I has to do is work a little bit overtime. Mr. Hawkins—

ESSIE. Don't you make me tired now, David. And hold your head still now.

DAVE [*pause*]. You know we needs a gun. Daddy ought to have one, the way folks is thieving around here. Remember last year when them men escaped from the state pen? You thought we needed one then! Come on, Momma, I get the gun and give it to Daddy—all right?

[*He pulls his head away from her hands and looks up at her, reaching simultaneously and stroking her arm. She starts to protest but pushes him again into a kneeling position and begins massaging his hair.*]

ESSIE [*smiling lightly at him*]. You so restless. Ain't never seen nobody so restless . . . like some kind of jackrabbit. Restless! . . . Always been that way . . . [*pause.*] Your father'll have a fit if he knew I let you have some money for one of them things. Who's gonna sell it to you?

DAVE. Mr. Joe said he would.

ESSIE. He did, huh?—the rascal! [*Pause, thinking.*] Folks work hard around here for two dollars. It just don't grow on no trees, David.

DAVE. Momma, I told you I'd—

[*She shushes him, and is silent, sighing heavily.* DAVE *turns away from her grasp and reaches up, rubbing her arm.*]

CUT TO

[*A close shot of her face—thoughtful, deciding.*]

CUT TO

[*A close shot of Dave's face—hopeful.*]

CUT TO

[*A medium shot of both,* DAVE *staring hopefully up at her. She responds after a moment by pushing his head toward the tub and beginning to rinse his hair.*]

ESSIE. All right, I'll let you get it, but—

DAVE [*rising happily, kissing her cheek*]. Oh, man! Oh, man, Momma, thanks!

ESSIE [*pushing him away*]. Hold your horses now—just hold it, and sit right down here and let me finish.

[*He sits happily. She continues to rinse his hair and then begins drying him off with a towel.*]

ESSIE. I'll let you, but you has to promise me one thing. You get that gun and you bring it straight back here, you hear? [*He nods eagerly.*] We're getting it for your father, and I don't want no misunderstanding. You listening to me, boy?

DAVE. Yes, ma'am. I'll go on up there tomorrow, soon as I finish my plowing—right after.

[*He rises quickly, taking the towel from her, and begins to dry his hair himself.*]

DAVE. You . . . you gonna give it to me now—the money?

ESSIE. Don't you get so rambunctious now. Just take your time.

[*She rises slowly, as if still trying to be sure of her decision. She stands, thinking, and then sighs, the decision made.* DAVE *dries his hair vigorously, his eyes anxiously on her. She turns away and raises the hem of her dress, rolling down her stockings, pulling out the wad of bills, slowly peeling off two of them, and then puts the rolled-up wad back into her stocking.*]

ESSIE [*turning to him*]. All right—for your father. So no whining, no lip, no nothing. And you get it and bring it straight back here and put it in my hand—tomorrow—right here! And I'll give it to him myself. You understand now?

DAVE [*eagerly*]. Yes, ma'am. [*Dropping the towel on a chair.*]

ESSIE. All right . . . here . . . You got your money.

[*She hands it to him. He takes it in disbelief—two dollars! He grins, moving quickly toward her, kissing her, and then stares incredulously, happily, at the two dollars before jamming them into his pants pocket.*]

DAVE. Thanks, Momma.

ESSIE. Yes, well . . . come here now. Sit yourself down and let me finish drying your head. You certainly ain't done it right. Come on, David, I ain't got time to fool.

[*He sits, happily, dreamily. She takes the towel and begins rubbing his head with it, making him wince slightly.*]

ESSIE [*sighing heavily. Off camera, over next shot*]. Like a jackrabbit . . . just like a jackrabbit . . .

TIME LAPSE CUT

EXTERIOR: NEXT DAY. DAVE RUNNING UP ROAD TOWARD MR. JOE'S STORE.

SOFT CUT TO

Dave running down steps of store with newly purchased gun in hand.

ON RICHARD WRIGHT and "ALMOS' A MAN"

Fred Stocking
Williams College, Massachusetts

"Almos' a Man" tells the story of David, a black farm laborer of seventeen who is ridiculed by his elders because he wants to be treated like a man. Being a "man," to Dave, would mean being free to make his own decisions, being treated as an equal by other laborers, and being no longer obliged to obliterate his personality in obeying his so-called superiors.

We immediately sympathize with Dave's desire to be treated with decency and respect. At the same time, however, we are torn with anguish because Dave is so naïve, fervently believing that he can achieve manhood merely by owning a gun! The very sight of firearms in a catalogue stirs in him a glowing faith that somehow a gun will release him from all frustrations and endow him with the self-assurance of maturity.

After Dave's first experiment with a cheap pistol results in a pathetic blunder that subjects him to fresh ridicule, he runs away, jumping onto a passing freight train. We last see him lying atop a box car, with no money, no knowledge of the world, and only an unloaded gun in his pocket, staring ahead at the rails that are "glinting in the moonlight, stretching away, away, to somewhere, somewhere where he could be a man." Our hearts sink, for we realize that Dave has little sense of the terrible ordeals and responsibilities of manhood which lie ahead. Yet we also applaud his desire to grow up and live his own life.

This moving psychological study of an adolescent, written early in Richard Wright's literary career, embodies a theme central to all his work: the search for that personal freedom which enables one to discover his own identity as a human being. This search was also a central feature of Wright's own life.

Born in 1908 on a cotton plantation in Mississippi where

his father was a tenant farmer, he grew up in conditions of squalor and poverty much like those we glimpse in "Almos' a Man." But poverty was only one of the forces which threatened to crush Wright's spirit. For in the early years of this century many Southern whites, determined to retain their power despite the abolition of slavery, ruthlessly imposed Jim Crow standards of conduct on all black people, dictating exactly where blacks could or could not eat, ride on trolleys and buses, or walk, as well as what kind of speech they must use. A black male could not say "Yes" or "No" to a white adult, for example, without adding "Sir" or "Ma'am." Furthermore, he must passively accept the degrading treatment of black women by whites, nor could he expect equal protection for blacks under the law. In an illuminating essay called "The Ethics of Living Jim Crow," Wright later pointed out that certain subjects must never be mentioned in conversations with whites:

> American white women; the Ku Klux Klan; France, and how Negro soldiers fared while there; . . . the entire northern part of the United States; the Civil War; Abraham Lincoln; U.S. Grant; General Sherman; Catholics; the Pope; Jews; the Republican Party; slavery; social equality; . . . the 13th and 14th Amendments to the Constitution; or any topic calling for positive knowledge or manly self-assertion on the part of the Negro.

Wright resented not only the terroristic methods by which these restrictions were enforced but also the cringing fear in his fellow blacks which often caused them to beat their own children into adopting the submissive attitudes whites demanded. In "Almos' a Man," for example, we notice how Dave's mother and father keep their son a "boy." Neither of them tries to understand his desire for mature self-realization.

Still another repressive force in young Wright's life was the religious fanaticism of his grandmother, with whom he spent a crucial period of his childhood. Pleasure was forbidden. No baseball. No marbles. Above all, no reading of fiction. All literature, except for the Bible and religious tracts, was denounced as the work of the Devil. Though a well-meaning woman, his grandmother was a raging tyrant.

Hence he eventually rebelled against all conventional religious teachings. And he was already reading in secret anything he could lay hands on, including (when he was eighteen) the writings of H. L. Mencken, who demonstrated for young Richard the amazing fact that unpopular ideas could find expression in print.

In 1927, when Wright was nineteen, he moved to Chicago, learning there the special problems that plagued a black living in a northern city. And when the Depression hit Chicago, he learned at first-hand both the humiliations of unemployment and the effects of poverty—more painful than anything he had known in the rural South.

Wright thus became persuaded that there was something deeply wrong with a society which preached freedom and equality of opportunity for all men, but actually denied these to a large percentage of the population. Believing that not only individual people but the very structure of society was responsible for the suffering around him, he joined the Communist Party in the early 1930s; a decade later he broke from the Party, having discovered that the Communists' requirement of absolute adherence to the party line was intolerable.

Meanwhile he had begun to write, and in 1937 he moved to New York in order to join the staff of the *Daily Worker* as Harlem Editor. He published several stories in the late 1930s, but achieved no major success until 1940, when his brilliant novel, *Native Son*, made him famous.

Because it so eloquently expressed the frustrations and resentments of millions of American blacks, *Native Son* spoke for black America much as Steinbeck's *The Grapes of Wrath* (1939) spoke for the nation's dispossessed whites. These two novels continue to stand out as the most powerful fiction that emerged from the Depression years, and *Native Son* is recognized as Wright's finest novel—as well as his most controversial.

Native Son features the blood-curdling murder of a white woman by a black man, Bigger Thomas. The novel's searing power is not derived, however, from the shocking description of the act itself, but from the detailed and subtle portrayal of the social, economic, and (especially) psychological forces which are ultimately responsible for this act. The title suggests that Bigger is symbolic of all Americans, and that his fate may well serve as a warning of the possible fate of anyone born into American society.

Although the novel has been praised for its effectiveness as social protest, its main concern is not the external conditions which shape Bigger's behavior but what goes on in his mind as a result of these conditions. "Almos' a Man," published in the same year as *Native Son*, shares this concern. Although Dave's need to be a man has clearly been stimulated by the degradation in which he lives, the story deals more directly with Dave's state of mind than with the social and economic forces producing this state. Both novel and story offer psychological portraits; in both we learn what it feels like to be a black male seeking to realize his own identity.

In the final scene of *Native Son* Bigger Thomas, condemned to die in the electric chair, is talking with his friend and lawyer, Max:

> "Mr. Max, you go home. I'm all right . . . Sounds funny, Mr. Max, but when I think about what you say I kind of feel what I wanted. It makes me feel I was kind of right. . . ." . . . "I ain't trying to forgive nobody and I ain't asking for nobody to forgive me. I ain't going to cry. They wouldn't let me live and I killed. Maybe it ain't fair to kill, and I reckon I really didn't want to kill. But when I think of why all the killing was, I begin to feel what I wanted, what I *am* . . ." . . . "I didn't know I was really alive in this world until I felt things hard enough to kill for 'em."

This passage not only concludes Wright's study of Bigger Thomas' own psychology but also defines a philosophical position, a view of life. For Bigger has lived in a northern ghetto where he, like Dave in "Almos' a Man," has not been allowed to discover his own identity as a human being:

> "We black and they white. They got things and we ain't. They do things and we can't. It's just like living in jail. Half the time I feel like I'm on the outside of the world peeping in through a knot-hole in the fence."

Treated as a nobody in such a world, not fit for a paying job or a decent education, Bigger is forced to commit a crime in order to feel that he really exists, that he is somehow important. However perverse his act may be, by murdering a white woman he has actually established some kind of significance for himself, just as Dave is trying to do in "Almos' a Man"—first by buying a gun, and then by running away.

Running. This, too, was a central feature of Richard Wright's life. In 1927 he moved from the South to Chicago, in 1937 from Chicago to New York, and finally in 1947 from New York to Paris, where he lived until his death from a heart attack in 1960. During these final years he became associated with Jean-Paul Sartre and other French writers known as existentialists. What appealed to Wright in their ideas was their involvement in the very kind of search in which Dave and Bigger Thomas participate: the search for self-realization. Search involves travel, movement, restlessness; and these French writers tended to regard rootlessness as an essential fact of all human life. Because all men are alone in an alien or indifferent universe, each man must formulate a set of values for himself and impose these values on his experience without the authority and support of a church or other institution to assure him that his values are "right."

Richard Wright's final years continued the search which Dave was just beginning at the end of "Almos' a Man." Wright traveled to Ghana, to Indonesia, and to Spain, and wrote books about these travels. But the central question of his writing remained the same: how individuals, either separately or in groups (particularly minority groups), can throw off the shackles holding them in bondage and discover or devise new meanings for their lives.

The best introduction to Richard Wright's career is his autobiography, *Black Boy* (1945), describing his southern boyhood before moving north. There is authentic drama on every page, yet the prose is straightforward and factual, never pretentious or "literary," and Wright's ear for the phrasing and the inflections of black speech is astounding.

His most important writings, in addition to *Native Son* (1940), include *Uncle Tom's Children* (1938), four short novels about life in the Mississippi River lowlands near Memphis, where black and white sharecroppers struggle in vain against the injustices and cruelties of their overlords;

Twelve Million Black Voices (1941), a folk history of American blacks, with photographs by Edwin Rosskam; *The Outsider* (1953), generally considered unsuccessful as a novel but of special philosophical interest in its presentation of Wright's rejection of Communism, and in the futile attempts of its central character to find coherence and purpose in a universe where "man is nothing in particular"; and *Eight Men* (1961), a collection of eight stories, written at various times, in which "Almos' a Man" appears as "The Man Who Was Almost a Man."

This change in the title is interesting. The word "Man" appears in all eight titles, and four of these open with the phrase, "The Man Who . . . ," giving them the flavor of fables and suggesting that each central character represents some aspect of mankind. Dave, for instance, could be any adolescent who feels the stirring of talents and powers within himself and is compelled to rebel against the indifference and contempt of his elders.

The most famous of these eight stories, "The Man Who Lived Underground," is clearly influenced by Dostoevsky's *Notes from Underground*. In Wright's narrative a life under ground becomes a metaphor for the life a black must live in a white man's world, or the life any man may be forced to live in an incomprehensible universe. When the central character, a black fugitive from the police, drops into a manhole and finds himself in the city sewer system, we realize that he is now literally experiencing the reality of what he has long been considered by his fellows: something filthy that must be discarded—in short, sewage. The events that follow swirl about in surrealistic, nightmarish patterns which reveal to the hero, in fantastic ways, the essential absurdity of civilization. This story is undoubtedly Wright's most compelling work of short fiction.

These two narratives, "The Man Who Was Almost a Man" and "The Man Who Lived Underground," define Wright's most persistent interests: the dramatizing of psychological states, particularly of blacks who have been treated with scorn, and the lonely search of any man, of any race, for an authentic identity in an alien universe.

SUGGESTIONS FOR FURTHER READING

By Richard Wright:

Black Boy: A Record of Childhood and Youth. New York: Harper, 1945.

Eight Men. Cleveland, Ohio: World Publishing Co., 1961.

Native Son. New York: Harper, 1940.

About Richard Wright:

Bone, Robert. *Richard Wright.* Minneapolis, Minn.: University of Minnesota Press, 1964. (University of Minnesota Pamphlets on American Writers, No. 74.)

Brigano, Russell Carl. *Richard Wright: An Introduction to the Man and His Works.* Pittsburgh, Pa.: University of Pittsburgh Press, 1970.

Margolies, Edward. *Native Sons.* Philadelphia: J. B. Lippincott, 1968.

Webb, Constance. *Richard Wright.* New York: G. P. Putnam's Sons, 1968.

THE DISPLACED PERSON

by Flannery O'Connor

The peacock was following Mrs. Shortley up the road to the hill where she meant to stand. Moving one behind the other, they looked like a complete procession. Her arms were folded and as she mounted the prominence, she might have been the giant wife of the countryside, come out at some sign of danger to see what the trouble was. She stood on two tremendous legs, with the grand self-confidence of a mountain, and rose, up narrowing bulges of granite, to two icy blue points of light that pierced forward, surveying everything. She ignored the white afternoon sun which was creeping behind a ragged wall of cloud as if it pretended to be an intruder and cast her gaze down the red clay road that turned off from the highway.

The peacock stopped just behind her, his tail—glittering green-gold and blue in the sunlight—lifted just enough so that it would not touch the ground. It flowed out on either side like a floating train and his head on the long blue reed-like neck was drawn back as if his attention were fixed in the distance on something no one else could see.

Mrs. Shortley was watching a black car turn through the gate from the highway. Over by the toolshed, about fifteen feet away, the two Negroes, Astor and Sulk, had stopped work to watch. They were hidden by a mulberry tree but Mrs. Shortley knew they were there.

Mrs. McIntyre was coming down the steps of her house to meet the car. She had on her largest smile but Mrs. Shortley, even from her distance, could detect a nervous slide in it. These people who were coming were only hired help, like the Shortleys themselves or the Negroes. Yet here was the owner of the place out to welcome them. Here she was, wearing her best clothes and a string of beads, and now bounding forward with her mouth stretched.

The car stopped at the walk just as she did and the priest

was the first to get out. He was a long-legged black-suited old man with a white hat on and a collar that he wore backwards, which, Mrs. Shortley knew, was what priests did who wanted to be known as priests. It was this priest who had arranged for these people to come here. He opened the back door of the car and out jumped two children, a boy and a girl, and then, stepping more slowly, a woman in brown, shaped like a peanut. Then the front door opened and out stepped the man, the Displaced Person. He was short and a little sway-backed and wore gold-rimmed spectacles.

Mrs. Shortley's vision narrowed on him and then widened to include the woman and the two children in a group picture. The first thing that struck her as very peculiar was that they looked like other people. Every time she had seen them in her imagination, the image she had got was of the three bears, walking single file, with wooden shoes on like Dutchmen and sailor hats and bright coats with a lot of buttons. But the woman had on a dress she might have worn herself and the children were dressed like anybody from around. The man had on khaki pants and a blue shirt. Suddenly, as Mrs. McIntyre held out her hand to him, he bobbed down from the waist and kissed it.

Mrs. Shortley jerked her own hand up toward her mouth and then after a second brought it down and rubbed it vigorously on her seat. If Mr. Shortley had tried to kiss her hand, Mrs. McIntyre would have knocked him into the middle of next week, but then Mr. Shortley wouldn't have kissed her hand anyway. He didn't have time to mess around.

She looked closer, squinting. The boy was in the center of the group, talking. He was supposed to speak the most English because he had learned some in Poland and so he was to listen to his father's Polish and say it in English and then listen to Mrs. McIntyre's English and say that in Polish. The priest had told Mrs. McIntyre his name was Rudolph and he was twelve and the girl's name was Sledgewig and she was nine. Sledgewig sounded to Mrs. Shortley like something you would name a bug, or vice versa, as if you named a boy Bollweevil. All of them's last name was something that only they themselves and the priest could pronounce. All she could make out of it was Gobblehook. She and Mrs. McIntyre had been calling them the Gobblehooks all week while they got ready for them.

There had been a great deal to do to get ready for them because they didn't have anything of their own, not a stick of furniture or a sheet or a dish, and everything had had to be scraped together out of things that Mrs. McIntyre couldn't use any more herself. They had collected a piece of odd furniture here and a piece there and they had taken some flowered chicken feed sacks and made curtains for the windows, two red and one green, because they had not had enough of the red sacks to go around. Mrs. McIntyre said she was not made of money and she could not afford to buy curtains. "They can't talk," Mrs. Shortley said. "You reckon they'll know what colors even is?" and Mrs. McIntyre had said that after what those people had been through, they should be grateful for anything they could get. She said to think how lucky they were to escape from over there and come to a place like this.

Mrs. Shortley recalled a newsreel she had seen once of a small room piled high with bodies of dead naked people all in a heap, their arms and legs tangled together, a head thrust in here, a head there, a foot, a knee, a part that should have been covered up sticking out, a hand raised clutching nothing. Before you could realize that it was real and take it into your head, the picture changed and a hollow-sounding voice was saying, "Time marches on!" This was the kind of thing that was happening every day in Europe where they had not advanced as in this country, and watching from her vantage point, Mrs. Shortley had the sudden intuition that the Gobblehooks, like rats with typhoid fleas, could have carried all those murderous ways over the water with them directly to this place. If they had come from where that kind of thing was done to them, who was to say they were not the kind that would also do it to others? The width and breadth of this question nearly shook her. Her stomach trembled as if there had been a slight quake in the heart of the mountain and automatically she moved down from her elevation and went forward to be introduced to them, as if she meant to find out at once what they were capable of.

She approached, stomach foremost, head back, arms folded, boots flopping gently against her large legs. About fifteen feet from the gesticulating group, she stopped and made her presence felt by training her gaze on the back of Mrs. McIntyre's neck. Mrs. McIntyre was a small woman of sixty with a round wrinkled face and red bangs that came almost down to two high orange-colored penciled eyebrows. She had a little doll's mouth and eyes that were a soft blue when she opened them wide but more like steel or granite when she narrowed them to inspect a milk can. She had buried one husband and divorced two and Mrs. Shortley respected her as a person nobody had put anything over on yet—except, ha, ha, perhaps the Shortleys. She held out her arm in Mrs. Shortley's direction and said to the Rudolph boy, "And this is Mrs. Shortley. Mr. Shortley is my dairyman. Where's Mr. Shortley?" she asked as his wife began to approach again, her arms still folded. "I want him to meet the Guizacs."

Now it was Guizac. She wasn't calling them Gobblehook to their face. "Chancey's at the barn," Mrs. Shortley said. "He don't have time to rest himself in the bushes like them niggers over there."

Her look first grazed the tops of the displaced people's heads and then revolved downwards slowly, the way a buzzard glides and drops in the air until it alights on the carcass. She stood far enough away so that the man would not be able to kiss her hand. He looked directly at her with little green eyes and gave her a broad grin that was toothless on one side. Mrs. Shortley, without smiling, turned her attention to the little girl who stood by the mother, swinging her shoulders from side to side. She had long braided hair in two looped pigtails and there was no denying she was a pretty child even if she did have a bug's name. She was better looking than either Annie Maude or Sarah Mae, Mrs. Shortley's two girls going on fifteen and seventeen but Annie Maude had never got her growth and Sarah Mae had a cast in her eye. She compared the foreign boy to her son, H.C., and H.C. came out far ahead. H.C. was twenty years old with her build and eyeglasses. He was going to Bible school now and when he finished he was going to start him a church. He had a strong sweet voice for hymns and could sell anything. Mrs. Shortley looked at the priest and was reminded that these people did not have an advanced religion. There was no telling what all they believed since none of the foolishness had been reformed out of it. Again she saw the room piled high with bodies.

The priest spoke in a foreign way himself, English but as if he had a throatful of hay. He had a big nose and a bald rectangular face and head. While she was observing him, his large mouth dropped open and with a stare behind her, he said, "Arrrrrrr!" and pointed.

Mrs. Shortley spun around. The peacock was standing a few feet behind her, with his head slightly cocked.

"What a beauti-ful birdrrrd!" the priest murmured.

"Another mouth to feed," Mrs. McIntyre said, glancing in the peafowl's direction.

"And when does he raise his splendid tail?" asked the priest.

"Just when it suits him," she said. "There used to be twenty or thirty of those things on the place but I've let them die off. I don't like to hear them scream in the middle of the night."

"So beauti-ful," the priest said. "A tail full of suns," and he crept forward on tiptoe and looked down on the bird's back where the polished gold and green design began. The peacock stood still as if he had just come down from some sun-drenched height to be a vision for them all. The priest's homely red face hung over him, glowing with pleasure.

Mrs. Shortley's mouth had drawn acidly to one side. "Nothing but a peachicken," she muttered.

Mrs. McIntyre raised her orange eyebrows and exchanged a look with her to indicate that the old man was in his second childhood. "Well, we must show the Guizacs their new home," she said impatiently and she herded them into the car again. The peacock stepped off toward the mulberry tree where the two Negroes were hiding and the priest turned his absorbed face away and got in the car and drove the displaced people down to the shack they were to occupy.

Mrs. Shortley waited until the car was out of sight and then she made her way circuitously to the mulberry tree and stood about ten feet behind the two Negroes, one an old man holding a bucket half full of calf feed and the other a yellowish boy with a short woodchuck-like head pushed into a rounded felt hat. "Well," she said slowly, "yawl have looked long enough. What you think about them?"

The old man, Astor, raised himself. "We been watching," he said as if this would be news to her. "Who they now?"

"They come from over the water," Mrs. Shortley said with a wave of her arm. "They're what is called Displaced Persons."

"Displaced Persons," he said. "Well now. I declare. What do that mean?"

"It means they ain't where they were born at and there's nowhere for them to go—like if you was run out of here and wouldn't nobody have you."

"It seem like they here, though," the old man said in a reflective voice. "If they here, they somewhere."

"Sho is," the other agreed. "They here."

The illogic of Negro-thinking always irked Mrs. Shortley. "They ain't where they belong to be at," she said. "They belong to be back over yonder where everything is still like they been used to. Over here it's more advanced than where they come from. But yawl better look out now," she said and nodded her head. "There's about ten million billion more just like them and I know what Mrs. McIntyre said."

"Say what?" the young one asked.

"Places are not easy to get nowadays, for white or black, but I reckon I heard what she stated to me," she said in a sing-song voice.

"You liable to hear most anything," the old man remarked, leaning forward as if he were about to walk off but holding himself suspended.

"I heard her say, 'This is going to put the Fear of the Lord into those shiftless niggers!' " Mrs. Shortley said in a ringing voice.

The old man started off. "She say something like that every now and then," he said. "Ha. Ha. Yes indeed."

"You better get on in that barn and help Mr. Shortley," she said to the other one. "What you reckon she pays you for?"

"He the one sont me out," the Negro muttered. "He the one gimme something else to do."

"Well you better get to doing it then," she said and stood there until he moved off. Then she stood a while longer, reflecting, her unseeing eyes directly in front of the peacock's tail. He had jumped into the tree and his tail hung in front of her, full of fierce planets with eyes that were each ringed in green and set against a sun that was gold in one second's light and salmon-colored in the next. She might have been looking at a map of the universe but she didn't notice it any more than she did the spots of sky that cracked the dull green of the tree. She was having an inner vision instead. She was seeing the ten million billion of them pushing their way into new places over here and herself, a giant angel with wings as wide as a house, telling the Negroes that they would have to find another place. She turned herself in the direction of the barn, musing on this, her expression lofty and satisfied.

She approached the barn from an oblique angle that allowed her a look in the door before she could be seen herself. Mr. Chancey Shortley was adjusting the last milking machine on a large black and white spotted cow near the entrance, squatting at her heels. There was about a half-inch of cigarette adhering to the center of his lower lip. Mrs. Shortley observed it minutely for half a second. "If she seen or heard of you smoking in this barn, she would blow a fuse," she said.

Mr. Shortley raised a sharply rutted face containing a washout under each cheek and two long crevices eaten down both sides of his blistered mouth. "You gonter be the one to tell her?" he asked.

"She's got a nose of her own," Mrs. Shortley said.

Mr. Shortley, without appearing to give the feat any consideration, lifted the cigarette stub with the sharp end of his tongue, drew it into his mouth, closed his lips tightly, rose, stepped out, gave his wife a good round appreciative stare, and spit the smoldering butt into the grass.

"Aw Chancey," she said, "haw haw," and she dug a little hole for it with her toe and covered it up. This trick of Mr. Shortley's was actually his way of making love to her. When he had done his courting, he had not brought a guitar to strum or anything pretty for her to keep, but had sat on her porch steps, not saying a word, imitating a paralyzed man propped up to enjoy a cigarette. When the cigarette got the proper size, he would turn his eyes to her and open his mouth and draw in the butt and then sit there as if he had swallowed it, looking at her with the most loving look anybody could imagine. It nearly drove her wild and every time he did it, she wanted to pull his hat down over his eyes and hug him to death.

"Well," she said, going into the barn after him, "the Gobblehooks have come and she wants you to meet them, says, 'Where's Mr. Shortley?' and I says, 'He don't have time . . .' "

"Tote up them weights," Mr. Shortley said, squatting to the cow again.

"You reckon he can drive a tractor when he don't know English?" she asked. "I don't think she's going to get her money's worth out of them. That boy can talk but he looks delicate. The one can work can't talk and the one can talk can't work. She ain't any better off than if she had more niggers."

"I rather have a nigger if it was me," Mr. Shortley said.

"She says it's ten million more like them, Displaced Persons, she says that there priest can get her all she wants."

"She better quit messin with that there priest," Mr. Shortley said.

"He don't look smart," Mrs. Shortley said, "—kind of foolish."

"I ain't going to have the Pope of Rome tell me how to run no dairy," Mr. Shortley said.

"They ain't Eye-talians, they're Poles," she said. "From Poland where all them bodies were stacked up at. You remember all them bodies?"

"I give them three weeks here," Mr. Shortley said.

Three weeks later Mrs. McIntyre and Mrs. Shortley drove to the cane bottom to see Mr. Guizac start to operate the silage cutter, a new machine that Mrs. McIntyre had just bought because she said, for the first time, she had somebody who could operate it. Mr. Guizac could drive a tractor, use the rotary hay-baler, the silage cutter, the combine, the letz mill, or any other machine she had on the place. He was an expert mechanic, a carpenter, and a mason. He was thrifty and energetic. Mrs. McIntyre said she figured he would save her twenty dollars a month on repair bills alone. She said getting him was the best day's work she had ever done in her life. He could work milking machines and he was scrupulously clean. He did not smoke.

She parked her car on the edge of the cane field and they got out. Sulk, the young Negro, was attaching the wagon to the cutter and Mr. Guizac was attaching the cutter to the tractor. He finished first and pushed the colored boy out of the way and attached the wagon to the cutter himself, gesticulating with a bright angry face when he wanted the hammer or the screwdriver. Nothing was done quick enough to suit him. The Negroes made him nervous.

The week before, he had come upon Sulk at the dinner hour, sneaking with a croker sack into the pen where the young turkeys were. He had watched him take a frying-size turkey from the lot and thrust it in the sack and put the sack under his coat. Then he had followed him around the barn, jumped on him, dragged him to Mrs. McIntyre's back door and had acted out the entire scene for her, while the Negro muttered and grumbled and said God might strike him dead if he had been stealing any turkey, he had only been taking it to put some black shoe polish on its head because it had the sorehead. God might strike him dead if that was not the truth before Jesus. Mrs. McIntyre told him to go put the turkey back and then she was long time explaining to the Pole that all Negroes would steal. She finally had to call Rudolph and tell him in English and have him tell his father in Polish, and Mr. Guizac had gone off with a startled disappointed face.

Mrs. Shortley stood by hoping there would be trouble with the silage machine but there was none. All of Mr. Guizac's motions were quick and accurate. He jumped on the tractor like a monkey and maneuvered the big orange cutter into the cane; in a second the silage was spurting in a green jet out of the pipe into the wagon. He went jolting down the row until he disappeared from sight and the noise became remote.

Mrs. McIntyre sighed with pleasure. "At last," she said, "I've got somebody I can depend on. For years I've been fooling with sorry people. Sorry people. Poor white trash and niggers," she muttered. "They've drained me dry. Before you all came I had Ringfields and Collins and Jarrells and Perkins and Pinkins and Herrins and God knows what all else and not a one of them left without taking something off this place that didn't belong to them. Not a one!"

Mrs. Shortley could listen to this with composure because she knew that if Mrs. McIntyre had considered her trash, they couldn't have talked about trashy people together. Neither of them approved of trash. Mrs. McIntyre continued with the monologue that Mrs. Shortley had heard oftentimes before. "I've been running this place for thirty years," she said, looking with a deep frown out over the field, "and always just barely making it. People think you're made of money. I have the taxes to pay. I have the insurance to keep up. I have the repair bills. I have the feed bills." It all gathered up and she stood with her chest lifted and her small hands gripped around her elbows. "Ever since the Judge died," she said, "I've barely been making ends meet and they all take something when they leave. The niggers don't leave—they stay and steal. A nigger thinks anybody is rich he can steal from and that white trash thinks anybody is rich who can afford to hire people as sorry as they are. And all I've got is the dirt under my feet!"

You hire and fire, Mrs. Shortley thought, but she didn't always say what she thought. She stood by and let Mrs. McIntyre say it all out to the end but this time it didn't end as usual. "But at last I'm saved!" Mrs. McIntyre said. "One fellow's misery is the other fellow's gain. That man there," and she pointed where the Displaced Person had disappeared, "—he has to work! He wants to work!" She turned to Mrs. Shortley with her bright wrinkled face. "That man is my salvation!" she said.

Mrs. Shortley looked straight ahead as if her vision penetrated the cane and the hill and pierced through to the other side. "I would suspicion salvation got from the devil," she said in a slow detached way.

"Now what do you mean by that?" Mrs. McIntyre asked, looking at her sharply.

Mrs. Shortley wagged her head but would not say anything else. The fact was she had nothing else to say for this intuition had only at that instant come to her. She had never given much thought to the devil for she felt that religion was essentially for those people who didn't have the brains to avoid evil without it. For people like herself, for people of gumption, it was a social occasion providing the opportunity to sing; but if she had ever given it much thought, she would have considered the devil the head of it and God the hanger-on. With the coming of these displaced people, she was obliged to give new thought to a good many things.

"I know what Sledgewig told Annie Maude," she said, and when Mrs. McIntyre carefully did not ask her what but reached down and broke off a sprig of sassafras to chew, she continued in a way to indicate she was not telling all, "that they wouldn't be able to live long, the four of them, on seventy dollars a month."

"He's worth raising," Mrs. McIntyre said. "He saves me money."

This was as much as to say that Chancey had never saved her money. Chancey got up at four in the morning to milk her cows, in winter wind and summer heat, and he had been doing it for the last two years. They had been with her the longest she had ever had anybody. The gratitude they got was these hints that she hadn't been saved any money.

"Is Mr. Shortley feeling better today?" Mrs. McIntyre asked.

Mrs. Shortley thought it was about time she was asking that question. Mr. Shortley had been in bed two days with an attack. Mr. Guizac had taken his place in the dairy in addition to doing his own work. "No he ain't," she said. "That doctor said he was suffering from over-exhaustion."

"If Mr. Shortley is over-exhausted," Mrs. McIntyre said, "then he must have a second job on the side," and she looked at Mrs. Shortley with almost closed eyes as if she were examining the bottom of a milk can.

Mrs. Shortley did not say a word but her dark suspicion grew like a black thunder cloud. The fact was that Mr. Shortley did have a second job on the side and that, in a free country, this was none of Mrs. McIntyre's business. Mr. Shortley made whisky. He had a small still back in the farthest reaches of the place, on Mrs. McIntyre's land to be sure, but on land that she only owned and did not cultivate, on idle land that was not doing anybody any good. Mr. Shortley was not afraid of work. He got up at four in the morning and milked her cows and in the middle of the day when he was supposed to be resting, he was off attending to his still. Not every man would work like that. The Negroes knew about his still but he knew about theirs so there had never been any disagreeableness between them.

But with foreigners on the place, with people who were all eyes and no understanding, who had come from a place continually fighting, where the religion had not been reformed—with this kind of people, you had to be on the lookout every minute. She thought there ought to be a law against them. There was no reason they couldn't stay over there and take the places of some of the people who had been killed in their wars and butcherings.

"What's furthermore," she said suddenly, "Sledgewig said as soon as her papa saved the money, he was going to buy him a used car. Once they get them a used car, they'll leave you."

"I can't pay him enough for him to save money," Mrs. McIntyre said. "I'm not worrying about that. Of course," she said then, "if Mr. Shortley got incapacitated, I would have to use Mr. Guizac in the dairy all the time and I would have to pay him more. He doesn't smoke," she said, and it was the fifth time within the week that she had pointed this out.

"It is no man," Mrs. Shortley said emphatically, "that works as hard as Chancey, or is as easy with a cow, or is more of a Christian," and she folded her arms and her gaze pierced the distance. The noise of the tractor and cutter increased and Mr. Guizac appeared coming around the other side of the cane row. "Which can not be said about everybody," she muttered. She wondered whether, if the Pole found Chancey's still, he would know what it was. The trouble with these people was, you couldn't tell what they knew. Every time Mr. Guizac smiled, Europe stretched out in Mrs. Shortley's imagination, mysterious and evil, the devil's experiment station.

The tractor, the cutter, the wagon passed, rattling and rumbling and grinding before them. "Think how long that would have taken with men and mules to do it," Mrs. McIntyre shouted. "We'll get this whole bottom cut within two days at this rate."

"Maybe," Mrs. Shortley muttered, "if don't no terrible accident occur." She thought how the tractor had made mules worthless. Nowadays you couldn't give away a mule. The next thing to go, she reminded herself, will be niggers.

In the afternoon she explained what was going to happen to them to Astor and Sulk who were in the cow lot, filling the manure spreader. She sat down next to the block of salt under a small shed, her stomach in her lap, her arms on top of it. "All you colored people better look out," she said. "You know how much you can get for a mule."

"Nothing, no indeed," the old man said, "not one thing."

"Before it was a tractor," she said, "it could be a mule. And before it was a Displaced Person, it could be a nigger. The time is going to come," she prophesied, "when it won't be no more occasion to speak of a nigger."

The old man laughed politely. "Yes indeed," he said. "Ha ha."

The young one didn't say anything. He only looked sullen but when she had gone in the house, he said, "Big Belly act like she know everything."

"Never mind," the old man said, "your place too low for anybody to dispute with you for it."

She didn't tell her fears about the still to Mr. Shortley until he was back on the job in the dairy. Then one night after they were in bed, she said, "That man prowls."

Mr. Shortley folded his hands on his bony chest and pretended he was a corpse.

"Prowls," she continued and gave him a sharp kick in the side with her knee. "Who's to say what they know and don't know? Who's to say if he found it he wouldn't go right to her and tell? How you know they don't make liquor in Europe? They drive tractors. They got them all kinds of machinery. Answer me."

"Don't worry me now," Mr. Shortley said. "I'm a dead man."

"It's them little eyes of his that's foreign," she muttered. "And that way he's got of shrugging." She drew her shoulders up and shrugged several times. "How come he's got anything to shrug about?" she asked.

"If everybody was as dead as I am, nobody would have no trouble," Mr. Shortley said.

"That priest," she muttered and was silent for a minute. Then she said, "In Europe they probably got some different way to make liquor but I reckon they know all the ways. They're full of crooked ways. They never have advanced or reformed. They got the same religion as a thousand years ago. It could only be the devil responsible for that. Always fighting amongst each other. Disputing. And then get us into it. Ain't they got us into it twict already and we ain't got no more sense than to go over there and settle it for them and then they come on back over here and snoop around and find your still and go straight to her. And liable to kiss her hand any minute. Do you hear me?"

"No," Mr. Shortley said.

"And I'll tell you another thing," she said. "I wouldn't be a tall surprised if he don't know everything you say, whether it be in English or not."

"I don't speak no other language," Mr. Shortley murmured.

"I suspect," she said, "that before long there won't be no more niggers on this place. And I tell you what. I'd rather have niggers than them Poles. And what's furthermore, I aim to take up for the niggers when the time comes. When Gobblehook first come here, you recollect how he shook their hands, like he didn't know the difference, like he might have been as black as them, but when it come to finding out Sulk was taking turkeys, he gone on and told her. I known he was taking turkeys. I could have told her myself."

Mr. Shortley was breathing softly as if he were asleep.

"A nigger don't know when he has a friend," she said. "And I'll tell you another thing. I get a heap out of Sledgewig. Sledgewig said that in Poland they lived in a brick house and one night a man come and told them to get out of it before daylight. Do you believe they ever lived in a brick house?

"Airs," she said. "That's just airs. A wooden house is good enough for me. Chancey," she said, "turn thisaway. I hate to see niggers mistreated and run out. I have a heap of pity for niggers and poor folks. Ain't I always had?" she asked. "I say ain't I always been a friend to niggers and poor folks?

"When the time comes," she said, "I'll stand up for the niggers and that's that. I ain't going to see that priest drive out all the niggers."

Mrs. McIntyre bought a new drag harrow and a tractor with a power lift because she said, for the first time, she had someone who could handle machinery. She and Mrs. Shortley had driven to the back field to inspect what he had harrowed the day before. "That's been done beautifully!" Mrs. McIntyre said, looking out over the red undulating ground.

Mrs. McIntyre had changed since the Displaced Person had been working for her and Mrs. Shortley had observed the change very closely: she had begun to act like somebody who was getting rich secretly and she didn't confide in Mrs. Shortley the way she used to. Mrs. Shortley suspected that the priest was at the bottom of the change. They were very slick. First he would get her into his Church and then he would get his hand in her pocketbook. Well, Mrs. Shortley thought, the more fool she! Mrs. Shortley had a secret herself. She knew something the Displaced Person was doing that would floor Mrs. McIntyre. "I still say he ain't going to work forever for seventy dollars a month," she murmured. She intended to keep her secret to herself and Mr. Shortley.

"Well," Mrs. McIntyre said, "I may have to get rid of some of this other help so I can pay him more."

Mrs. Shortley nodded to indicate she had known this for some time. "I'm not saying those niggers ain't had it coming," she said. "But they do the best they know how. You can always tell a nigger what to do and stand by until he does it."

"That's what the Judge said," Mrs. McIntyre said and looked at her with approval. The Judge was her first husband, the one who had left her the place. Mrs. Shortley had heard that she had married him when she was thirty and he was seventy-five, thinking she would be rich as soon as he died, but the old man was a scoundrel and when his estate was settled, they found he didn't have a nickel. All he left her were the fifty acres and the house. But she always spoke of him in a reverent way and quoted his sayings, such as, "One fellow's misery is the other fellow's gain," and "The devil you know is better than the devil you don't."

"However," Mrs. Shortley remarked, "the devil you know is better than the devil you don't," and she had to turn away so that Mrs. McIntyre would not see her smile. She had found out what the Displaced Person was up to through the old man, Astor, and she had not told anybody but Mr. Shortley. Mr. Shortley had risen straight up in bed like Lazarus from the tomb.

"Shut your mouth!" he had said.

"Yes," she had said.

"Naw!" Mr. Shortley had said.

"Yes," she had said.

Mr. Shortley had fallen back flat.

"The Pole don't know any better," Mrs. Shortley had said. "I reckon that priest is putting him up to it is all. I blame the priest."

The priest came frequently to see the Guizacs and he would always stop in and visit Mrs. McIntyre too and they would walk around the place and she would point out her improvements and listen to his rattling talk. It suddenly came to Mrs. Shortley that he was trying to persuade her to bring another Polish family onto the place. With two of them here, there would be almost nothing spoken but Polish! The Negroes would be gone and there would be the two families against Mr. Shortley and herself! She began to imagine a war of words, to see the Polish words and the English words coming at each other, stalking forward, not sentences, just words, gabble gabble gabble, flung out high and shrill and stalking forward and then grappling with each other. She saw the Polish words, dirty and all-knowing and unreformed, flinging mud on the clean English words until everything was equally dirty. She saw them all piled up in a room, all the dead dirty words, theirs and hers too, piled up like the naked bodies in the newsreel. God save me! she cried silently, from the stinking power of Satan! And she started from that day to read her Bible with a new attention. She poured over the Apocalypse and began to quote from the Prophets and before long she had come to a deeper understanding of her existence. She saw plainly that the meaning of the world was a mystery that had been planned and she was not surprised to suspect that she had a special part in the plan because she was strong. She saw that the Lord God Almighty had created the strong people to do what had to be done and she felt that she would be ready when she was called. Right now she felt that her business was to watch the priest.

His visits irked her more and more. On the last one, he went about picking up feathers off the ground. He found two peacock feathers and four or five turkey feathers and an old brown hen feather and took them off with him like a bouquet. This foolish-acting did not deceive Mrs. Shortley any. Here he was: leading foreigners over in hoards to places that were not theirs, to cause disputes, to uproot niggers, to plant the Whore of Babylon in the midst of the righteous! Whenever he came on the place, she hid herself behind something and watched until he left.

It was on a Sunday afternoon that she had her vision. She had gone to drive in the cows for Mr. Shortley who had a pain in his knee and she was walking slowly through the pasture, her arms folded, her eyes on the distant low-lying clouds that looked like rows and rows of white fish washed up on a great blue beach. She paused after an incline to heave a sigh of exhaustion for she had an immense weight to carry around and she was not as young as she used to be. At times she could feel her heart, like a child's fist, clenching and unclenching inside her chest, and when the feeling came, it stopped her thought altogether and she would go about like a large hull of herself, moving for no reason; but she gained this incline without a tremor and stood at the top of it, pleased with herself. Suddenly while she watched, the sky folded back in two pieces like the curtain to a stage and a gigantic figure stood facing her. It was the color of the sun in the early afternoon, white-gold. It was of no definite shape but there were fiery wheels with fierce dark eyes in them, spinning rapidly all around it. She was not able to tell if the figure was going forward or backward because its magnificence was so great. She shut her eyes in order to look at it and it turned blood-red and the wheels turned white. A voice, very resonant, said the one word, "Prophesy!"

She stood there, tottering slightly but still upright, her eyes shut tight and her fists clenched and her straw sun hat low on her forehead. "The children of wicked nations will be butchered," she said in a loud voice. "Legs where arms should be, foot to face, ear in the palm of hand. Who will remain whole? Who will remain whole? Who?"

Presently she opened her eyes. The sky was full of white fish carried lazily on their sides by some invisible current and pieces of the sun, submerged some distance beyond them, appeared from time to time as if they were being washed in the opposite direction. Woodenly she planted one foot in front of the other until she had crossed the pasture and reached the lot. She walked through the barn like one in a daze and did not speak to Mr. Shortley. She continued up the road until she saw the priest's car parked in front of Mrs. McIntyre's house. "Here again," she muttered. "Come to destroy."

Mrs. McIntyre and the priest were walking in the yard. In order not to meet them face to face, she turned to the left and entered the feed house, a single-room shack piled on one side with flowered sacks of scratch feed. There were spilled oyster shells in one corner and a few old dirty calendars on the wall, advertising calf feed and various patent medicine remedies. One showed a bearded gentleman in a frock coat, holding up a bottle, and beneath his feet was the inscription, "I have been made regular by this marvelous discovery!" Mrs. Shortley had always felt close to this man as if he were some distinguished person she was acquainted with but now her mind was on nothing but the dangerous presence of the priest. She stationed herself at a crack between two boards where she could look out and see him and Mrs. McIntyre strolling toward the turkey brooder, which was placed just outside the feed house.

"Arrrrr!" he said as they approached the brooder. "Look at the little biddies!" and he stooped and squinted through the wire.

Mrs. Shortley's mouth twisted.

"Do you think the Guizacs will want to leave me?" Mrs. McIntyre asked. "Do you think they'll go to Chicago or some place like that?"

"And why should they do that now?" asked the priest, wiggling his finger at a turkey, his big nose close to the wire.

"Money," Mrs. McIntyre said.

"Arrrr, give them some morrre then," he said indifferently. "They have to get along."

"So do I," Mrs. McIntyre muttered. "It means I'm going to have to get rid of some of these others."

"And arrre the Shortleys satisfactory?" he inquired, paying more attention to the turkeys than to her.

"Five times in the last month I've found Mr. Shortley smoking in the barn," Mrs. McIntyre said. "Five times."

"And arrre the Negroes any better?"

"They lie and steal and have to be watched all the time," she said.

"Tsk, tsk," he said. "Which will you discharge?"

"I've decided to give Mr. Shortley his month's notice tomorrow," Mrs. McIntyre said.

The priest scarcely seemed to hear her he was so busy wiggling his finger inside the wire. Mrs. Shortley sat down on an open sack of laying mash with a dead thump that sent feed dust clouding up around her. She found herself looking straight ahead at the opposite wall where the gentleman on the calendar was holding up his marvelous discovery but she didn't see him. She looked ahead as if she saw nothing whatsoever. Then she rose and ran to her house. Her face was an almost volcanic red.

She opened all the drawers and dragged out boxes and old battered suitcases from under the bed. She began to unload the drawers into the boxes, all the time without pause, without taking off the sunhat she had on her head. She set the two girls to doing the same. When Mr. Shortley came in, she did not even look at him but merely pointed one arm at him while she packed with the other. "Bring the car around to the back door," she said. "You ain't waiting to be fired!"

Mr. Shortley had never in his life doubted her omniscience. He perceived the entire situation in half a second and, with only a sour scowl, retreated out the door and went to drive the automobile around to the back.

They tied the two iron beds to the top of the car and the two rocking chairs inside the beds and rolled the two mattresses up between the rocking chairs. On top of this they tied a crate of chickens. They loaded the inside of the car with the old suitcases and boxes, leaving a small space for Annie Maude and Sarah Mae. It took them the rest of the afternoon and half the night to do this but Mrs. Shortley was determined that they would leave before four o'clock in the morning, that Mr. Shortley should not adjust another milking machine on this place. All the time she had been working, her face was changing rapidly from red to white and back again.

Just before dawn, as it began to drizzle rain, they were ready to leave. They all got in the car and sat there cramped up between boxes and bundles and rolls of bedding. The square black automobile moved off with more than its customary grinding noises as if it were protesting the load. In the back, the two long bony yellow-haired girls were sitting on a pile of boxes and there was a beagle hound puppy and a cat with two kittens somewhere under the blankets. The car moved slowly, like some overfreighted leaking ark, away from their shack and past the white house where Mrs. McIntyre was sleeping soundly—

hardly guessing that her cows would not be milked by Mr. Shortley that morning—and past the Pole's shack on top of the hill and on down the road to the gate where the two Negroes were walking, one behind the other, on their way to help with the milking. They looked straight at the car and its occupants but even as the dim yellow headlights lit up their faces, they politely did not seem to see anything, or anyhow, to attach significance to what was there. The loaded car might have been passing mist in the early morning half-light. They continued up the road at the same even pace without looking back.

A dark yellow sun was beginning to rise in a sky that was the same slick dark gray as the highway. The fields stretched away, stiff and weedy, on either side. "Where we goin?" Mr. Shortley asked for the first time.

Mrs. Shortley sat with one foot on a packing box so that her knee was pushed into her stomach. Mr. Shortley's elbow was almost under her nose and Sarah Mae's bare left foot was sticking over the front seat, touching her ear.

"Where we goin?" Mr. Shortley repeated and when she didn't answer again, he turned and looked at her.

Fierce heat seemed to be swelling slowly and fully into her face as if it were welling up now for a final assault. She was sitting in an erect way in spite of the fact that one leg was twisted under her and one knee was almost into her neck, but there was a peculiar lack of light in her icy blue eyes. All the vision in them might have been turned around, looking inside her. She suddenly grabbed Mr. Shortley's elbow and Sarah Mae's foot at the same time and began to tug and pull on them as if she were trying to fit the two extra limbs onto herself.

Mr. Shortley began to curse and quickly stopped the car and Sarah Mae yelled to quit but Mrs. Shortley apparently intended to rearrange the whole car at once. She thrashed forward and backward, clutching at everything she could get her hands on and hugging it to herself, Mr. Shortley's head, Sarah Mae's leg, the cat, a wad of white bedding, her own big moon-like knee; then all at once her fierce expression faded into a look of astonishment and her grip on what she had loosened. One of her eyes drew near to the other and seemed to collapse quietly and she was still.

The two girls, who didn't know what had happened to her, began to say, "Where we goin, Ma? Where we goin?"

They thought she was playing a joke and that their father, staring straight ahead at her, was imitating a dead man. They didn't know that she had had a great experience or ever been displaced in the world from all that belonged to her. They were frightened by the gray slick road before them and they kept repeating in higher and higher voices, "Where we goin, Ma? Where we goin?" while their mother, her huge body rolled back still against the seat and her eyes like blue-painted glass, seemed to contemplate for the first time the tremendous frontiers of her true country.

II

"Well," Mrs. McIntyre said to the old Negro, "we can get along without them. We've seen them come and seen them go—black and white." She was standing in the calf barn while he cleaned it and she held a rake in her hand and now and then pulled a corn cob from a corner or pointed to a soggy spot that he had missed. When she discovered the Shortleys were gone, she was delighted as it meant she wouldn't have to fire them. The people she hired always left her—because they were that kind of people. Of all the families she had had, the Shortleys were the best if she didn't count the Displaced Person. They had been not quite trash; Mrs. Shortley was a good woman, and she would miss her but as the Judge used to say, you couldn't have your pie and eat it too, and she was satisfied with the D.P. "We've seen them come and seen them go," she repeated with satisfaction.

"And me and you," the old man said, stooping to drag his hoe under a feed rack, "is still here."

She caught exactly what he meant her to catch in his tone. Bars of sunlight fell from the cracked ceiling across his back and cut him in three distinct parts. She watched his long hands clenched around the hoe and his crooked old profile pushed close to them. You might have been here *before* I was, she said to herself, but it's mighty likely I'll be here when you're gone. "I've spent half my life fooling with worthless people," she said in a severe voice, "but now I'm through."

"Black and white," he said, "is the same."

"I am through," she repeated and gave her dark smock that she had thrown over her shoulders like a cape a quick snatch at the neck. She had on a broad-brimmed black straw hat that had cost her twenty dollars twenty years ago and that she used now for a sunhat. "Money is the root of all evil," she said. "The Judge said so every day. He said he deplored money. He said the reason you niggers were so uppity was because there was so much money in circulation."

The old Negro had known the Judge. "Judge say he long for the day when he be too poor to pay a nigger to work," he said. "Say when that day come, the world be back on its feet."

She leaned forward, her hands on her hips and her neck stretched and said, "Well that day has almost come around here and I'm telling each and every one of you: you better look sharp. I don't have to put up with foolishness any more. I have somebody now who *has* to work!"

The old man knew when to answer and when not. At length he said, "We seen them come and we seen them go."

"However, the Shortleys were not the worst by far," she said. "I well remember those Garrits."

"They was before them Collinses," he said.

"No, before the Ringfields."

"Sweet Lord, them Ringfields!" he murmured.

"None of that kind *want* to work," she said.

"We seen them come and we seen them go," he said as if this were a refrain. "But we ain't never had one before," he said, bending himself up until he faced her, "like what we got now." He was cinnamon-colored with eyes that were so blurred with age that they seemed to be hung behind cobwebs.

She gave him an intense stare and held it until, lowering his hands on the hoe, he bent down again and dragged a pile of shavings alongside the wheelbarrow. She said stiffly, "He can wash out that barn in the time it took Mr. Shortley to make up his mind he had to do it."

"He from Pole," the old man muttered.

"From Poland."

"In Pole it ain't like it is here," he said. "They got different ways of doing," and he began to mumble unintelligibly.

"What are you saying?" she said. "If you have anything to say about him, say it and say it aloud."

He was silent, bending his knees precariously and edging the rake along the underside of the trough.

"If you know anything he's done that he shouldn't, I expect you to report it to me," she said.

"It warn't like it was what he should ought or oughtn't," he muttered. "It was like what nobody else don't do."

"You don't have anything against him," she said shortly, "and he's here to stay."

"We ain't never had one like him before is all," he murmured and gave his polite laugh.

"Times are changing," she said. "Do you know what's happening to this world? It's swelling up. It's getting so full of people that only the smart thrifty energetic ones are going to survive," and she tapped the words, smart, thrifty, and energetic out on the palm of her hand. Through the far end of the stall she could see down the road to where the Displaced Person was standing in the open barn door with the green hose in his hand. There was a certain stiffness about his figure that seemed to make it necessary for her to approach him slowly, even in her thoughts. She had decided this was because she couldn't hold an easy conversation with him. Whenever she said anything to him, she found herself shouting and nodding extravagantly and she would be conscious that one of the Negroes was leaning behind the nearest shed, watching.

"No indeed!" she said, sitting down on one of the feed racks and folding her arms, "I've made up my mind that I've had enough trashy people on this place to last me a lifetime and I'm not going to spend my last years fooling with Shortleys and Ringfields and Collins when the world is full of people who *have* to work."

"How come they so many extra?" he asked.

"People are selfish," she said. "They have too many children. There's no sense in it any more."

He had picked up the wheelbarrow handles and was backing out the door and he paused, half in the sunlight and half out, and stood there chewing his gums as if he had forgotten which direction he wanted to move in.

"What you colored people don't realize," she said, "is that I'm the one around here who holds all the strings together. If you don't work, I don't make any money and I can't pay you. You're all dependent on me but you each and every one act like the shoe is on the other foot."

It was not possible to tell from his face if he heard her. Finally he backed out with the wheelbarrow. "Judge say the devil he know is better than the devil he don't," he said in a clear mutter and trundled off.

She got up and followed him, a deep vertical pit appearing suddenly in the center of her forehead, just under the red bangs. "The Judge has long since ceased to pay the bills around here," she called in a piercing voice.

He was the only one of her Negroes who had known the Judge and he thought this gave him title. He had had a low opinion of Mr. Crooms and Mr. McIntyre, her other husbands, and in his veiled polite way, he had congratulated her after each of her divorces. When he thought it necessary, he would work under a window where he knew she was sitting and talk to himself, a careful roundabout discussion, question and answer and then refrain. Once she had got up silently and slammed the window down so hard that he had fallen backwards off his feet. Or occasionally he spoke with the peacock. The cock would follow him around the place, his steady eye on the ear of corn that stuck up from the old man's back pocket or he would sit near him and pick himself. Once from the open kitchen door, she had heard him say to the bird, "I remember when it was twenty of you walking about this place and now it's only you and two hens. Crooms it was twelve. McIntyre it was five. You and two hens now."

And that time she had stepped out of the door onto the porch and said, "MISTER Crooms and MISTER McIntyre! And I don't want to hear you call either of them anything else again. And you can understand this: when that peachicken dies there won't be any replacements."

She kept the peacock only out of a superstitious fear of annoying the Judge in his grave. He had liked to see them walking around the place for he said they made him feel rich. Of her three husbands, the Judge was the one most present to her although he was the only one she had buried. He was in the family graveyard, a little space fenced in the middle of the back cornfield, with his mother and father and grandfather and three great aunts and two infant cousins. Mr. Crooms, her second, was forty miles away in the state asylum and Mr. McIntyre, her last, was intoxicated, she supposed, in some hotel room in Florida.

But the Judge, sunk in the cornfield with his family, was always at home.

She had married him when he was an old man and because of his money but there had been another reason that she would not admit then, even to herself: she had liked him. He was a dirty snuff-dipping Court House figure, famous all over the country for being rich, who wore hightop shoes, a string tie, a gray suit with a black stripe in it, and a yellowed panama hat, winter and summer. His teeth and hair were tobacco-colored and his face a clay pink pitted and tracked with mysterious prehistoric-looking marks as if he had been unearthed among fossils. There had been a peculiar odor about him of sweaty fondled bills but he never carried money on him or had a nickel to show. She was his secretary for a few months and the old man with his sharp eye had seen at once that here was a woman who admired him for himself. The three years that he lived after they married were the happiest and most prosperous of Mrs. McIntyre's life, but when he died his estate proved to be bankrupt. He left her a mortgaged house and fifty acres that he had managed to cut the timber off before he died. It was as if, as the final triumph of a successful life, he had been able to take everything with him.

But she had survived. She had survived a succession of tenant farmers and dairymen that the old man himself would have found hard to outdo, and she had been able to meet the constant drain of a tribe of moody unpredictable Negroes, and she had even managed to hold her own against the incidental bloodsuckers, the cattle dealers and lumber men and the buyers and sellers of anything who drove up in pieced-together trucks and honked in the yard.

She stood slightly reared back with her arms folded under her smock and a satisfied expression on her face as she watched the Displaced Person turn off the hose and disappear inside the barn. She was sorry that the poor man had been chased out of Poland and run across Europe and had had to take up in a tenant shack in a strange country, but she had not been responsible for any of this. She had had a hard time herself. She knew what it was to struggle. People ought to have to struggle. Mr. Guizac had probably had everything given to him all the way across Europe and over here. He had probably not had to struggle enough.

She had given him a job. She didn't know if he was grateful or not. She didn't know anything about him except that he did the work. The truth was that he was not very real to her yet. He was a kind of miracle that she had seen happen and that she talked about but that she still didn't believe.

She watched as he came out of the barn and motioned to Sulk, who was coming around the back of the lot. He gesticulated and then took something out of his pocket and the two of them stood looking at it. She started down the lane toward them. The Negro's figure was slack and tall and he was craning his round head forward in his usual idiotic way. He was a little better than half-witted but when they were like that they were always good workers. The Judge had said always hire you a half-witted nigger because they don't have sense enough to stop working. The Pole was gesticulating rapidly. He left something with the colored boy and then walked off and before she rounded the turn in the lane, she heard the tractor crank up. He was on his way to the field. The Negro was still hanging there, gaping at whatever he had in his hand.

She entered the lot and walked through the barn, looking with approval at the wet spotless concrete floor. It was only nine-thirty and Mr. Shortley had never got anything washed until eleven. As she came out at the other end, she saw the Negro moving very slowly in a diagonal path across the road in front of her, his eyes still on what Mr. Guizac had given him. He didn't see her and he paused and dipped his knees and leaned over his hand, his tongue describing little circles. He had a photograph. He lifted one finger and traced it lightly over the surface of the picture. Then he looked up and saw her and seemed to freeze, his mouth in a half-grin, his finger lifted.

"Why haven't you gone to the field?" she asked.

He raised one foot and opened his mouth wider while the hand with the photograph edged toward his back pocket.

"What's that?" she said.

"It ain't nothin," he muttered and handed it to her automatically.

It was a photograph of a girl of about twelve in a white dress. She had blond hair with a wreath in it and she looked forward out of light eyes that were bland and composed. "Who is this child?" Mrs. McIntyre asked.

"She his cousin," the boy said in a high voice.

"Well what are you doing with it?" she asked.

"She going to mah me," he said in an even higher voice.

"Marry you!" she shrieked.

"I pays half to get her over here," he said. "I pays him three dollar a week. She bigger now. She his cousin. She don't care who she mah she so glad to get away from there." The high voice seemed to shoot up like a nervous jet of sound and then fall flat as he watched her face. Her eyes were the color of blue granite when the glare falls on it, but she was not looking at him. She was looking down the road where the distant sound of the tractor could be heard.

"I don't reckon she goin to come nohow," the boy murmured.

"I'll see that you get every cent of your money back," she said in a toneless voice and turned and walked off, holding the photograph bent in two. There was nothing about her small stiff figure to indicate that she was shaken.

As soon as she got in the house, she lay down on her bed and shut her eyes and pressed her hand over her heart as if she were trying to keep it in place. Her mouth opened and she made two or three dry little sounds. Then after a minute she sat up and said aloud, "They're all the same. It's always been like this," and she fell back flat again. "Twenty years of being beaten and done in and they even robbed his grave!" and remembering that, she began to cry quietly, wiping her eyes every now and then with the hem of her smock.

What she had thought of was the angel over the Judge's grave. This had been a naked granite cherub that the old man had seen in the city one day in a tombstone store window. He had been taken with it at once, partly because its face reminded him of his wife and partly because he wanted a genuine work of art over his grave. He had come home with it sitting on the green plush train seat beside him. Mrs. McIntyre had never noticed the resemblance to herself. She had always thought it hideous but when the Herrins stole it off the old man's grave, she was shocked and outraged. Mrs. Herrin had thought it very pretty and had walked to the graveyard frequently to see it, and when the Herrins left the angel left with them, all but its toes, for the ax old man Herrin had used to break it off with had struck slightly too high. Mrs. McIntyre had never been able to afford to have it replaced.

When she had cried all she could, she got up and went into the back hall, a closet-like space that was dark and quiet as a chapel and sat down on the edge of the Judge's black mechanical chair with her elbow on his desk. This was a giant roll-top piece of furniture pocked with pigeon holes full of dusty papers. Old bankbooks and ledgers were stacked in the half-open drawers and there was a small safe, empty but locked, set like a tabernacle in the center of it. She had left this part of the house unchanged since the old man's time. It was a kind of memorial to him, sacred because he had conducted his business here. With the slightest tilt one way or the other, the chair gave a rusty skeletal groan that sounded something like him when he had complained of his poverty. It had been his first principle to talk as if he were the poorest man in the world and she followed it, not only because he had but because it was true. When she sat with her intense constricted face turned toward the empty safe, she knew there was nobody poorer in the world than she was.

She sat motionless at the desk for ten or fifteen minutes and then as if she had gained some strength, she got up and got in her car and drove to the cornfield.

The road ran through a shadowy pine thicket and ended on top of a hill that rolled fan-wise down and up again in a broad expanse of tasseled green. Mr. Guizac was cutting from the outside of the field in a circular path to the center where the graveyard was all but hidden by the corn, and she could see him on the high far side of the slope, mounted on the tractor with the cutter and wagon behind him. From time to time, he had to get off the tractor and climb in the wagon to spread the silage because the Negro had not arrived. She watched impatiently, standing in front of her black coupe with her arms folded under her smock, while he progressed slowly around the rim of the field, gradually getting close enough for her to wave to him to get down. He stopped the machine and jumped off and came running forward, wiping his red jaw with a piece of grease rag.

"I want to talk to you," she said and beckoned him to the edge of the thicket where it was shady. He took off the cap and followed her, smiling, but his smile faded when she turned and faced him. Her eyebrows, thin and fierce as a spider's leg, had drawn together ominously and the deep vertical pit had plunged down from under the red bangs into the bridge of her nose. She removed the bent picture from her pocket and handed it to him silently. Then she stepped back and said, "Mr. Guizac! You would bring this poor innocent child over here and try to marry her to a half-witted thieving black stinking nigger! What kind of a monster are you!"

He took the photograph with a slowly returning smile. "My cousin," he said. "She twelve here. First Communion. Six-ten now."

Monster! she said to herself and looked at him as if she were seeing him for the first time. His forehead and skull were white where they had been protected by his cap but the rest of his face was red and bristled with short yellow hairs. His eyes were like two bright nails behind his gold-rimmed spectacles that had been mended over the nose with haywire. His whole face looked as if it might have been patched together out of several others. "Mr. Guizac," she said, beginning slowly and then speaking faster until she ended breathless in the middle of a word, "that nigger cannot have a white wife from Europe. You can't talk to a nigger that way. You'll excite him and besides it can't be done. Maybe it can be done in Poland but it can't be done here and you'll have to stop. It's all foolishness. That nigger don't have a grain of sense and you'll excite . . ."

"She in camp three year," he said.

"Your cousin," she said in a positive voice, "cannot come over here and marry one of my Negroes."

"She six-ten year," he said. "From Poland. Mamma die, pappa die. She wait in camp. Three camp." He pulled a wallet from his pocket and fingered through it and took out another picture of the same girl, a few years older, dressed in something dark and shapeless. She was standing against a wall with a short woman who apparently had no teeth. "She mamma," he said, pointing to the woman. "She die in two camp."

"Mr. Guizac," Mrs. McIntyre said, pushing the picture back at him. "I will not have my niggers upset. I cannot run this place without my niggers. I can run it without you but not without them and if you mention this girl to Sulk again, you won't have a job with me. Do you understand?"

His face showed no comprehension. He seemed to be piecing all these words together in his mind to make a thought.

Mrs. McIntyre remembered Mrs. Shortley's words: "He understands everything, he only pretends he don't so as to do exactly as he pleases," and her face regained the look of shocked wrath she had begun with. "I cannot understand how a man who calls himself a Christian," she said, "could bring a poor innocent girl over here and marry her to something like that. I cannot understand it. I cannot!" and she shook her head and looked into the distance with a pained blue gaze.

After a second he shrugged and let his arms drop as if he were tired. "She no care black," he said. "She in camp three year."

Mrs. McIntyre felt a peculiar weakness behind her knees. "Mr. Guizac," she said, "I don't want to have to speak to you about this again. If I do, you'll have to find another place yourself. Do you understand?"

The patched face did not say. She had the impression that he didn't see her there. "This is my place," she said. "I say who will come here and who won't."

"Ya," he said and put back on his cap.

"I am not responsible for the world's misery," she said as an afterthought.

"Ya," he said.

"You have a good job. You should be grateful to be here," she added, "but I'm not sure you are."

"Ya," he said and gave his little shrug and turned back to the tractor.

She watched him get on and maneuver the machine into the corn again. When he had passed her and rounded the turn, she climbed to the top of the slope and stood with her arms folded and looked out grimly over the field. "They're all the same," she muttered, "whether they come from Poland or Tennessee. I've handled Herrins and Ringfields and Shortleys and I can handle a Guizac," and she narrowed her gaze until it closed entirely around the diminishing figure on the tractor as if she were watching him through a gunsight. All her life she had been fighting the world's overflow and now she had it in the form of a Pole. "You're just like all the rest of them," she said, "—only smart and thrifty and energetic but so am I. And this is my place," and she stood there, a small black-hatted, black-smocked figure with an aging cherubic face, and folded her arms as if she were equal to anything. But her heart was beating as if some interior violence had already been done to her. She opened her eyes to include the whole field so that the figure on the tractor was no larger than a grasshopper in her widened view.

She stood there for some time. There was a slight breeze and the corn trembled in great waves on both sides of the slope. The big cutter, with its monotonous roar, continued to shoot it pulverized into the wagon in a steady spurt of fodder. By nightfall, the Displaced Person would have worked his way around and around until there would be nothing on either side of the two hills but the stubble, and down in the center, risen like a little island, the graveyard where the Judge lay grinning under his desecrated monument.

III

The priest, with his long bland face supported on one finger, had been talking for ten minutes about Purgatory while Mrs. McIntyre squinted furiously at him from an opposite chair. They were drinking ginger ale on her front porch and she kept rattling the ice in her glass, rattling her beads, rattling her bracelet like an impatient pony jingling its harness. There is no moral obligation to keep him, she was saying under her breath, there is absolutely no moral obligation. Suddenly she lurched up and her voice fell across his brogue like a drill into a mechanical saw. "Listen!" she said, "I'm not theological. I'm practical! I want to talk to you about something practical!"

"Arrrrrrr," he groaned, grating to a halt.

She had put at least a finger of whisky in her own ginger ale so that she would be able to endure his full-length visit and she sat down awkwardly, finding the chair closer to her than she had expected. "Mr. Guizac is not satisfactory," she said.

The old man raised his eyebrows in mock wonder.

"He's extra," she said. "He doesn't fit in. I have to have somebody who fits in."

The priest carefully turned his hat on his knees. He had a little trick of waiting a second silently and then swinging the conversation back into his own paths. He was about eighty. She had never known a priest until she had gone to see this one on the business of getting her the Displaced Person. After he had got her the Pole, he had used the business introduction to try to convert her—just as she had supposed he would.

"Give him time," the old man said. "He'll learn to fit in. Where is that beautiful birrrrd of yours?" he asked and then said, "Arrrrr, I see him!" and stood up and looked out over the lawn where the peacock and the two hens were stepping at a strained attention, their long necks ruffled, the cock's violent blue and the hens' silver-green, glinting in the late afternoon sun.

"Mr. Guizac," Mrs. McIntyre continued, bearing down with a flat steady voice, "is very efficient. I'll admit that. But he doesn't understand how to get on with my niggers and they don't like him. I can't have my niggers run off. And I don't like his attitude. He's not the least grateful for being here."

The priest had his hand on the screen door and he opened it, ready to make his escape. "Arrrr, I must be off," he murmured.

"I tell you if I had a white man who understood the Negroes, I'd have to let Mr. Guizac go," she said and stood up again.

He turned then and looked her in the face. "He has nowhere to go," he said. Then he said, "Dear lady, I know you well enough to know you wouldn't turn him out for a trifle!" and without waiting for an answer, he raised his hand and gave her his blessing in a rumbling voice.

She smiled angrily and said, "I didn't create his situation, of course."

The priest let his eyes wander toward the birds. They had reached the middle of the lawn. The cock stopped suddenly and curving his neck backwards, he raised his tail and spread it with a shimmering timbrous noise. Tiers of small pregnant suns floated in a green-gold haze over his head. The priest stood transfixed, his jaw slack. Mrs. McIntyre wondered where she had ever seen such an idiotic old man. "Christ will come like that!" he said in a loud gay voice and wiped his hand over his mouth and stood there, gaping.

Mrs. McIntyre's face assumed a set puritanical expression and she reddened. Christ in the conversation embarrassed her the way sex had her mother. "It is not my responsibility that Mr. Guizac has nowhere to go," she said. "I don't find myself responsible for all the extra people in the world."

The old man didn't seem to hear her. His attention was fixed on the cock who was taking minute steps backward, his head against the spread tail. "The Transfiguration," he murmured.

She had no idea what he was talking about. "Mr. Guizac didn't have to come here in the first place," she said, giving him a hard look.

The cock lowered his tail and began to pick grass.

"He didn't have to come in the first place," she repeated, emphasizing each word.

The old man smiled absently. "He came to redeem us," he said and blandly reached for her hand and shook it and said he must go.

If Mr. Shortley had not returned a few weeks later, she would have gone out looking for a new man to hire. She had not wanted him back but when she saw the familiar black automobile drive up the road and stop by the side of the house, she had the feeling that she was the one returning, after a long miserable trip, to her own place. She realized all at once that it was Mrs. Shortley she had been missing. She had had no one to talk to since Mrs. Shortley left, and she ran to the door, expecting to see her heaving herself up the steps.

Mr. Shortley stood there alone. He had on a black felt hat and a shirt with red and blue palm trees designed in it but the hollows in his long bitten blistered face were deeper than they had been a month ago.

"Well!" she said. "Where is Mrs. Shortley?"

Mr. Shortley didn't say anything. The change in his face seemed to have come from the inside; he looked like a man who had gone for a long time without water. "She was God's own angel," he said in a loud voice. "She was the sweetest woman in the world."

"Where is she?" Mrs. McIntyre murmured.

"Daid," he said. "She had herself a stroke on the day she left out of here." There was a corpse-like composure about his face. "I figure that Pole killed her," he said. "She seen through him from the first. She known he come from the devil. She told me so."

It took Mrs. McIntyre three days to get over Mrs. Shortley's death. She told herself that anyone would have thought they were kin. She rehired Mr. Shortley to do farm work though actually she didn't want him without his wife. She told him she was going to give thirty days' notice to the Displaced Person at the end of the month and that then he could have his job back in the dairy. Mr. Shortley preferred the dairy job but he was willing to wait. He said it would give him some satisfaction to see the Pole leave the place, and Mrs. McIntyre said it would give her a great deal of satisfaction. She confessed that she should have been content with the help she had in the first place and not have been reaching into other parts of the world for it. Mr. Shortley said he never had cared for foreigners since he had been in the first world's war and seen what they were like. He said he had seen all kinds then but that none of them were like us. He said he recalled the face of one man who had thrown a hand-grenade at him and that the man had had little round eye-glasses exactly like Mr. Guizac's.

"But Mr. Guizac is a Pole, he's not a German," Mrs. McIntyre said.

"It ain't a great deal of difference in them two kinds," Mr. Shortley had explained.

The Negroes were pleased to see Mr. Shortley back. The Displaced Person had expected them to work as hard as he worked himself, whereas Mr. Shortley recognized their limitations. He had never been a very good worker himself with Mrs. Shortley to keep him in line, but without her, he was even more forgetful and slow. The Pole worked as fiercely as ever and seemed to have no inkling that he was about to be fired. Mrs. McIntyre saw jobs done in a short time that she had thought would never get done at all. Still she was resolved to get rid of him. The sight of his small stiff figure moving quickly here and there had come to be the most irritating sight on the place for her, and she felt she had been tricked by the old priest. He had said there was no legal obligation for her to keep the Displaced Person if he was not satisfactory, but then he had brought up the moral one.

She meant to tell him that *her* moral obligation was to her own people, to Mr. Shortley, who had fought in the world war for his country and not to Mr. Guizac who had merely arrived here to take advantage of whatever he could. She felt she must have this out with the priest before she fired the Displaced Person. When the first of the month came and the priest hadn't called, she put off giving the Pole notice for a little longer.

Mr. Shortley told himself that he should have known all along that no woman was going to do what she said she was when she said she was. He didn't know how long he could afford to put up with her shilly-shallying. He thought himself that she was going soft and was afraid to turn the Pole out for fear he would have a hard time getting another place. He could tell her the truth about this: that if she let him go, in three years he would own his own house and have a television aerial sitting on top of it. As a matter of policy, Mr. Shortley began to come to her back door every evening to put certain facts before her. "A white man sometimes don't get the consideration a nigger gets," he said, "but that don't matter because he's still white, but sometimes," and here he would pause and look off into the distance, "a man that's fought and bled and died in the service of his native land don't get the consideration of one of them like them he was fighting. I ast you: is that right?" When he asked her such questions he could watch her face and tell he was making an impression. She didn't look too well these days. He noticed lines around her eyes that hadn't been there when he and Mrs. Shortley had been the only white help on the place. Whenever he thought of Mrs. Shortley, he felt his heart go down like an old bucket into a dry well.

The old priest kept away as if he had been frightened by his last visit but finally, seeing that the Displaced Person had not been fired, he ventured to call again to take up giving Mrs. McIntyre instructions where he remembered leaving them off. She had not asked to be instructed but he instructed anyway, forcing a little definition of one of the sacraments or of some dogma into each conversation he had, no matter with whom. He sat on her porch, taking no notice of her partly mocking, partly outraged expression as she sat shaking her foot, waiting for an opportunity to drive a wedge into his talk. "For," he was saying, as if he spoke of something that had happened yesterday in town, "when God sent his Only Begotten Son, Jesus Christ Our Lord"—he slightly bowed his head—"as a Redeemer to mankind, He . . ."

"Father Flynn!" she said in a voice that made him jump. "I want to talk to you about something serious!"

The skin under the old man's right eye flinched.

"As far as I'm concerned," she said and glared at him fiercely, "Christ was just another D.P."

He raised his hands slightly and let them drop on his knees. "Arrrrr," he murmured as if he were considering this.

"I'm going to let that man go," she said. "I don't have any obligation to him. My obligation is to the people who've done something for their country, not to the ones who've just come over to take advantage of what they can get," and she began to talk rapidly, remembering all her arguments. The priest's attention seemed to retire to some private oratory to wait until she got through. Once or twice his gaze roved out onto the lawn as if he were hunting some means of escape but she didn't stop. She told him how she had been hanging onto this place for thirty years, always just barely making it against people who came from nowhere and were going nowhere, who didn't want anything but an automobile. She said she had found out they were the same whether they came from Poland or Tennessee. When the Guizacs got ready, she said, they would not hesitate to leave her. She told him how the people who looked rich were the poorest of all because they had the most to keep up. She asked him how he thought she paid her feed bills. She told him she would like to have her house done over but she couldn't afford it. She couldn't even afford to have the monument restored over her husband's grave. She asked him if he would like to guess what her insurance amounted to for the year. Finally she asked him if he thought she was made of money and the old man suddenly let out a great ugly bellow as if this were a comical question.

When the visit was over, she felt let down, though she had clearly triumphed over him. She made up her mind now that on the first of the month, she would give the Displaced Person his thirty days' notice and she told Mr. Shortley so.

Mr. Shortley didn't say anything. His wife had been the only woman he was ever acquainted with who was never scared off from doing what she said. She said the Pole had been sent by the devil and the priest. Mr. Shortley had no doubt that the priest had got some peculiar control over Mrs. McIntyre and that before long she would start attending his Masses. She looked as if something was wearing her down from the inside. She was thinner and more fidgety and not as sharp as she used to be. She would look at a milk can now and not see how dirty it was and he had seen her lips move when she was not talking. The Pole never did anything the wrong way but all the same he was very irritating to her. Mr. Shortley himself did things as he pleased—not always her way—but she didn't seem to notice. She had noticed though that the Pole and all his family were getting fat; she pointed out to Mr. Shortley that the hollows had come out of their cheeks and that they saved every cent they made. "Yes'm, and one of these days he'll be able to buy and sell you out," Mr. Shortley had ventured to say, and he could tell that the statement had shaken her.

"I'm just waiting for the first," she had said.

Mr. Shortley waited too and the first came and went and she didn't fire him. He could have told anybody how it would be. He was not a violent man but he hated to see a woman done in by a foreigner. He felt that that was one thing a man couldn't stand by and see happen.

There was no reason Mrs. McIntyre should not fire Mr. Guizac at once but she put it off from day to day. She was worried about her bills and about her health. She didn't sleep at night or when she did she dreamed about the Displaced Person. She had never discharged anyone before; they had all left her. One night she dreamed that Mr. Guizac and his family were moving into her house and that she was moving in with Mr. Shortley. This was too much for her and she woke up and didn't sleep again for several nights; and one night she dreamed that the priest came to call and droned on and on, saying, "Dear lady, I know your tender heart won't suffer you to turn the porrrrr man out. Think of the thousands of them, think of the ovens and the boxcars and the camps and the sick children and Christ Our Lord."

"He's extra and he's upset the balance around here," she said, "and I'm a logical practical woman and there are no ovens here and no camps and no Christ Our Lord and when he leaves, he'll make more money. He'll work at the mill and buy a car and don't talk to me—all they want is a car."

"The ovens and the boxcars and the sick children," droned the priest, "and our dear Lord."

"Just one too many," she said.

The next morning, she made up her mind while she was eating her breakfast that she would give him his notice at once, and she stood up and walked out of the kitchen and down the road with her table napkin still in her hand. Mr. Guizac was spraying the barn, standing in his swaybacked way with one hand on his hip. He turned off the hose and gave her an impatient kind of attention as if she were interfering with his work. She had not thought of what she would say to him, she had merely come. She stood in the barn door, looking severely at the wet spotless floor and the dripping stanchions. "Ya goot?" he said.

"Mr. Guizac," she said, "I can barely meet my obligations now." Then she said in a louder, stronger voice, emphasizing each word, "I have bills to pay."

"I too," Mr. Guizac said. "Much bills, little money," and he shrugged.

At the other end of the barn, she saw a long beak-nosed shadow glide like a snake halfway up the sunlit open door and stop; and somewhere behind her, she was aware of a silence where the sound of the Negroes shoveling had come a minute before. "This is my place," she said angrily. "All of you are extra. Each and every one of you are extra!"

"Ya," Mr. Guizac said and turned on the hose again.

She wiped her mouth with the napkin she had in her hand and walked off, as if she had accomplished what she came for.

Mr. Shortley's shadow withdrew from the door and he leaned against the side of the barn and lit half of a cigarette that he took out of his pocket. There was nothing for him to do now but wait on the hand of God to strike, but he knew one thing: he was not going to wait with his mouth shut.

Starting that morning, he began to complain and to state his side of the case to every person he saw, black or white. He complained in the grocery store and at the courthouse and on the street corner and directly to Mrs. McIntyre herself, for there was nothing underhanded about him. If the Pole could have understood what he had to say, he would have said it to him too. "All men was created free and equal," he said to Mrs. McIntyre, "and I risked my life and limb to prove it. Gone over there and fought and bled and died and come back on over here and find out who's got my job—just exactly who I been fighting. It was a hand-grenade come that near to killing me and I seen who throwed it—little man with eye-glasses just like his. Might have bought them at the same store. Small world," and he gave a bitter little laugh. Since he didn't have Mrs. Shortley to do the talking any more, he had started doing it himself and had found that he had a gift for it. He had the power of making other people see his logic. He talked a good deal to the Negroes.

"Whyn't you go back to Africa?" he asked Sulk one morning as they were cleaning out the silo. "That's your country, ain't it?"

"I ain't goin there," the boy said. "They might eat me up."

"Well, if you behave yourself it isn't any reason you can't stay here," Mr. Shortley said kindly. "Because you didn't run away from nowhere. Your granddaddy was brought. He didn't have a thing to do with coming. It's the people that run away from where they come from that I ain't got any use for."

"I never felt no need to travel," the Negro said.

"Well," Mr. Shortley said, "if I was going to travel again, it would be to either China or Africa. You go to either of them two places and you can tell right away what the difference is between you and them. You go to these other places and the only way you can tell is if they say something. And then you can't always tell because about half of them know the English language. That's where we make our mistake," he said, "—letting all them people onto English. There'd be a heap less trouble if everybody only knew his own language. My wife said knowing two languages was like having eyes in the back of your head. You couldn't put nothing over on her."

"You sho couldn't," the boy muttered, and then he added, "She was fine. She was sho fine. I never known a finer white woman than her."

Mr. Shortley turned in the opposite direction and worked silently for a while. After a few minutes he leaned up and tapped the colored boy on the shoulder with the handle of his shovel. For a second he only looked at him while a great deal of meaning gathered in his wet eyes. Then he said softly, "Revenge is mine, saith the Lord."

Mrs. McIntyre found that everybody in town knew Mr. Shortley's version of her business and that everyone was critical of her conduct. She began to understand that she had a moral obligation to fire the Pole and that she was shirking it because she found it hard to do. She could not stand the increasing guilt any longer and on a cold Saturday morning, she started off after breakfast to fire him. She walked down to the machine shed where she heard him cranking up the tractor.

There was a heavy frost on the ground that made the fields look like the rough backs of sheep; the sun was almost silver and the woods stuck up like dry bristles on the sky line. The countryside seemed to be receding from the little circle of noise around the shed. Mr. Guizac was squatting on the ground beside the small tractor, putting in a part. Mrs. McIntyre hoped to get the fields turned over while he still had thirty days to work for her. The colored boy was standing by with some tools in his hand and Mr. Shortley was under the shed about to get up on the large tractor and back it out. She meant to wait until he and the Negro got out of the way before she began her unpleasant duty.

She stood watching Mr. Guizac, stamping her feet on the hard ground, for the cold was climbing like a paralysis up her feet and legs. She had on a heavy black coat and a red head-kerchief with her black hat pulled down on top of it to keep the glare out of her eyes. Under the black brim her face had an abstracted look and once or twice her lips moved silently. Mr. Guizac shouted over the noise of the tractor for the Negro to hand him a screwdriver and when he got it, he turned over on his back on the icy ground and reached up under the machine. She could not see his face, only his feet and legs and trunk sticking impudently out from the side of the tractor. He had on rubber boots that were cracked and splashed with mud. He raised one knee and then lowered it and turned himself slightly. Of all the things she resented about him, she resented most that he hadn't left of his own accord.

Mr. Shortley had got on the large tractor and was backing it out from under the shed. He seemed to be warmed by it as if its heat and strength sent impulses up through him that he obeyed instantly. He had headed it toward the small tractor but he braked it on a slight incline and jumped off and turned back toward the shed. Mrs. McIntyre was looking fixedly at Mr. Guizac's legs lying flat on the ground now. She heard the brake on the large tractor slip and, looking up, she saw it move forward, calculating its own path. Later she remembered that she had seen the Negro jump silently out of the way as if a spring in the earth had released him and that she had seen Mr. Shortley turn his head with incredible slowness and stare silently over his shoulder and that she had started to shout to the Displaced Person but that she had not. She had felt her eyes and Mr. Shortley's eyes and the Negro's eyes come together in one look that froze them in collusion forever, and she had heard the little noise the Pole made as the tractor wheel broke his backbone. The two men ran forward to help and she fainted.

She remembered, when she came to, running somewhere, perhaps into the house and out again but she could not remember what for or if she had fainted again when she got there. When she finally came back to where the tractors were, the ambulance had arrived. Mr. Guizac's body was covered with the bent bodies of his wife and two children and by a black one which hung over him, murmuring words she didn't understand. At first she thought this must be the doctor but then with a feeling of annoyance she recognized the priest, who had come with the ambulance and was slipping something into the crushed man's mouth. After a minute he stood up and she looked first at his bloody pants legs and then at his face which was not averted from her but was as withdrawn and expressionless as the rest of the countryside. She only stared at him for she was too shocked by her experience to be quite herself. Her mind was not taking hold of all that was happening. She felt she was in some foreign country where the people bent over the body were natives, and she watched like a stranger while the dead man was carried away in the ambulance.

That evening Mr. Shortley left without notice to look for a new position and the Negro, Sulk, was taken with a sudden desire to see more of the world and set off for the southern part of the state. The old man Astor could not work without company. Mrs. McIntyre hardly noticed that she had no help left for she came down with a nervous affliction and had to go to the hospital. When she came back, she saw that the place would be too much for her to run now and she turned her cows over to a professional auctioneer (who sold them at a loss) and retired to live on what she had, while she tried to save her declining health. A numbness developed in one of her legs and her hands and head began to jiggle and eventually she had to stay in bed all the time with only a colored woman to wait on her. Her eyesight grew steadily worse and she lost her voice altogether. Not many people remembered to come out to the country to see her except the old priest. He came regularly once a week with a bag of breadcrumbs and, after he had fed these to the peacock, he would come in and sit by the side of her bed and explain the doctrines of the Church.

SCENES FROM *THE DISPLACED PERSON,*

*a film script based on the O'Connor story by Horton Foote**

Mrs. McIntyre, the widowed owner of a Georgia dairy farm, has just welcomed a new hired hand and his family, Polish refugees from Europe, brought to her farm by a local priest. She introduces them to Mrs. Shortley, the wife of another of her employees, while her black fieldhands look on from a distance. When Mrs. McIntyre takes the Polish family to the tenant shack they will occupy, the following scenes begin.

5. MOVING SHOT—MRS. SHORTLEY.

As she goes toward the mulberry tree, she stops about ten feet away and calls out to the two black men.

MRS. SHORTLEY [*calling*]. Well . . . Yawl have looked long enough. What you think about them?

[ASTOR *and* SULK *come out toward her.*]

ASTOR. We been watching. Who they now?

MRS. SHORTLEY. They come from over the water. Only one of 'em seems like can speak English. They're what is called displaced persons.

ASTOR. Displaced persons. Well now, I declare. What do that mean?

MRS. SHORTLEY. It means they ain't where they were born at and there's nowhere for them to go. Like if you was run out of here and wouldn't nobody have you.

---

* An eminent dramatist known for his works for the New York stage, for the screen, and for television, Horton Foote is the author of such plays as *A Trip to Bountiful* and *A Young Lady of Property,* and such film dramatizations as those of Harper Lee's *To Kill a Mockingbird* and Faulkner's "Tomorrow."

ASTOR. It seem they here though. If they here they somewhere.

SULK. Sho is. They here.

MRS. SHORTLEY. They ain't where they belong to be at. They belong to be back over yonder where everything is still like they been used to. They don't have an advanced religion I can tell you that.

ASTOR. They don't?

MRS. SHORTLEY. No. I can't tell you exactly what all they believe; but I know this much—none of the foolishness has been reformed out of it. Over here it's more advanced in all ways than where they come from. But yawl better look out now. There's about ten billion more just like them and I know what Mrs. McIntyre said.

SULK. Say what?

MRS. SHORTLEY. Places are not easy to get nowadays, for white or black, but I reckon I know what she stated to me.

ASTOR. You liable to hear most anything.

MRS. SHORTLEY [*in angry voice*]. I heard her say . . . "This is going to put the fear of the Lord into those shiftless niggers."

[ASTOR *starts off*.]

ASTOR. She say something like that every now and then. Ha! Ha! Yes, indeed.

[MRS. SHORTLEY *continues on to* SULK.]

MRS. SHORTLEY. You better get on in that barn and help Mr. Shortley. What you reckon she pays you for?

SULK. He the one sent me out. He the one give me somethin' else to do.

MRS. SHORTLEY. Well, you better get to doing it then.

[*He moves on after* ASTOR. MRS. SHORTLEY *stands there reflecting. The peacock jumps up into the mulberry tree, his tail hanging in front of* MRS. SHORTLEY.]

CLOSE SHOT—PEACOCK TAIL.

CLOSE SHOT—MRS. SHORTLEY.

[*She is unaware of the peacock or his tail. She is having an inner vision. Her face is set and has the fierce look of a prophet.*]

MRS. SHORTLEY [*calling in her vision*]. They have come to take your place. You'll have to find another. Go on now. I warned you.

[*She is drained and tired after the visionary experience. She starts for the barn.*]

6. EXTERIOR: BARNYARD. DAY.

Mrs. Shortley looks over toward the barn where her husband is milking.

7. INTERIOR: BARN MILKING AREA. DAY. MRS. SHORTLEY'S POINT OF VIEW.

She can see Mr. Shortley in the barn adjusting the last milking machine on a large black and white spotted cow, near the entrance, squatting at her heels, a half-inch of cigarette adhering to the center of his lower lip.

BACK TO MRS. SHORTLEY NOW AT THE ENTRANCE.

She continues to watch him closely for a second and he is not aware of her.

MRS. SHORTLEY. Chancey, if she seen or heard of you smoking in this barn, she would blow a fuse.

MR. SHORTLEY [*turns and sees his wife*]. You gonna be the one to tell her?

MRS. SHORTLEY. She's got a nose of her own.

ANGLE—MR. SHORTLEY.

As he lifts the cigarette stub with the sharp end of his tongue, draws it into his mouth, closes his lips tightly, rises, steps outside to his wife.

TWO-SHOT—MR. AND MRS. SHORTLEY.

He gives his wife a good appreciative stare and spits the smoldering butt into the grass.

MRS. SHORTLEY. Aw, Chancey. Haw. Haw.

[*She digs a little hole for it with her toe and covers it up. He starts back into the barn and she follows after him.*]

INTERIOR: BARN MILKING AREA. DAY.

Mr. Shortley squats at the cow again. She comes over to him and continues to watch him milk.

MRS. SHORTLEY. Well, the Gobblehooks have come and she wants you to meet them, says, "Where's Mr. Shortley?" I says . . .

MR. SHORTLEY [*interrupting*]. Tote up them weights.

MRS. SHORTLEY. An' she don't call them Gobblehooks no longer.

MR. SHORTLEY. What does she call them?

MRS. SHORTLEY. Whatever their last name is. She can say it just as plain as that priest can. The boy's called Rudolph and the girl, Sledgewig. I just as soon name a child of mine boll-weevil as Sledgewig. You reckon he can drive a tractor when he don't know English? I don't think she's going to get her money's worth out of them. That boy can talk but he looks delicate. The one can work, can't talk, and the one can talk can't work. She ain't no better off than if she had more niggers.

MR. SHORTLEY. I would rather have niggers if it was me.

MRS. SHORTLEY. She says it's ten million more like them, displaced persons. She says that there priest can get her all she wants.

MR. SHORTLEY. She better quit messin' with that there priest.

MRS. SHORTLEY. He don't look smart. Kind of foolish.

MR. SHORTLEY. I ain't going to have no Pope of Rome tell me how to run no dairy.

MRS. SHORTLEY. They ain't Eyetalians, they're Poles. From Poland. Where all them bodies were stacked up at. Like we seen at the newsreel at the picture show. You remember all them bodies?

MR. SHORTLEY. I give them three weeks.

DISSOLVE:

INTERIOR: CAR. MRS. SHORTLEY AND MRS. MCINTYRE. DAY.

Mrs. McIntyre drives the car towards the fields.

MRS. MCINTYRE [*with enormous enthusiasm*]. I want to

see that cutter I just bought in action. For the first time I have somebody can operate it. Mr. Guizac is a wonder. He can drive a tractor, use the rotary hay-baler, the combine, the mill or any other machine I got around the place.

MRS. SHORTLEY. I hope they don't all break down.

MRS. MCINTYRE. I don't worry about that. He is an expert mechanic. A carpenter. A mason. He is thrifty and he is energetic. He will save me twenty dollars a month on repair bills alone. Getting him was the best day's work I have ever done in my life. He can work milking machines and is the cleanest thing I ever saw, and he doesn't smoke.

[*This last remark is not lost on* MRS. SHORTLEY. *She scowls.*]

INTERVIEW WITH HORTON FOOTE*

INT: Horton, you've done many, many original plays —for the stage, for television, for film. When you're working on an adaptation, do you prepare yourself in any way that you wouldn't when you are doing an original work?

FOOTE: I think that the first preparation is almost a kind of mystical one; you have to feel somehow that you can enter into another writer's terrain, and take on the beat of another writer's heart. Whenever I have not obeyed that and tried just to do something, it has never worked for me.

INT: How do you get yourself up to enter that mystical experience?

FOOTE: You have to know that there are certain writers you feel very close to and others not. I can admire terribly, let's say, a writer like Norman Mailer, but I would never be able to enter into his world, creatively. I mean I can admire him, I can read him, but I can sense the differences in our temperaments. It just isn't a question of being Southern, either. I could never enter into Truman Capote's world, though I can admire him greatly, which I do, and respect him as a craftsman, which I do. So you just have to sense that. I don't really know that you can analyze it logically.

INT: Is there anything about the day-to-day working process when you're working on a dramatization like *The Displaced Person* that's different from when you're writing an original script?

FOOTE: Yes, because there are certain things that you know are established. When you are working on something of your own, it's like going into an uncharted world, and part of the secret is to find the form, the structure. When you are restructuring a story in dramatic form, you are

---

* An eminent dramatist known for his works for the New York stage, for the screen, and for television, Horton Foote is the author of such plays as *A Trip to Bountiful* and *A Young Lady of Property*, and such film dramatizations as those of Harper Lee's *To Kill a Mockingbird* and Faulkner's "Tomorrow." This interview was conducted by Calvin Skaggs on April 15, 1977.

involved in the process of construction, but there are so many things that you assimilate differently. When you're working on something of your own, you call upon a lot of unconscious things that you have been storing up and thinking about. Well, here a great deal more is conscious, and you have to approach consciously what must have been an unconscious process for the original writer. But there are times . . . for instance when I was dramatizing Faulkner's story, "Tomorrow," the character of the woman became alive to me, even though Faulkner gives only one little paragraph to her. He told me enough about her so that my imagination just began to work, and she became somebody I knew. Nothing like that was done with *The Displaced Person* because Flannery O'Connor's world was so ordered that you simply couldn't. She's as structured a writer as I know of.

INT: And the form is very, not rigid perhaps, but very distinct.

FOOTE: It comes strictly from her own vision of life. The thing that for me was very interesting in working on her was whatever it is in her vision, whether it's the Catholicism or whatever it is, that goes beyond what I normally am involved with. So this was a great adventure, to try to figure out what this point of view was. You know, a lot of people don't respond to her. They feel she's very cold and cruel, you know that. I don't think that at all.

INT: You don't think she's cruel?

FOOTE: Oh no, not really. I think she's unsentimental and I think she's tough as anything on people, but really, somewhere down there, there is an enormous sense of compassion.

INT: It's an unsentimental compassion.

FOOTE: That's right. Almost classic in a sense. I always go back to that comment of Thomas Merton's that she's like Sophocles, that she is not like anybody contemporary. There is something totally unique about her.

INT: That Sophoclean sense comes, I think, out of one's feeling that the form in her work is so inevitable.

FOOTE: When she's at her best. When you take her lesser works, she can be sentimental and vague and fuzzy.

INT: Let me ask another question about your working process. Do you ever visualize a particular actor or actress playing a character you're creating?

FOOTE: Oh no, it never crosses my mind. People do. I might say, well, oh my God, this is Miss Lily. Oh, I knew this woman, oh yes. Or yes, the Shortleys, well this is Mr. Culpepper or Mr. Tillman or Mr. Anybody.

INT: Do you visualize locales that you remember? A particular shack, or spot? Does a specific place come into your mind?

FOOTE: Sure. Cottonfields. . . . You know I was born in cottonfields, so I remember the smell of them and the sound of them and the sound of these machines coming in. And I knew dairy farms like Mrs. McIntyre's. In this case I was immediately reminded that after the Second World War some cousins of mine had brought in some people from Poland to work as tenants.

INT: This was in the South? In Texas?

FOOTE: Yes. So I knew what kind of man the displaced person was, and because my wife is Polish, I knew intimately through her family another side of Polish life.

INT: You told me once how hard-working the Polish immigrants were.

FOOTE: Yes. Because my wife's family brought over a nephew of her father's, a man who had survived the concentration camps, and the minute he hit this country, he began to go. In a way, the American Poles were flabbergasted to see it.

INT: Since you could identify with so many aspects of Flannery O'Connor's world, did you have any problems once you had made that first leap you describe?

FOOTE: Well, I would have preferred to have the script longer. But as you know my main problem was that I felt this curious kind of division in the story. I felt there were two endings to the work. In fact, the story as first published ended with the death of Mrs. Shortley. Knowing that helped me in some way make this bridge, and I began to understand why she extended the story. Also, Glenn Jordan (the director) insisted that Mrs. McIntyre be the line we follow throughout. But the person who took me over first was Mrs. Shortley, as you know. I simply adore her. I adore all of her crudity and all of her vulgarity and all her stupidity, and she doesn't offend me. You know, I just do understand her. So it took me a while to dig out and to follow Mrs. McIntyre's line and see that she is the structural force that unifies everything.

INT: At first did the story go dead? After Mrs. Shortley disappeared?

FOOTE: Yes. But what I really had to do was to go back and to understand that Mrs. McIntyre was there all the time.

INT: So it's like underlining what is there and carving away.

FOOTE: Yes.

INT: I want to ask you about some of the visual things in the story. Say the newsreels Mrs. Shortley refers to.

FOOTE: Well, if you include that newsreel visually, then the counterpoint to that is Mrs. Shortley's vision. Those are two different styles, and I think now that Glenn was absolutely right. But the dreams and visions did intrigue me, and in another kind of world I guess you'd have said, "Let's play around with this, and we can cut it later." But you would have had to really find a whole kind of style to treat those things in. And I don't know whether it would have worked. What happens in the film is you know something is going on.

INT: And it remains mysterious.

FOOTE: Yes.

INT: Well, the story is flagrant with visual symbols, like the dreams and the newsreel, and the peacock. Did you feel stimulated by all this visual material?

FOOTE: Oh yes; see, this is what I love about her. Again, it's this vision of people, that makes you always say, wow, it's deeply rooted in the reality I know.

INT: Was there anything in Flannery's work that worried you—for example, her treatment of blacks?

FOOTE: Well, it worries you in a sense because this is how a lot of people think about the blacks. Yet you have to say to yourself that there are a lot of blacks like this too. And she's not sparing of them. Unfortunately, the enormous injustice is not a racial injustice; the enormous injustice is that some people are born with a certain gift, and other people are not. Black or white, there is nothing you can do about it. And this is what I think you find you have to say about her, that human nature is of itself not enough. That beyond it is some kind of transcendental thing.

INT: Is it accurate to say that Flannery O'Connor believes human nature is not enough, and then she makes us accept, without understanding, that there is something beyond?

FOOTE: This terrible vision she has! You see, it's not to say that I don't share any of her religious perceptions or ideas, but her religion is so bleak. It is so totally without our consent. I mean, who in the world is going to be grabbed by this terrible consuming fire, by whatever it is that takes on to these people, and by this unsentimental God. It becomes the transcendental light and it becomes the vision; it becomes the sparing of nothing. All of the things we hold dear as human beings just have no meaning. And it picks the most unlikely people to carry it forth. For example, Mrs. Shortley.

INT: Let's talk about some of the cruxes in the story. And I suppose the most dramatic one is that accident. To what degree did you worry over it?

FOOTE: Oh, I agonized over it.

INT: Over how accidental that accident is?

FOOTE: As a writer, I don't think I ever made a choice. I simply said, well, here are the facts presented to me, technically: I know that he was under the machine; I know that Mr. Shortley came up on another machine; I know that they were all there; I know that you could say the brakes didn't work on the machine Mr. Shortley was on; I know that the machine rolled down; and I guess I know that three people watched this and didn't stop it. Now, whether it happened so quickly that they couldn't, whether they simply didn't know how to, whether they were willful conspirators . . . I think it's very clear in the film. In the film you do know they know it.

INT: They know it's happening.

FOOTE: Yes, and that they're destroyed by it. And I think that this works very, very well. This is the director's contribution. I still am never sure in the story whether it's true or not. And I read it over and over. So I thought, well, I'll just let everybody do what I'm doing: make up their own minds about it.

INT: When you are doing a dramatization like this, do you find certain things you have to leave open-ended and certain things you have to interpret clearly?

FOOTE: It just depends on the moment itself. When something is as structurally inevitable as this moment, you have to trust it. You begin to see all kinds of overtones in this. First of all, bringing the machines into a world and displacing mules with them. You say to yourself, there are many things man really can't manage. The machine was created by man, and if the machine had never been there, they would never have gotten rid of him this way.

INT: Fascinating, because of course the Shortleys and the blacks belong in the world of the mule. And it's Mrs. McIntyre who is so interested in the efficiency of the machines. Yet the machine destroys the Pole.

FOOTE: These are the searches you make, you know, and you don't ever write this out because O'Connor doesn't ever do it. I think if you impose this on the story you'll ruin it.

INT: One of the other cruxes I'd like to ask you about is what really happens to Mrs. McIntyre after that accident. We understand what happens to Mrs. Shortley; it can be explained physiologically. She gets so angry, and she is a big overweight woman, and it's hot. When she relaxes, she has some kind of a stroke. Now what happens to Mrs. McIntyre?

FOOTE: Let's go back to Mrs. Shortley, because you know what Flannery O'Connor says happens to her. She sees the frontiers of her true country. No matter what we see physically happening to her, she's in the process of a vision. Flannery O'Connor loves all the violence in the Bible. That doesn't worry her. She does believe that most Christians are kind of sentimental and do-gooders, and she's not interested in all that. In some ways Mrs. Shortley is her woman because Mrs. Shortley is not above violence. And I think that Mrs. McIntyre is appalled at that, and why she's paralyzed is that she can't enter into that; she's appalled at the violence she became involved in. The priest is trying to give her something to make the journey palatable to her, which is purgatory, and nobody knows whether the poor thing is being reached or not. She's in a state of suspension, of inaction. She cannot justify what she saw and the results of what happened. So that everything she lived by—the efficiency, the machines, the getting up and going—it all just stopped. This whole thing of breaking, of distorting . . . I guess Flannery O'Connor says that religion does break us and distort us and transcend us. And remakes us. But Mrs. McIntyre really wants an orderly world. Firing is not part of that. Her people just leave when the time comes, like the mules. Flannery O'Connor will have nothing to do with that order. She's interested in something more primal.

INT: In something transfiguring.

FOOTE: But whatever all of these things mean, as a writer she is always able to find the human line for you to follow. I think one of the most magical moments in the film is when Mrs. McIntyre lies on the bed, and she puts her hand on her heart, and she's just sobbing and crying like a little girl. You feel her heart is broken, in a curious kind of way, by the fact that she can't manage life and that these people keep on disappointing her just when she thinks she has things under control. Finally, it's just too much for her. All the complexities of life just descend on her like a flood. So that she is really the displaced person. It's just all taken away from her, and she has no country. Mrs. Shortley has a country; the priest has a country.

INT: But we don't leave Mrs. McIntyre seeing the frontiers of her true country.

FOOTE: No sir. She's just there. It's all too much for her. And in that sense she's enormously human, don't you feel?

INT: Yes.

FOOTE: I had a great-grandfather, a man named Speed, from Kentucky. He was a planter, and I guess not a very good one. He had a plantation in Texas, and we always had a joke in our family that whenever it rained he used to just pull the blinds down and go to bed. He just couldn't cope with the fact that the rain was ruining the cotton. And whenever there was a crisis, we would always say, "Well, I feel just like Grandfather Speed. I just want to go to bed and pull the blinds down, no matter what." And I feel that's Mrs. McIntyre. She just goes to bed.

INT: Could you comment on one last question? When you saw the film, when you saw the realization of your work for the first time, what pleased you most?

FOOTE: The sense that Mrs. McIntyre was the correct person to follow. That there was a great sense of unity to the work. And that we all recognized no matter how saddened Flannery O'Connor was, she did not exaggerate. Her humor sometimes seems exaggerated because she was so enormously sensitive and because she dared to pick things off that we'd rather forget. All of us, you know, want so much another kind of society, that we're apt to forget some whites do feel this way about blacks or some blacks do feel this way about whites. You see this in Astor. You just feel the cost of living this way is bending this man, and in the film he has a kind of haunting frailty. And you just want to say, oh, I wish we weren't this way, but we are this way.

ON FLANNERY O'CONNOR and "THE DISPLACED PERSON"

James M. Cox
Dartmouth College, New Hampshire

"The Displaced Person" is an excellent means of entry to Flannery O'Connor's work, for this story is a true introduction to her world. She has other stories which would serve as well, but none better, for this is unquestionably one of her best short stories. And the short story was her true form. Although she wrote two novels—*Wise Blood* and *The Violent Bear It Away*—both had their origin in short stories, which means that Flannery O'Connor's imagination originally expressed itself through that form; she seized upon it and put her life into it. We could even say that she died into it, for the fact is that fifteen years of her twenty-year writing life were spent in the grip of a deadly disease which she knew would kill her. Her work is thus her true life burning in the consciousness of death.

If that is the first fact of her biography, the second is that she was a Southerner—deeply Southern from the deep South. With the exception of two years (1945–47) spent in the creative writing program at the University of Iowa and three years (1947–50) spent in New York and Connecticut, all her life was lived in Georgia. The South, Georgia, Milledgeville, a dairy farm outside Milledgeville where she raised peacocks—that is the residential line of her life. A farm in the South is, as Mrs. McIntyre reminds us in "The Displaced Person," a *place*.

The third fact of Flannery O'Connor's life is that she was a Roman Catholic, and she was as insistent about that fact as Mrs. McIntyre is about her place. Being a Catholic in a dominantly Protestant South redoubled her sense of estrangement from the modern world. Finally there was the fact that she was a writer, not a saint. Her form was fatally secular, and her profound religious sense of herself caused her to be permanently estranged from the public identity she knew she was determined to have. All these facts meant that her life, which she translated into her work, was estranged from the work which was to become her life. That is all we know and all we need to know.

Now to "The Displaced Person." The logic of the story is as clear as it is relentless. It begins with the intrusion of a displaced person into a southern rural area—an area with which we associate racial bigotry, ignorance, and poverty. That area is Flannery O'Connor's given, and she reinforces all the negative associations we could possibly have. The story also exploits the great sentiment of our time, which is the modern sympathy for the true outcasts and refugees of the earth. In other words, in one of its aspects, the story exposes the bigotry of the South's poor whites (the Shortleys) and shabby gentility (Mrs. McIntyre) as they are threatened by the presence of the Displaced Person (Mr. Guizac). Seen in this light, the Shortleys are the first victims. The ignorant suspicion, self-complacency, and vicious fear with which Mrs. Shortley contemplates the presence of Mr. Guizac disclose her as the American version of that mentality which we would rather attribute to those in Europe who had put Mr. Guizac in a concentration camp. Her fear for herself and her husband leads her to try to excite fear in the Negroes, Sulk and Astor, in an effort to league them with her against the threatening intruder.

But the truth is that Mrs. Shortley's fear is in many ways justified. Mr. Guizac's industry and efficiency are a very real threat. Mrs. McIntyre, pleased with the prospect of a real worker in a world of laziness, lying, and general incompetence, is perfectly ready to use Mr. Guizac's presence as a weapon not only to threaten but to drive out the Shortleys. Instinctively aware of the whole pattern of her future, Mrs. Shortley can indeed feel prophetic. Her indelible memory of the pictures from the concentration camp she has witnessed in a *March of Time* newsreel becomes the reality she dies into as she and her family are making their escape from the world which is at the threshold of driving them out. The climactic scene in which she violently dies is living proof that the Shortleys are displaced persons.

It is then Mrs. McIntyre's turn to feel the full force of the intruding stranger. Complacently satisfied with the efficiency of her new tenant, she is all the more unprepared for the revelation that he is about to bring his niece over to marry the Negro, Sulk. Modern though she is in her desire to make her farm lucrative by mechanizing it under the direction of Mr. Guizac's sure-handed skill, she cannot yet face the vision of racial intermarriage. Thus she affirms the racial bigotry which keeps her region spiritually blighted and backward. In her initial complacency she had said of Mr. Guizac, "That man is my salvation." But confronted with the social disruption which would accompany the financial salvation, she rejects Guizac and allies herself with Mr. Shortley, who has returned to seek vengeance for the death of his wife—"God's Own Angel," in his words. Mrs. McIntyre needs Mr. Shortley precisely because she cannot actually fire Mr. Guizac. She has depended in the past on her tenants having had the simple grace to leave when it was clear they were unwanted. If they made off with something from the place, that was but one more proof of how much an owner is put upon in this world. At least it had left her secure in not having had to be the Judge.

Once again, then, she is in the position of wanting to be rid of someone. But Mr. Guizac is a different tenant. He cannot understand the ways of the new world. It remains for Mr. Shortley to go about getting rid of him, and Shortley manages the affair so that the tractor itself does the office of execution. But in the instant that the tractor wheel inexorably crushes Mr. Guizac, neither Shortley nor Sulk nor Mrs. McIntyre is spared the communal recognition of their collusion in his death. They are, in that instant, a true community; they have jointly participated in his violent end, for his death is their wish. Yet their mutual recognition of each other isolates them forever and annihilates the "place." Shortley and Sulk simply leave; Mrs. McIntyre is left with the place, barren after she sells her livestock and equipment at a loss, a place she leaves spiritually as she sags into the increasing blindness of despair with only a Negro to wait on her, and only the priest to visit her in order to "explain the doctrines of the church."

The meaning of the story is surely clear. Everyone in the story is somehow a displaced person. Thus the title of the story, which initially seems to apply only to Mr. Guizac, comes to apply to everyone, with the possible exception of the priest. But more important, everyone in the story is forever at the point of displacing someone else. Thus the condition of post-war Europe, which echoes the moral violence of the modern world, is brought by Flannery O'Connor into a "backward" region of the rural South with all the force of an invasion.

This force by which the backward region is made the arena where the universal modern condition is literally enacted is nothing less than the imaginative act of displacement which transforms what would be a story about a displaced person into a revelation of displacement. For if the story were merely about a displaced person coming to a Georgia farm and causing complications, then the meaning of displacement would be nothing but a moral, a truth which the story illustrates. But the story is neither allegorical nor didactic. It neither presupposes a moral order behind its surface nor instructs us in how to live. Instead it reveals in its action both a sense and a sensation of violent vision. That violence is the very pressure it exerts upon every reader, and exerts so powerfully that many readers will attempt to find a moral rather than experience a vision. That is, they will want the story to be "about" the South or "about" the condition of modern man who has lost his relation to religious reality. Such wishes will turn into readings of the story which see Mrs. Shortley's vision as selfish prophecy, Mrs. McIntyre's demise as some morally deserved punishment for her greed, and Mr. Guizac as the presence of someone "like" Christ. Yet such a system of relationships is merely a protection erected against the violent pressure of the story. It is likely to make of Shortley a "Devil figure" and Guizac a "Christ figure," as if the two were symbolic echoes of some prior reality.

Of course such strategies are understandable, for readers can feel the presence of a kind of religious reality in the story almost as much as they can feel the presence of the South in it. Almost as much, but decisively not as much. For the realistic South, which is the place of the story, has displaced the religious reality to the extent that the relationship between the two is violently recognized rather than comfortably discerned. Thus, if Mr. Guizac is to be related to Christ—and I by no means wish to deny the relationship—he is so deeply and truly different that the relationship is felt like a thunderclap. If, in other words, Guizac is the Second Coming, then we must know that when Christ comes again we will not recognize Him, for He will not have a halo and He will not be mouthing scripture. And if Mrs. Shortley's vision is seen to be somehow selfishly motivated—and of course we are made by the very order of Flannery O'Connor's conception to want to see it that way—the reality of her vision displaces whatever moral or psychological explanation of it we might erect on the basis of what we want to believe is the nature of her character. She *has* the vision. That is the fact and that is the point. We might want to claim that Mrs. Shortley's ignorant fundamentalism and bigoted imagination make her blind to the beauty of the peacock, which the priest of course sees and equates with the redemption of Christ. Yet Mrs. Shortley's vision surrounds the figure she sees in the heavens with bright wheels, and we had better not fail to recognize that those wheels are related to the fierce planets of the peacock's tail. Once again the relationship is violent—as violently present as Mrs. Shortley's vision.

Whatever primitive fundamentalism we must recognize in Mrs. Shortley, we had better not forget that it is primitive and that it is fundamental. Like so many fundamentalists in Flannery O'Connor's world, she knows the Bible without having to read it. Thus, when she starts to read her Bible in the story, it is because she is already prepared to prophesy, not because she needs the Bible to prepare her for prophecy.

To begin to see the nature of Mrs. Shortley and her vision is to begin to see why, as well as how, the story exerts such relentless pressure. We cannot finally tell who is good and who is bad in the story. If we too easily see the priest as good, then we have to ignore his perfect willingness to see the Displaced Person he brought to Mrs. McIntyre's farm displace the Negroes and the Shortleys. His beatific serenity is undisturbed by that prospect. To protect the priest from such scrutiny would be akin to lavishing upon the Negroes moral superiority which we have imported from a prior structure of values. The fact is that we can never quite tell what is going on inside the priest or the Negroes—or Mr. Guizac either, for that matter. They are all powerful presences in the story. They are there and they greatly matter, for they are profoundly implicated in the action. They speak and they act, but they do not reveal themselves to us. They are so deeply mechanical in their speech and action that we have to attribute to them whatever virtue and inner life we would see in them. We might want to redeem them from the mechanical space they occupy, but we could never know whether such redemptive attributes were merely our own comfortable rationalizations to protect us from the fire and violence of the story.

Flannery O'Connor knows in the very heart of her imagination that we will have to make such attributions. She knows that we are modern in our values, which is to say that we believe more in society and history than we can ever believe in God. She knows, moreover, that this modern world will not change. She knows that society and history are the secular forms in which we believe and on which we depend for revelation. Thus our judgment of the South—the place of her fiction—would gravitate inevitably toward the crime of its history, the intolerance within its society, and the ignorance of its religious life. She knows, in other words, that we are all enlightened "northerners," no matter where we may come from, and that we believe in life, not death; in art, not religion; in time, not eternity; in mercy, not judgment. She likes this knowledge; sometimes she seems to like it so well that she gloats over it. Certainly she takes a certain satisfaction in it. There is both knowledge and pleasure in her imaginative security, giving her a firm hold on her region. Such assurance gives her the economy, the concentration, and the compression which characterize her style. It enables her at every moment both to define her region and to give it a bold, sharp edge.

Since the modern world will not change, it becomes the permanent condition against which she sets her South—a South of place much more than a South of time. Her South is not a region which has lost to the North nearly so much as it has lost to itself. Its people are therefore not alienated but estranged—from themselves, from the reader, and, I think, from their author. Their compelling reality—which is something quite different from their social reality—has its source in the moral breach she creates between us and them. Recognizable as they are in their adherence to social stereotypes—hence their strong, almost comic regional vernacular—they are exceptions in the moral order. That is what makes them, their society, and their region truly different. She has selected them precisely by virtue of their moral difference; and her selection emphasizes the true distance of the region from our moral universe. They confront us as freaks and cripples who wear their physical oddity like a badge, or as ignorant and morally self-satisfied to the point of being offensive.

Yet the distance between them and us becomes increasingly uncomfortable. Though there are funny moments in almost every Flannery O'Connor story—as when Mr. Shortley performs the trick of hiding the cigarette in his mouth—it would be a strange person indeed who saw her work as primarily humorous. And while there are fierce exposures of human depravity, it would be an insensitive person who saw her as a satirist. Instead of exploiting a laughter that would relax us, or an indignation that would satisfy us, Flannery O'Connor inflames the initial difference between us and her characters until it is as violent as the space between the characters themselves. That is why her work glares at us with the force of a rebuke, as if it were saying that the grotesque deformations we are made to see are the effects of our own distorted vision.

But that is not all. Their distortion comes to us as a kind of stark reality because we have so little reality ourselves. Her characters and region are so powerful in our vision because our own lives are so *averted*; hence we feel aversion in relation to them. Mutilated, impoverished, judged, and punished though they are, they may at any moment be given the gift of seeing, of bearing witness. They have access to revelation because God can come to them not as themselves but as truly Other—in His power and His terror and His glory. He does not come to them because they are good; that would be the sentimentality our weakened religious sensibility would want to believe. He comes to them because He is real. He comes to them not so much in peace as with a sword, and His vision often strikes them dead. Thus they often see as they die. This is true of Mrs. Shortley, whose angry heart explodes in order for her to contemplate for the first time the frontiers of her true country. If Mrs. McIntyre cannot see at the end of the story, she may see at the end of her life. For death is the true displacer of persons. That is why it is no accident that the judge lies grinning beneath his desecrated monument at the center of the cornfield; in that center, toward which Mr. Guizac relentlessly circles with his silage cutter, he has become the judge indeed.

All of this brings us back to Flannery O'Connor, who is somehow on the other side of the story. If we cannot exempt ourselves from the implications of the action of the story, we should not exempt her from the implications of having invented it. Surely the violent estrangement we are made to feel in reading her work, she must have felt in writing it. Her very act of imagination was to displace her true vision into the secular form of the short story. Edgar Allan Poe, reviewing Nathaniel Hawthorne's tales, had invented the rationale of the short story. Whereas Hawthorne had deeply felt the moral problem of the artist cut off from God, and had sought allegorical connections which would relate art to a prior moral structure, Poe determined to make art the invention of the artist, an aesthetic object whose beauty would render whatever moral substance it might contain secondary, even incidental. A hundred years later, Flannery O'Connor seizes upon the very form with which Poe had shockingly severed us from religion to shock us back into relation with it. She punishes her characters until they need God enough to see Him; and she wants her short stories to punish us enough to see the God which art always somehow kills even as it weakly represents Him. That is why she has so little use for secular art and why she was so insistent about her Catholicism. She wanted art to be truly real and her characters not Christ figures but Christs. Thus she deformed them, even crucified them, until they could see through the sentiment of the church to the blazing vision which originates and is originated by religion. To have found herself displaced in this form of secular art must have made her need her religion too. It must have made her need grace and redemption as much as her stories can ever remind us that we need them.

SUGGESTIONS FOR FURTHER READING

By Flannery O'Connor:

The Complete Stories of Flannery O'Connor. New York: Farrar, Straus and Giroux, 1971.

Mystery and Manners: Occasional Prose, ed. Sally and Robert Fitzgerald. New York: Farrar, Straus and Giroux, 1969.

The Violent Bear It Away. New York: Farrar, Straus and Cuhady, 1960.

Wise Blood. New York: Farrar, Straus and Cuhady, 1962.

About Flannery O'Connor:

Eggenschwiler, David. *The Christian Humanism of Flannery O'Connor*. Detroit: Wayne State University Press, 1972.

Feeley, Kathleen. *Flannery O'Connor: Voice of the Peacock*. New Brunswick, N.J.: Rutgers University Press, 1972.

Friedman, Melvin A. and Lewis A. Lawson, eds. *The Added Dimension: The Art and Mind of Flannery O'Connor*. New York: Fordham University Press, 1966.

Martin, Carter W. *The True Country: Themes in the Fiction of Flannery O'Connor*. Nashville: Vanderbilt University Press, 1969.

THE MUSIC SCHOOL

by John Updike

My name is Alfred Schweigen and I exist in time. Last night I heard a young priest tell of a change in his Church's attitude toward the Eucharistic wafer. For generations nuns and priests, but especially (the young man said) nuns, have taught Catholic children that the wafer must be held in the mouth and allowed to melt; that to touch it with the teeth would be (and this was never doctrine, but merely a nuance of instruction) in some manner blasphemous. Now, amid the flowering of fresh and bold ideas with which the Church, like a tundra thawing, responded to that unexpected sun, the late Pope John, there has sprung up the thought that Christ did not say *Take and melt this in your mouth* but *Take and eat*. The word is *eat*, and to dissolve the word is to dilute the transubstantiated metaphor of physical nourishment. This demiquaver of theology crystallizes with a beautiful simplicity in the material world; the bakeries supplying the Mass have been instructed to unlearn the science of a dough translucent to the tongue and to prepare a thicker, tougher wafer—a host, in fact, so substantial it *must* be chewed to be swallowed.

This morning I read in the newspaper that an acquaintance of mine had been murdered. The father of five children, he had been sitting at the dinner table with them, a week after Thanksgiving. A single bullet entered the window and pierced his temple; he fell to the floor and died there in minutes, at the feet of his children. My acquaintance with him was slight. He has become the only victim of murder I have known, and for such a role anyone seems drastically miscast, though in the end each life wears its events with a geological inevitability. It is impossible, today, to imagine him alive. He was a computer expert, a soft-voiced, broad-set man from Nebraska, whose intelligence, concerned as it was with matters so arcane to me, had a generous quality of reserve, and gave him, in my apprehension of him, the dignity of an iceberg, which floats so serenely on its hidden mass. We met (I think only twice) in the home of a mutual friend, a professional colleague of his who is my neighbor. We spoke, as people do whose fields of knowledge are miles apart, of matters where all men are ignorant—of politics, children, and, perhaps, religion. I have the impression, at any rate, that he, as is often the case with scientists and Midwesterners, had no use for religion, and I saw in him a typical specimen of the new human species that thrives around scientific centers, in an environment of discussion groups, outdoor exercise, and cheerful husbandry. Like those vanished gentlemen whose sexual energy was exclusively spent in brothels, these men confine their cleverness to their work, which, being in one way or another for the government, is usually secret. With their sufficient incomes, large families, Volkswagen buses, hi-fi phonographs, half-remodelled Victorian homes, and harassed, ironical wives, they seem to have solved, or dismissed, the paradox of being a thinking animal and, devoid of guilt, apparently participate not in this century but in the next. If I remember him with individual clarity, it is because once I intended to write a novel about a computer programmer, and I asked him questions, which he answered agreeably. More agreeably still, he offered to show me around his laboratories any time I cared to make the hour's trip to where they were. I never wrote the novel—the moment in my life it was meant to crystallize dissolved too quickly—and I never took the trip. Indeed, I don't believe I thought of my friend once in the year between our last encounter and this morning, when my wife at breakfast put the paper before me and asked, "Don't we know him?" His pleasant face with its eyes set wide like the eyes of a bear gazed from the front page. I read that he had been murdered.

I do not understand the connection between last night and this morning, though there seems to be one. I am trying to locate it this afternoon, while sitting in a music school, waiting for my daughter to finish her piano lesson. I perceive in the two incidents a common element of nourishment, of eating transfigured by a strange irruption, and there is a parallel movement, a flight immaculately direct and elegant, from an immaterial phenomenon (an exegetical nicety, a maniac hatred) to a material one (a bulky wafer, a bullet in the temple). About the murder I feel certain, from my knowledge of the victim, that his offense was blameless, something for which he could not have felt guilt or shame. When I try to picture it, I see only numbers and Greek letters, and conclude that from my distance I have witnessed an almost unprecedented crime, a crime of unalloyed scientific passion. And there is this to add: the young priest plays a twelve-string guitar, smokes mentholated cigarettes, and seemed unembarrassed to find himself sitting socially in a circle of Protestants and nonbelievers—like my late computer friend, a man of the future.

But let me describe the music school. I love it here. It is the basement of a huge Baptist church. Golden collection plates rest on the table beside me. Girls in their first blush of adolescence, carrying fawn-colored flute cases and pallid folders of music, shuffle by me; their awkwardness is lovely, like the stance of a bather testing the sea. Boys and mothers arrive and leave. From all directions sounds—of pianos, oboes, clarinets—arrive like hints of another world, a world where angels fumble, pause, and begin again. Listening, I remember what learning music is like, how impossibly difficult and complex seem the first fingerings, the first decipherings of that unique language which freights each note with a double meaning of position and duration, a language as finicking as Latin, as laconic as Hebrew, as surprising to the eye as Persian or Chinese. How mysterious appears that calligraphy of parallel spaces, swirling clefs, superscribed ties, subscribed decrescendos, dots and sharps and flats! How great looms the gap between the first gropings of vision and the first stammerings of percussion! Vision, timidly, becomes percussion, percussion becomes music, music becomes emotion, emotion becomes—vision. Few of us have the heart to follow this circle to its end. I took lessons for years, and never learned, and last night, watching the priest's fingers confidently prance on the neck of his guitar, I was envious and incredulous. My daughter is just beginning the piano. These are her first lessons, she is eight, she is eager and hopeful. Silently she sits beside me as we drive the nine miles to the town where the lessons are given; silently she sits beside me, in the dark, as we drive home. Unlike her, she does not beg for a reward of candy or a Coke, as if the lesson itself has been a meal. She only remarks—speaking dully, in a reflex of greed she has outgrown—that the store windows are decorated for Christmas already. I love taking her, I love waiting for her, I love driving her home through the mystery of darkness toward the certainty of supper. I do this taking and driving because today my wife visits her psychiatrist. She visits a psychiatrist because I am unfaithful to her. I do not understand the connection, but there seems to be one.

In the novel I never wrote, I wanted the hero to be a computer programmer because it was the most poetic and romantic occupation I could think of, and my hero had to be extremely romantic and delicate, for he was to die of adultery. Die, I mean, of knowing it was possible; the possibility crushed him. I conceived of him, whose professional life was spent in the sanctum of the night (when, I was told, the computers, too valuable to be unemployed by industry during the day, are free, as it were, to frolic and to be loved), devising idioms whereby problems might be fed to the machines and emerge, under binomial percussion, as the music of truth—I conceived of him as being too fine, translucent, and scrupulous to live in our coarse age. He was to be, if the metaphor is biological, an evolutionary abortion, a mammalian mutation crushed underfoot by dinosaurs, and, if the metaphor is mathematical, a hypothetical ultimate, one digit beyond the last real number. The title of the book was to be "N + 1." Its first sentence went, *As Echo passed overhead, he stroked Maggy Johns' side through her big-flowered dress.* Echo is the artificial star, the first, a marvel; as the couples at a lawn party look upward at it, these two caress one another. She takes his free hand, lifts it to her lips, warmly breathes on, kisses, his knuckles. *His halted body seemed to catch up in itself the immense slow revolution of the earth, and the firm little white star, newly placed in space, calmly made its way through the older points of light, which looked shredded and faint in comparison.* From this hushed moment under the ominous sky of technological miracle, the plot was to develop more or less downhill, into a case of love, guilt, and nervous breakdown, with physiological complications (I had to do some research here) that would kill the hero as quietly as a mistake is erased from a blackboard. There was to be the hero, his wife, his love, and his doctor. In the end the wife married the doctor, and Maggy Johns would calmly continue her way through the comparatively faint . . . Stop me.

My psychiatrist wonders why I need to humiliate myself. It is the habit, I suppose, of confession. In my youth I attended a country church where, every two months, we would all confess; we kneeled on the uncarpeted floor and propped the books containing the service on the seats of the pews. It was a grave, long service, beginning, *Beloved in the Lord! Let us draw near with a true heart and confess our sins unto God, our Father. . . .* There was a kind of accompanying music in the noise of the awkward fat Germanic bodies fitting themselves, scraping and grunting, into the backwards-kneeling position. We read aloud, *But if we thus examine ourselves, we shall find nothing in us but sin and death, from which we can in no wise set ourselves free.* The confession complete, we would stand and be led, pew by pew, to the altar rail, where the young minister, a black-haired man with very small pale hands, would feed us, murmuring, *Take, eat; this is the true body of our Lord and Saviour Jesus Christ, given unto death for your sins.* The altar rail was of varnished wood, and ran around three sides, so that, standing (oddly, we did not kneel here), one could see, one could not help but see, the faces of one's fellow-communicants. We were a weathered, homely congregation, sheepish in our Sunday clothes, and the faces I saw while the wafer was held in my mouth were strained; above their closed lips their eyes held a watery look of pleading to be rescued from the depths of this mystery. And it distinctly seems, in the reaches of this memory so vivid it makes my saliva flow, that it was necessary, if not to chew, at least to touch, to embrace and tentatively shape, the wafer with the teeth.

We left refreshed. *We give thanks to thee, Almighty God, that Thou hast refreshed us through this salutary gift.* The church smelled like this school, glinting with strange whispers and varnished highlights. I am neither musical nor religious. Each moment I live, I must think where to place my fingers, and press them down with no confidence of hearing a chord. My friends are like me. We are all pilgrims, faltering toward divorce. Some get no further than mutual confession, which becomes an addiction, and exhausts them. Some move on, into violent quarrels and physical blows; and succumb to sexual excitement. A few make it to the psychiatrists. A very few get as far as the lawyers. Last evening, as the priest sat in the circle of my friends, a woman entered without knocking; she had come from the lawyers, and her eyes and hair were flung wide with suffering, as if she had come in out of a high wind. She saw our black-garbed guest, was amazed, ashamed perhaps, and took two backward steps. But then, in the hush, she regained her composure and sat down among us. And in this grace note, of the two backward steps and then again the forward movement, a coda seems to be urged.

The world is the host; it must be chewed. I am content here in this school. My daughter emerges from her lesson. Her face is fat and satisfied, refreshed, hopeful; her pleased smile, biting her lower lip, pierces my heart, and I die (I think I am dying) at her feet.

JOHN UPDIKE'S
THE MUSIC SCHOOL

*Screenplay by John Korty**

1. The translucent edge of an old-fashioned lace curtain lifts very slowly in the morning breeze coming through an open window.	The last notes of the title music fade out and the natural sounds of early morning fade in.
2. The entire bedroom is seen from one corner. There are two figures lying still under the covers, barely visible in the dim light of early morning.	
3. The camera moves over two chairs used as clothes-stands for the night. The room is gradually getting a little brighter.	

* Among the most honored of contemporary American filmmakers, John Korty is known for such films as *Crazy Quilt* and *River Run* and such television works as *The Autobiography of Miss Jane Pittman* and *Farewell to Manzinar*. His most recent feature film is *Alex and the Gypsy*.

4. The first time we see the man he is already awake, staring at the moving curtain. He swings his eyes over toward the nightstand.	
5. A CU of the digital clock on the nightstand silently flipping from 5:47 to 5:48.	
6. A tighter shot of the man's face as his eyes move from the clock over toward his wife.	
7. Her bare shoulders and neck with wisps of hair on them, moving slightly in the path of her slow breathing.	
8. XCU of water running and splashing over his face and hands in the wash basin.	Sounds of water cut in sharply.
9. A wider shot of his head and shoulders rising into the frame of the bathroom mirror still dripping wet. He dries himself with a towel.	
10. A child's poster about the whale as an endangered species, pan down to a young girl still asleep in her bed.	
11. Her father standing in the doorway, looking at her while he buttons his shirt, and then walking on.	

Shot	Sound
12. A high angle of the front yard as the door opens and Alfred walks out with shirt and pants on, but his feet still bare. He steps off the porch onto the lawn.	Outdoor sounds of early morning.
13. A CU of his bare feet moving across the grass which is still wet with dew.	
14. He walks from full figure into a CU as he picks up the paper. He stands there for a moment, taking in the serenity of the morning. A bird is calling and he tries to locate it.	
15. The camera pans the tree tops.	
16. Back to Alfred who gives up trying to find the bird and walks back toward the house.	
17. A bowl of fruit in the kitchen. The folded newspaper drops on the table and he takes a grapefruit from the bowl. The camera lifts up to show him going to the other side of the kitchen, turning on a small radio, and putting the grapefruit on a cutting board.	Music cue begins.
18. A CU of the knife slicing the grapefruit in half. As it falls open the first rays of sun slanting through the kitchen window turn the grapefruit half into a translucent circle of yellow and pink in his hands.	

19. He picks up one half of the grapefruit, puts it in a porcelain bowl with a serrated grapefruit spoon. He walks back towards the table. Spooning out the grapefruit, he sits at the table again and unfolds the newspaper.

20. The sunlight bounces off the newsprint and lights his face. His eyes roam over the collage of the front page. Suddenly, they stop at one point and hold there, reading intently.

    Music cue. Stops abruptly.

21. A yellow sheet of writing paper is rolled into an old-fashioned upright typewriter.

22. A wider angle shows the writer in his upstairs study, a small room, consisting of bookshelves, a day bed and a desk which looks out through the dormer window to a yard and street below. He sits there motionless, staring out the window.

23. A CU on his fingers perched above the keys of the typewriter flexing slightly but not pressing any keys. The camera pans up to his face, looking first at the blank page and then out the window.

24. A long shot of two boys walking to school. They go in and out of patches of light on the sidewalk and the smaller boy swings his lunchbox as he tries to match his strides to the larger one.	
25. A reverse angle on Alfred, through the dormer window, centered behind his typewriter. Suddenly, he begins to type something.	
26. An XCU of typewriter keys clacking against the yellow paper with a brittle noise. The type has the uneven, thick-and-thin quality of well-worn keys and we see the first sentence as it appears on the page.	"My name is Alfred Schweigen and I exist in time."
27. A plastic glass of wine is being poured from a half-gallon jug of Mountain Red. From the MCU on Alfred's hands at the table, we pull out to show him at an informal party of fifteen to twenty people. He looks around for someone to pour for, but there's no one else at the table. He moves off across the living room and the shot becomes a wider angle showing the whole party.	Amid the party noise, a twelve-string guitar is heard playing an up-tempo folk tune.
28. A cut-away to a woman that he notices as he crosses the room. His wife does not seem to be at the party.	

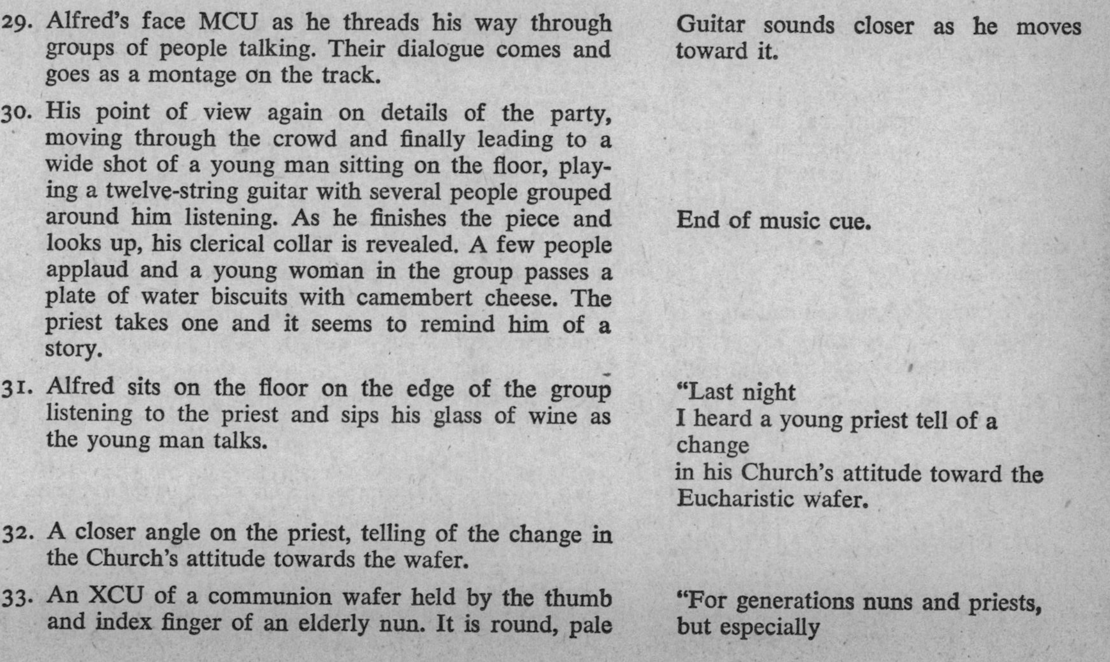

29. Alfred's face MCU as he threads his way through groups of people talking. Their dialogue comes and goes as a montage on the track.	Guitar sounds closer as he moves toward it.
30. His point of view again on details of the party, moving through the crowd and finally leading to a wide shot of a young man sitting on the floor, playing a twelve-string guitar with several people grouped around him listening. As he finishes the piece and looks up, his clerical collar is revealed. A few people applaud and a young woman in the group passes a plate of water biscuits with camembert cheese. The priest takes one and it seems to remind him of a story.	End of music cue.
31. Alfred sits on the floor on the edge of the group listening to the priest and sips his glass of wine as the young man talks.	"Last night I heard a young priest tell of a change in his Church's attitude toward the Eucharistic wafer.
32. A closer angle on the priest, telling of the change in the Church's attitude towards the wafer.	
33. An XCU of a communion wafer held by the thumb and index finger of an elderly nun. It is round, pale	"For generations nuns and priests, but especially

and translucent. The camera pulls out to show the nun demonstrating to a class of young children the rituals of communion.	[the young man said] nuns,
34. A pan across the small faces looking up to the nun and showing that special combination of awe, embarrassment and an eagerness to please.	"have taught Catholic children that the wafer must be held in the mouth and allowed to melt;
35. A medium shot starting on the nun as she offers the wafer to one of the small boys. As he opens his mouth, she places it on his tongue. Unconsciously he begins to chew it. With this, she gently but firmly holds his jaw in her hand.	"that to touch it with the teeth would be (and this was never doctrine, but merely a nuance of instruction) in some manner blasphemous.
36. A closer angle on the nun watching him with a slight smile.	
37. CU on the boy's face still in the awkward position with her hand on his jaw. He looks around helplessly and waits for the wafer to melt.	"Now, amid the flowering of fresh and bold ideas with which the Church, like a tundra thawing,
38. A pan away from the children over to some of the decorations of the schoolroom—brightly-colored	"responded to that unexpected sun, the late Pope John,

children's paintings of religious scenes, book illustrations and finally to a photograph of Pope John.	
39. A low angle up toward a colored poster of Jesus.	"there has sprung up the thought that Christ did not say *'Take and melt this in your mouth'* but *'Take and eat.'*
40. What seems like a reverse angle, looking down at the face of A. as he sits at his typewriter. His gaze drops to the page in front of him and he begins to type again.	"The word is *eat* and to dissolve the word is to dilute the transubstantiated metaphor of physical nourishment.
41. CU of his fingers working the keys of the typewriter in an easy rhythm. We tilt up to his face just as he finishes these last two lines. He seems to like what he's written.	"This demiquaver of theology crystallizes with a beautiful simplicity in the material world;
42. A large mixing machine in a convent bakery. It is full of dough which is being pulled and twisted in the rotary motion of the machine. A middle-aged nun comes into the picture and pours a pitcher of milk into the bowl and then goes back for more.	(EFX of machine come in loud.) (Type level in #41.) "The bakeries supplying the mass have been instructed to unlearn the science of a dough translucent to the tongue

	and to prepare a thicker, tougher wafer,
43. Following nun, shot widens to show the activity in the bakery, analyzing the materials going into the wafers.	"a host, in fact, so substantial it *must* be chewed to be swallowed."
44. CU of a timer going off. Pan to a nun opening a large oven, sliding out a tray of the new wafers, and setting it on a table to cool.	Loud noise of timer alarm (bell or buzzer).
45. A closeup of her picking up one of the new wafers and sampling it, chewing it with great concentration.	
46. A closeup of A. looking down at what he's written, possibly biting one fingernail. He seems depressed, finally pushes his chair away from the writing desk and gets up. We move with him and see more of the room as he walks around straightening papers, putting books away.	
47. CU of a vase of dead flowers on the other side of the room. He pulls the flowers out of the vase and drops them in a wastebasket.	
48. He turns and looks back at the typewriter, moves across the room, and leans over it, reading what he has written so far. He looks out the window.	

49. His wife, still in her morning robe, inspects the flower beds around the yard below.	
50. XCU on his face as the next sentence forms in his mind.	"This morning I read in the newspaper that an acquaintance of mine had been murdered."
51. Suddenly one pane in a large window is punctured neatly by a bullet.	The sound of the shot explodes at full volume, and then,
52. At one end of a dinner table, a five-year-old child in pajamas suddenly turns his head in reaction.	echoes into silence for the rest of this sequence. No voices or other EFX are heard.
53. A man with a glass of wine to his lips has been hit by the bullet and grabs his head, falling off his chair.	
54. The wife at the other end of the table, feeding a baby, takes a second to comprehend and then screams and backs away.	
55. The first child, crying now, scrambles away from the table knocking over a glass of milk.	
56. CU of the milk spilling over the edge of the table in a white stream.	

57.	The typewriter carriage is slammed back to the right. The line about the man being murdered has just been typed and is visible on the paper.	The sudden sound of typewriter carriage return.
58.	MS of A. sitting at the typewriter, pausing a moment before making his next transition. His face is sober yet working towards something.	"My acquaintance with him was slight. He has become the only victim of murder I have known, and for such a role anyone seems drastically miscast, though in the end each life wears its events with a geological inevitability.
59.	The man we have just seen murdered is now sitting very much alive in an easy chair at a suburban dinner party. He sips from an iced drink as he talks and occasionally looks across the room where other guests are seated. The camera pulls out to reveal A. seated next to him, also with a drink in his hand, listening to the man and commenting occasionally.	"He was a computer expert, a soft-voiced, broadset man from Nebraska, whose intelligence, concerned as it was with matters so arcane to me, had a generous quality of reserve, and gave him, in my apprehension of him, the dignity of an iceberg,

Shot	Audio
	which floats so serenely on its hidden mass. . . ."
60. Wide angle shot of the entire living room with about eight other guests sitting and talking.	(Classical music plays softly in the background. Music cue.)
61. MCU of the Nebraska scientist as he talks to A.	"We spoke, as people do whose fields of knowledge are miles apart, of matters where all men are ignorant— of politics, children, and, perhaps, religion.
62. MCU on A. as he watches the man.	
63. The camera moves over the man, his clothes, and mannerisms from A's viewpoint.	
64. CU of the scientist's children in a small glass frame at the front of a cluttered desk. The camera pulls away to show him thumbing through books, moving papers from one pile to another, generally looking for something.	"I have the impression, at any rate, that he, as is often the case with scientists and Midwesterners, had no use for religion,
65. Reveals the entire room which has some tables and computers in various stages of assembly or repair.	

The man moves to one of the tables and begins examining small transistors.	
66. He reaches under the table to a briefcase which has a combination lock on it, works the combination and takes out some papers. He sets the briefcase back down on the other side of an aluminum tennis racket.	and I saw in him a typical specimen of the new human species that thrives around scientific centers, in an environment of discussion groups, outdoor exercise, and cheerful husbandry.
67. He is now working with a pocket tabulator, checking it against the paperwork in front of him, and then reaching out to the controls of one of the computer panels at the end of the table.	"Like those vanished gentlemen whose sexual energy was exclusively spent in brothels, these men confine their cleverness to their work, which, being in one way or another for the government, is usually secret."
68. His face as he does this shows a total involvement in his work.	
69. The front panel of a very modern hi-fi amplifier resting on an antique cabinet in the living room of the dinner party.	The background music is more audible now.

70. Shows A. and the scientist looking at the hi-fi, standing now, as some of the guests are moving into the dining room.

"They seem to have solved,
or dismissed,
the paradox of being a thinking animal
and, devoid of guilt,
apparently participate not in this century
but in the next.

71. MCU of the scientist as he refers to some standing screens next to the antique cabinet and explains to A. that they are really speakers and the music is coming from them.

72. CU of A. feeling the thinness of the screens and leaning his ear close to the surface to hear the music.

73. The hostess comes by and reminds the two men that dinner is about to begin; escorts them into the dining room. The camera swings around to reveal the entire table, with candelabra, set for ten.

"If I remember him with individual clarity, it is because once I intended to write a novel about a computer programmer,
and I asked him questions,
which he answered agreeably.
More agreeably still,
he offered to show me around his laboratories

	anytime I cared to make the hour's trip to where they were.
74. A two-shot as the men finish up their conversation and move to their assigned seats at the dinner table.	
75. A CU of A. as he sits at his place. His expression is strangely serious. He looks up to his wife across the table.	
76. MCU of her mocking his seriousness.	
77. He gives her the smile she asks for, and unfolds his napkin.	
78. CU of the candles in the middle of the table burning slowly.	
79. MCU of A.'s hands examining a folder of scribbled notes and rough drafts. He reads over certain pages, takes out others and drops them in the wastebasket.	"I never wrote the novel— the moment in my life it was meant to crystallize dissolved all too quickly— and I never took the trip.
80. CU of his face as he reads the material, and finally closes the file with a trace of self-consciousness.	"Indeed, I don't believe I thought of my friend

once in the year between our last
encounter
and this morning."

81. The other half of the grapefruit is picked up by a woman's hand and placed in a bowl. The shot widens to show his wife carrying it to the kitchen table where A. is still sitting, now drinking a cup of coffee.

82. MCU of her taking the newspaper from the table and beginning to scan it. When she gets to the story of the murder, she looks up to A. in shock.

WIFE: "Don't we know him?"

83. CU of A. responding—just a look and a nod.

84. She turns the paper around to him and we see the victim's photograph for the first time in the strange black-and-white formality of the newspaper page.

The sound of a child's piano piece fades in slowly. Music cue.

85. Wide angle of the basement corridor of the music school. A. sits alone on an old brown and white pew. The camera moves slowly toward him, until it becomes a MCU.

"I do not understand the connection between last night and this morning, though there seems to be one.

86. A possible repeat of the nun holding the transparent wafer.

"I perceive in the two incidents
a common element of nourishment,
of eating transfigured

87. A possible repeat of the bullet puncturing the window pane.	by a strange irruption, and there is a parallel movement, a flight immaculately direct and elegant, from an immaterial phenomenon (an exegetical nicety, a maniac hatred) to a material one (a bulky wafer, a bullet in the temple).
88. A closer angle on A.'s face as he looks around the hallway listening to music and thinking. He looks down to:	"About the murder I feel certain, from my knowledge of the victim, that his offense was blameless, something for which he could not have felt guilt or shame.
89. A pile of sheet music on the pew beside him. His hand enters the frame and he leafs through some of the manuscripts.	"When I try to picture it, I see only numbers and Greek letters, and conclude that from my distance I have witnessed an almost un- precedented crime, a crime of unalloyed scientific passion.

90. CU of A. looking down at the music pages and then up again to the sound of music.	
91. The priest again in the middle of his performance with a cigarette in his mouth as he plays.	"And there is this to add: the young priest plays a twelve-string guitar, smokes mentholated cigarettes,
92. A pan of the audience listening to him.	and seemed unembarrassed to find himself sitting socially in a circle of Protestants and nonbelievers—
93. The Nebraska scientist leaving work, picking up the briefcase in one hand and the aluminum tennis racket in the other, closing the door behind him.	like my late computer friend, a man of the future."
94. The door in the music school basement opens and a janitor enters the hallway, walks through nodding silently to A. and goes out the other door.	The mix of the music lessons comes back. "But let me describe the music school . . .
95. A., hearing a new piece of music emerge from one of the rooms down the hall, gets up and walks toward the door, feeling the music on all sides of him	"I love it here. The sounds arrive like hints of another world,

as a strange accompaniment to his progress through the empty corridor.	a world where angels fumble, pause, and begin again."
96. CU from inside the music room toward the door as A.'s face appears in the small window looking through.	One piece of music becomes predominant out of the mix of student pieces.
97. MS of that student performing on a flute (for instance). The music teacher in the background, watching the student.	"Listening, I remember what learning music is like, how impossibly difficult and complex seem the first fingerings, the first decipherings
98. CU on the music in front of the student.	of that unique language which freights each note with a double meaning of position and duration.
99. XCU on the student, his eyes moving back and forth across the sheet of music.	How mysterious appears that calligraphy, how great looms the gap between the first gropings of vision and the first stammerings of percussion!"

100. A. moving to a new window and looking through.	Another piece of music becomes predominant.
101. Reveals another room with a student playing a cello and another teacher.	
102. Through 119. Continuation of this montage of teachers, students, music, instruments, and various shots of A. watching through the windows. The students will range from the age of eight, including his young daughter, up to about seventeen. The instruments used will probably be cello, piano, flute, clarinet and possibly something like a harp or violin. Also in this montage we will probably show antique- and modern-style metronomes being used in the music lessons.	"Vision, timidly, becomes percussion, percussion becomes music, music becomes emotion, emotion becomes—vision.
120. The montage of straining violin bows and tentative piano chords finally gives way to a fast and carefree downhill run on the twelve-string guitar by the young priest. The buoyancy of the music emerging from the instrument, over which the priest's fingers prance so confidently, carries the camera across the room to A.'s face, watching with a strange mixture of envy and incredulity.	"Few of us have the heart to follow this circle to its end. I took lessons for years, and never learned.
121. A closer shot of the priest playing the guitar.	

122. A wider angle on the audience. Several of them are tapping their fingers or their feet in time to the music, but A. is not.

123. CU of A.'s hands tapping in silent rhythm on the steering wheel of his car. The camera pulls out to reveal him driving and occasionally looking over at his daughter.

124. His daughter as she looks out the window on her side of the car.

125. CU of a small pile of piano music on the front seat between them.

"My daughter is just beginning the
piano. These are her first lessons,
she is eight, she is eager and hopeful.
Silently she sits beside me
as we drive the nine miles to the town
where the lessons are given;"

126. A closer angle on A. as he looks in her direction.

(Fade in music cue.)

127. LS of the car entering the deep shade of a forest on a small road.

"silently she sits beside me,
in the dark,
as we drive home . . .

128. The girl's point of view, past the cool colors of dark greens and blues washing over the car, out to the houses and trees racing past.

129. CU of her face looking out the window.	"I love taking her, I love waiting for her, I love driving her home through the mystery of darkness toward the certainty of supper."
130. XCU of A.'s face lost in reverie as he drives.	
131. A sudden spray of light across the screen.	(A loud drumming noise cuts off the music.)
132. A. reacts to the noise, suddenly looking up from the typewriter, to the window of the dormer.	
133. A wider shot of the dormer window as the water drips down the panes and reveals the figure of his wife waving up at him from below holding the garden hose. She laughs.	"I do this taking and driving because today my wife visits her psychiatrist. She visits a psychiatrist because I am unfaithful to her.
134. He looks at her for a moment without expression and then waves almost as an afterthought.	"I do not understand the connection, but there seems to be one.
135. She has turned her back and is walking away, but then turns and looks at him one more time, unhappy that he didn't appreciate her joke.	
136. MCU back on A. slightly thrown off balance by what has just happened, trying to regain his concentration. He looks down at the typewriter.	

137. CU of another typewriter. On this one, however, the keyboard is more mathematical and complex. A pull-back reveals the typewriter to be part of a huge computer center with a solitary man sitting at the desk.	"In the novel I never wrote, I wanted the hero to be a computer programmer because it was the most poetic and romantic occupation I could think of, and my hero had to be extremely romantic and delicate, for he was to die of adultery." (Electronic music slowly fades in but stays low and not perceptible as music yet.)
138. CU of the man as he works, trying to shake some thought from his head and concentrate once more on what he is doing.	"Die, I mean, of knowing it was possible; the possibility crushed him.
138.5 A flash cut of a bare shoulder and part of one breast.	
139. CU of a digital clock reading out the time down to tenths of seconds so that the digits seem to animate into a dance cycle.	"I conceived of him, whose professional life was spent in the sanctum of the night

(when, I was told,
the computers,
too valuable to be unemployed by
industry during the day,
are free,
as it were,
to frolic and to be loved),
devising idioms whereby
problems might be fed to the machines
and emerge,
under binomial percussion,
as the music of truth.

139.5 Another flash cut of bare legs.

140. The man's concentration is broken and he stares at the machines around him, finally getting up and moving away.

141. XCU of the punched paper tape emerging from the computer. The coded dots along its length seem to synchronize with small electronic sounds coming from the cabinets. The tape spins out into coils and arabesques across the polished floors as the camera

pans up to reveal the man wandering between the rows of the computer elements.

"I conceived of him as being too fine,
translucent,
and scrupulous
to live in our coarse age.
He was to be,
if the metaphor is biological,
an evolutionary abortion,
a mammalian mutation crushed underfoot
by dinsosaurs,
and, if the metaphor is mathematical,
a hypothetical ultimate,
one digit beyond the last real number."

141.5 Another glimpse of the nude woman showing a bare back.

142. Another angle of the hero wandering through banks of tape transports and computer equipment.

143. A hint of the face of the nude woman.

144. LS of hero leaving through a door at one end of the room.

145. through 146. Miscellaneous closeups of the machinery in the computer center.

147. XCU of a plastic tube being bent in a woman's hands. As it bends, something inside breaks and it begins to glow with a strange light. A pull-back shows her handing the glowing light-stick to the hero of the novel as he enters the gate of the garden party. He takes it from her and begins to move off through the crowd.	(The electronic music changes and becomes more obvious. Music cue.)
148. Wide shots of the party reveal that everyone there is holding a similar light-stick. Some of the people wave them slowly under their noses, others hold them up to the sides of their face and move them around. The clothes of the people are futuristic but in a very subtle way. Some of the clothes have a slight reflective or phosphorescent quality and some of the makeup is slightly reflective.	
149. Through the crowd we see the focus of the hero's attention—a beautiful woman on the edge of the crowd. We approach her as he does. She is the woman we have seen in the mental flashes.	
150. The camera pans with him until he joins her. They look into each others eyes, lit by the chemical light-sticks, and then both turn toward the sky, as his arm goes around her waist.	"The title of the book was to be *N + 1*. Its first sentence went, 'As Echo passed overhead,

	he stroked Maggy Johns' side through her big-flowered dress.'
151. A shot past the trees of the garden into the night sky where we see Echo, the artificial star, perceptibly moving through the natural constellations with an extra amount of brightness.	
152. Back on the lawn, a closeup of Maggy taking his free hand in hers, lifting it to her lips, breathing on it, kissing his knuckles.	
153. XCU of the hero's face as he looks down at Maggy Johns and then up to the sky and the artificial star again.	"His halted body seemed to catch up in itself the immense slow revolution of the earth, and the firm little white star, newly placed in space, calmly made its way through the older points of light, which looked shredded and faint in comparison.
154. A closer cut to the star moving through the natural constellations.	

155. through 165. A montage which becomes more and more obviously melodramatic, as does A.'s voice summarizing the rest of the novel. We do not go into any other scenes of the novel visually, but we use the lawn party to show clandestine looks between husband, wife, doctor, Maggy Johns, the hidden clasping hands, the hurried kisses behind shrubbery, etc. There is also a style of movement and acting in this sequence which makes it more theatrical than the rest of the film.
The final scene is Maggy Johns making her way calmly through the crowd, finally dropping the glowing light-stick from her hand.

"From this hushed moment
under the ominous sky of technological miracle,
the plot was to develop more or less downhill,
into a case of love, guilt,
and nervous breakdown,
with physiological complications
(I had to do some research here)
that would kill the hero
as quietly as a mistake is erased
from a blackboard.
There was to be the hero, his wife,
his love,
and his doctor.
In the end the wife married the doctor,
and Maggy Johns would calmly
continue her way through the
comparatively faint . . ."

(The music is cut off.)

166. XCU the words, "Stop me," being hammered into the paper on A.'s typewriter.

"Stop me.

167. CU of his reaction to what he has just written. He rises and walks away, wandering around the room for a bit, and finally flopping down on a small daybed on the other side of the room.	"My psychiatrist wonders why I need to humiliate myself.
168. CU of him in that position looking up at the ceiling.	"It is the habit, I suppose, of confession."
169. Reserved for miscellanous.	
170. The ceiling and stained-glass windows of a small country church. The camera tilts down to show a congregation of twenty to thirty people. At a signal from the minister they all begin to settle, scraping and grunting, into the backwards kneeling position. The time is about 1949 but the strangeness of the men's suits and the women's fashions makes it seem even further in the past.	(Church organ music cue.)
171. MCU which picks out A. as a thirteen-year-old adolescent, kneeling at a side pew.	
172. MS of the minister leading the service.	"Beloved in the Lord! Let us draw near with a true heart

	and confess our sins unto God, our Father . . .
173. CU of the thirteen-year-old as he turns and looks behind him.	
174. A pan across some of the faces around him.	"But if we thus examine ourselves, we shall find nothing in us but sin and death, from which we can in no wise set ourselves free."
175. At another signal from the minister, the congregation is led, pew by pew, to the altar rail for the communion.	(The organ music finishes.)
176. Realizing that his row is in the first group, he moves to join them.	
177. MCU of the minister beginning the words of the communion.	"Take, eat, this is the true body of our Lord and Savior Jesus Christ, given unto death for your sins."
178. A.'s point of view of the first people at the altar rail receiving their communion.	
179. CU of A. looking up as the minister approaches him.	

180. CU of the minister repeating the words once more, directly to A. Camera pans down to show the wafer in his hand.

181. XCU of the wafer being placed on A.'s tongue. He draws it into his mouth, still holding his chin high, wondering where to look and what to do.

182. Another pan across the faces of his fellow communicants.

"I remember the faces I saw
while the wafer was held in my mouth.
They were strained.
Above their closed lips
their eyes held a watery look of
pleading to be rescued
from the depths of this mystery.
And it distinctly seems,
in the reaches of this memory so vivid
it makes my saliva flow,
that it was necessary,
if not to chew,
at least to touch,
to embrace
and tentatively shape the wafer
with the teeth."

183.	CU on A.'s face. We notice a slight and surreptitious movement of his jaw, as the wafer is melting inside his mouth.	
184.	On the new organ chord, in a wide shot, we see the entire congregation filing out, shaking hands with the minister standing outside the door. The bright light of day streaming in.	(Organ starts again. Music cue.) "We left refreshed."
184.5	MCU of A. watching them leave.	
185.	One of the last out, silhouetted by himself, A. leaves the dim sanctuary and disappears through the arched door into the sunlight outside.	"We give thanks to thee Almighty God, that thou hast refreshed us through this salutary gift."
186.	[An optional shot which might follow the youth through a cemetery attached to the church.]	
187.	A full-figure shot of A. as a man, back in the sanctuary of the Baptist church where the music school is located, staring just past the camera.	(The organ music slowly falls away.)
188.	From his point of view, an arched door very similar to the one in the church of his childhood. This one is closed, defined only by lines of light seeping through the cracks of the door.	

189. A closer shot back to A. as his gaze moves from the door upward to a stained-glass window.	"I am neither musical nor religious. Each moment I live, I must think where to place my fingers and press them down with no confidence of hearing a chord."
190. The stained-glass window from his point of view.	
191. CU of A.'s face looking up at the window and then around the church.	
192. A CU of someone back at the first party which relates to something that A. has just seen in the church, possibly a painting or a piece of statuary.	(Slow guitar music and party noise fade in. Music cue.)
193. A pan of more faces at the party, all listening to the guitar.	"My friends are like me. We are all pilgrims, faltering toward divorce. Some get no further than mutual confession,
194. CU of the priest playing a slower and sadder song.	which becomes an addiction, and exhausts them.
195, 196. More shots of individuals and couples at the party.	Some move on, into violent quarrels, and physical

197. The door opens suddenly and a woman enters. She sees the priest and shows surprise.	blows; and succumb to sexual excitement. A few make it to the psychiatrists. A very few get as far as the lawyers.
198. CU of the priest still playing the guitar, but looking up in her direction, almost as surprised as she is. 199. Closer on the woman as she takes two backward steps.	"Last evening, a woman entered without knocking; she had come from the lawyer's, and her eyes and hair were flung wide with suffering, as if she had come in out of a high wind."
200. A wide shot of people looking up at her and then away, so as not to embarrass her any further.	
201. CU of A. looking at her just a little bit longer than the others.	
202. A wider shot of her regaining her composure and sitting down among them.	"But then, in the hush, she regained her composure and sat down among us."
203. A wide angle of the stairs and hallway of the music school. A. is gradually revealed coming down the stairs.	(The guitar music is replaced by the mix of music students.)

204. A brief slow-motion repeat of her two steps backwards and then again the forward movement. There is a strange grace to her gestures.

"And in this grace note,
of the two backwards steps
and then again the forward movement,
a coda seems to be urged."

205. A pan of the doors of the practice rooms, showing only glimpses of the people inside.

(The sounds from the various practice rooms thin out and finally only one melody is left.)

206. CU of A. standing in the empty hallway, listening to the end of the last piece of music. Finally there is a moment of silence, and the moment of realization shows on his face.

"The world is the host;
it must be chewed."

207. In a wide angle, the doors of the study rooms begin to open and gradually the hallway is filled with the sounds of children's voices, footsteps.

(Sound EFX come in sudden contrast to the silence.)

208. Pan over children closing their music cases, banging into each other, looking around for their parents.

209. A few of their parents enter from outside to take the children home.

210. A. moves away from the center of activity and sits again on the brown and white pew, waiting for his daughter.

(The noise of children and parents gradually dies down.)

211. The door to her room opens and she comes out, looks around and sees him.

212. CU of her first look. She seems satisfied, refreshed, hopeful. She bites her lip with a pleased smile and begins to walk toward him.

213. A wider shot as she approaches him and he stands up. Just at that moment several sheets of music slide out of her hand and onto the floor. Before she can stoop, A. kneels and picks up the papers for her.

214. A closer angle from her point of view down toward him. He picks up the papers and begins to hand them back to her. There is a look on his face that we have not seen there before.

215. Suddenly, we are outside and their car is making its way through the dusk.

216. CU inside the car of A. driving.

217. The daughter sitting beside him, again in silence as they make their way home.

218. Their point of view of the house with windows glowing as they pull into the driveway.

219. Pan as they walk from the car to the front door, opening it wide and going inside.

220. A close shot through a window of the house. The daughter going her way, but A. stopping and looking carefully at his wife.

221. A wider shot through another window of all three of them sitting down to dinner and beginning to eat. At this point, the tail credits begin to roll, over shots farther and farther away to show their house as one among many, ending with a high angle of a suburban community at evening-time. And the final credits end.

ON JOHN UPDIKE and "THE MUSIC SCHOOL"

Joyce B. Markle
Loyola University, Chicago

For almost a generation, John Updike has been considered one of the leading literary figures in contemporary America. A prolific writer, he has already produced eight book-length works of fiction, several dozen short stories, book reviews, prose essays, poetry, and children's books. His wide readership includes not only professional critics and students of literature but also a reading public large enough to keep each new novel on the best-seller list for months. Criticized by some readers for being too melodramatic and by others for being too philosophical, Updike has apparently managed to maintain a delicate balance between the romantic and the reflective, between the appeal of the popular novel and the critical esteem of more esoteric fiction.

Updike was born in 1932 in Shillington, Pennsylvania, a remote suburb of Reading. His parents moved to a nearby farm in Plowville when he was thirteen. He grew to love Pennsylvania and has become something of a regionalist, using its people and landscapes as the explicit or implied setting for much of his fiction. He graduated from Harvard in 1954 and went with his wife of one year to the Ruskin School of Drawing and Fine Arts in Oxford, England. Updike had long been interested in drawing and painting; his innate talents as a graphic artist along with his intense training at Ruskin have invested his fiction with a highly visual quality—a concentration on color, texture, form, space, and motion which gives it a cinematic character. In 1955 he joined the staff of the *New Yorker* where he worked for more than two years, absorbing the sights and sounds of New York and acquiring polish and sophistication as a writer. In 1957 he moved to his present home in Ipswich, Massachusetts, where he began writing fiction full time.

Updike is a highly autobiographical writer, and his various travels as well as the births and advancing ages of his four children are chronicled, one way or another, in his fiction. Also chronicled is his reluctant emergence from the Christianity which seemed so natural to previous Americans, into the practical but comfortless existentialism which marks the scientific modern era. This dialectic—between the reassuring God-given order of religion and the manmade order of the sciences—forms the basic tension of Updike's fiction.

In Updike's work, religion assures humans of their special place in creation and justifies their desperate refusal to accept death as final; but it remains unproven, fails to alleviate man's sense of alienation from his world, and requires a trusting society, not a cynical one. Science thrives in a cynical era, where it can demonstrate the workability of its propositions, and fits man nonchalantly into the physical universe of matter and motion, chemicals and processes; but it is cold and sterile, denies both hope and anguish, and gives man no reassuring way to deal with the fact of his own mortality.

Taken as a sequence, Updike's book-length fictions show gradually aging protagonists, living through the era of transition from a society which still instinctively yearns for its older religions to one that accepts atheistic humanism as its norm. The main characters are usually survivors from the fading era of belief; they are reluctant to abandon their upward-directed vision which invests humans with special dignity, which thus makes them lovable, and which would give meaning to their death. Although these characters are shown to be life-givers—people who can offer, through their love, this sense of specialness—they also appear to be unhappy: at odds with their community, doubtful of their own instincts, and overwhelmed by a dread of death. Often these protagonists are pitted against an antagonist who recurs in various forms as a modern man of science who does not believe "in anything" and who is unprepared to deal with the disorderly and unpredictable world of human emotion. In "The Music School" Alfred Schweigen is the humanist who longs for a belief or a world view that would give purpose and dignity to human life; the computer expert is this story's version of the man of science.

It is a curious feature of Updike's style that although his

central characters seek meaning beyond the physical, Updike himself relies heavily on physical details to formulate his meaning. Through careful handling of his imagery, he enables the visual details of his settings to establish values and control reader response.

Updike's talent and training in the graphic arts is complemented by an enthusiasm for motion pictures. The highly cinematic quality of his fiction is therefore no accident. Though "The Music School" is, in its short-story form, less obviously cinematic than Updike's novels, the story consists of the meditations of an artist who, like Updike, instinctively puzzles over matters of order and arrangement. Meticulous descriptions of settings have been a characteristic of Updike's style from the beginning. Like any artist he outlines his characters against a background which gives their features meaning; he relies heavily on details of color to establish such backgrounds. In addition to color, Updike's imagery systems often reveal a highly elaborated spatial pattern.

Indeed, Updike sometimes appears to be writing a scenario for a film rather than the text of a short story or novel. In addition to the detailed settings, panned slowly and with obvious pleasure, he often includes the characters' moment-to-moment perceptions and movements—the kind of material scriptwriters supply for films. Updike allows us to absorb things slowly, visually. He frequently stops the action to study the setting or pauses to watch the characters' mundane comings and goings, the intimate moments of play or anger which all together make up the quality of one's life. Yet with the deft economy which marks art, he designs these scenes in such a way as to control and shape the reader's perceptions until each story's delicate logic seems no longer arbitrary or unique; the story can successfully pretend the realism of a documentary, which views scenes, not sets; people, not characters.

"The Music School" is a picture of a man's mind. Its scenery is internal, not external; its dialogue is a monologue spoken to oneself; and its visual elements depict memories and meditations which, as a group, portray the man Alfred Schweigen. It is important to notice that it is not really the computer expert we learn about but Schweigen's reactions to the computer expert. Though

Schweigen says "let me describe the music school," after a few words we get not one of Updike's familiar detailed descriptions, but an impressionistic sense of Schweigen's experience while he waits there and meditates on the nature of music.

Schweigen's reflections center around two dominant metaphors—music and food (eating)—and two subdominant metaphors—religion and mathematics. Music represents order and harmony; religion and mathematics resemble music because they provide an orderly system for viewing reality. The computers produce, Schweigen imagines, "the music of truth." And when the churchgoers would assume a kneeling position, he recalls, "there was a kind of accompanying music."

The computer expert in Schweigen's imagination has the cool assurance of Updike's recurrent character, the scientist. Schweigen describes him as "a typical specimen of the new human species" participating "not in this century but in the next." The priest in "The Music School" is also called "a man of the future"; he displays the secular nonchalance associated with the figure of the scientist. Perhaps more comfortable at a party than in church, at home with Protestants and nonbelievers, he plays a guitar and smokes while casually chatting about the Eucharist. Such men of theory as the priest and the computer expert appear to Schweigen sublime—lacking a sense of an animal nature. "They have solved or dismissed the paradox of being a thinking animal," he decides. Such men seem to strike a basic harmony with the orderly universe they see. They are able, like the priest, to play chords every time. Schweigen sees them as "scrupulous," "fine," and "translucent." Yet the translucent host is being discarded as inappropriate to the reality which Christ saw and which Schweigen also recognizes. What Schweigen senses is a tough, coarse, opaque world with disorderly passions beyond the comprehension of men like the computer expert to whom shame and guilt are also unknown.

Schweigen says he had once tried to learn music. He had also once been religious. But he has long ago given up being either musical or religious; apparently he cannot feel comfortable with systems which envision an orderly universe. Although he feels unable to learn music himself, however, he loves his daughter's hopeful attempts to play.

She returns from her lesson "refreshed" just as the church-goers of Schweigen's early memories leave the service refreshed. Though these are no longer Schweigen's modes, he admires those who find them still efficacious. And he realizes that each of us chews the world in his own way.

Yet the story does not have a simple melody line; there is a faint counterpoint of irony. Alfred Schweigen, for all his intelligence and sensitivity, is not a very good novelist. His intended novel sounds trite and precious—even, it would seem, to him. If he is an artist who cannot come to terms with the concept of an orderly universe, then how will he produce the patterned verbal music of literature? And one wonders whether such a cool and aloof man chews the world as he says one must. Even his confessional and meditative essay is strangely formal and distant. He will tell us nothing of that moment so important it almost produced a novel, although he is not above teasing our curiosity a bit by mentioning it. Nor will he admit that his adulteries could cause his wife to suffer enough that she seeks someone else for guidance and support.

For all of his joy at his daughter's lessons, his voice remains anemic, dry, tired, overly formal, and tense. He says he is not religious, yet he reveals a longing for the religion which formerly gave him harmony with the universe and with himself. Caught between two worlds, he knows he is too old-fashioned to become a modern man even as he senses that his older rhythms of belief and behavior have receded, have diminished to a distant music.

"The Music School" offers us an encompassing metaphor for Updike's view of his own art—perhaps the reason he used the title for a whole collection of short stories. The change to a chewy host and the death of the computer expert are both products of a transubstantiation—from the world of ideas to the world of matter. Art, too, is such a transubstantiation. In sonata, or novel, or film, one moves from the realm of idea through the corridors of form to those flashes of sound or color which are the stuff of experience. The artist grapples with the tough and confusing world, searching for those combinations which, when struck, produce music.

SUGGESTIONS FOR FURTHER READING

By John Updike:

The Centaur. New York: Knopf, 1963.

Museums and Women and Other Stories. New York: Knopf, 1972.

The Music School: Short Stories. New York: Knopf, 1966.

Pigeon Feathers and Other Stories. New York: Knopf, 1962.

Rabbit Redux. New York: Knopf, 1971.

Rabbit, Run. New York: Knopf, 1960.

About John Updike:

Markle, Joyce B. *Fighters and Lovers: Themes in The Novels of John Updike*. New York: N.Y.U. Press, 1973.